# Figure It Out

An Omegaverse Sports Romance

C.R. Ship

# FIGURE IT OUT: AN OMEGAVERSE SPORTS ROMANCE


Edited by Jason Frey
Cover & Interior Design by C.R. Ship



cr-ship.com

ISBN: 979-8-2958-7645-5

PRINTED IN THE UNITED STATES OF AMERICA
10 9 8 7 6 5 4 3 2

For my wonderful husband, our love story is my favorite.

And to a fandom that taught me the value of my words and myself. I will make our ships sail in every world.

# GLOSSARY

**Omegaverse** - A universe in which everyone is born with a secondary gender beyond just male and female. There are three categories: Alpha, Omega, and Beta. A person's secondary biological gender is what determines their reproductive function in society.

**Alpha** - In society, Alphas are seen as the genetic lottery winners. They are typically dominant, with the expectation of being considered the breadwinner in any relationship. While alpha males cannot become pregnant, alpha females can carry a child.

**Omega** - A typical omega is expected to be small, gentle, and soft, usually the caregiver. While omegas have achieved greatness in several fields, they are generally excluded from more masculine or alpha-dominated roles. This is primarily due to the stereotype that they have the singular need to find an alpha and settle down to produce children and care for their family. Regardless of birth gender, male or female omegas can become pregnant and birth children.

**Beta** - Betas have neither the elevated hormones nor the testosterone levels of an omega or an alpha. While they will give off scents, they are often more muted than those of the other genders. Betas are by far the most common in the Omegaverse, while alphas and omegas are the extremes on either side of the secondary gender spectrum. Similar to alphas, male betas cannot birth children, but female betas can.

**Heat** - A quarterly biological time for omegas, starting at puberty, when their bodies begin to become fertile and ready to find a mate. While the media has vastly exaggerated an omega's reaction to heat, their bodies do go through changes ranging from scent change to producing sexual discharge, also known as slick, in preparation for an alpha.

**Knot** - During sexual intercourse with an omega, the base of a male alpha's penis swells. This effectively locks the alpha and their partner together, increasing the chance of a successful pregnancy.

**Scent** - A side-effect of secondary gender, alphas, betas, and omegas release unique, involuntary hormones based on their mood. Omegas have limited control over their scent, allowing them to release specific hormones that can either calm or entice alphas and betas. However, they are not always able to mask their scent, especially during their heat.

# CHAPTER ONE

## ~~~~~~ ROWAN ~~~~~~

'*Just ten minutes 'til we get there.*' Rowan looked out the window of the moving bus, watching the town he would spend the next several years in go by.

'*My new home.*'

He settled back in his seat, resisting the urge to watch his already dying phone, tracking the minutes until the bus arrived at the campus drop-off station.

Deciding to distract himself, he looked up at the hanging TVs, which were set on some trashy rerun channel. The blond winced inwardly when he realized what they were showing, at a low volume and with subtitles.

"One alpha," The TV announced, showing a handsome man in a suit, holding a single flower, smiling at the camera. It soon panned out to show a group of people behind him, all dressed to the nines, staring at the alpha with bedroom eyes. "Sixteen single omegas!" Next, the camera showed each cast member's face. "Which one will he choose?"

Rowan groaned as he squinted up at it, hating how shows like that portrayed omegas.

"These omegas can't keep their hands off me. I mean, how could they?" The alpha from the show said in a side interview. "I'm all that they were made to want and more."

A redhead in another interview smiled slyly at the camera, "These other omegas don't know it, but I came here to win, not to play around. And to prove it, I'm starting my heat on day one," He said with a wink. "That alpha won't be able to keep his hands off me."

Another omega showed up next in their interview, "I mean, it's every omega's dream to have an alpha like that pick you to be their omega, right?" They asked the camera as if it were obvious.

Rowan shook his head, looking back out the window. Shows like that weren't his thing. It just perpetuated omega stereotypes, like most media outlets did. Rowan was a proud omega, and his grandma raised him to never let his secondary gender define how he acted or his worth. He wasn't just some baby-making, wilting flower waiting for an alpha. If an omega wanted to be a housewife and parent, that was fine with him. Just as long as they didn't try to force him into a box specifically meant for his type to stay in. Rowan had his eyes on a whole other level of achievement, and he didn't have time to let sexism hold him back from any of his dreams.

The bus turned to pass the University's large gate, proudly showing its crest. Rowan quickly began gathering up his belongings. When it came time to exit the bus at the designated drop-off, he ignored the annoyed bus driver's look. It probably didn't help that, two hours ago, when Rowan got on the bus, the driver commented that omegas shouldn't travel alone. Rowan also probably didn't help the situation by replying that he didn't need a babysitter. It may have been a bit rude, but Rowan really didn't need someone watching out for him. He'd been doing fine on his own for some time now.

He didn't need anyone to fight his battles for him.

But it was time to put his troubles behind him, because he had arrived.

After a short and, frankly, uninspiring stop at what was left of the new student welcoming committee, Rowan made his way to the reason he had traveled halfway across the state for college.

Rowan stood before the massive stadium, his wide blue eyes taking in the grand building.

He stood outside in the light rain under his yellow umbrella for over fifteen minutes. The white steps leading up to the arena doors glistened with rainwater. Banners hung down from the sides, proudly displaying a mighty figure striking a pose.

Nobody else was around; there were no events for the day, and no one in their right mind would stand out in the rain for no reason. At the moment, Rowan wouldn't have been able to say whether he was in his right mind for being there, either.

As he looked up at the gray sky above, his mind replayed all the moments that led him there.

*"Grandma! Grandma! It's here; I got accepted!" Rowan screamed, waving his acceptance letter for Asher University. He had been waiting all day by the mailbox for his letter. Now that it was finally there, he could hardly believe that several years of intense training had brought him to his next journey.*

*A little old beta woman sat in her chair, putting together a puzzle of a cat, her soft blue eyes looking back at Rowan with kind confusion.*

*"Do you know what this means? Emily Star is going to be my coach! This is my shot at the big leagues!" Rowan announced with a glassy cover of joy over his eyes.*

*"Who are you?" the older woman asked with a soft smile.*

*Rowan lowered his acceptance letter, his once excited eyes turning down in sadness, but he forced his smile anyway. "It's me, Gran Gran. Rowan, your grandson."*

*She just hummed, turning back to her puzzle. The blond gave her a soft kiss on the head before walking out to call his friends.*

*It wasn't until later that he found the price of attending such a prestigious school. If his grandmother were lucid, he was sure she would tell him, 'No work, no gain. Nothing's free.'*

*He called Emily, holding back his tears.*

*"E-Emily, I can't afford this. I've been on the phone with financial aid all day. Even if I knew the difference between a Pell Grant and an unsubsidized loan, I don't think I could cover half of what it would cost to keep me going." He stuttered through the call, looking at the acceptance letter on the fridge that was hanging from a 'Señor Frogs' magnet. "I can't work a job, train under you, AND go to school full time."*

*"Let's not borrow trouble just yet, kid. I know the school doesn't offer figure skating scholarships yet, but let me call around and see what strings I can pull." Her peppy voice was undeterred by the stressful situation.*

*"We're not going to let something as trivial as money stop you from training for the gold!"*

*A few days later, the blond got word back from his future coach that she had figured it all out. Though he had to admit, he was surprised when she explained her plan.*

*"H-hockey?" Rowan nearly spat out; his face scrunched up as if tasting a ripe lemon on his tongue. "But... I've never played before." He recalled seeing a few games on the agelessly thick TVs that hung over the carpeted area in the ice arena where he worked. Their volume couldn't outdo the slightly broken speaker blasting songs from new-age pop to 80's top charts, though. The blond had never actually paid any attention to the gruff sport that just so happened to share a key element with his own passion.*

*"That's fine! It's a full-ride hockey scholarship! It's all the school had left, so I pulled a lot of favors to get it." She sounded so happy she could burst.*

*He wondered how she couldn't see the major flaw in the plan. Would he have to be the one to bring it up?*

*Rowan looked at his snoozing grandma and back to the phone. "But... but what about... you know," He squeezed his hand around the phone, trying not to let the nervous tone drip into his voice. "I'm an omega."*

*"So?" Emily paused, genuinely questioning it. Rowan already knew how progressive his new coach was; she was renowned for her background in gender equality. But hearing it firsthand made him feel a small sense of pride in having scored her as his mentor. However, another part of him wanted to grab her and try to shake some sense into her.*

*"I've never heard of an omega hockey player," he whispered, feeling anxiety fill his stomach.*

*"Me neither," Emily hummed in thought before busting out laughing. "Guess you'll be breaking all kinds of glass ceilings!" Her infectious laughter was back.*

*If she didn't see a problem with it, maybe it wasn't as big an issue as he thought.*

*So, he said the words that would either land him on a podium or in a hospital bed.*

*"Okay, coach."*

Rowan clutched his shirt, wringing it between his fingers as he continued to stare at the intimidating building. His other hand gripped the umbrella like his life depended on it.

'*This is it.*' He thought, smiling tightly. '*Where my dreams of skating professionally begin. With this step, I'll be one closer to the gold.*'

He bit down on his lower lip, taking several deep breaths before walking up the stairs. He stopped when he reached the top and stared at his reflection in the glass door. His long blond hair ruffled in the wind.

With a final sigh, he pulled open the door and stepped inside, closing and shaking off his umbrella. His wet shoes squeaked against the floor as his eyes took in the grandness of the arena. He was overcome by a sense of wonder at the beauty of it all, and he hadn't even seen the ice yet. The concession stands alone put his small-town rink to shame.

Following the signs to the rink, he stopped when he noticed his future coach, Emily Star, standing there, peeking through the double doors and grinning mischievously.

He beamed with excitement. He hadn't seen his new coach since his last performance three months ago; their only conversations had been over text and calls. She had come to his junior division show at the request of his first coach to see if he lived up to expectations, and he apparently didn't disappoint.

Rowan couldn't express how excited he was to meet one of his idols up close when she approached him after the show. Emily had won a gold medal in the Olympics at the tender age of nineteen. Rowan had a poster of her back in his old room and wished he had brought it for her to sign. Sadly, that poster was packed away with his other meager belongings, which had been sent to his new dorm.

A dorm that he hadn't even had a chance to see since the bus had been so slow.

"Coach Emi!" He called out, and the brown-haired coach looked at him with sparkling eyes. She had insisted early on that he should refer to her by her nickname since that's what all her friends used.

Of course, it was only natural that calling her by a nickname would mean that he would earn one as well. Though he never really understood where she came up with the name.

"Sparky!" Her enthusiastic nickname from their first meeting snuck into every one of their phone calls and texts. Rowan sort of wished she would come up with a cooler nickname, but it was better than some of the names she'd called the other skaters.

Stopping before her, Rowan couldn't stop the excitement in his chest as the anxiety fizzled back in the presence of his first real coach.

“Welcome to Asher University!” She spread her arms out. “My original stomping grounds!”

# CHAPTER TWO

## ~~~~~~ ROWAN ~~~~~~

Rowan's eyes widened as he stared at the interior of the massive complex. "You trained here?"

Emily nodded, putting her fists on her hips and causing her curly brown hair to bounce with the movement. "First one here at sunup and last one to leave at night." Her bright eyes opened from the wide grin. "Similar to what your schedule will look like, kid." She pulled out a bronze key with a tacky school keychain and tossed it over. Rowan's hands fumbled as it bounced from left to right before landing in his open palms. "You're gonna need the keys to the kingdom if you want to rule the land. This'll get you into the stadium for practice whenever you want, day or night."

Rowan clenched his hand into a fist around the key, giving her a determined smile. "I'm ready! Point me in the direction of the ice!" He could feel his skin fizzle, almost as if he were conducting electricity through his veins.

Maybe Sparky wasn't such a bad nickname, after all.

"Whoa, whoa! Slow down there, Sparky! Love the enthusiasm, but let's skate before we lutz." She giggled at her own joke. "Got your gear?"

Rowan held up his black duffel bag, the old stitching around the seams looking ready to break at any second. "Right here!" He gave it a pat, sliding his new key into the front zipper and securing it with a zip.

"Excellent! Coach Archer's talking to the team right now. Explaining their new addition." She threw her two thumbs over her shoulders to the doors behind her. "Ready to go in?"

Rowan's smile dropped as he stuffed his hands into the front pocket of his yellow and black hoodie, twisting the fabric nervously. "Um, well-"

Emily's eyes softened as she reached out, placing a hand on the omega's shoulder. "I know it's not an *ideal* situation." She pushed out the word 'ideal' as if it were forced. "But it's a full-ride scholarship. It got you here, and while hockey isn't the softest sport, you'll still have ice under your skates." Emily's scent was calming, like fresh-baked bread and sugar. It made him think of standing on the kitchen chair as a kid, watching his mother knead biscuit dough. Her soft hand would reach out and poke the tip of his small nose, leaving behind a small dot of flour.

Rowan looked into Emily's motherly face, instantly wishing he had his mother there with him, but instead, he just swallowed his doubts and nodded. "Right."

"Besides!" Emily's face brightened back up. "Coach Archer said he won't really play you. Can't have that body broken to pieces before qualifications come around, right?"

The blond's eyes widened. "He won't play me?" He felt relief sag across his body. "You didn't tell me that!" He wished she had mentioned it before his long bus ride here with tense shoulders and a leg that wouldn't stop bouncing with nerves.

The person sitting beside him on that bus probably would have appreciated it, too.

“I didn’t?” She put a finger to her chin, her teal nail polish standing out against her mocha skin. “Oh, well, I assumed you’d figure it out on your own. Hockey’s a dangerous sport. No point in training you if you’re just going to break an arm or a leg. What kinda coach would I be if I put a cast around your arm before I put a medal around your neck?”

He wanted to tell her he didn't know, and knowing earlier would have saved him several sleepless nights. Instead, he bit it back and focused on the moment. "You're right."

“Of course I’m right!” She said with a proud grin. “Now, did you stop by your dorm yet?” Emily peeked past the door again, so Rowan assumed she was waiting for some sign.

"Nah, my bus got delayed. When I got here, the last of the student welcome committee had already taken my bags to my dorm. Plus, the guy from the welcoming committee seemed…less than welcoming." He thought of the golden key and several welcome packets in his skating bag. "Probably didn’t want to stand out in this rain any longer than he already had. Anyway, I didn't want to be late, so I came right here."

"I love a prompt student!" She slapped his arm before gasping and throwing open the doors. "That's our cue! Come on, Sparky!"

Rowan didn't even have time to question her before she grabbed his sleeve and jerked him into the stadium. As they passed several rows of chairs, Rowan saw the large rink, surrounded by several stories of bleachers and a massive Jumbotron hanging above the middle. The blond couldn't help but drop his mouth open at the sheer size of it all. Sure, he had seen several arenas during his competition tours, but this place was the largest one to date by far. This place could hold two of his old rinks, and to know it would be his new home made his heart jump happily into his throat.

Rowan knew he was exuding a happy omega scent, and he didn't even care. Lighting could strike him right then and he'd thank the heavens for pinching him so he would know it wasn't a dream.

It wasn't until the scent of alpha slapped his nose that he looked away from the bleachers to the line of sweaty men standing geared up on the ice, staring at him. No, men was a light understatement…they were GIANTS! Their gear doubled their size, and they looked just as intimidating. The blond brought his shoulders up to his ears, straightening his back to try and make himself as tall as possible. However, it was pathetic compared to the other players.

What the hell did they feed these guys?

'*Omegas,*' he thought before he brushed the idea away.

Emily waved her free hand up in the air. "Harlan! Hey, I got your signal! We're here!"

Standing in front of the players was an older Asian man with long black hair that looked like he had just rolled out of bed; his tired eyes looked back at Emily. The figure skating coach pushed open the metal door to the rink and continued walking. Rowan had walked in his Converse on ice before, and he had the balance to stay upright with Emily as she strode across the rink in her thick rain boots. The closer they got, the more Rowan could see the mixed faces of his new teammates.

"What signal?" Coach Archer sighed in annoyance. "I told you to come in when you're ready."

His eyes dropped to Rowan as they stopped before him, his eyes taking in the small size of his new player.

"Damn. I didn't think he'd be so-" Archer stopped as Emily interrupted.

"Amazing?" She gasped loudly, shaking her hand that held Rowan, "Awe-inspiring? No, wait, SPECTACULAR?" She gushed, and Rowan blushed at her compliments as he forced a smile, rubbing the back of his head with his other hand.

"Small," The alpha coach finished, his tone as dead and annoyed as he looked. Rowan couldn't help but deflate a bit under his glare, though he still tried to stand strong. "How tall are you, anyway? 5'3?" The hockey coach asked.

"Um," Rowan muttered. "5'1, actually"

No one spoke, and Rowan resisted the urge to turn his eyes down in submission to the alpha male. He wasn't about that gender inequality bullshit, so instead of playing the submissive omega, he held his head high and kept eye contact with the coach.

"I like to think of him as fun-sized!" Emily said, scratching the back of her neck before laughing. "He's the perfect height for his sport, though, so no height shaming." The beta let Rowan go and presented him as if he were an award. "Let me introduce you to your newest player: Rowan West!" She turned to Rowan. "Rowan, this is your second coach, Harlan Archer."

Murmuring poured out from the players, and Rowan's eyes looked away from his coach to the line of athletes. His gaze instantly fell on a set of green eyes set in a glare that ran a chill down the omega's spine. He quickly looked at the player next to him, and his hair bristled when he locked with a set of angry hazel eyes.

He decided it was probably best not to look at any of them just yet.

Forcing a bright smile, he looked back to his coach and held his hand out. "Thank you for this opportunity, coach!"

Harlan stared at Rowan's hand as if it were a foreign object. The scent of burning coffee singed the omega's nose. It wafted off the coach in waves as if he was trying to figure out what that outstretched hand meant. Rowan had a moment of panic as he worried the coach was going to brush him off. However, after several anxiety-filled seconds, the coach grabbed his hand in a hard shake.

"Don't mention it… seriously, don't." His eyes flickered to Emily, who was beaming at their interaction. "If I were smarter and didn't owe Emily here the favor, I'd have said no to this arrangement."

Rowan felt sweat accumulate behind his neck as he pulled his hand back, "O-oh."

"Aw, don't be like that, Harlan, babe!" Emily winked. "I showed you his training video! You even said so yourself; the kid's got moves."

Looking between the adults, the omega watched a sneer pass over Coach Archer's face. "I said he can skate."

"Tomato, potato!" Emily shrugged, looking at Rowan. "I gotta go; gotta teach my next class in fifteen." She slapped Rowan's shoulder and gave him a thumbs-up, nearly knocking the blond over. "Knock em' dead, Tiger!" She pushed off, gliding across the ice in her thick black boots and humming some random tune.

Rowan watched the beta go, inhaling deeply before turning back to his team and forcing a big grin on his face. He gave them a small wave and said, "It's great to meet you all! I promise I won't be any trouble!"

As he stared at the row of players, he finally took in all the faces of his team and was relieved to see that not all of them were sneers or glares. In fact, there was a redheaded alpha smiling at him from down the line.

Archer looked at his team and grunted, his alpha stance making him almost tower over the others in a show of clear authority. "As I was saying, West will be our new player. And I expect you all to accept the circumstances."

A thin beta with sharp features raised his hand, an uncertain look on his face. "Um, sir?"

Archer looked at him, and the player must have taken that as a chance to speak. "Did my last concussion never heal, or is he an omega?"

Rowan bristled but kept his smile on. He thought of wearing a scent patch, but he figured there wasn't a point. They were going to know just by looking at him. Even before he presented, everyone knew he was destined to be an omega from a young age. It was pretty obvious; from his boyish soft looks to his short height, his body screamed 'omega.'

He did have more muscle than the average omega, though, especially in his legs from all the skating. Still, he knew what people would assume from the first glance.

The angry-looking, sandy blond alpha next to green eyes shot his own hand up quickly, talking without Archer's look of approval. "Yeah, what's up with that?"

A murmur of agreement picked up, making Rowan wish he were at least a couple of inches taller, so they were not literally looking down at him.

Archer groaned before looking at Rowan. "You wanna take this?"

Rowan was surprised, but he looked at his coach with a nod before facing his team again. "Um, well, yes. I am an omega, but I don't think that really matters."

The thin player raised his hand again, leaning on his hockey stick. "I've never heard of an omega playing hockey," he said with mischievous curiosity. His eyes darted over to the sandy blond with a knowing look with most of the team nodding in agreement. Rowan had met his share of shit-stirrers in his life, especially on the ice, and he assumed he just found one on this team.

He didn't let it bother him too much, though. There was at least one in every group.

The green-eyed alpha that kept drawing Rowan's attention, though, stayed quiet. Instead, his stare grew more intense, and he seemed to command respect with nothing but a glare. Rowan felt a chill pass over his skin as he tried to look everywhere but at the tall alpha. "Yeah, I guess, but there's a first time for everything, and I've been skating my whole life. Plus, I need this scholarship." He put his hands on his hips, trying to stand as tall as possible.

"So, for the sake of it, let's get the awkwardness out of the way. Elephants don't belong on the ice, so let's address this one now. Ask me anything at all, I'm an open book!"

Silence filled the air as the team diverted their eyes away from the small omega. Their cheeks flushed pink; Rowan was sure all of their questions had something to do with his heats or taboo subjects. Male omegas were already scarce, so their traits were vastly over-exaggerated by the media. To many, omegas were just wilting flowers, hardly able to hold a shovel without a strong alpha there to pick up the heavy end. Omegas were seen as baby-making incubators in the eyes of the world, thanks in no small part to the traditional roles shown off in classic TV shows and the older generation spouting off about what things were like in 'the good old days.'

Rowan hated it, and while he competed in what many considered to be a softer sport, it involved just as much blood, sweat, and tears as any 'real' sport.

Rowan cocked his head, looking them over and avoiding those green eyes for the sake of his sanity. "Come on. Isn't anyone at least going to ask about my heats?"

The players winced at the word, and Rowan resisted the urge to giggle at their delicate sensibilities.

'*And they say omegas are fragile*,' he thought, rolling his eyes. Part of him wished Imani were here to rip them to shreds. She loved making alphas feel awkward under her bubbly personality.

The player at the end with the brown hair raised a hand. Rowan snapped his fingers and pointed at him with a finger gun. "Yes?"

"Won't your heat prevent you from practicing or attending away games?" He cocked his head, seemingly unaffected by the awkwardness his other teammates were feeling. All except green eyes over there, of course.

Rowan snapped his fingers again, almost like a nervous tic, grinning at the alpha. "Fantastic question! No to both of those. You see, a heat isn't like how the mainstream media portrays it. I don't wither and wilt as I wait for a knot for a whole week." He chuckled when a blush appeared on many of their faces. "At most, I'm mildly uncomfortable and a bit horny, but given our ages, aren't we all?" He left the joke hanging in the air, thankful when the skinny guy and redhead let out a laugh.

"I'm just like you guys." Rowan motioned to himself, "Except, I don't know much about hockey, but I'm a high-level figure skater, and I just know with a little work we'll be great friends!"

The sandy blond alpha snorted loudly. "Figure skater? Coach, is he shitting us?"

"Language, Wilson." Archer sighed. "But yes, West is here on a hockey scholarship, but his main focus is to compete as a figure skater under Coach Star's training."

"So he's an airhead and a ballerina," Wilson snorted, and was joined by a few laughs covered by many hands.

Rowan blushed but glared at the sandy blond. "For your information, yes, I did take several years of dance. And, just by looking at your blocky frame, I know I could skate figure eights around you in my sleep."

"The FUCK did he just say?" Wilson exploded as the redhead beside him brought a hand out to stop the alpha from charging forward.

Archer held up a hand. "Alright, enough questions. We're melting ice time. I still have you for another hour. Get in position, I want us to do seven sets of speed drills." The team groaned and broke formation as Archer looked to Rowan. "Bring your skates?"

Rowan nodded, pulling his duffel out before him. "Yeah, but I figured I'd head out soon. I haven't even been to my dorm yet." He also hoped to meet his roommate before it got too late. People usually weren't at their best right before bed, and he hoped to at least start that relationship on the right foot.

Archer raised a brow. "What?"

Rowan felt the ball of anxiety roll in his stomach. "Um," He poked his two index fingers together. "Coach Emi told me… um…That I-" He looked at the skaters already doing sprints back and forth on the ice and back to his coach. "I have practice first thing in the morning, and I thought I'd get to bed early." It had been his plan, but it felt more like a desperate request as the words tumbled out. There was something about this guy that made it feel like you needed to ask for permission to breathe.

Archer glared down at him, eyes narrowing. "You think you're not training with the team?"

Rowan balked, a nervous smile spreading as he scratched the back of his head. "That's a lot. I mean, every day I have practice with Coach Emi at sunup for five hours, and then classes, and then schoolwork before bed. Not to mention the evening runs, the gym, the gymnastics…I barely have time to eat as it is." He felt his confidence slipping the more he spoke. "I can't do figure training and hockey training at the same time."

The smell of burning coffee was back as Archer bent at the waist until he was at eye level with Rowan. "Listen here, kid," His voice was low, so low, in fact, that the sound of blades on the ice behind him hardly allowed Rowan to hear him, but he forced his brain to focus. "I gave up a kid with a lot of prospects just so you could join Coach Star out here. She showed me your tapes, and she believes in you. She said you could go to the Olympics if she works you hard enough."

Rowan felt his throat tighten up, happy that Emily believed in him so much. The emotion was short-lived when Archer grunted, and Rowan flinched under his glare.

"But don't think for a second you get out of training with my team," Archer's tone turned dark. "I don't give out free rides. Whatever they do, you do. I might not play you, but I'll work you so hard you'll wish you drowned in student loan debt. So, hear me when I say this: you'll be here at the scheduled times every day. And if I so much as sense you slacking, I'll snatch that scholarship back so fast it'll make your axel's spin. Do I make myself clear?"

The figure skater gulped, feeling dread and fear wash over him as he nodded stiffly.

"Look at the bright side; this can count as your evening run. Now get your skates on." He turned back to the team, blowing his whistle. "Kage! Sideline!"

Rowan slid to the side, focusing on not falling in his black Converse.

Reaching the gate, he sat down on the long bench, slipping off his shoes and quickly replacing them with his slightly scuffed figure skates. Once laced up, he left his bag under the bench next to the other players' stuff and pushed out onto the ice. He felt ten times better the second his blades touched the smooth surface. He was still anxiety-riddled and scared of what this meant for his schedule, but he was just glad to be standing on the thin steel again.

That was until-

"What the fuck are those!?" A voice crackled loudly. The skinny guy echoed, "What are thoooose?!"

Rowan stopped before the team as some players rolled to a stop or kept skating at half speed. Wilson pointed at his skates, an evil laugh echoing off the large roof. "You brought figure skates to practice? What an idiot!"

Rowan blushed, looking down to see that the men all had on thick black skates, layered with padding, while his looked so… formal.

Archer sighed, blowing his whistle. "Start over. Don't make me double the set."

A loud bunch of groans rang out, but the team continued, though now without green eyes. He and Coach Archer skated over to Rowan, and the black-haired player stopped in front of the omega, regarding him with an angry look. Despite that, Rowan could clearly see the attractive features behind the mean eyes. He was, as his friend Imani would put it, a goddamn 'snack', or a full entree, in this case.

"Hey," Rowan said as charismatically as possible. Now that he was close enough, Rowan could smell the scent of coffee and rain on him. It was nice, and if it weren't for the overlay of sweat coating the ice, he would lean in for a better sniff. He thought better of it, though; this guy looked like he could do some real damage with his height and mass.

'*Be still, my beating heart,*' Rowan thought as he softly bit his lower lip.

Archer motioned to the player. "This is Beckett Kage, our captain. He'll be giving you an overlay of what the team does. Filter any dumb questions through him first before coming to me. I don't have time to hold your hand through this." With that, he skated away to the others, blowing his whistle. “Adam, don’t slack on those roundabouts!”

Rowan looked up at Beckett and tried to figure out why he was scowling at him. But even with a scowl, he was drop-dead handsome. So instead of a normal greeting, Rowan leaned heavily on his humor and held his hand out and wiggled his fingers, giving a flirtatious smile. "So, I guess that means we're holding hands then?"

Beckett looked down at his hand and back at him. "Cute," he said, and Rowan blushed, figuring he was being sarcastic as he dropped his hand. He was trying to ignore the hair raised on the back of his neck at the deep voice this guy had, but he was failing miserably. It was like melted chocolate on liquid hot sex! Rowan could feel his stomach flip, wanting to hear more.

“Sorry,” Rowan chuckled forcefully, “I tend to rely on humor when things are awkward.”

Beckett shrugged, “Alright.” After a few more seconds of silence, he spoke again. “So, what do you know about hockey?”

Rowan poked his fingers together again nervously, trying to hide what this guy's voice did to him. “Um, well, there's ice, and skates, and a puck. Oh, and sticks!”

The captain waited for more as Rowan’s face turned redder. “Erm- and one team tries to get the puck into the other team’s net?”

“Correct.” Beckett nodded. “What about rules?”

The blond’s face went blank, and Beckett sighed. Rowan instantly felt guilty for taking so much of his time, but also annoyed because he felt like a team captain was supposed to rally their teammates.

"Skate with me. I need to stay warmed up." The alpha motioned with his head to the other end, where the team wasn't practicing.

'*Don't mind if I do,*' Rowan thought, hoping this guy would keep talking. Even if he was kind of a jerk.

Rowan was relieved to move as they finally glided down to the opposite net. Rowan glanced up at the captain, noticing how the omega barely came up to this giant's shoulders. His wild black hair was all over the place as he held his helmet in his other hand. Reaching the end, Beckett circled the omega and the goal.

"I'm gonna run you through the basics of the game," Beckett said. Rowan nodded along.

The black-haired player was throwing out words that Rowan knew had meaning, but for the life of him, he couldn't see how they all applied to this game.

Rowan couldn't help but feel like a fish being circled by a shark, so he joined the captain halfway through, skating alongside him. The annoyed look on the alpha's face didn't waver as he finished the rules and penalty talk. His sentences were short, but he seemed to know what he was talking about, so Rowan tried not to focus on the fact that his guy had a bedroom voice made by the gods.

Rowan was proud that he got the basics right in their earlier conversation. The whole game involved the players trying to hit a small, frozen piece of rubber, called the puck, into each other's goals. They got rough, and that was okay, unless they got too rough, and then it wasn't.

Also, there would apparently be some icing at some point, which he was looking forward to. He also wondered why someone was going to get a check, but figured it might have something to do with the scholarship. He would have to bring up 'checking' to Emily.

"Got it?" He asked, and Rowan halted his skating, nodding.

"I think so."

"You think?" Beckett sneered, and Rowan bristled in annoyance.

"I mean, yeah, I think I got it. It's not like I can just pick it up, no problem, after a chat. I'll need time."

Beckett blinked down at him with that blank look, and Rowan had the sudden urge to call him a very harsh name, but he bit back. He didn't want to make enemies with his captain on the first day. Finally, after a few tension-filled seconds, the captain looked back at the team that was now running a drill on the ice. "Well, if you *think* you've got it, let's get to practice."

Rowan looked down at his ripped jeans and baggy hoodie. If he had known he would be training, he would have brought a change of clothes.

Oh well, it would do no good to dwell in the past.

He joined Archer, and the coach instructed Rowan to join the team in their drills.

"He thinks he's got it," Beckett said in passing to the coach, who eyed Rowan, making sure the blond was sure of what he meant. Rowan gave a thumbs-up as the coach shrugged and blew his whistle.

"Welcome to hell!" Wilson sneered as he skated by the omega.

Rowan shivered, watching as all the players began slapping their sticks on the ice to intimidate him. It was a chaotic, echoing, banging sound that rang in Rowan's ears like drums of war. He looked up at his captain to see him giving the blond a knowing look. Rowan heard it in his head as 'You *thought* you got it.'

'*Fuck this guy!*' Rowan snorted, ready to show he could handle a little extra training.

How hard could it be?

# CHAPTER THREE

An hour later, Rowan was gasping for air, lying on his back on the ice and staring up at the stadium's roof. His chest and feet were on fire, and his hands felt cramped from holding that stick so tightly. He didn't so much do drills as avoid getting pummeled by the racing skaters around him.

The loud chirp of a whistle soared across the ice before a voice called out, "Alright, that's it for the day. Hit the showers!"

Rowan sat up on the ice, watching as the nameless guys from his team skated by him toward their bags on the sidelines.

"Just think, Blondie," Wilson skated by him, hardly looking like he broke a sweat. "That was just the last hour. You missed the other two." He chuckled darkly. "Well, there's always tomorrow." He paused at the door. "Ya know… unless you wanna save us the hassle and quit now." Looking away, he headed to the locker rooms with the others as Rowan pouted, glaring at his back.

Beckett stopped by him and looked down at the blond before holding a hand out. Rowan scoffed and jutted his chin out. “I can get up on my own!”

As soon as he said it, a look passed on the black-haired skater's face, and Rowan regretted his harsh words. "Hey, um-"

Beckett turned and skated off, not bothering to look back at the omega. Rowan cursed under his breath before standing up, stopping only when Archer glided past him. “Bring your A game tomorrow, kid. I don’t plan on going easy on you again.”

Rowan scoffed loudly, holding his arms up. “That was easy?” He motioned to the ice, where he was sure he had left half a gallon of sweat. Once the ice was clear, Rowan lowered his arms and looked around him, taking in the wide rink and empty seats.

Taking several deep breaths, he controlled his racing heart and whispered to himself, “Go for the gold, Rowan.” He smiled before pushing off. He stopped at the benches, changed from his skates to his shoes, and took his bag.

Since he didn’t have a change of clothes, he skipped the showers, but he wondered if the team was talking about him. Instead, he stopped by Archer’s office to get some release papers. He read through the fields and quickly scribbled down Imani as his emergency contact. He then signed the documents and several mandatory player contract sheets. He left them on the coach’s desk, his eyes lingering on a picture of a cute girl with long brown hair holding a cat. There were other pictures, but Rowan didn’t want to get caught snooping, so he just dropped the papers and walked out quickly. He could already see some players freshly showered and walking back to their dorms in different directions.

Shaking his head, he left the stadium and quickly walked toward the dorms across campus. His legs hurt, but not as much as his hands. That hockey stick was a bitch to hold onto without dropping.

After getting lost several times, he finally approached the outskirts of the dorms and looked up at the old brownstone bricks.

'*So, this is home for the next four years?*' he questioned before smiling. "Could be worse."

Entering the building with a scan of his student ID, he immediately saw the large 'out of order' sign above the elevator button. He groaned before turning around to find the stairs. As much as he wanted to rest his legs, he knew the quicker he got up the three flights, the sooner he could get a shower and change.

Each step of the stairs was grueling on his sore legs, and the lack of air conditioning in the stairwell wasn't helping his sweat-soaked clothes from sticking to his skin. Finally, after what felt like an eternity of climbing, he exited the stairwell and took a deep, refreshing breath of cool, circulated air.

He looked at the sign on the wall for directions and made his way to his room. Stopping at his door, he smiled brightly at the brass numbers across the wood.

Finally, a place of his own!

Along with Rowan being super stoked to train under *the* Emily Star and attend a high-level university, he recently learned that the scholarship included boarding in the university's dorms. Rowan had been so excited!

However, a brief flash of guilt clouded his mind as he thought back to his grandma, wondering what she was doing. Did she even notice he was gone, even in her most lucid moments?

Shaking off the thoughts of his home life, he shoved his key in the lock and burst through the door, only to have his smile falter as the smell of alpha slapped him in the face.

"Wha-" Looking around the small dorm, he found a spacious room with two beds on opposite ends and a window dead center of the room. On the left side, the bed was made, and the walls bare, signifying it was untouched.

However, the right side was littered with books, posters, and hockey memorabilia hanging from the sidewall.

“What the hell? What is this, a locker room?” He was about to take another step back when something hard hit his back. He looked up to see two familiar green eyes looking down at him.

Rowan could feel his whole face heat up like a Christmas light as he stumbled forward into the dorm. Beckett walked forward, holding a heavy-looking duffel bag. His confused and tired eyes looked from Rowan to the floor by the door, where two suitcases sat.

“Hm, roommate?” Beckett asked, cocking his head and scratching under his chin, though his voice was a lot quieter than it had been on the ice. Almost docile, as if afraid someone would hear.

The omega sputtered, looking from his suitcases on the floor to Beckett and the room. “Me- you- this- I can’t-” It was like Rowan completely forgot how to speak. He took two deep breaths and forced a charming smile on his face.

“Sorry, there must be a slight mix-up.”

Beckett raised a single brow before shrugging and walking over to his bed to dump his duffel onto it.

Rowan chuckled nervously, trying to explain more to himself than to Beckett. "I'm an omega, and you're an-"

"Alpha?" Beckett finished for him, dropping down onto his bed, finally looking at the blond with that same passive face. "So?"

"So?" Rowan scoffed, "It's, it's-"

"I thought you were just like us," Beckett regurgitated Rowan's earlier words to the team, and the figure skater blushed.

"I am! But-"

Beckett laid across the bed, kicking his shoes off to fall over the side and bringing his large hands up to cross behind his head. It pissed the blond off that this guy was hardly talking at all! Wasn't he just as put off about having to share the room with an omega? Of course, some alphas would do somersaults to have that situation. It was almost like a bad plot to a cheesy porno, the thought of which was enough to light Rowan's face up again.

"But this is weird! Um… I'm sure it's a mistake. Aren't there guidelines against commingling?"

Beckett shook his head and shrugged as if he didn't even know if there was an answer to the question.

"How can you be so easy about this? Doesn't it bother you?" Rowan put his hands on his hips.

Beckett looked like he wanted to say something, but he just blinked at the blond, making Rowan assume he didn't see the situation the same as him.

"Pfft- wow! It should bother you!" Rowan chuckled in astonishment. "For one... What about the smell?" He scrunched up his nose. "You can't say the sweet smell of omega isn't going to drive you crazy."

Beckett hummed. "Not really. You smell nice."

Rowan's face went red to his roots as heat exploded over his skin. "Um, thank you?"

Instead of answering, Beckett just lay there fully dressed on his made bed. If it wasn't for his open eyes, Rowan would have wondered if he had fallen asleep.

"Well, no offense, but I'm gonna talk to the dean tomorrow. See if I can't straighten this out."

Beckett rolled away from Rowan to face the wall, showing he heard him but just didn't respond.

Rowan felt a spike of fear run through him at the prospect of sleeping there with a stranger—not just any stranger, either—an alpha! His scent must have given him away because Beckett was sitting up, looking at him with that unreadable look.

"I can sleep out in the common room tonight," He offered, his voice low like a soft rumble that oddly calmed Rowan's anxiety.

Rowan felt his heart sputter as he played with the sleeve of his hoodie. "No, you don't need to do that. I'm fine."

Beckett cocked his head, and Rowan waved a hand. "No, no, really, it's fine. Thanks, though."

The fact that he was willing to offer spoke volumes about his character. Rowan felt his mouth quirk up in a small, hesitant smile. "Just… just warning you, though; I know karate." He held up his fists in warning as the captain shrugged and lay back down. Rowan didn't know karate, or any other martial art, for that matter. He figured he could be a black belt in bluffing, though.

When he was sure the conversation was over, Rowan took in the rest of the white, rectangular room. There were two desks on either side of the room and a small couch by the door with a coffee table. To the far right sat a door, which, upon opening, he found to be what had to have been the world's smallest bathroom.

"Jeez, how do you shower in this thing?" Rowan asked before he could filter himself. But since it was already out, he went with it. "I mean, I guess I can fit under that showerhead, but you definitely can't."

Looking over his shoulder at Beckett, he found him lying on his back again and staring at him. The blond blushed as the captain shrugged again.

Figuring he wasn't getting much out of the alpha, Rowan took in the rest of the bathroom. The walls were lined with what looked like cheap acrylic tile, giving the room the white and teal design of a kid's dentist. The sink was the only thing separating the shower from the toilet, and Rowan thought he could probably lie across all three at once, even with his small stature.

Rowan looked back at the small shower and felt that familiar sensation, imagining the alpha naked in the small space. Picking up a suitcase, he brought it into the bathroom and went to lock the door behind him, only to discover that there was no lock.

"Son of a bitch!" He hissed before saying screw it and hopping in the shower to wash the day away.

After a quick scrub-down, he discovered the hot water lasted only ten minutes. He jumped out and found there was only a single towel, which he assumed was Beckett's. Looking around, he nervously took it and dried himself off, hoping it was alright since he planned on getting some dorm supplies later, including a towel.

Once dressed in his sweatpants and oversized Nationals shirt, he peeked out of the bathroom. He found Beckett changed and lying in bed, holding his phone over his face and watching a video.

Not saying much, Rowan moved his suitcases to the foot of his bed and smiled at Beckett nervously. “Hope you don’t mind; I used your towel.”

Beckett looked over, and Rowan saw his green eyes flick down, roaming over his body briefly before going back to his phone. "S'fine."

Rowan crawled into his own twin bed, feeling the springs with each movement. It wasn't uncomfortable, just different from what he was used to.

Snuggling into his bed, he pulled out his phone from the side pouch of his duffel and checked the time.

“Sorry about the alarm ahead of time. Hope you don’t mind; I get up hella early.” He offered a smile to his roommate, who just glanced at him with those far-away eyes and went back to his phone screen.

Not that it was a perfect response, but Rowan let out a loud sigh, wondering what this guy's problem was. Maybe he was always like this? It was hard to say, given the short time they'd had together.

“Alright, well… night, Beckett!” He forced out another smile before pulling the covers over his head to hide away from the scent of alpha, rain, and coffee.

“Night,” Beckett said, the deep voice sending chills down the omega’s arms.

Damn that man and his sexy deep voice.

Yeah, he was one thousand percent asking for a room change because there was no way he could live with an alpha, especially one from his team. It could only end badly if it stayed like this; Rowan couldn't afford distractions right now.

And Beckett was the worst kind of distraction… A hot one.

# CHAPTER FOUR

"Nice one, Sparky!" Emily called out from the sidelines as Rowan landed another perfect salchow.

Rowan smiled brightly, excited to hear such praise from his idol. "Thanks, Coach!"

Emily looked at her watch and nodded. "Well, it's just about time for your first class, kid. Better hit the showers and head out."

"Already?" Rowan whined, gliding towards the rink's door. "I feel like we just started."

Emily smiled softly, touching his shoulder when he stepped off the ice. "It'll always feel that way, no matter how tired or hungry you get. There's never enough time on the ice." She sighed as if recalling a distant memory before slapping his shoulder. "Come on, you'll be late!"

Rowan took off his skates and rushed to the locker room, wincing at the strong scent of alpha. Covering his nose, he walked to the back of the empty room, where his name was taped on the front of a metal locker door. Quickly jumping in the shower, he rinsed off the sweat and used one of the provided towels to dry off. Changing into his jeans and band hoodie, he was already rushing out of the stadium towards his Intro to English with Doctor Vance Archer. The name did cause him to double-take. What would the odds be of them being related to the toughest coach on the planet?

On his way over, he couldn't help but think of his morning.

As soon as dawn broke, he was up and dressed, constantly looking at his alpha roommate. Beckett seemed to sleep like the dead, even though he had been up really late watching videos on his phone. He swung by the housing department's office to find the advisor wasn't in yet, but his secretary showed up with fresh tea in hand. She told Rowan that the dorms were full and that if he left his current dorm, he would be responsible for his own accommodations. Rowan couldn't afford an apartment with his already hectic schedule. Hell, even finding time to study or eat would be a miracle!

Walking into his Intro to English class, Rowan was met with a large auditorium filled with students. He couldn't help but squeal to himself at how cool and adult it all was—like something out of those college movies he had seen. Looking around the room, he searched for an open seat. The class would be starting in two minutes, and he found nearly every seat taken.

Except…

His eyes widened when he located not one but two open seats, both on either side of a brooding-looking alpha with deep green eyes that looked right at him.

Rowan blushed, looking away quickly to see if he missed a seat somewhere. Nothing was popping out as he frantically glanced around.

"Welcome to Intro to English!" a loud voice shouted, and Rowan felt sweat break out on his neck as the teacher looked at the blond standing along the classroom's stairs. "Find your seat, little friend!"

Rowan quickly apologized and made his way across the aisle of filled seats, whispering, 'excuse me' and 'pardon me,' before sitting next to Beckett. He sat up rigidly before telling himself not to be rude. The scent of coffee and rain slowly seeped into his bones like a forgotten presence.

Turning to his roommate and captain, he forced a smile and whispered, "Hey, roomie."

Beckett glanced at him before facing forward again. Rowan pouted at the lack of greeting before facing forward. A sweet girl next to him waved, and Rowan greeted her, along with the small group in the row behind them.

Instantly, he gained smiles all around, no doubt from his sunny disposition. People always smiled when Rowan was around; he was literally like a big ball of energy that transferred to everyone… '*Well, almost everyone,*' he thought, glancing at his hockey captain.

"I highly suggest making friends in this class, so you always have someone to lean on for support!" The teacher shouted, suggesting they take five minutes to trade numbers.

Rowan perked up, looking at the girl next to him, who smiled earlier. Rowan instantly handed over his number as she did the same. The group behind them passed Rowan a piece of paper with their numbers on it, and he promised to text his number over. Beckett sat stone-still, staring at the front with that same unreadable expression on his face. Rowan found it weird that he didn't even attempt to talk to anyone around him.

‘*Some people are just loners,*’ he thought with a shrug as the teacher continued.

The rest of the class went on like that. The professor went over the curriculum for the semester while Rowan doodled in his agenda. English was his best subject, so this class would be something he could breeze past as a recovery period after morning training.

Since he felt confident in zoning out, the figure skater checked his peripheral vision for the dozenth time since sitting next to his new captain. The alpha’s scent was so strong that Rowan had to subtly lean the lower half of his face into his sleeve, which he pulled over his hand.

It wasn’t like his scent was more pronounced than anyone else's in the room; it just stuck out to Rowan more than the other alphas or betas. It lingered in the air around him, and Rowan would be lying if he said it wasn't distracting.

Beckett stared intently at the front of the large room. Only once did he look down at Rowan, and the figure skater blushed, averting his eyes to seem like he wasn’t looking at the alpha.

Rowan was so excited when class ended that he nearly sprang up, startling Beckett, who looked at him with a raised brow.

Rowan chuckled nervously. "Um, see you later!" He waved, stepping out shyly around their desk toward the stairs. Once he left, he wondered if he should have waited for Beckett, but he shook the thought off and bolted for the cafeteria.

‘*The guy’s a lone wolf. He’d probably try and shake me off the first chance he got,*’ Rowan mused with a huff.

Standing in line with his tray, he hummed in excitement at all the amazing smells.

"Sweet, sweet food!" He hummed, taking out his meal plan card and looking over the stations.

Although the school received high praise for its education and sports, the food seemed to leave something to be desired. Rowan confidently walked up to the counter, only to see the kitchen staff dumping the food into a nearby bin. Appalled, Rowan managed to swipe a banana nut muffin and an apple before they joined the rest of the food in the trash.

Looking at the bare slots along the line, he groaned. He looked at a woman in a hair net, scrubbing an empty cereal tube. "Excuse me, when will they be laying out more food?"

She smiled sweetly. "Sorry, sugar; we toss breakfast at eleven, and lunch isn't out till twelve."

The blond looked up at a clock on the wall. "But it's only 10:55!"

"What can I say?" the woman replied with a shrug. "To be early is to be on time."

Rowan resisted the urge to frown, knowing that it wasn't her fault, and thanked her before taking his meager findings to the scanner. Plopping down at an empty table, he looked around the large room before biting into his apple. Then, while enjoying his first meal that wasn't a power bar, he took out a book and picked up where his receipt bookmark left him.

Twenty before twelve, he started to collect his things and stand up when the door to the cafeteria burst open.

"Hey, check it out; it's Twinkle Toes!" A familiar voice growled.

Rowan stood up, holding his books to his chest as he met eyes with five of his new teammates, one of whom he knew the name of; Ryker Wilson.

The omega raised a hand in what he hoped would be a warm greeting. "Morning, guys!"

Wilson scoffed, turning away as his teammates followed. The redhead in the group gave Rowan a shrug that must have meant sorry as he followed his teammate.

Rowan sighed, shook his head, and left the cafeteria to head to his math class.

# CHAPTER FIVE

The day flew by after his break, with his final class letting him out with just enough time to head over to the stadium for his second day of training. Archer was standing outside the locker room, seemingly waiting for him. Rowan felt anxiety swell in his stomach. Was the coach going to kick him off the team? Did Rowan offend him yesterday? Did he not work hard enough?

"H-hey, coach," Rowan said with hopeful confidence. "West," Archer regarded him. "A word."

"Oooo, someone's in trouble," The thin beta from yesterday sang, walking into the locker room with one of the red-haired guys.

"McAllister, keep it to yourself," Archer chided, looking back to Rowan. "Come in." He motioned to the locker room.

Rowan blushed but followed the coach into the white-tiled room, which stank of alpha, soap, and sweat. A few players were already there, some half-dressed, putting on their gear. Rowan averted his eyes to the back of Archer's head, following the coach to the back.

In the back of the locker room, there was a door before the showers. Archer opened it, and Rowan saw a gear room filled with skates and padding.

"We train in gear, so you'll need to get fitted." He motioned with his head to follow as the door shut behind them.

Archer pushed through the padding, looking between Rowan's small frame and the stuff they had available. He grunted with annoyance before he continued to search. Rowan just stood there, holding his backpack on one shoulder. The scent of burning coffee was almost familiar to Rowan if he thought about it. He resisted the urge to sniff, worried he might get caught, and discreetly kept it to himself.

"Something wrong, sir?" He asked after a few minutes of Archer cursing under his breath.

"You're smaller than we usually get, but-" He pulled out some padding, a training jersey, and some pants. "This should fit."

Rowan heard the gear thump loudly as it fell before him. He nearly bristled at the idea of skating with all that gear. Who did they think he was, Goku?

"Thanks, sir!" Rowan watched him go to the skates and squint at them. "What size skate are you?"

"Eight."

"Eight?" He balked loudly, looking at him in surprise.

Rowan blushed again, bringing his shoulders to his ears. "I'm small, kind of an omega trait," He bit out under his breath.

Archer rubbed his chin. "We don't have that, but we can order you a pair. Until then, just wear your regular skates."

"Yes, sir." Rowan was relieved; at least he would be comfortable with one piece of his equipment.

"Also..." Archer paused at the door. "If you want, you can change in here, away from the others." The older alpha seemed hesitant but clear. "Anyone gives you any trouble for being an omega, just come see me. I don't put up with that kind of shit."

Rowan felt touched that this gruff, intimidating man could offer such a kind option for him.

"Thank you, I might just take you up on that." He nodded as Archer left, shutting the door behind him.

The hockey pants were a bit loose, but Rowan tightened them with the Velcro belt around the sides. The big socks were next, along with his shin guards and skates. Once his lower half was done, he slid on a compression shirt. It hugged his slight frame and felt soft, like one of Rowan's skating costumes. He smiled before looking at the shoulder pads and pausing.

"How do you-" He asked no one, lifting the heavy item and noticing the straps and string on the front.

After trying to get it on unsuccessfully, he swallowed his pride and opened the door to poke his head out.

Lucky him, the only person left in the locker rooms was his roommate. Rowan bit on the inside of his cheek as the tall alpha finished lacing his neck guard.

Rowan sighed; it was now or never. "Psst!"

Beckett raised his eyebrow at Rowan, his normal angry look still in place. "Hm?"

Rowan offered what he hoped was a sweet smile. "Hey, Captain, mind helping me?"

Beckett walked over; his movements slowed by his skates. He stopped before Rowan, looking down at the shoulder pads.

"I've never worn one of these... could you show me?"

The captain accepted the heavy padding and held it up over Rowan. "Stand still."

A chill went down his spine at the deep voice as his mind went somewhere pretty perverted. He did as the alpha asked.

He slid the padding over his blond's head, resting it on his shoulders. Rowan grunted under the weight but kept upright as Beckett fastened the Velcro around his sides tightly.

"It's tight," Rowan muttered, feeling his face heat up as Beckett leaned in and reached for the laces in the middle

"Good," Beckett said firmly. "Won't fall off."

Rowan pouted and averted his eyes, so he wasn't looking at his captain's handsome face. Yes, the captain was handsome; he'd be blind not to see that. His face was always in a perpetual state of pissed, though, and it threw Rowan off.

Rowan always fell for the sweet-guy smile. Not once since meeting this guy had he ever cared for the tough-guy persona, though something about Beckett made Rowan's heart race and his stomach twist. Maybe it was the sight of those eyes looking down at him with such intensity.

"There." Beckett took a step back, looking over his work.

Rowan felt like the walls were closing in on them as he offered a sweet smile to the alpha. "Thanks for the help, man."

Beckett looked to the side, and after a second, he asked softly, almost hesitantly. "Need help... with anything else?"

"Beckett!" Rowan playfully slapped the alpha's arm, shocking the captain to look back at him in surprise. "I'm not that kind of omega," He teased.

For the first time, a splash of red scattered across the bridge of Beckett's nose, and he brought the back of his hand up to try to cover it, looking away. "I-I didn't mean-" He trailed off nervously.

Rowan felt his chest swell as he admired how cute Beckett looked when he was all flustered. The omega was practically giggling and giving the alpha a wink. "I was just playing! I think I've got the rest." He held up his elbow pads. "I'll see you on the ice!"

Beckett nodded, "Don't forget your helmet."

"I won't!" He waved to the captain and watched him walk out of the locker room, picking up his helmet and gloves on the way.

Once he was gone, Rowan placed a hand over his racing heart. "Well... that was unexpected," He muttered as he slipped on his elbow pads.

# CHAPTER SIX

## ROWAN

Walking in hockey gear was just as awkward as he thought it would be. Rowan stumbled on his skates like a new baby deer. However, he managed to get the hang of it before leaving the locker room and making his way to the ice, where the team was already stretching.

"Hey, guys!" Rowan projected an air of confidence as he stepped nervously on the ice. His legs buckled a bit, unfamiliar with the weight on such a smooth surface. All of his muscles tried to balance him the same as they had a million other times on the ice, but everything was so different with the weight of the gear. His erratic movements must have been amusing, because his team responded with a small wave of laughter.

"Oh my god! Look at him!" McAllister, the thin player from earlier, pointed at him. "He's precious!" He leaned on the spiky redhead for support.

"Aw, come on, it's not so bad!" The redhead chortled.

"Can he even do inside edges?" Wilson shouted, pointing at him while looking at Archer, who seemed just as disappointed in Rowan's appearance. "Coach, look at him!"

Rowan puffed out his cheeks in annoyance like a pufferfish and skated over to stand near Archer, holding his stance as rigid as he could. “I’ll have you know, even like this, I could skate circles around you!”

Those seemed to be the magic words, turning Wilson’s sneer into a sadistic smirk. “Oh yeah? Come over here and say that to my face, Twinkle Toes!”

“Gladly!” Rowan started to skate over when Archer grabbed the back of his shoulder pads, holding him back with barely any effort.

“As much as we would all love to see that,” the coach said to Wilson before turning his head to speak to everyone. “We have drills to run.”

Rowan stopped fighting Archer, who let him go once the blond’s struggles ceased. Rowan looked up at the coach, who pointed to some small black cylinders that sat on the ice.

“Watch,” he said before looking at Beckett.

“Captain! Inside Edges!” Archer shouted. Beckett moved like lightning to the black shapes. He seamlessly wove through the obstacles in a precise crisscross pattern. After he finished, Archer nudged Rowan toward the challenge. “Your turn.”

Rowan smiled. “Piece of cake!” he proclaimed before pushing forward.

As before, Rowan skated with the grace of a burning cement truck. He attempted to copy Beckett’s moves, knowing beyond a shadow of a doubt that his body could do what his mind ordered. His face grew hot as he shuffled across the ice, embarrassed at the grace that had been stolen from him by the weights they covered him with.

Even from halfway across the rink, Archer's groan was impossible to ignore. It was echoed by the snickering of his teammates, who looked ready to fall over their sticks in enjoyment at Rowan's expense.

"Beckett," the coach grumbled. The team captain glided across the ice and slid to a stop, kicking up powdered ice in the process. "Please get him adjusted."

Beckett looked at Rowan, who was slowly skating in circles, trying to get some sense of balance back. Beckett grimaced before looking back at his coach and nodding. He skated over to Rowan, grabbed him by the arm, and guided him to the far side of the ice. They stopped at the far wall, ignoring the sounds of Archer's whistle demanding the other players get to their drills, commenting, 'show's over!' very loudly.

"Okay, Rookie. Skate around the net, let me see your footwork," Beckett said. Rowan slowly made a circle around the net with Beckett staring at his skates and form the whole way. Finally, the blond came to a stop in front of the team captain.

"Ta-da," Rowan said as he raised a hand up theatrically. He was embarrassed, but he did his best not to show it. Beckett looked up and met Rowan's eyes, causing that same familiar sizzle to encase his chest cavity.

"You win a lot of medals with that work?" He asked smugly. Rowan's face scrunched up, shocked to see what must have been Beckett's amused face.

"It's these pads! They're just heavy enough to throw my balance off," he said before pointing a finger at Beckett. "And I'll have you know I've won tons of competitions. My body is a finely-tuned machine," he said as he gestured up and down his body with open hands.

Beckett rolled his eyes and said, "Yeah, okay." He moved over to the blond and spun halfway around so they stood shoulder-to-shoulder. He imitated the blond's upright pose.

"We don't skate upright, Rookie. We skate for speed, and that means low center of gravity," Beckett said before doing a slight squat and leaning forward. "Standing upright is fine when you're still, but you need to get lower when you move."

Rowan looked at the larger player and copied his stance. He skated forward a step and slipped a little, but he caught himself.

"Skate to the blue line and back. Take your time, get used to the motions," Beckett said. Rowan started to move, and Beckett added, "and stop thinking so gracefully!"

Rowan smiled and pushed off, moving his arms and legs in ways that would typically cost him points without question in competition. The crouch was weird at first, but after a few strides, he found himself more balanced, though not much faster than he was before. He got to the blue line, did a small U-turn, and skated back, feeling his confidence come back little by little. He stopped in front of Beckett and excitedly asked, "How was that?"

Beckett nodded in approval. "You won't be out-maneuvering anyone, but better." He pointed to the blue line. "However, turns like that take too long. You gotta get better at stopping on a dime before shoving yourself in the other direction. Speed and time are everything." Rowan nodded and smiled.

"Got it. Thanks."

Beckett crossed his arms and looked at the blond. They stood in silence for a moment before Beckett raised an eyebrow.

"Well?" he asked before motioning to the blue line with his head. "Again!"

Rowan jumped, turning as he repeated his movements down to the blue line, gaining more confidence with each trip. On his fourth try, Beckett joined him, skating alongside the blond's hesitant movements. Rowan felt the need to break the silence.

"I think this is the most I've heard you spout since meeting you yesterday. And that's saying something, considering you're my roomie." Rowan did a sharp turn but nearly lost his footing. Fortunately, he managed not to fall on his butt in front of his hot captain.

Beckett shrugged, honestly looking a little annoyed. Rowan hoped it wasn't because of how slowly they were moving.

"I don't talk much." He muttered, looking down at his skates. "You seemed pretty alright back there with it."

Beckett scoffed, cocking his head sideways to the blond. "That doesn't count. It's easy to talk on the ice. Everywhere else not so much."

"I feel you! Talking can be hard." Rowan nodded.

Beckett let out a sound between a hum and a chuckle, which did things to Rowan's insides. The blond was so distracted that he nearly ran into the net as they turned around to go back to the blue line. "What's so funny?"

"S'nothing." Beckett shook his head. "You just don't seem the type to have any problem talking."

Rowan blushed, glad his helmet covered most of his face with the bright lights casting a glare on the guard. "I'm not perfect. My mouth speaks before my filter catches it, and I still panic internally. What if I say the wrong thing? What if my ADHD takes the wheel and changes the conversation? What if I slip and say something embarrassing?" Rowan chuckled nervously, looking up at the alpha next to him. "Talking is hard."

"Hmm," Beckett hummed. "Well, you make it look... effortless."

Those electrical zaps in his stomach sparked to life as he looked up at his captain and gave him the biggest smile. "Hey, thanks, man. You know, you're not so bad."

Beckett looked away, a faint blush on his face as he looked down at his skates. It was strange seeing an alpha look down and away from an omega's gaze. So much so that Rowan reached a hand out and poked his arm, "You okay?"

The captain looked back at him, bringing a gloved hand to the back of his helmet. "You think I'm alright?"

Rowan felt his infectious smile pull across his face. "Yeah, and frankly, I'm relieved. I thought you hated me."

Beckett stopped skating and made Rowan stop as well. "You thought I didn't like you?"

The blond blushed, lifting the visor of his helmet to get a good look up at the alpha. "Well, yeah, you kind of have this face when you look at me."

The alpha looked down, eyebrows drooping as if crestfallen, but those intense eyes to any new person would seem angry. “I don’t have the best-” He struggled with finding the right words. “Honestly, I have the emotional expressions of a rock.”

Rowan’s mouth dropped open in shock and realization. “Oh! You have a resting bitch face!”

The face his captain made was set between stunned and pissed off, making Rowan think he hit a sore spot and quickly backpedaled. "Sorry, that was harsh. See? No filter. What about resting mean face?"

That seemed to work better as the alpha let his shoulders slump. "I guess you could say that."

Everything seemed to make sense now. “I see, I see. I bet your friends have an easier time reading you than strangers.”

Rowan was about to go back to skating when he heard the alpha mutter something. Rowan turned to look over his shoulder pads at him, “What was that?”

“I don’t really have friends.” The words came out forced, as if he were embarrassed to say them.

“What?” Rowan whispered, feeling sadness pool in his stomach as well as shock and disbelief. “But what about your team?” He motioned to the others at the other end of the ice, oblivious to their conversation.

Beckett shrugged, “I don’t think they like me. They don’t really talk to me outside of practice.”

“Aw, well, join the club, because if they don’t like a charmer like you, then that means they hate my guts.”

Rowan chuckled, starting up his skating again while Beckett joined him.

“You’ll win them over,” Beckett muttered.

“How about we both win them over?” Rowan asked, looking up at the alpha with a glint of excitement in his blue eyes.

Maybe it was the omega getting scent-drunk off coffee and rain, or maybe it's the way the brooding alpha looked at Rowan. Regardless, the blond wanted to make this captain smile, and before he knew it, words started tumbling out.

"I don't follow." Beckett took off his helmet, squinting his eyes down at the small blond.

Rowan chuckled, glad to finally get a clear look at his handsome face. "We team up! I think we can help each other out here." He motioned between them. "You help me get the hang of this hockey stuff, at least enough for me to not lose my scholarship, and I'll help you get some friends."

"You want to help me?" Beckett seemed hesitant. "Why?" The look he gave the omega showed years of not trusting anyone, and it pained him to see it.

'*Because it means I get to stay close by your side.*' His inner omega mewed, desperate for more of that alpha scent.

"Because, besides Coach Emi, you're the first person who's actually had a conversation with me since I got here. You seem nice now that we're getting to know each other." Rowan felt the bridge of his nose heat up under the cold temperature of the arena.

"What about finding a new roommate?" Beckett asked almost hesitantly.

"That's long out the window. I was shot down." He sighed sadly, now feeling guilty for even trying in the first place.

Looking to his captain, he noticed an almost sad look cross his face, and Rowan quickly touched his arm with his gloved hand. "But that was before! Now that we're friends, I don't think it should be a big deal. You don't mind me being an omega, do you?"

Rowan couldn't explain the look Beckett gave him, looking from the hand touching his arm to Rowan's blue eyes. "You… you say we're friends?"

"Well, duh!" Rowan scoffed, taking his hand back. "But you didn't answer my question."

Beckett quickly shook his head. "N-no, I don't have an issue with you being an omega." He looked sideways and back quickly. "Are you alright with me being an alpha?"

"I'll have to get used to the smell, but thankfully, your scent is calming." Rowan chuckled under his breath. "So yes, you're cool in my book, Beck."

"Beck?" Beckett whispered, as if tasting the name. "No one's ever called me that."

"Well, if you can call me Rookie, I can call you Beck. Or do you prefer Alpha?" He purred the word, causing the captain's cheeks to heat up in a way that made Rowan bark out a laugh as the alpha tried to hide it behind his large glove.

"Aw, come on, don't hide it! Show me that cute face!" Rowan grabbed onto his arm to try to pry it away.

"No, thank you," Beckett grumbled out. "Maybe we should move on to another drill?"

"Whatever you say, Beck!" Rowan laughed infectiously, happy that he finally made his first friend in this place.

Maybe hockey wouldn't be so bad after all!

# CHAPTER SEVEN

## ~~~~~~ ROWAN ~~~~~~

Once Rowan felt he had leveled up from baby deer to skittish raccoon in the bulky gear, he and Beckett moved on to a different drill.

Rowan felt it was important to ask as many questions as possible since Beckett would become as silent as a mime once they were off the ice.

"So, tell me about the team," Rowan said, holding his new hockey stick and mimicking the way Beckett leaned forward with his own stick parallel to the ground. Beckett pointed at the other players.

"Well, that's all of them," he said. The other players skated around the far half of the ice, quickly accelerating and stopping on a dime. Some of them fired pucks at the net while others stretched on the ice.

Rowan observed them all before asking, "Okay, but who are they? What do they do?"

Beckett sighed and pointed at the two players in the bulkiest gear. "That's Briggs and Rhodes; they're our goalies. Their whole job is to keep the puck out of the net. That's why their gear is so heavy; everybody's shooting frozen pieces of rubber at them at a hundred miles an hour all game." Rowan thought they must be insane to willingly jump into that path.

Beckett gestured to a couple of players who were running skating drills and doing a lot of backward skating. "Those four," he said, pausing as the angry blond player shouted at a teammate who bumped into him, "are our defensemen. Their main role is to keep the puck out of our zone and act as our first line of defense against the other team. They can also try to score or protect the offensive players, but they generally hang back near the rear of the play."

He pointed specifically at the aggressive blond. "That bundle of joy is Wilson. The other defensemen are," he pointed at them individually as he spoke. "Sanchez, Jones, and Harrington."

Rowan watched as Wilson shoved Sanchez into the sideboard before rerunning the drill.

"Wilson seems...passionate," Rowan observed. Beckett snorted out a breath of laughter.

"Yeah. As he'll proudly tell you, he had the most fights in the league last year."

Rowan nearly fell on the ice as he spun toward Beckett. “Fights?!”

Beckett nodded. “Yeah, fights. It can be a rough sport, especially when you have people like Wilson on the ice. But I’ll tell you, I’ve never seen another player make the other team flinch like he does.”

Rowan shuddered at the thought of it. He turned back and pointed at the players firing pucks at the net. “What about them? Who are they?”

Beckett motioned to a player with chestnut hair and a scar around his left eye. “That’s Jeon. He’s a center.” Beckett pointed at himself with his thumb. “Which is also my thing. I’m just better at it.”

Rowan rolled his eyes. "And you’re so humble about it, too."

"Humility doesn't score goals. I do," Beckett replied. Then, he pointed at the others and listed off their names. "That's McAllister, Cooper, Dominguez, and Walker. They're wings to the center."

Rowan raised an eyebrow. "Wings? Like, dating?" He expected a smile, but Beckett's lips stayed as flat as a week-old bottle of opened soda.

"More like pilots. We have to work as a team, communicate, pass the puck, and create formations. We're the offensive line, and it's not a job any one person can do on their own."

Beckett rattled off a handful of other names, but Rowan knew he wouldn't be able to remember them all. He just nodded along as Beckett pointed out a few players and gave him a quick checklist of their positions.

Rowan looked over at the players as they passed the puck to each other before one of them fired a shot at the net with a loud, 'Crack!' The puck smacked into the metal bar, and a clang rang out through the arena.

"Crossbar, Jeon!" Archer shouted from the side. "That's five Herbies!" Jeon hung his head and skated to the blue line.

"Herbies?" Rowan asked.

"It's a skating drill," Beckett replied. He shook his head, "It was a sloppy shot on an empty net. Jeon's better than that."

Rowan watched the player rapidly skate back and forth across the ice. The blond omega looked back at Beckett after a few moments.

"So, how many of you go on the ice at once?"

"Six. A center, a goalie, two wings, and two defensemen." Beckett replied.

Rowan nodded. “Got it. And who has the most important job?”

"They're all important," Beckett said quickly, like it was the textbook answer. After a moment, though, he went on. "But people have their own opinions about it." He didn't look at Rowan as he spoke, staring at his players as they trained. Rowan figured it was because he was their captain; he must have to watch that stuff.

Rowan couldn't help but look up and down his body, covered by the baggy jersey he wore with his gear. The guy was a freaking giant, and he was even bigger with those skates on!

Rowan leaned in a bit. “What’s yours?”

Beckett glanced at him before looking back to the team. "Selfishly, I say it's the center; the most famous player ever was a center. They're the playmakers, they're always in the action, and they're often the team captain because of it." There was a brief moment of silence before he continued. "But I can get the argument about the goalie being the most important person out there, too. It doesn't matter how much we score if the other team can get more goals."

Rowan smiled and pointed at Beckett. “Ha! So, he does have some humility!” he said triumphantly. Beckett rolled his eyes and gently nudged him with the hockey stick.

“Come on, Rookie, enough talk. We’ve got work to do.”

Rowan felt his heart leap into his throat, thrilled that Beckett was becoming more comfortable with him as they went on. Beckett skated toward the drills as Rowan repeated the player names in his head to make sure he would remember them all.

Time went a lot quicker than yesterday's practice, and this time Rowan managed to stay on his feet instead of collapsing when Archer ended the practice with a blow of the whistle. He knew Beckett went easy on him, and Rowan appreciated the chance to get used to the game.

Rowan leaned against the wall along the ice, watching the team skate off one by one. He found himself constantly looking at the captain, watching him. The guy had barely broken a sweat all practice.

"That was… enlightening." Rowan sighed, feeling the burn in his legs from holding all that weight up.

Beckett shrugged. "You seem to be getting it alright."

Archer passed them as they stepped through the doorway to exit the rink, looking at Rowan with an unreadable expression. Rowan expected the coach to say something snarky and braced himself for the vocal impact.

"Nice hustle, kid. Beckett, good leadership skills," he said before turning his back to them and skating off the ice.

"Wow, was that a compliment?" Rowan stepped off the ice, followed by Beckett.

At the silence, he turned to the massive captain and saw his unsure face. "Aw, come on. I know we're not on the ice anymore, but you can still talk to me, right?"

Beckett's nose turned pink as he shrugged. Rowan found his odd silence cute, but he already missed that deep voice.

"Alright, we'll work on that." He walked with Beckett toward the locker room, where he paused. Beckett looked back at him and tilted his head to the door. Rowan nodded, following him in and keeping his eyes averted down.

The sound of the showers flowed out through the door, and Rowan felt his face turn bright red as he walked down to his locker, passing the line of changing alphas and betas. He opened the locker and slipped his duffel bag out before silently making his way to the equipment room in the back. No one paid him any mind; they were too busy with their own conversations as they changed and showered.

Rowan stood in the equipment room, nervously pulling at his jersey as he waited. While he had never been shy in a locker room, he had never been around so many alphas with so little clothing.

His hometown ice rink was just for community use, so the locker room had only three showers and a single row of lockers for the few who used it, including Rowan and his fellow rink buddies. Most of them were betas, and he never had an issue walking around them in a towel.

To pass the time, he watched his friend Imani's TikToks, where she was skating to a Ricky Martin song in a very revealing pair of shorts. For the number of followers and sponsors she had, Rowan could only applaud her choices in life. Frankly, though, he wondered why she didn't go pro and instead pursued a more commercial route.

She actually had a role as a background character in a skating movie, but it wasn't wise to get her talking about that. You'd be stuck there forever as she showed you the whole film just to get to the forty-second shot of her twirling around in the background while the main characters talked. Huffing out a laugh, Rowan left a heart and a comment to show his support. PinkIce was one of the fastest-growing figure skaters on social media. Rowan was honored that he could call her one of his closest friends.

When the commotion in the locker room died down, Rowan took off the rest of his clothes, wrapped the stadium-provided towel around his waist, and poked his head from the room. Looking both ways, he was satisfied to find no one around, allowing him to use the showers that reeked of alpha.

If Imani were there, she would have walked her butt-ass naked body down there from her own locker, gender roles be damned. That confidence transferred to Rowan as they grew up, and he felt proud to call himself an omega. Why should he feel bad about the cards dealt to him at birth? All he could do was be proud of himself. Though at the same time, pride and safety were two separate things. While his team didn't seem like the type to try anything, he would rather avoid any awkwardness.

After a quick scrub-down, he changed into his jeans and hoodie, then grabbed his backpack. Opening the locker room door, he nearly bumped into the giant wall called Beckett.

"Oh! Beck! You waited for me?" Rowan cocked his head, shoving his hands into the front pocket of his hoodie.

Beckett held his duffel bag on one shoulder and looked to the side before shrugging.

Rowan gave the alpha a bright smile. "Well, I'm glad you didn't ditch me! Wanna get some dinner?"

The captain nodded once, waiting for Rowan to make the first move, and followed beside him. It was refreshing to see an alpha who wasn't always trying to stay at least a step ahead of an omega. Rowan hated it when they did that, even if it was done subconsciously. Beckett wasn't like the typical alpha, which was fine with Rowan.

The whole way to the mess hall, Rowan babbled on about hockey questions, getting only brief answers from the alpha in return. Beckett's voice grew lower when someone would pass by them, his eyes darting nervously in their direction. It was as if they were going to catch him in the act of making any sound.

Once inside, Rowan was thrilled to see actual food, swiping his meal card and filling up on a big bowl of spaghetti and breadsticks. Beckett got a large bowl of rice and chicken, double the portion of what Rowan would consider normal. But he assumed a guy as large as Beckett had to go heavy on the carbs and protein.

Sitting at a cleared-out table, Rowan dove into his food, moaning obscenely. "Gods, I needed this! Can you believe they stop serving breakfast at eleven?" He pointed a breadstick at the alpha, who just listened.

"I train from the ass-crack of dawn until my first class, and just when we get out of English, they stop serving breakfast! By the time lunch comes out, I'm already on my way to my next class, and then to hockey practice. This is my first real meal all day," Rowan whined, nibbling on the bread to savor it.

Beckett seemed taken aback and gave the omega a concerned head tilt. At least, Rowan assumed it was out of concern. It was a familiar look his friends would give him when he would show up late or 'misplace' his school lunch money. It was a look he wasn't at all fond of; he didn't need anyone's pity.

“Oh, it’s fine! I just need to double down on carrying snacks. I used to do it all the time back home.” He leaned into his palm, twirling a fork around the noodles. “Maybe we can get a mini fridge for our dorm, stock up on some essentials.”

Beckett nodded as he ate his rice and listened intently.

A roar of conversation echoed through the room. Rowan looked over and saw half the hockey team bustling in, heading for the food. They all took seats on the other side of the room, not even acknowledging the two players. Rowan pouted at them but looked at Beckett. "How long have you been playing on the team?"

Beckett muttered a low, “Six months.”

“How’d you make captain so quickly?”

The alpha shrugged, and Rowan sighed. "You know, we need to communicate to keep a friendship going."

A moment of panic flittered across Beckett's face. "Um," He whispered. "I knew the coach before coming here."

"Oooo, didn't peg Archer for playing favorites. What are you, family friends or something?"

Beckett looked down at his food. "Something like that."

“Well, he doesn’t seem like the type to put his social life over the game, so you must be good.” Rowan shoved another fork of pasta in his mouth.

Beckett poked at his chicken and looked over his shoulder at the team. Rowan leaned to the side to look and noticed they were being watched. Rowan quickly raised his hand after swallowing his food. "Hey, guys!"

Wilson sneered, turning away before motioning for Jeon and Briggs to focus and get back to their own food.

The omega sighed, smiling in exhaustion as he looked back at his only friend in this place. “So, I get why they don’t like me. But why don’t they like you?” Rowan pointed his fork at the captain.

Beckett chewed his food slowly, seemingly avoiding talking as Rowan waited as patiently as he could. His left leg bounced animatedly under the table before he groaned. “Come on, while I’m young.”

“I don’t think Wilson likes me.” Beckett sounded out the words so softly that Rowan had to lean closer to hear. “Because I’m captain.”

“So?” Rowan prodded, waiting for more.

“I assume he wants that position.”

"But you're good, right?"

"Hm?" Beckett looked down at the blond.

Rowan could almost swing his feet under the table with how high the bench was from the floor; the tips of his Converse squeaked obnoxiously every few seconds. "You're a good captain. Otherwise, you wouldn't be leading the team. So, we can't be too sure that's the reason." Rowan hummed, looking up in thought before a metaphorical lightbulb went off over his head. "I have an idea! Let's go over there!"

A look of horror passed across Beckett’s face. “Wha-”

"Yeah, come on!" Rowan quickly stood up, swinging his duffel bag over his shoulder before picking up his food tray and waiting for Beckett.

The alpha looked at Rowan like he was crazy. “Now?”

“No time like the present!” He motioned for the captain to follow before beginning his trek.

The sound of scuffling filled the air as Beckett quickly stood, grabbed his own bag and tray, and followed the blond.

The hockey team's conversation echoed through the cafeteria, even from several tables away. However, the chatter came to a deathly silence when the blond and raven-haired player stopped near the players. Rowan smiled brightly while Beckett looked like he wanted to disappear into the floor with how hard he was looking down at his tray.

The other players looked at them, faces ranging from mild confusion to outright annoyance. Finally, after several seconds, Rowan took it upon himself to break the silence.

"Hey, guys! Mind if we join you?" Rowan asked happily, looking at each of their faces.

"Uh, sure," The redhead, whom he recalled was Briggs, said, but he flinched when Wilson elbowed him in the side. "Ow! What?"

Wilson looked from the goalie to the two standing students. “Why?”

Rowan lowered his tray to the empty seat next to another player. "Well, as your new teammate, I feel we should get to know each other."

The blond alpha scoffed, looking from Rowan to the captain. “What about you?”

Beckett's face was blank. His eyes narrowed down at Wilson, who narrowed them back. To anyone walking by, it would appear as if they were in a staring contest. Finally, after several long seconds, Wilson growled and stood up, nearly knocking over his soda. "The fuck you looking at?"

Beckett just continued to stare, and Rowan nervously looked between the two. “Beck?” He whispered.

"See? Always a goddamn attitude with this guy!" Wilson growled loudly. Briggs brought up a hand to push the blond back down into his seat, chiding him by explaining fights off the ice are so not cool.

Rowan pouted, looking back to the group. “Beck? Nah! He’s a big old softie!”

The guy named McAllister looked nervously up at Beckett. “You sure? Guy looks ready to rip our throats out.”

Jones, the beta at the end of the table, looked ready to shit bricks when Beckett came over. "He doesn't usually talk to us outside of practice."

"Tch! Some captain!" Wilson rolled his hazel eyes, going back to his rice.

Rowan was about to suggest they all talk when Beckett slammed his tray down, and nearly the whole table flinched, including Rowan. He glared at Wilson before turning on his heel and walking away.

“B-Beck, wait!” Rowan abandoned his own tray, running after his friend, “Beck!”

Once outside the mess hall, Rowan managed to catch the alpha, grabbing the sleeve of his jacket and pulling him to a stop. Beckett looked over his shoulder to the omega, and Rowan could actually see the pain there, past the annoyed look.

"Beck," He said softly. "Come on. They're just being dicks."

"They're my team," he said, nearly startling Rowan. "And they hate me."

"Yeah, well, they hate me, too." The blond chuckled, trying to lighten the situation. "Fuck 'em. If they don't like us, then we can just like each other!" He quickly blushed, waving his hands before him, releasing the other sleeve. "I mean like friends! We have each other's back!"

Beckett seemed to think about this for a moment before his shoulders sagged, and he nodded.

Rowan was relieved that he calmed the captain down. He looked down at his watch. "Hey, we got a few hours before the stores near here close. Wanna help me get some stuff?"

Beckett looked back at the mess hall and back at him. “What about your food?”

“Pssf, I’m stuffed! Stick a fork in me, I'm done,” The blond lied through his teeth, motioning with his head to the sidewalk that led off campus. “Come on, I need a towel. I can’t keep using yours.”

"I wouldn't mind," Beckett said as he walked alongside the short figure skater. He wore a pink splotch of color on his nose that resembled Rowan's own blush.

"Dude!" Rowan punched his shoulder but laughed through it, loving how Beckett caved to his joke with a less-pensive look.

# CHAPTER EIGHT

## ~~~~~~ BECK ~~~~~~

Beckett was amazed; for once, the day had not gone how he had imagined.

When he woke up this morning to his blond roommate gone but with his still-packed bags at the end of his bed, he assumed he was off to get his room re-assigned. Guilt bubbled up in his stomach that he might have made the small omega uncomfortable before bed. Maybe he should have gone out to sleep in the common room, regardless of what Rowan said.

After getting dressed for the day, Beckett brushed his teeth and, when he spat into the sink, he reached for his towel. He froze when he caught a scent on it. His eyes widened as he sniffed it, his face flushed at the knowledge that the blond had used his towel to dry off last night. Quickly, he tossed the fluffy fabric into the laundry basket outside the bathroom door.

No use getting attached to another person who was going to leave him.

After breakfast, he went to his first class to find it mostly empty. His papa was up front writing his name on the board. Beckett made him promise not to make a big deal of him taking his class. He put it off last semester, but he could only do that for so long. Taking a seat near the top rows, he watched as people filed into the room one by one. The more seats that were taken, the more he noticed people giving him worried looks, hoping to find one more open chair so they wouldn't have to sit with him.

It was fine; it was just another thing he'd gotten used to thanks to his big, gruff, alpha appearance. He wouldn't want to sit with himself, either. Hopefully, his papa wouldn't read too much into it and assign seats or anything to get him to be more social. He'd probably pull something sneaky, like ask everyone to talk to the people around you, or group projects, to get his son out of his bubble.

When a familiar scent hit his nose, he looked up from his book to see his new teammate and roomie standing there and looking up at him with wide eyes.

"Welcome to Intro to English!" A loud voice shouted from the front as the equally blond teacher spread his arms out in welcome. "Find your seat, little friend!" He said to Rowan, who nodded quickly and apologized.

Beckett had his lower face pushed into his palm to keep his tired head propped up; he hadn't slept much the night before.

Watching the blond make his way through the tight squeeze of students to the only available seat made the alpha smile into his palm, though the grin wasn't apparent to anyone else.

The blond sat down and gave a weak smile before whispering, "Hey, roomie."

Beckett just glanced at him, his hand dropping once his smile was gone. He looked back at the teacher as his nerves swelled in his stomach. He couldn't believe he was addressing him in front of people! Was he just being nice? Rowan seemed like the nice kind of guy who would do that.

"I highly suggest making friends in this class, so you always have someone to lean on for support!" The teacher exclaimed, suggesting they take five minutes to trade numbers.

And there it was… He narrowed his eyes down at his papa, who was smirking back up at Beckett as if saying, 'You can thank me later.'

The captain felt a cold sweat break out behind his neck as he nervously looked at Rowan, who was accepting numbers from his seatmate, a nice-looking beta girl. Two people then leaned over their desks from behind to pass numbers to the skater. Rowan received them all with promises to text them his number in return.

A sudden urge to have the blond's number rose within him as he picked up his pen, but he froze when he tried to write his number. His hand almost shook, barely touching the tip of the paper.

His nerves got the better of him as he lowered his pen and sighed, staring at the small pile of papers next to Rowan's notebook in envy. Beckett looked behind him at the same people in hopes they would pass him a note, too.

Instead, they all froze and gave the alpha a scared look.

"What's his deal?" A guy whispered, looking away nervously.

"No idea, he's scary, though," a girl said, scooting her chair away even though they were behind him.

Rowan didn't seem to notice and happily picked up his pen to doodle in his notebook. He swung his legs in the tall chair, his Converse scratching against the carpeted floor.

Beckett felt himself close down, focusing on the teacher to hide his disappointment about trying and failing to communicate with someone. As always.

What was even worse was that his papa saw it all happen and would no doubt ask later.

When class was over, he was shocked out of his depressing thoughts when the blond beside him jumped up. Rowan chuckled nervously. "Um, see you later!" He waved, stepping shyly around their desk to the stairs.

Beckett felt his hand twitch, finding himself wanting to wave back, but instead, he bit the inside of his cheek to hide his smile. The omega didn't need to say bye, but he did.

Rowan was a nice person.

He nodded to himself, waiting for most of the students to leave before making his way out of the classroom and heading to the gym to work out. Thankfully, his papa had a small gaggle of students waiting to talk to him, so Beckett managed to get out of that interaction. It was usually dead at the gym around this time since people liked to work out either early in the day or late in the evening. This gave him the room he needed to get his pre-practice workout done.

After a quick protein shake and some coffee, he did some homework outside the campus coffee shop. He could have gone back to his dorm, but he wanted to give Rowan a chance to get his things together for the move.

The last thing he wanted was to make the small omega feel awkward. Before he knew it, he was already running late for their next practice.

He made it back to the dorm building and picked up his duffel bag from his room, noticing that Rowan's stuff was still there before making his way to the rink. He was usually the first one there so he could be the first on the ice, but the captain stopped by Archer's empty office. He needed to collect some plays that the coach had printed off and texted Beckett to pick up.

Getting to the locker rooms, he dropped his stuff before his locker and noticed the new name on the next locker over. It was apparently Rowan's new locker, which had previously been empty since his team seemed adamant on distancing themselves from their captain. The tape had the blond's name on it, boasting proudly in Archer's handwriting.

McAllister, Briggs, and Wilson were ready first. The goalie called out to him as they passed by, "Hurry up, Captain!"

He nodded once, but Wilson snapped at Briggs. "Pfft, why even bother? Guy thinks he's better than us."

Beckett clenched his hands around his jersey before turning back to his locker.

"See? What a bitch," Wilson groaned at the lack of a challenge, and the others followed. Jeon, Sanchez, and Rhodes left next, along with the last stragglers.

Beckett was lacing up his neck guard when he heard it. It was faint, but it was just loud enough to hear in the quiet room.

“Psst.”

He paused, looking over his shoulder and seeing Rowan leaning out the door with a kind smile.

"Hey, Captain, mind helping me?"

Beckett walked over, though his skates slowed his movements as he approached Rowan, stopping just before the omega and looking down at the shoulder pads.

"I've never worn one of these... can you show me?"

The captain accepted the heavy padding and held it up over Rowan. "Stand still."

Rowan tensed up, and Beckett wondered if he scared the small blond. The captain quickly covered his possible error by placing the shoulder pads over Rowan's head and tightening them.

When he got to the laces, he was trying to remember the last time he was this close to someone who wasn't trying to check him on the ice.

"It's tight," Rowan muttered, his face a light pink. Beckett wondered if he was warm in the layered clothing.

"Good," Beckett said firmly. "Won't fall off."

"There." Beckett stepped back, looking over his work.

Rowan's pout was distracting, but once the task was complete, he smiled up at Beckett as if he hung the moon. It made the alpha's heart beat heavily. "Thanks for the help, man."

Beckett looked to the side, and after a second, he asked softly, almost hesitantly, "Need help... with anything else?"

"Beckett!" Rowan playfully slapped the alpha's arm, shocking the captain to look back at him in surprise. "I'm not that kind of omega." Beckett felt heat explode across his face as he brought the back of his hand up to try and cover it, looking away.

"I-I didn't mean like that."

Rowan let out the cutest laugh before winking up at him. "I was just playing! I think I got the rest." He held up his elbow pads. "I'll see you on the ice!"

Beckett nodded. "Don't forget your helmet," he said, trying to find something to say in an attempt to sound cool.

"I won't!" He waved to the captain as Beckett quickly turned away to leave before he could do more to embarrass himself.

Once on the ice and assigned to help the rookie, Beckett felt a wave of confidence he could only harness on the ice itself. Out there, he could truly be the person he wanted to always be. Or, at least, the self he wanted people to see. He even told Rowan about it when the topic came up. "It's easy to talk on the ice. Everywhere else not so much."

The blond stumbled over his words, rambling about how talking can be hard. Beckett found it wildly cute and managed to let the figure skater ramble his way out of the loop of things to say.

"-What if I slip and say something embarrassing?" Rowan chuckled nervously, looking up at the alpha next to him. "Talking is hard."

"Hmm," Beckett hummed. "Well, you make it look... effortless."

And he did. Rowan made talking and interacting with people look as easy as breathing. Beckett was jealous of people like him, who could just open their mouths and say whatever they wanted without panicking. It had always been hard for Beckett to talk, only communicating with Archer's help when he was a kid, even if it was exclusively on the ice.

Then Rowan had to go and say all those nice things to Beckett, making him feel excited that he might just have made his first friend. Shaking his head at the stupid thought, he was surprised by Rowan's next remark.

"How about we both win them over?" Rowan asked, looking up at the alpha with a glint of excitement in his blue eyes.

"I don't follow."

"We team up! Looks like we can help each other out here," he motioned between them. "You help me get the hang of this hockey stuff, at least enough to not lose my scholarship, and I'll help you get some friends. We'll start with the team and branch out from there."

"You want to help me?" Beckett seemed hesitant. "Why?" He felt his defenses come up, pushing down his hopeful excitement.

"Because, besides Coach Emi, you're the first person who's actually talked to me like a person. You seem nice now that we're getting to know each other," Rowan said innocently. The bridge of his nose turned a slight pink, making him look even cuter under the bright lights of the ice rink.

"What about finding a new roommate?" Beckett asked almost hesitantly.

"That's long out the window. I was shot down," he sighed sadly. Beckett felt bad, knowing he wasn't the first choice for anyone wanting a roommate. He had actually scared off two others last semester. They didn't even fully make it through the door before making a run for it when they saw him. He felt terrible that Rowan was stuck with him. He only looked back up when he felt a hand touch his arm. He saw Rowan with that damned perfect smile gazing up at him. "But that was before! Now that we're friends, I don't think it's a big deal. You don't mind me being an omega, do you?"

And there it was…

"You… you say we're friends?" Beckett felt his heart clench and his breath hitch. How long had he waited to hear someone say those words to him? Years of rejection flew through his thoughts; memories of kids ditching him on the playground or avoiding him in school due to his 'resting mean face,' as Rowan had perfectly put it. He was always feared and pushed away. He was an outcast, unwanted.

To finally hear someone say that they were his friend was enough to make the captain choke on his air.

"Well, duh!" Rowan scoffed as if he didn't just electrify Beckett's sense of well-being.

And that was the story of how Beckett gained his first friend. He didn't care if they were both gaining something from it, just as long as he could call Rowan his friend. He even got a nickname! Beckett wanted to smile, but from previous comments, he knew he smiled like a deranged killer, so he curbed that habit long ago.

# CHAPTER NINE

## ~~~~~~ BECK ~~~~~~

So, there they were, in their dorm room. Beckett sat on his twin bed, watching the blond unpack his bags. Beckett would be lying if he said he wasn't getting more and more excited as the blond took out belongings to put away.

Several times on their outing to the local market, he had to stop himself from giving that murderous smile he was so well-known for at his old middle school.

The whole time they were out, the blond talked non-stop about… well, anything, really. That was alright for Beckett, since he preferred to listen instead.

Rowan took out a tube from his suitcase and dumped out several posters he had rolled up safely inside. Beckett raised a brow at the blond, who gave him a challenging look. "What?" He picked up the first one, proudly showing it was of a figure skater doing some kind of spin. "You can have posters, but I can't?" He motioned to the four posters behind Beckett's bed of various hockey teams and players.

Beckett quickly shook his head and gestured for Rowan to continue.

Rowan had already changed into his pajamas and stood on his bed with a small roll of tape that he fished out from the desk. He quickly got to work placing them haphazardly on the wall. They were all very crooked, of course.

"Hand me another, will you, Beck?" He asked, and the captain jumped at the mention of his nickname, quickly handing another laminated poster to the blond.

“Thanks”, he gave another sweet smile, taping this one above the other. Beckett picked up the next one and prepared to hand it over.

"You know, I have like a ton more posters at home. I couldn't bring them all, but maybe when I go home for a visit, I'll bring some back," Rowan rambled, putting up another and another before putting his hands on his hips and smiling at the wall. "It already looks like home."

The blond took a step back on the bed, catching his heel on the bunched-up comforter and tumbling backward with a yelp. Thankfully, two big, strong arms managed to catch him in a simple bridal carry. Rowan looked up into Beckett’s blinking green eyes as his face exploded in red. "Oops?" He laughed nervously as the hockey player set him back down on his feet.

"'S’fine," Beckett said, though he was sure the blond could see the light pink on the tip of his nose as he pulled away and took a step back.

Rowan quickly turned back to the suitcase to focus on something else. He pulled out two picture frames, turned around, and placed them on the nightstand next to his bed.

Beckett bent at the waist to look at them. “Friends?” he asked, almost longingly.

The figure skater looked at the first picture and smiled, picking it back up and handing it to Beckett to let him know it was alright to look at the image.

"Yeah, my old team," he shrugged. "It was small, just Juliette, Ember, Imani, Thea, and Claude." He pointed out each face of the other figure skaters, all in their sparkly uniforms and wearing medals. They crowded around Rowan, who wore a similar black costume. Each of them held a hand up and gave a V with their index and middle fingers. A championship banner hung from the ceiling behind them. "We conquered the ice so many times."

Beckett couldn't help but feel jealous, staring at their happy group. How often did he look at a group of friends and wish beyond all hope that he could be part of it? Rowan was obviously popular no matter where he went. He looked at the other picture still sitting on the nightstand.

Rowan followed his line of sight, and his smile took on a different light, though Beckett couldn't tell what it meant.

"That's my grandma."

In the picture was a smiling old woman with her gray hair tied back. She kneeled over a flourishing garden while a small Rowan sat at her side with a plastic shovel.

"You look close," Beckett commented as he handed back the first picture.

Rowan accepted it, setting it perfectly on the table by the bed. "Yeah, super close. She raised me."

Beckett cocked his head at that, apparently vocalizing his curiosity with his expression.

He could see the tension in Rowan's shoulders, obviously uncomfortable with the topic, so Beckett dropped it. Sitting back on his bed, he looked at Rowan as if waiting for him to change the subject again.

Rowan picked up some shopping bags and dumped out his small purchases on the messy bed. There were several towels and some storage bins to tuck under his tall bed.

"So, I've been rambling on and on all evening!" Rowan laughed, a pink flush coming up to his face as he began to organize some of the bins with clothes for different seasons. "Tell me about you, Mr. Alpha Captain."

Beckett felt his stomach flip at the nickname. Normally, he couldn't care less if someone brought up that he was an alpha. But when this small omega said it, his stomach felt like it came down with a case of the hiccups. Not in a wholly bad way, though.

All he could do was blink, not knowing what to say. He went to open his mouth, but he froze and closed it just as fast. He elected to shrug weakly with his large, strong shoulders instead.

"Aw, come on!" Rowan lowered a shirt he was folding and pouted. Beckett had to admit it was one of the cutest sights he had ever seen. He quickly looked away from the adorable display. "How do you expect this to work unless you give me something?"

Give him something?

Beckett cocked his head to the side. "Like… what?" He managed to force out.

Rowan shrugged dramatically before tapping a finger to his chin. "Where did you grow up? Family? Hobbies besides hockey? What are you majoring in? Oh, oh!" His eyes burned brightly with excitement as he dropped his shirt and scurried over to sit beside Beckett on the bed. “Favorite color!”

Beckett leaned away, eyes wide at the sudden attack of questions. He reached up and gripped at his own arm, rubbing it nervously. Rowan seemed so excited, and it would be a shame to disappoint him by not answering at least one question. He swallowed a lump in his throat and looked away. He opened his mouth with every intention of answering, but nothing came out.

Rowan waited patiently, but when it became apparent after a while that Beckett wasn't going to crack, the blond nodded and got off his bed. The captain had a moment of panic as he watched the blond pick up his shoes. Was this it? Did he finally realize Beckett was a lousy friend, and he was leaving? Did he fuck up again?

The hockey captain squeezed his arm, feeling his hand shake as he opened his mouth, trying to force anything out to stop the blond from leaving.

Rowan looked over his shoulder at Beckett and gave him that kind smile. “Get your shoes on! Hurry!”

“W-wha-” Beckett couldn’t even get the words out before Rowan knotted the dirty laces of his Converse and slid on a black jacket, zipping it up over his shirt.

Beckett was in a perpetual state of shock until the omega picked up the hockey player's own jacket and tossed it to him. The blond then picked up his skates from the top of his bag by the door. "Bring your skates, too." He opened the door before throwing another grin over his shoulder to the alpha. "And hurry up, slowpoke."

Beckett snapped from his surprise and quickly put on his jacket and sneakers before taking out his heavy skates, giving their dorm another look before closing the door behind him. Turning around, he nearly ran into

Rowan, who was standing there, laced skates hanging over his shoulder and a wide and mischievous grin on his cute face.

"'Bout time!" he slapped the back of his hand to the alpha's stomach. "Come on."

Beckett had a dozen questions, but he just followed, allowing the omega to lead him down the stairs of their building and out into the dark, chilled air of the campus. It wasn't completely deserted, but the duo did get the occasional glance as people probably wondered about their jackets and pajama bottoms. Beckett just lifted his hood and followed.

It didn't take long to get to the ice arena, and the captain looked at the omega with a raised brow once they arrived. He looked around the abandoned area outside the arena, unsure what they were doing there. The building closed after hockey practice, locked down tight.

Rowan opened the glass door with a twist of his wrist and a grin in his direction before holding up a small key on a plastic keychain of a skate. "I know what you must be thinking," he pocketed the key before motioning for Beckett to come in, which the alpha did. The blond shut the door behind him, the sound echoing off the empty corridors. "Coach Emi gave me a key my first day here," he said, leading them toward the next set of doors, which were propped open to reveal the half-lit ice rink. "She expects me to practice in any spare time I have, even if that time doesn't line up with the hours of the building."

They stopped at the waist-high barrier, looking out at the perfectly Zambonied ice. The white floor was a glistening paradise to the alpha captain; the desire to get on the ice made his legs itch. It was the need to get out there and let it all go.

Rowan moved first, sitting down on a bench next to the wall and removing his shoes. Beckett followed, lacing up his hockey skates. They were a far cry from Rowan's small, delicate ones.

Once laced and ready, the two slid open the side door before stepping onto the ice. When Beckett gilded onto it, he let out a loud sigh, his breath coming out like a dragon's in the cold air.

"Better?" Rowan asked, his smile as evident in his tone as on his face. Beckett didn't even need to look as he pushed off his right foot to skate toward the center.

"Yeah," he said, his lip curving up slightly as he looked up at the giant Jumbotron overhead. The black screen reflected the glow from the stadium lights. "Much better."

"Good." Rowan skated ahead before turning gracefully and sliding backward, facing his captain. "Now we can talk."

Beckett felt his stomach hiccup again as he nodded. "I'd like that."

# CHAPTER TEN

## ROWAN

Rowan was happy to see Beckett's ice personality return. He could see the alpha's shoulders droop in relief once his skates touched the freshly Zambonied ice. He had been worried that it wouldn't help, but the blond remembered how open he had been earlier. Rowan wanted to see that Beckett again, the one with the look of ease and confidence. He would do anything to bring it out.

"Better?" Rowan asked.

"Yeah," He said, looking up above them to the Jumbotron. "Much better."

"Good." Rowan skated ahead before turning gracefully and skating backward, facing his captain. "Now we can talk." And maybe he could show him that he wasn't a total and complete klutz on skates.

"I'd like that."

Rowan nodded, glad that he was right about this little experiment. "Sooo, where were we?" He made an exaggerated thinking look before pointing a finger at Beckett, making sure to keep his wits about him while skating in reverse. "Ah, yes. Tell me about yourself!"

Beckett hummed, looking down at his skates. “I like being on the ice. Nothing very interesting besides that.”

"I highly doubt that," Rowan said as he wagged his brow, looking the captain up and down. He was very interesting, and it wasn't just in the looks department. "You're a ball of mystery! A modern-day Casanova. I bet you have to beat callers off with hockey sticks." He laughed at his own joke.

Beckett blushed, and Rowan thought about how cute it was to see an alpha like him, so tall and strong-looking, flustered under a few sweet words. Any other alpha would have preened and soaked up the attention of an omega. Rowan never found alphas like those very attractive. Beckett was definitely checking all the right boxes.

"Not really." Beckett shrugged, skating closer to the blond while still keeping some distance between them.

"Alright, so no jealous significant other I need to worry about, got it. I have to warn you, I'm a very clingy person with my friends. I sometimes come off very physical. It's my love language, as Imani always says."

“I don’t mind.” Beckett sounded amused, not trying to take advantage of Rowan’s trusting nature or his words. The more he talked to Beckett, the more he felt drawn to him.

Rowan cleared his throat, hoping his face wasn’t as red as it felt. “So, I know we’re working on getting you some more friends. But what about family? Parents?”

Beckett made a face down at the ice before sighing. “I don’t really talk about family.”

Rowan felt a tether of familiarity under that gaze, and he instantly understood the need to avoid topics with a cryptic answer like that. He nodded, "Alright, gotcha. Let's change the subject," he looked to the side and hummed before gasping in excitement and back at the captain. "What are you studying? WAIT!" He held his hand up and giggled at the shocked look in those green eyes. "Let me guess."

He brought a finger to his chin, twisting his skates to the side to circle around the captain like a vulture, taking in every aspect of the tall, handsome alpha. He could see the faint blush on Beckett's face, and he smirked before pulling up beside him so they could skate together. "Let me see your hand," he said before he held his own out, wiggling his fingers in excitement.

"Why?" Beckett asked while reaching his hand out to the omega, who snatched and inspected it, trailing a line down the middle finger to the center of his palm. Finally, they came to a soft stop, and Rowan felt himself shiver under the gentle drag of his finger. By nature, Rowan was a natural flirt, so he couldn't help pushing the boundaries of this new friendship.

Rowan wondered if the calm and shy alpha would take advantage of this and flirt back or stay reserved and silent. He felt the calloused pads on Beckett's individual fingers before holding his own hand up to the larger one, matching their fingers up and splaying the fingers out. His hand was so much smaller than Beckett's.

Looking up at Beckett, he could see those same red cheeks as his eyes were locked onto their hands, but he didn't make a move or a sound. Rowan worried for a moment if he broke the alpha before feeling the hand twitch, and he chuckled. "Chef?"

“What?” Beckett finally looked up from their hands to the blond. “You’re here to study culinary arts?” He asked as if it were obvious. Beckett cocked his head.

“No?”

It was enough to make the blond break his hand away and brace them on his knees as he bent over, laughing loudly at the look of utter confusion his captain was giving him. "Wow! Are you for real?"

Beckett shoved his hand into his jacket pocket, face instantly pouting, and Rowan had to bite back a vocal swoon at how handsome he looked. "Sorry, man, I swear I'm not laughing at you. Well- that's a lie," he wiped a tear from the corner of his eye from his laughing fit. "Your expressions are priceless. It's fun to push your buttons."

The captain's eyebrow ticked up, obviously not finding it as funny, but also not annoyed as he shook his head. "Push too many of them, and I might push back." He leaned forward slightly.

Rowan felt his lower stomach curl at the suggestive tone; he wanted to slide close and lean into his amazing scent. "Is that a promise?"

Beckett breathed out through his nose in a long sigh. "Wanna take another guess? Or is chef all you had?"

“I was also thinking astronomy. Because your ass is out of this world.”

Beckett brought a hand up and covered his mouth as he looked away and snorted.

Rowan instantly lit up, knowing that Beckett was hiding that smile that he had been dying to see. "Hey, come on! No fair! If I have the guts to put out these terrible jokes, you should have the balls to show me you enjoy them."

Beckett coughed to hide his laugh, shaking his head. “No." He hid his lower face in the crook of his elbow, though his shoulders were still shaking.

“Fine, then I guess I’ll just keep going!” Rowan skated around the captain. “Are you a biochem major? Because I’ve got my ion you, babe.”

Beckett snorted loudly into the sleeve of his jacket, and Rowan felt the excitement swell up in him like he was the hunter for once, and this big, strong alpha was his prey.

“Maybe you’re a computer science major! Is your middle name also Wi-Fi? Because I’m feeling a connection.” He motioned between them.

“Stop,” Beckett chuckled, shaking his head. “These are so terrible.”

"I'll stop when you show me that smile!" Rowan wagged a finger at him. He reached out and pulled at the arm covering his prize. Surprisingly enough, it was easy to pull away, revealing-

"Oh!" Rowan's eyes widened, and Beckett quickly dropped his smile, nervously scratching at the back of his head.

"Yeah, I know. It's kind of scary," Beckett said nervously.

“Scary?” Rowan asked as if he were crazy. “It’s damn adorable!”

“What?” Beckett looked at him in surprise.

Rowan grasped the sleeve of Beckett’s jacket and shook it. “Do it again! It was so cute!”

"You-" He paused, looking around as if he wasn't sure the moment was real. "You like my smile?"

“Yeah!” Rowan nodded. “It’s so real!” He lowered his hands on his jacket, “Why would you say it’s scary?”

Beckett looked down at the hands holding his jacket sleeve. "People," he paused, "People say I scare them when I smile. So, I just kind of stopped."

Rowan puffed his cheeks out, glaring up at him as if that answer offended him. "Who was it? Want me to beat them up?" He released Beckett's jacket, holding up his tiny fists. "I'll throw down! These hands are rated E for everyone!" He did a test jab to the air. "No one says mean things about my friends! Just ask Imani! One time, someone said she put the cow in Salchow, and I went off on them! I mean-” Rowan looked up at him with wide eyes. “That’s not even how it’s pronounced. We hate that! I mean, the insult, too, but mostly the name pronunciation.” He shook his fist at the roof. "I hate bullies!"

He only managed to stop his ramblings when the alpha smiled again. Rowan paused. "What?"

Beckett shook his head gently, "Nothing, it's just… You keep surprising me."

Rowan felt his ears burn pink as he lowered his fists and shoved them into his front pockets, then smiled gently. “Is that good?”

“Yeah,” Beckett nodded. “I mean, I like it.”

"Good," Rowan nodded along with him. "Let's keep skating." He motioned with his chin before pushing off and gliding forward. "I like it when you talk."

And talk they did, skating circles around the rink, openly laughing at dumb jokes and puns so painful they should have been a crime. Rowan couldn't remember the last time he had this much fun with someone on the ice.

Sure, his friends were a riot, but everyone got into their own zone on the ice, focusing on the routine or their precious amount of practice time. Right there, neither of them was worried about practice or learning new moves. It was just Beckett and Rowan in the moment, laughing and talking.

Rowan had a feeling Beckett didn't talk this much with anyone; he just seemed excited to keep talking, not once looking at the time or mentioning how late it was getting. Watching Beckett on the ice versus Beckett on regular ground was like night and day. The other Beckett was quiet, nervous, and timid. Meanwhile, this Beckett was playful, vocal, and even a little flirty at times.

By what felt like the fiftieth time they circled the rink, Rowan thought he knew enough about Beckett to ace a short quiz on him if their teacher, for some reason, slapped one in front of him. Surprisingly enough, they had a lot in common, from their taste in books to their similar taste in music. The only things they really differed on were pizza toppings and the order in which a burger should be built.

"You can't tell me you put lettuce on the bottom like a savage," Rowan snorted.

"It just makes sense, followed by the cheese before the patty. Mustard on top, no pickles, ever," he said as he held an imaginary burger before him. "The perfect sequence of flavor."

"No, no, no, see, this is where I think you're a sociopath. The lettuce belongs on top, and, um, ew, cheese under a burger. Whoever made you a burger like that, I wanna slap them. It's a crime punishable by food death," Rowan said dramatically.

“Food death? Pray tell, what is food death?” Beckett snorted.

"You're fed your most hated food until you pop! Like that chick in the Willy Wonka movie! You'll swell up like a big ball and explode!" Rowan made an explosion sound, blowing his hands up as if for demonstration.

Beckett laughed loudly, throwing his head back while his shoulders shook, no longer attempting to hide it from the world or Rowan. It made the blond nearly swoon as he admired the beautiful face and lyrical tone.

Rowan was about to crack another joke when the alarm on his phone went off. He gasped, digging in his pocket for the device, pulling it out to stop the loud chime. Again, he gasped loudly and showed the screen to Beckett. "Yo! It's five in the morning!"

Beckett's eyes widened just as much, leaning down to see the screen. "Shit!" He hissed, looking down at his own phone that he dug out of his own pocket. "I didn't even realize-" He looked back to Rowan with worried eyes. "Do you have practice?"

Rowan nodded, “In half an hour.”

"Let's head back." Beckett pulled at his sleeve, and Rowan nodded as he followed him to the edge, sad to see their night over so quickly.

Once they stepped off, he looked over his shoulder to Beckett. "Looks like Cinderella's glass skate lasted past midnight." He laughed. "I had fun."

The silence met him as he plopped down on the bench next to his shoes. "Beck?"

The captain sat next to him and nodded, a soft smile on his face. Rowan felt his shoulders fall, sad to see that even now, with all that time together, his friend still couldn't really talk off the ice. Instead of showing his disappointment, though, he perked up and quickly put on his shoes.

They rushed back to their dorm, the hardly pink sky above a harsh contrast to the night that they had left when they had gone inside. Once in, Rowan ran to the dorm's shower, reveling in the warm water, before jumping out and changing into his skating gear. Then, rushing out of the bathroom, he picked up a different zip-up jacket and looked at Beckett sitting on his bed, blinking away the sleep that had now started to appear.

Rowan felt guilty for taking up his night like that as he bit his lower lip and smiled. "Sorry for keeping you out so late."

Beckett grumbled before shrugging. "S'fine," He scratched his chin. "I had…" He seemed to be struggling with his words. "Fun."

Rowan felt like Christmas had come early as he giggled, slinging his jacket on and zipping it up. "Get some sleep! I'll see you later!" Rowan paused on the way to the door. They only had their English class twice a week, and he wasn't actually sure when he would see his new friend outside of that class and practice.

"When's your first class?" He asked nervously. "Mine's right after practice again. It's some math thing."

Beckett lay back in bed, looked up at the blond, and yawned. “Ten,” he mumbled.

"Mine too! I get out at eleven-thirty, sooo, um..." He blushed, looking to the clock to see he had five minutes to run to the arena. He threw doubt out the window and leaned over their shared desk, writing on the corner of a notebook paper before tossing the pen down and pointing to the page, "My number. Text me!" He pointed at him. "I mean it," he said in a playful, threatening voice.

Beckett said nothing, but the creeping smile that pulled on his face was answer enough. Rowan winked before turning around, snatching up his duffel bag and skates, and running from the dorm.

# CHAPTER ELEVEN

The omega was out of breath by the time he reached the doors. Emily strolled up behind him with a cup of coffee in hand.

“Morning, Rowan!” She said cheerfully, unlocking the doors and walking in with him. “Sleep alright?”

Rowan, thankfully, was used to all-nighters. He pulled a few with Imani and Juliette to keep his grades up. It was either that or his first coach would have him benched for some competitions. "Yeah! Like a log!" He chirped back.

"How's your roommate?" She asked. "I hear you got one of the last dorms on campus." She nudged his side as they walked through the deserted arena. "Lucky you," the beta teased.

Rowan blushed as he thought of his roommate and smiled up at her. "Yeah, lucky me. He's great."

"Oooo, don't go starting any love affairs. The only love in your life right now is the ice." She looked out to the rink and blanched. "Aw, man! Did the Zamboni guy not clear the ice?" She motioned to the multitude of ice marks in the rink.

Rowan winced, quickly speaking up to cover for the Zamboni driver. "No, no, no, that was me. I came back after he cleaned the ice for some practice."

Emi looked at him with big sparkly eyes, dewy with unshed tears. "Oh, Rowan! I knew you were a hard worker!" She set her coffee down on the ledge and wrapped her arms around the omega, nearly picking him off the ground in a bear hug.

She dropped him back down with determination on her face. "I did the same thing when I was your age. It's why I gave you the key!" She clasped a hand on his shoulder, and somehow, her smile appeared to grow even wider. "You're a hard worker, kid. I'm proud of you."

Guilt swam across Rowan's stomach at the lie. Instead of letting it show, he gave a thumbs-up and promised himself he would come back and actually practice that night.

"Let's get to it, kid." She walked over to the speaker system in the corner and plugged in her phone. "I got a new playlist that I put together for your senior debut. Let's hit shuffle and see what fits. Wanna start warm-ups?"

Rowan felt the strain in his legs from yesterday's hockey practice and an all-night skate session, but he nodded, excitement building as some music began to play. "Let's go!"

For the next three hours, he let Emi direct his movements. She even put on her own skates and hopped on the ice with him to show first-hand experience, which nearly gave Rowan a fanboy attack. He was getting to skate with his idol! He forgot all about the burn in his legs and just skated, remembering the same feeling he'd had with Beckett on that very ice. It was quite addicting.

By the time they were done, he was shaky on his legs and nearly falling over.

Emi turned off the music and gave him a giant slap on the back that nearly sent him tumbling over as she collected her things. "Great job on the ice today, kid!" She looked down at his shaky legs. "Though you seem a bit tired. Did Archer work you over yesterday?" She pouted. "He knows your situation. It's not like you're actually playing," She snickered at the idea. "I'll talk to him. Tell him to ease off."

"No!" Rowan held out a hand, not realizing he shouted until he saw the shocked look on Emi's face. He quickly covered his nerves with a smooth smile. "I mean, don't worry. It's a bit of work, but I could use more strength training to get me moving faster. It's discipline, and my first coach always said the pain you feel today will be the strength you feel tomorrow."

"Wise man." She nodded. "Kind of fortune cookie-ish, but he's not wrong."

She shouldered her own bag. "Alright, but let me know if it gets too hard." She softly patted Rowan's arm. "I'm proud of you, kid." She left with a final thumbs-up as Rowan went to the locker room to shower before changing into jeans and his hoodie for class.

Looking at his phone, he sighed, knowing he wouldn't have time to run to the cafeteria before class. He could always wait around afterward for lunch since he didn't have any classes later in the day. His first semester was very light since he was bogged down with two different practices for different sports.

Walking from the locker room, he nearly ran into the wall before him, stopping just short of an inch and looking up to see Beckett.

"Beck?" Rowan smiled, feeling the warmth seep back into his bones, chasing the cold arena feeling away. "What are you doing here? Don't you have class soon?" He cocked his head.

Beckett seemed nervous but lifted a brown paper bag. Rowan looked at it and back at those emerald eyes. "For me?"

Beckett nodded, a pink flush on his cheeks as Rowan accepted it and opened the bag. Inside, he took a whiff and groaned loudly. "Is this a bacon, egg, and cheese sandwich?" He clenched the bag close to hold the heat in as he held it to his heart.

Beckett nodded, and Rowan giggled, opening it back up and digging out the warm food as he took a quick bite and moaned again. "I could kiss you right now."

Beckett scoffed, his flush deepening as he turned his back to the skater, and Rowan laughed around the food, looping his free arm around Beckett's own.

"Come on," he said after swallowing his food. "I'll let you walk me out. Maybe to my class if it's in the direction of yours," He winked up as he took another bite.

Beckett let out a chuckle but nodded, escorting him out as the blond happily ate the hearty food. He wondered if it was from the school cafeteria or off-campus somewhere. But no matter where it came from, it was from Beckett, and it was heavenly. He thought of Rowan and remembered that he missed breakfast yesterday because of practice. It was a sweet gesture, and the omega couldn't help but purr at the thought of their alpha taking care of them.

Wait… their alpha? Since when did he subconsciously make that decision?

Looking up at Beckett, Rowan felt his stomach hiccup again as he slowly chewed his food. His handsome face looked straight ahead before realizing he was being watched and looking down at Rowan. The captain gave the small omega a soft smile.

Rowan swooned, blushing while looking away and shoving the rest of the food in his mouth.

"Don't choke," Beckett said quietly.

Rowan's face resembled that of a hamster with puffy cheeks as he chewed. Once he swallowed, he said what was on his mind. "Fun fact: I have no gag reflex, making it easy for me to choke. Soooo," He winked up at Beckett, hugging the large arm to his small body. "Take that however you will."

Beckett snorted but laughed, shaking his head, though his cheeks were tinted pink. It made Rowan happy as he pulled Beckett in the direction of his math building.

# CHAPTER TWELVE

After class, Rowan returned to his dorm to get some much-needed sleep. He knew he would need it for his upcoming hockey practice.

Pushing open the door, he dropped his backpack, kicked off his shoes, and threw himself onto his bed, not even bothering with the blanket. Sleep closed in on him fast as he took several deep breaths. His mind focused on the calming scent of Beckett filling the room. It made his inner omega purr with happiness.

He wasn't sure how long he was out for, but the sound of the door closing jolted him awake. He snorted, sat up, and looked right at an awkward-looking Beckett as he stood there with another brown paper bag in hand.

Rowan rubbed the sleep from his eyes, "What? What time is it?"

He fished his phone out from under him and gasped. "Shit! We have practice soon!" He also noticed three missed texts from an unknown number and blinked at them before flipping the phone around to Beckett. "This you?"

The alpha nodded, walking to the blond and holding out the bag. Rowan accepted it and peeked inside. "What's this?"

"Food," he said calmly, sitting on his own bed and pulling out his phone, typing away on it.

Rowan dumped the bag onto the desk, and half a wrapped sandwich and a bag of chips fell out. He smiled at the offer and unwrapped the grilled sandwich as he sat back on his bed to eat, looking at the missed texts and their delivery times.

**Unknown:** Getting lunch. You hungry? - 1:33 pm

**Unknown:** This is Beckett by the way. - 1:34 pm

**Unknown:** You alive? - 1:45 pm

Rowan chuckled and added Beckett to his contacts as 'Beck,' with an emoji of a hockey stick along with a purple heart framing each side of his name. He took a bite from the half sandwich and nodded. "This is good. Thanks!" He bit into another piece before setting it aside to open the chips. "You get this in the cafeteria?"

Beckett shook his head, "Food truck."

"Cool, love me some food truck grub," his smile turned mischievous. "Can you talk when you put in your order?"

Beckett shook his head, "Online orders, usually."

"Ohhh, three words? I'm impressed." He winked, trying not to make it sound mean as he popped a chip in his mouth.

Beckett just gave a half smile before going back to his phone. Rowan didn't want to push, so he ate his food and tossed the trash before standing up. "Ready for practice?"

Beckett nodded before standing up as well, towering over the small omega. Beckett grabbed his stuff, and they left, taking their time on the way to the ice rink to let Rowan digest his food properly. Once at the rink, they parted at the lockers so Rowan could change in the equipment room.

He changed and popped his head out, gasping when he noticed the undressed men in the locker room. All eyes turned to him as he coughed into his hand, knowing it would just be worse if he went back in.

Instead, he stepped out, breathing through his mouth to try and forget he was surrounded by the scent of alpha. He nodded to McAllister and waved. “Hey.” He looked at Wilson, who was shirtless and glaring down at the omega. “Nice pecs, man.” He gave it a second before adding. “Do they come in men’s?”

"Ha! Nice one," Briggs said, and Rowan wished he could kiss the redhead for lightening the mood. A few chuckles sounded, and everyone went back to getting ready.

McAllister snickered, shoving his jersey. "Do they come in men's," he repeated under his breath. "Funny shit right there."

Rowan looked at Beckett, who was waiting by the door, looking at Rowan like he was crazy. Rowan was about to wink and mouth 'it's fine' before he felt a presence behind him. He looked up to see a frowning Wilson towering over him.

Scrambling back, he imagined that if this were an anime, there would be steam coming from the other blond's nose.

"What did you say to me, Small Fry?" He asked in a low voice.

Rowan giggled nervously. "I said," he looked at his wrist. "Look at the time, I’d better get going." He gave a giant grin before stepping back to Beckett, who looked amused at the flustered omega.

Rowan blushed, glaring up at his roommate as he walked by. "Not a word," he whispered as he walked by Beckett, who smugly made a zipper motion across his mouth.

The omega let out a sigh as soon as he touched the ice. His muscles felt the burn from all the recent activity, but in a good way. Looking over his shoulder, he found Beckett already leaning down, tapping one of the many pucks spread across the ice back and forth with his stick.

Rowan looked at his stick and grinned as he slid across the rink. "Right here, Captain." He called, and Beckett actually smiled before gently pushing the puck over to Rowan, who, shockingly enough, managed to catch it. He tried tapping it back and forth like Beckett, but it kept sliding away from him.

Rowan tried until a whistle sounded and Beckett tapped his back, motioning over to the line of players who had already gotten to the blue line.

Blushing at having been watched, he forgot the puck and skated over with the captain before getting in line. Archer looked at his clipboard, caught the team up on their upcoming games, then pointed at the omega. "West!"

"Sir!" Rowan stood up straight, saluting like someone in the army would. It gained him a few chuckles, mainly from McAllister and Briggs.

Archer sighed in annoyance, motioning to the far side of the rink where several pucks were lined up on a blue line, "You're working on puck control. Anything really, just stay out of our way. Everyone else-" He looked to the others, "We're running drills." Then, he motioned to Beckett, "Set them up, Captain."

Beckett nodded, pointing out to the ice. "Let's start from the top and work our way down."

Rowan skated down, out of the way, barely missing a check from Wilson as he ducked away. The omega stuck his tongue out at him and knew if Wilson wasn't wearing big gloves, he would probably be flipping him off.

Rowan was thankful for the light work as he lined up his shots. He went down the line of pucks before retrieving them and coming back. It was good practice in his gear. But by the sixth time, he found himself looking out at the real practice and was amazed to see the action unfolding.

The brute force his teammates used was impressive; they shoulder-checked each other and moved like lightning in the rink. He watched Beckett and couldn't help the blush that came when he admired how fast the alpha was sweeping the puck from under Jeon.

Getting past Wilson was impressive; the blond had the temperament of a bull on the ice. Rowan didn't even realize he was leaning on his stick until Archer came over and knocked it over, nearly toppling the omega before telling him to get back to work.

By the end of practice, everyone was a sweaty mess. The players were huffing, faces pink from exhaustion, some barely standing on their skates. Rowan, meanwhile, was the perfect display of content as he smiled up at an exhausted-looking Beckett.

Archer blew his whistle, causing two players to topple over when he signaled it was the end of practice. He pointed over to Rowan. “Since you look like you haven't had enough, collect all the pucks and training gear before hitting the showers."

While Rowan was annoyed at being kept late, he couldn't argue about the fairness.

Wilson skated by him with his tongue out, and a proud middle finger extended, his gloves now tucked under his arm. Rowan just winked at him. He watched his teammates go, including Beckett, who threw him a quick glance while Rowan waved.

Coach Archer hung back even though the alpha looked way past a nap of his own. He checked in with Rowan to see if he had any questions, which he certainly did. Rowan stood straight up like an eager student and asked, "What was that move the players were doing? Where they moved back-and-forth."

The coach looked mildly annoyed by the question as he sighed. "That's called a deke, it's a basic offensive maneuver to confuse the goalie," he replied.

"It's so elegant." Rowan smiled up at the alpha. "Reminds me of this one show my friend Julie did where she-"

"Any more questions, kid? That pertains to my actual job?" The coach interrupted, the bags under his eyes speaking more than his words.

The omega blinked up at him before offering a smile, not at all put off by the gruff attitude. "Ya know, I can recommend some great treatments for eyebags. It'll do wonders for your-" The words died on his tongue as the coach turned away.

But before he got far, he called back to the skater, "No questions? Good, great. Clean up the equipment and leave it in the equipment room."

Standing there at the blatant brush off, the blond snorted, crossing his arms. “And they say omegas are sensitive.” He rolled his eyes, getting to work at a snail's pace.

Rowan picked up the black net bag and glided around the ice, picking up pucks at random. It took a bit of time since his gear prevented him from bending smoothly. Once one bag was filled, he set it aside and went to work getting the cones. With his back turned, he didn't see the figure sneak back in and snatch up the black bag of pucks.

"Hey, Twirl Hurl!" Rowan heard before he stood up, holding a bunch of small orange cones in hand. Turning around, he found Wilson leaning against the half wall around the ice, holding the bag of pucks.

“Ohhh, Wilson, did you miss me?” Rowan asked, fluttering his eyelashes.

"Nah, just remember I forgot something." He pulled the bag’s drawstring and upended it onto the ice with a flick, letting the pucks fall and slide across the ice. He threw the bag to the side and said, "There." He wiped his hands together as if brushing the dust off. "Now you have a horrible night." He flipped him off once more.

Rowan was too shocked to say anything, but as the alpha walked away, he managed to call out, "Asshole!" He cupped his hand around his mouth, but it was no use; the damage was done, and Rowan looked around in annoyance.

He was hoping to be done so he could walk back with Beckett, but he figured he missed his shot on that one.

Sighing, he looked up at the arena ceiling and let out a hiss, cursing Wilson.

"Let me guess," a different voice said, startling Rowan as he looked around. Beckett walked out onto the ice, wearing sneakers, his duffel bag hanging on the half-wall door. He picked up a puck and gave a pointed look to Rowan. "Wilson?"

"The guy is such a dick!" Rowan growled, skating over and setting the cones along the side before bending down to pick up a few pucks. Beckett walked over; his grace on the ice was evident, even without skates.

"Yeah, he has an attitude with anyone that questions anything about him." Beckett held out the black mesh bag for the blond to dump the pucks in.

Rowan blushed. "You didn't have to stay behind. I got this. You must be tired from that practice."

Beckett shrugged. "It's just another day, really." He bent down and picked up another puck. "I wanted to see if you wanted to walk back together."

Rowan couldn't fight the grin as he nodded. "I'd like that."

Going back to the pucks, he asked over his shoulder, "So, what were all those drills about? Seemed pretty intense."

"Coach makes us run a hundred more," Beckett replied casually as he started collecting the pucks together with Rowan's stick, which he had left on the ice somewhere.

Rowan continued to scoop the pucks into the bag. "But what are they for? I saw you all skate up and down the ice fifty times and do nothing but pass the puck to each other. Aren't you supposed to be, I don't know, shooting it at the goal?"

"We call it a net," Beckett replied. It could have easily sounded condescending, but Beckett had more of an instructional tone than a bullying one. “A goal is the point we get for getting the puck into the net.”

“Okay,” Rowan said. “So why weren’t you shooting at the net with all that passing and skating?”

"Because," Beckett said as he kneeled down in front of Rowan. He picked up a puck and tossed it into the bag, but his eyes stayed on Rowan. "Hockey is a team sport. We make these formations, and we need to know exactly where we're supposed to be."

Beckett looked down at the pucks and set them into specific spots. He looked back up and locked eyes with Rowan again. "If everyone's in the right place, we can pass it to each other without wasting time on finding a teammate. And if we do that right," Beckett quickly grabbed one of the pucks and tossed it into the bag without breaking eye contact. "Scoring's a piece of cake."

Rowan looked down at the bag, partly in understanding and partly to hide the light-pink hue in his cheeks. He quickly cleared his throat and looked up. “Why doesn’t every team do that? They could score all the time.”

If Rowan didn’t know better, he would have sworn that a small smirk appeared on Beckett’s face as the larger player looked down at the pucks again and started picking them up. “Now you’re getting it; that’s the game. People think hockey is just about skating fast and shooting straight, but it’s as much a mental game as it is a physical one.”

Rowan half-snorted. “Then how does Wilson keep up?”

Beckett looked up without the smile Rowan had been hoping to see. He didn’t look mad, but it didn’t seem like he found the joke funny, either. “Look,

Wilson's brash and has a bit of a thick skull, but he's no idiot. If his anger didn't always get the best of him, he would probably be the captain of this team."

"No way, not against you. You're amazing," Rowan said without thinking, and his face started feeling warm. He quickly thought about pressing it to the ice to cool it off, but instead cast his gaze to the pucks again. Before Beckett could respond to the comment, Rowan blurted, "What about the other drill? With the pucks in the line?"

Beckett was quiet for a moment, and Rowan worried that the captain was getting annoyed. But, after what felt like a lifetime, Beckett replied, "The game might not be all about shooting straight into the net, but you really can't win without doing that, too. You line the pucks up and shoot them into the net from different parts of the blue line to build muscle memory. That way, when it's game time, your shots can fly true without you even having to think about it."

Rowan nodded as he shoveled the pucks. Beckett added, "Bet you wish you had practice like that for your compliment a moment ago, huh?"

Rowan's head snapped up to look at Beckett, but the team captain was pushing the last of the pucks into the bag. And for the second time, Rowan was sure there was something resembling a smirk on Beckett's face.

"Cheeky!" The omega slapped the alpha's shoulder, giving him a wink. "If it wasn't for the whole 'no talking' thing, I bet you'd have to fight the others off with a hockey stick to be your partner."

Beckett's face lightened as he scratched the back of his head, "Funny."

"No, no, no, I mean it." Rowan looked around to make sure they had the last of the pucks before smiling up at him. "Looks like we're all set."

Beckett took the bag from Rowan. "I'll go put these up. You go change," he offered.

As he skated off the ice, Rowan gave his roommate a big grin in thanks. He quickly showered and changed back to his hoodie and jeans, shoving his gear into the large locker before coming out to find Beckett leaning next to the water fountains, looking absolutely smoldering.

Rowan stopped before him, startling the captain from his thoughts. "I'm famished. Wanna get some food first?"

Beckett nodded, and the two left the arena for the mess hall. Inside, they could hear the hockey team already talking loudly about practice. Rowan and Beckett got their food in to-go Styrofoam containers before walking by the rowdy table.

"Hey, Rowan!" McAllister waved, and the duo paused, looking back.

Rowan blinked a few times before smiling widely and waving back. "Hey- um, McAllister, right?"

The skinny beta was smacked by a half-eaten piece of garlic bread, courtesy of Wilson, who sat down the table from him. "Why are you talking to them, bonehead?" He snapped before he looked up, noticing their to-go containers. "Look, they're not only too good to talk to us at practice, but now they think they're too good to eat in the same room as us," he sneered.

Rowan scoffed, rolling his eyes. "Babe," he took a step to the table, feeling the presence of his alpha shadow behind him like a silent backup bodyguard. "I can't help it that we intimidate you."

A hush fell over the table as all wide eyes looked at Rowan like he had a death wish. Wilson stood up, leaning forward with his hands pressed to the wooden tabletop. "What did you say?"

Rowan told himself that he was summoning all his courage, but it might have just been his exhaustion talking. His filter was at zero percent. "I mean, come on. This whole charade," He motioned up and down to Wilson's stance. "Is the equivalent of a playground bully."

Rowan giggled, looking at all the shocked faces. "Like pulling a girl's pigtails to show you like her. My friend here, Beckett-" He motioned with his chin to the shocked alpha behind him. "And I am a force to be reckoned with on the ice. I can see why you'd feel threatened by me coming along. I would feel intimidated, too, after seeing my game. But don't feel too bad; I have no intention of replacing you."

“Rowan,” Beckett whispered, voice strained.

Wilson's reaction was the equivalent of a bomb going off. Briggs and Jeon, on either side, had to grab onto his arms to make him sit back down as he ground his sharp teeth at the blond. Rowan felt Beckett take a step forward to half shield him from the display of another alpha's fangs. Rowan wasn't scared, though; he knew Wilson was all bark and no bite.

“Me and you! On the ice! Right now!” Wilson shouted, slamming a fist against the table.

Rowan shrugged. "Sorry, I have practice in the morning. Gotta rest up. But maybe next time." He winked. "Until then, try to control that jealousy. My guy here would hate to put you in your place." He smacked Beckett's arm as the alpha looked at Rowan like he was going to say something, but he quickly shook his head at Wilson.

"I- I wouldn't-" His voice was low as Wilson glared at him.

"You? Ha! You're his muscle? Alright! Me and you tomorrow! I challenge you, one on one!" He hollered.

Beckett sighed, seemingly already used to this, as he nodded. "Okay."

Rowan instantly felt bad, looking between the two and remembering he was meant to help Beckett make friends, not enemies. Maybe he let his mouth write a check that Beckett couldn't cash.

He cleared his throat. "Come on, Beck," Rowan pulled at the tall alpha's sleeve.

"Yeah, run away!" Wilson called out as the duo left the mess hall.

Rowan blushed at the ground. "Sorry, I kind of do that sometimes. My mouth works before my brain even thinks."

Beckett sighed. "S'fine."

"No, it's not. I'm really sorry. If you want, I can-"

"Don't, it's fine," Beckett assured him, and Rowan nodded as they made their way back to the dorm, where they changed into their pajamas for the night.

Rowan pulled up a movie on his old beat-up laptop for them to watch. They sat sideways on Beckett's twin bed, with the computer propped on the desk. It was a quiet night as they shared food, since Rowan couldn't decide whether he wanted the spaghetti and meatballs or the fettuccine Alfredo. So, they each got one and split it, along with the garlic bread.

Rowan was happy resting his sore legs. He looked down at his bruised feet, wiggling his toes to get more circulation to them.

Beckett looked down as well, and Rowan blushed, "Sorry, are they too gross?" He motioned to the bruised feet.

Beckett shook his head. "Does it hurt?" He asked with concern in his voice.

Rowan shrugged. "Yeah, but only when I'm relaxing them. I don't remember a time when my feet didn't have at least one bruise or blister on them."

"I understand." Beckett nodded, lifting the side of his shirt where a sizable purple bruise sat.

Rowan hissed and poked it, making Beckett wince as he lowered his shirt to give the blond a playful look. Rowan chuckled and looked back at the old 90's movie they had on. "Call us the bruised buddies."

Beckett leaned back against the wall and took a bite of his food.

It was a quiet night, and Rowan looked forward to many more like it. He was starting to get attached to Beckett, maybe even harboring a slight schoolboy crush on him.

Which he would never say aloud.

# CHAPTER THIRTEEN

## ~~~~~~ BECK ~~~~~~

When Beckett woke up the next morning, Rowan was already gone, having snuck out for his morning practice. The alpha sniffed the air, catching hints of the omega still in the room with residual dinner traces from the night before. He smiled, burying his face into the pillow, feeling content for the first time in a long while.

Usually, waking up to silence didn't bother him, but he missed the sounds of another person shifting around. Rowan was a fidgeter, always moving, even in his sleep; he had to toss and turn and mutter half words. It was cute.

While it was still silent, he knew he wasn't truly alone. Sitting up, he stretched his large body, bones popping back after a long night of tossing and turning in weird positions. Looking over to his roommate's side of the room, he smiled at the thrown pajamas on the half-made bed.

Standing up, he made his own bed and actually finished it, unlike Rowan. He changed into some basketball shorts and an old hockey team hoodie he'd had for ages. He glanced back and, with a roll of his eyes, he finished making up Rowan's bed. Slipping on his sneakers, he grabbed his headphones and phone before flipping through his playlist for the right tune to run to.

He liked running on the campus early, and when you ran with headphones, it was less likely anyone would talk to you.

Beckett liked that Rowan understood his issue; it made what they had a lot easier to build on, knowing how shy Beckett was.

*'You're not shy; you're traumatized,'* a voice in his head spoke that sounded strangely like his childhood therapist. An old woman with a penchant for fixing broken children like Beckett.

The captain started off on a light jog, going around the dorm's back path to the university's outskirts. He lifted his hood and took in the distinct smell of rain. They'd been getting a lot of it recently.

Beckett let his mind wander as he ran, thinking about his to-do list for the day. He liked to take control of his day by mentally reviewing his schedule. He had English with Rowan in two hours, and afterward, another class before lunch, and-

His train of thought stopped when he found himself standing before the arena doors. Pausing his run, he felt his breathing even out as he looked around, expecting someone to see him and question his need to be there. Even though he was the captain of the damn hockey team, he questioned why he was there, too. Giving one final look over his shoulder, he pushed open the doors.

He was immediately slapped by the cold air seeping from the inner rink. Walking down the long, empty halls, he passed a custodian cleaning out the trash receptacles. He caught the faintest sounds of music, something soft and catchy. Coming to a set of propped doors, he walked out to the rink. A flash of gold sped by, and he looked over, his breath leaving him at the sight before him.

Rowan gracefully spun on the ice, playing out a choreography that was obviously painstakingly planned and practiced. The alpha came closer to the half wall, holding onto it as he watched the omega twirl, arms going from open to closed as he leaned into his turns and spins. Several times, he performed jumps and quick turns that looked extremely complicated. The song matched each arm movement and footwork. At one point, he did a spin in place that went so fast he could hardly see the blond's face.

It wasn't until the music stopped that Rowan looked up from his spiral with wide eyes, chest heaving to catch his breath. He looked… ethereal, like he was in his own world just on the ice. His mind was a thousand miles away, leaving everything else behind. Beckett could relate to that feeling more than anyone else, but to see someone else lose themself on the ice like that-

"Excuse me!" A voice called out, and Beckett froze up, shoulders going rigid.

He was caught.

Slowly, he turned his head to where Rowan was looking to see a 30-something beta standing by the speaker system the DJ used, hands on her hips and looking extremely intimidating. "This is a closed practice."

"Oh, um…" Beckett felt his whole face heat up as he looked over to find Rowan staring at him. Instead of being mad for interrupting him, Rowan's face beamed like pure sunshine.

"Beck!" He skated over, gliding to a stop by the half wall, looking over his shoulder at the beta woman.

"It's alright, coach! I know him. It's my roomie that I told you about; Beckett Kage!" He motioned from Beckett to the woman walking around the wall towards him, now with a friendly smile. "Beck, this is my coach, the great Emily Star."

Beckett quickly raised a hand in greeting, shoulders still stiff as a board, guilt pouring over him for interrupting. "Hello-" He bit his tongue. "Sorry," he forced out, feeling his dry throat swallow. "For interrupting." He was close enough to the ice to get something out.

Emily waved him off. "S'fine. Kid's good though, right?" She jerked her thumb to a blushing Rowan, who had dots of sweat along his face from the fast skating.

"Coach!" Rowan whined as he laughed. "I could have done better." He poked his index fingers together nervously, looking up at Beckett. "I didn't know I had an audience."

Beckett couldn't help but think the red flush on the omega's face was adorable. He cleared his throat, looking away while rubbing the back of his neck. "You were… Good," he forced out.

This made Rowan's face turn into a damn explosion of excitement as he leaned over the half wall closest to him. "You haven't even seen the whole routine!" He looked at his coach. "Can he stay?" Then, he snapped his face back to Beckett. "You can stay, right?"

Emily shrugged. "Fine by me."

Beckett looked between the two grinning faces as he nodded, and Rowan cheered, pushing back from the ice. "Start from the top!" He swooped his fingers in a rewind gesture as Emily motioned for Beckett to follow her.

Walking back to the equipment, Beckett looked across at Emi's coaching notes spread out with Rowan's stats and some action shots of him from past competitions. It was impressive to see the blond hold so many medals in one picture on a podium. The coach picked up her phone and replayed the song. Peeking over her shoulder, Beckett confirmed it was that band his little sister Erin was currently obsessed with. That Korean boy band she played on an unnecessary loop whenever he went home for family dinners.

Looking back on the ice, Beckett watched as Rowan did a few slow arm movements before he glided across the ice in lazy circles. When the music picked up, he became more engaged, his skates leaving the ice in jumps and swirls that left Beckett almost dizzy just watching. He couldn't help but lean into the half wall again, mesmerized by the sunflower on ice.

"He's good," Emily said, but Beckett couldn't bring himself to look away. Her voice was soft in a fond, motherly way. "He's gonna go far, that kid. I know professionals who can't land half the jumps he does."

Beckett believed it, even without having seen a single figure skating routine. Watching Rowan skate was quickly becoming a hyper-fixated hobby; he could feel it. This couldn't be the only time he watched him skate.

The omega's eyes were incredibly focused with each spin and jump. He landed each of them with precision and grace. Beckett couldn't believe this was the same guy who fumbled his way on the ice over the past few days. It was like night and day seeing what he could actually do when in his element.

By the end of the song, Rowan fist-pumped the air, blowing out a large gush of air as he glided over to them. Beckett could feel his face warm up as he watched Rowan's chest heave and saw droplets of sweat fall from his hair. It was almost painful to see the blissed-out expression he wore on his face.

There's a famous term, 'so pretty it hurts.' Beckett believed that he could apply that to this situation as he stared at the omega.

"How was I?" He asked, stopping at the half-wall, and accepted the water bottle Emily handed him.

Beckett swallowed the lump in his throat as he gave a genuine smile and a thumbs-up. "You're great."

Rowan blushed harder, lowering his water bottle and slapping Beckett's arm. "See? I told you I had actual skill! Don't let my fumbling icecapades out on the hockey rink fool you. I'm a master of my craft," He giggled, and it was like music to Beckett's ears.

Emily, who Beckett had honestly forgotten was there, cleared her throat, and the two looked to her. "Sorry, but I have to cut this short," She slapped Beckett's arm this time. "Nice meeting you, Beck," she used Rowan's nickname for him in a teasing way that made him flush as she winked and looked back at Rowan.

"No practice tomorrow; rest up. I laid out a workout routine for you to follow." She tapped the white binder she had left balanced on the half wall. "Stretches for the morning and before bed, along with some recommended workout instructions. You may have 'skill' like you said, but that alone won't cut it in the big leagues, Sparky." She picked up her bag and skittered by the table. "I'll text you." She slapped Rowan's arm and walked backward, waving. "Byyyeeee!"

"Bye, coach! You can count on me!" Rowan waved back before looking up at Beckett, giving the alpha a coy smile. "So?"

"So," Beckett repeated, looking to the side, wondering what brought that look to the omega's face.

"We're alone again." He giggled. "On the ice."

Beckett couldn't help the smile that bubbled past his own usual serious facade. "Well… I'm not… on the ice," He managed, glancing at the blond.

Rowan pouted, pushing away from the wall. "Then come on," He skated backward, wagging his brow at him. "Join me, Captain."

Beckett perked up at the idea of a chase. He scoffed. "Wait here." He pointed to the ice before turning and walking toward the locker room.

"Ooo, was that an alpha command?" Rowan joked, knowing full well it wasn't. "Oh, Alpha, my alpha!" He giggled, skating around the rink in a lazy lean.

Beckett opened his locker and fished out an old pair of skates he kept there as alternates. Then, coming back and changing into them, he pushed out onto the ice, exhaling the weight of the world left behind him.

"Aw, that's a pretty picture." Rowan appeared beside him, holding his hands up as an invisible camera. "Click."

"What are you doing?" Beckett asked, cocking his head to the side as Rowan lowered his hands.

"Taking a mental picture," Rowan replied, turning to skate backward again. "You have such a nice smile."

Beckett blushed, looking to the side. "You always this bubbly this early?"

"When I know I get to skate, I am!" Rowan turned back around so they could skate side by side around the rink. "I'm naturally filled with electricity."

"I believe it," Beckett said, clearing his throat and drawing Rowan's gaze back up at him. "But you really were good. Like, insanely good." He felt the blush creep back to his face.

"Awww, thanks!" Rowan fiddled with the string on his yellow hoodie. "That means a lot coming from you."

"Why?"

"Aw, don't make me say it." Rowan scratched the back of his head.

Beckett scoffed. "I'm the one with the talking issue. You have, like, a chronic opposite to my problem, so spill."

Rowan ugly laughed with snorts and everything. "Alright, true. Well, you're good. Like insanely good," he repeated Beckett's words with a mock deep voice before chuckling and returning to his usual tone. "You're captain for a reason."

"Do they have captains in figure skating?" Beckett asked, worried it was a dumb question.

The small omega grinned, eyes crinkling at the edges from pure joy. "Yeah, in a way. My old team back home had Juliette as the captain. Well, she was more like the team Mom, and Imani was the dad." He sighed happily. "Of course, when she got recruited by a gold medalist from Japan, I was given the title, though it was hard to live up to her grace."

"I'm sure you did great," Beckett offered.

"Pfft, no way! Julie was like no other! She could sew tears on costumes and bake these cookies that just pack a punch! Oh, and she was always running these fundraiser boosters for us." Rowan looked happily at the ice.

"She sounds nice," Beckett felt a bubble of jealousy fill him, thinking of some other person taking care of his- erm...of Rowan. Beckett was pretty good with a needle and thread when his jerseys got a hole. He could help Rowan, and as for the baking, how hard could boxed brownies be?

The alpha made a mental note to get some from the store later, only breaking from the thought when Rowan kept going. "I didn't have a lot of money growing up. She always made sure I had a way to pay for my equipment without outright buying it for me. I kind of have this pride thing about handouts."

Beckett stopped his skating, and Rowan followed, tucking his hands away into the sleeves of his hoodie like sweater paws. He looked like he was caught with his hand in the cookie jar, like he said something he wasn't meant to.

Rowan looked down and played with his sleeved hands. "It's why I'm here on a hockey scholarship," Rowan said softly as if prying ears were listening. "I can't afford to study here with Emi, and my only option is the hockey team." He bit his lower lip, looking up at Beckett with big blue eyes. "If I get cut from the team, I'll have to move back home."

Panic surged through Beckett. He finally made a friend for the first time in his life, and it could easily be ripped from him because of money?

“I won’t let that happen,” he found himself saying before he could think. Rowan’s eyes widened as he cocked his head. “Yeah?”

Beckett nodded quickly. "I promised to teach you, didn't I?" He watched Rowan nod and continued. "I'll make you a pro before you know it."

The slow smile that came to Rowan’s face was enough to make Beckett’s heart skip as he resisted clutching his chest in shock at the emotional blow.

Rowan reached down and took his hand without removing his own from his hoodie sleeve. "Thanks, Beck."

The moment between them broke when the blond’s tender smile turned mischievous. “You’re gonna be the Shen Xue to my Zhao Hongbo?”

Beckett cocked his head to the side. “Your who to your what?”

Rowan laughed loudly, pulling his hand away, leaving Beckett's hand strangely cold as the blond did an axle spin, landing and skating backward, eliciting a "Show off" from the alpha. "They're a famous skating duo! Won the world figure skating competition with three gold medals back-to-back."

Beckett shrugged, watching the blond skate around him like a shark circling its prey. "I can be the Wayne Gretzky to your Mark Messier." Rowan raised a brow, so he answered the silent question. "They won four Stanley Cups together. Can't get any more iconic than that."

Rowan shrugged. "So, Zhao Hongbo," He motioned to himself before pointing to Beckett. "Wayne Gretzky."

Beckett nodded. “Alright, we’ll make it work.”

Rowan laughed at their joke as Beckett looked down at his watch and smirked. “Hey, if we leave now, we can catch breakfast before our first class.”

The blond gasped, coming to a skidding stop and kicking up some ice. “Pancakes?”

“All you can eat.”

“What are we waiting for?” Rowan took his hand again. “Let’s go!”

Beckett skated alongside him, happy that he had come here this morning. Before stepping off the ice, he spoke up, "Hey, Rowan?"

The omega turned around, the sweet smell of sunflowers and sugar blossoming around Beckett. “Yeah?”

Beckett blushed a bit but figured he should ask while he had the nerve. “Can I come with you next time you practice?”

Rowan nodded excitedly, “Yeah! I’d love that!” His smile turned sly as he wagged his brow. “Maybe you can help me with some lifts with those strong arms.”

Beckett sputtered, stepping off the ice and losing his ability to respond as Rowan laughed.

He couldn’t remember ever having such a perfect morning.

# CHAPTER FOURTEEN

## ROWAN

Rowan felt his eyes droop once again as he stifled a yawn behind his thick textbook. Not that the professor would be able to pick him out from the room filled with students. It was only his second time in that class, but he was still overwhelmed by the number of people taking it together.

He leaned his chin into his palm and looked down at his notes. Last night, Rowan fell asleep later than expected, managing to talk Beckett into starting X-Files with him. It didn't take much convincing to get Beckett to do anything unless it involved talking.

Having never seen it, the alpha was obviously entertained by Rowan's freestyle version of the theme song and was willing to sit through some episodes. The omega was surprised at how focused he had been on the show. Rowan was the one to call it quits when he kept nodding off against the alpha's surprisingly comfortable shoulder.

It wasn't his fault, though! Beckett was just so perfect; he smelled amazing, like coffee and rain. And he was always running so warm, while Rowan would freeze in any AC environment. For a guy who practically lived on the ice, Rowan got cold very easily, but the constant skating leveled it out for him. That and the thermal leggings Juliette gave him for his birthday last year.

He was just having a hard time focusing on anything. Heck, even that morning, Rowan nodded off while tying his hair back, fingers being held up by the elastic of the hair tie until Beckett nudged him, nearly snapping the hairpiece when he jerked awake.

While he didn't have practice that morning, he was still on a schedule and did his mandatory yoga in the room. It was comical to see Beckett wake up and see Rowan bent in a weird position. The way his eyes widened, and his flushed face looked away as if to give him privacy. Rowan laughed it off, promising he would find a better spot for his yoga in the future.

Rowan didn't even realize class was dismissed until everyone started standing up. He looked around, feeling guilty for zoning out. He quickly wrote down the assignment from the board before the professor could erase it. Then he was up from his seat, shoving his book into his backpack.

He froze when he recognized two familiar faces in the large crowd. He couldn't look this golden opportunity in the eye and not charge ahead like an angry bull!

Ducking under and around people with quick apologies, the omega saddled up before the two hockey players, grinning widely.

"Hey! McAllister, Briggs, right?" He asked, holding the strap of his bag on one shoulder while the other hand waved. "Didn't realize we had this class together."

The Alpha and Beta paused, giving small smiles of their own. "Hey, yeah. Fancy meeting you here, Twinkle Toes."

Rowan winced playfully. "Aw, pet names already?" He put a hand over his heart. "At least make them original."

McAllister laughed at that, nodding. "I'll come up with some zingers."

Rowan looked around, thinking it might be a good opportunity to make some more friends on the team. "You guys have anywhere to be right now? Maybe we can get some Frappuccinos?"

Their faces dropped slightly, and their smiles turned forced. "Yeah, um, maybe another time."

"Oh, plans?" Rowan asked, cocking his head.

McAllister looked nervously at Briggs, who broke the silence. "Eh, I mean, look-" The redhead forced a broader smile. "You seem super cool."

"A real chill guy," McAllister inputted quickly. "But-" He stretched, uneasiness in his tone. "But what?" Rowan raised a brow.

The redheaded alpha scratched the back of his head, looking like he'd rather be anywhere else. "We- me and the guys…think it's kinda weird."

Rowan's eyes widened. "About me being an omega?"

Briggs's eyes widened, and he shook his head. "No, no, not at all! In fact, I think it's kind of metal."

"Super metal!" McAllister chimed in again.

"We don't care what your second gender is, we just… care about the game."

"I see," Rowan lied, not at all getting it, nodding his head.

"Yeah, it's just you got here on a hockey scholarship," Briggs pressed. "We were kind of hoping for you know… an actual player… not a-"

"Figure skater?" Rowan finished.

"Yeah." Both McAllister and Briggs said together.

"I get what you mean. It can't be easy having me as a teammate." Rowan felt his insecurities pick up, the ones he had left behind as a ten-year-old on the ice, watching all the kids with their families come to pick them up, while his grandma forgot yet again.

"Once again-" Briggs placed a hand on Rowan's shoulder. "You're a cool dude. Just not a hockey player. We gotta pick up the slack now and, while I get why you did it, it just feels kind of-"

"Shady," McAllister finished again for the redhead.

Rowan nodded more, feeling like a bobblehead. "No, no, I get it, it's cool. Too soon."

"Yeah," Briggs nodded, moving to step around Rowan, "Maybe when the season's mostly over, we can chill. But until then… yeah." He looked back once more. "Tell Kage good luck on the shoot out!"

McAllister waved as the two left the blond to collect his shattered hopes on the floor. He wasn't upset that he couldn't become friends with them; he was upset that he might break his promise to Beckett. If he couldn't even get them to like the blond omega, what chance did he have of getting Beckett on their good side?

Rowan sighed as he left the large auditorium to head down to the campus coffee shop. If nothing else, at least he could drown his sorrows in an extra caramel drizzle Frappuccino. As he stood in line, he texted Beckett with a flourish of emojis.

**Rowan:** At the cafe. What chu want baby boi?

**Beck:** Coffee black

Rowan rolled his eyes at the simple text, looking up to see he was three people behind. He looked back down to respond, but before he could, another text came.

**Beck:** Boby boi? Is that my new name?

Rowan blushed as he looked around, expecting to see someone giving him a knowing look.

**Rowan:** You don't like?

**Beck:** I think you're more of the baby boi in this relationship.

**Rowan:** Ohhh so we have a relationship now?

**Beck:** You know what I mean

**Rowan:** No, I think I need you to spell it out for me

Rowan bit his lower lip, feeling his natural flirtation take over. Imani always said he could charm the pants off anyone if he tried.

**Beck:** Coffee black

Rowan let out a boisterous laugh, which he quickly quelled, realizing he was still in a public place.

**Rowan:** Smooth

**Rowan:** I'm gonna put sugar in your coffee.

**Beck:** A crime punishable by death

**Rowan:** or a harsh spanking?

**Rowan:** :)

**Beck:** I'm sure you'd like that too much.

Damn, Rowan adored this side of Beckett! It was like how he was on the ice: quick-witted and sassy. It was something Rowan found wildly attractive. Of course, his strong, silent persona was equally smoldering in a mysterious kind of way.

**Beck:** Baby boiii

“Next!” The barista called just as Rowan started to fan himself.

He stepped up, smiling forcefully as he shoved his phone into his pocket. “Can I get a caramel Frappuccino, large, and a large black coffee?”

The barista nodded and smiled as Rowan paid and went down to the end of the counter to wait. While he waited, he smoothly responded with a carefully calculated message.

**Rowan:** Boiii I'm about to bust!

**Rowan:** You better stop.

He sent a flurry of cat memes with shocked faces.

They called out his order, which he grabbed in a paper cup holder and headed back to the dorm. He arrived just as Beckett finished changing.

'*Damn, just missed a good show!*' He thought, pouting as he handed the coffee to Beckett.

The alpha accepted it with a small thanks, lifted it to his mouth, and paused as he screwed his face up.

Rowan looked up from his frappe, licking the whipped cream off the straw. "What? I swear I didn't put any sugar or anything actually flavorful in your mud water."

Beckett arched his brow as he showed the cup to Rowan, who blushed bright red at the prominent number written on it with a 'call me' under it.

Looking up at the blinking alpha, Rowan laughed, shrugging his shoulders. “Maybe they knew the coffee was for you?”

At the blank look he received, Rowan rolled his eyes. "What? It's completely possible! You have to be the only one here who orders a plain black coffee." He gasped dramatically. "Maybe you have a secret barista admirer!"

"No." Beckett shook his head, sipping his coffee.

Rowan nodded, walking around picking up his duffel bag while dropping his backpack on the bed. "Coffee shop romance! So cute!" He snickered. "If only you were a vampire, it could go from a book to a movie overnight."

Beckett scoffed, a smile finally peeking out from his grimace as he followed Rowan out to the hockey rink.

The walk to the rink was filled with more teasing as they finished their drinks and entered the building. Upon walking in, they saw that half the team was already in the locker room. Rowan nervously found Wilson as the center of attention.

"It's about damn time, zombie!" Wilson shouted. "Ready to finally get your ass whooped?"

"Hey!" Rowan glared playfully. "That's Captain Zombie to you!" He slapped Beckett's arm. "Show a little respect!"

McAllister and Briggs snickered from next to Wilson before he glared at them.

"Save the talking for the ice!" The sandy blond alpha shouted as he walked past the two. The scent of burning sugar followed him out, and Rowan screwed up his nose in a wrinkle.

"Interesting set of words!" Rowan called out, before looking at a skeptical Beckett and raising his arms. "Get it?" He chuckled. "Because you… don't talk?" He asked, his laugh dying as Beckett started putting his stuff in his locker. "Unless it's on the ice?" He jabbed a thumb over his shoulder.

Rowan grabbed his own stuff and headed to the equipment room. "You're secretly laughing on the inside. I can tell."

Beckett just ignored him, taking his shirt off as Rowan ducked away.

After changing, the duo made their way to the ice to find the rest of the team already waiting. Rowan couldn't help but feel nervous as he looked between the two alphas. Maybe this wasn't such a good idea. What if Wilson won? Would Beckett lose his title? All because Rowan couldn't keep his big trap shut.

Regardless, they glided towards the group. Wilson smirked evilly at them, "Ready for me to wipe the floor with your tears?"

"Sadly, I use Johnson and Johnson, no more tears," Rowan attempted a joke that received mild laughter from his two main kind-of friends before holding his hands up. "And I think we're good."

“Eh?” Wilson cocked his head.

"No, it's fine," Beckett assured, and Rowan looked up at the alpha, his scent not changing at all to show an ounce of nervousness. Rowan, meanwhile, was sure he smelled like burning sugar with the weird looks some gave him.

“Beck?” He whispered, and the alpha captain looked down at him. “You sure this is alright?”

Beckett smirked, a small canine peeking out. “I’ve beaten Wilson enough to know I’m very sure.”

Wilson was fuming. "Big talk for a fucking asshole! Come on! Let your shooting do the talking!" He looked over to Briggs. "Yo, muscle head!"

Briggs stood upright, rigidly. “Yeah?”

Wilson pointed to the net. The redhead nodded, lowering his cage-like mask, "Alright, keep your jets on."

Rowan nervously looked around. “So how does this work, exactly?” He played with the hem of his jersey, one skate tip tapping the ice gently.

Beckett put his helmet on and clipped the strap shut under his chin.

“We take turns trying to score with Briggs in net. We each get three shots, and whoever scores more wins,” the alpha said calmly.

Rowan nodded in understanding before fear covered his face.

“Wait, aren’t Briggs and Wilson friends? Wouldn’t he let Wilson score?” the blond asked, worried that he had found a gaping flaw in the plan.

Beckett glanced at him sideways and said, “Don’t let Briggs hear you say that. He’s a pro; he wouldn’t let something like that get in the way of his work. And besides,” he pointed at the ice. “Out here, Briggs won’t see either of us as friends. Anyone who tries to get a puck in his net is nothing but an opponent.”

Rowan looked out at Briggs, and the blond could see exactly what Beckett meant. The normally playful redhead had a fierce intensity in his eyes.

As off-putting as it was to see that unexpected intensity, Rowan did feel some relief from Beckett’s words. At least it would be a fair match.

“What if...Wilson...you know,” Rowan sputtered, not wanting to accidentally jinx anything.

“Wins?” Beckett finished. Rowan nodded.

Beckett glanced back at the blond and gave the faintest smirk. “He won’t.”

# CHAPTER FIFTEEN

'*He won't,*' Rowan resisted the urge to fan himself as this gorgeous alpha looked at him with those vibrant green eyes.

That one action sent a swirl of butterflies coursing through the omega, making him feel light as air. '*What can I say? Confidence is fucking sexy as hell.*' Rowan thought, and he knew he would eagerly drop to his knees if he was told to do so at that moment.

Without another word, Beckett skated across the ice and over to the penalty box. Wilson skated out and dropped the puck at center ice before skating back a few feet.

There was silence in the rink, a stillness that made Rowan's stomach tense up. He looked at the rest of the team and, while they didn't show it, he was sure they were feeling it, too.

The tension was palpable.

Then, like a sudden crack of a whip, Wilson launched forward. He quickly got control of the puck with his stick and raced toward the goal. Briggs got in a low, box-like stance.

Rowan watched in awe as Wilson slid the puck from side to side in sweeping motions. Even with the hard, black puck sliding across the brilliant white ice, Rowan still had difficulty following the activity.

Wilson swung to the left. Briggs moved to that side of the net and hugged his side against the net's post.

Suddenly, Wilson dashed to the right and, just a second later, fired the puck at the net. Briggs reacted quickly and followed the movement, but he was a microsecond too slow. The puck grazed past his shoulder and flew into the top-right corner of the net. The light behind the net lit up.

Wilson threw his fists into the air. "Yeah!" He pointed at Beckett, who was already standing up. "I drew first blood."

Beckett exited the box and let Wilson in. Even not being next to them, Rowan heard Beckett say, "But can you keep up the pace, Assistant Captain?" before watching him skate to the center of the ice. Briggs passed the puck to Beckett, who stopped it with a SMACK on his stick.

Rowan glanced over at Wilson and saw that his trademark fury had replaced the look of confidence that had been there a moment ago.

"You've lost it, Captain! You've gone as soft as your little twirl boy!" he shouted from the box. Beckett's face didn't show any sign of recognition.

He stared at Briggs intensely, and the hush fell over the arena again.

Much like Wilson, Beckett sprang forward with outrageous acceleration. However, once he had the puck, he took a much more direct approach to the net than Wilson had. Rather than large sways, he just dribbled the puck in small movements, and he picked up speed.

Rowan's eyes darted back and forth between Beckett and Briggs. He remembered how confusing Wilson's movements had been on the ice and how he had still just barely scored against the goalie.

'*Oh no,*' Rowan thought as he watched Beckett's straight-on approach. '*Beckett isn't doing anything like that! How can he score if Briggs can see where the puck is the whole time?*'

Beckett was just a few feet from the net when he veered to the left. Briggs followed without missing a beat. Then, with just the flick of his wrists, Beckett fired the puck low between the goalie's legs. Briggs dropped, but the puck was already in the net by the time his knees hit the ice.

The light came on again.

Rowan jumped up in the air. "Yes! You've got this, Beckett!" He felt an exhilaration he had never gotten from watching a sport like that before. He was invested; he cared what happened and knew what the consequences could be. He felt like he usually did when he watched his friends perform, on the edge of his very seat.

Beckett skated over to the goalie and patted him on the shoulder. "You've got to watch that five-hole, Briggs," he said. Briggs nodded before turning around and retrieving the puck.

Beckett skated back to the box and swapped places with Wilson. "Slick move. Let's see if you have any others," Wilson snarled.

Beckett held the box door, feet still on the ice. "We both know you couldn't beat me on my worst day," he said before stepping off the ice. Wilson stared at him for a moment before hitting the board with his stick and sliding to center ice.

The puck hit Wilson's stick, and this time, there wasn't any dramatic pause. Wilson immediately burst forward, again moving back and forth with the puck. However, while his first run had a certain grace to it, this one was much more aggressive and chaotic.

Wilson got close to the net and suddenly fired the puck at the left side of the net. It ricocheted off Brigg's stick, hit the top crossbar, and landed just inside the net.

Wilson spun around and pointed at Beckett. "And so begins the fall of the mighty Captain Kage, huh?!"

Beckett quietly stood up and exited the box. Wilson skated over, and Rowan was impressed by how much he made it look like a strut. He remembered how much practice it took to get that right in one of his routines when he was younger, and all Wilson needed was his ego.

Wilson effortlessly hopped into the box. Beckett was already skating to center ice, and Wilson got a cocky grin. "What, no witty quip this time?"

Beckett stopped at center ice. He shook his head and smiled coyly. "No, that was great. I think you might even be able to play hockey one day."

The puck hit Beckett's stick and stopped perfectly while he was still looking at Wilson. The captain skated back a bit and stared at Briggs.

Rowan looked at the goalie, too, and saw raw frustration on his face. The redhead wasn't playing around. He looked ready to throw whatever he could at that puck to stop it.

Rowan looked back to Beckett just as the alpha shot forth. He grabbed the puck and moved to the left side of the ice. Briggs followed the movement and slid forward out of the net a bit. Beckett skated forward at full speed, and as he got closer, Briggs slid backward into the net. Then, at the last moment, Beckett darted to the right and leaned into the stick, ready to fire.

But Briggs wouldn't be caught off guard this time. He dove to the other side of the net, blocking Beckett's entire view of the goal.

Unfortunately for the goalie, Beckett didn't shoot. Instead, he darted around the back of the net and came out the other side. Briggs was quick to move over to the other end, but it was too late.

The light lit up again.

"Come on!" Wilson shouted from the box, smacking his hands on the glass. Beckett skated back, and Wilson growled at him.

"What happened to that confidence?" Beckett asked as he paused by the open door. "Maybe hockey just isn't your thing. I know someone who might be able to coach you in figure skating instead."

Rowan couldn't believe that anyone's face could turn such a dark shade of red. He thought the ice might melt if Wilson touched it with his skin.

The angry blond skated to center ice and stopped the puck. "This one," he said as he pointed to the puck, "goes through the back of the net."

He looked back at the goalie and rocketed forward. It was a wild, emotional skate. Rowan wasn't sure if he should be impressed by the incredible speed or embarrassed by the poor form. There was no side-to-side movement. There was a straight line from where Wilson was and where he was going to be, and God help anything else on that line.

Rowan looked at Briggs and was surprised to see him looking calm. His shoulders were relaxed, his face was blank, but his eyes didn't blink behind that mask.

Wilson got halfway between the blue line and the net when he fired the puck. Despite having been raised away from hockey, Rowan still knew the term 'slapshot,' and he could only guess that he was seeing one of those at that moment. One moment, the puck had been in front of Wilson, who had quickly raised his stick up. The next moment, there was a loud crack, and the little black puck was gone.

There was a THUD, and Rowan looked at the net, but the black rubber wasn't sitting on the white ice behind the goalie. Instead, Briggs stood with his gloved left hand raised in the air. There was another dramatic silence in the rink before Briggs opened his gloved hand and let the puck drop down to the ice.

'*How did he even see that?*' Rowan thought in shock. He was sure the puck had moved at the speed of light, but Briggs was even faster than that.

"Shit!" Wilson said as he threw his stick at the wall where the other players stood. He skated back to the box while Jeon calmly opened the door to the ice and retrieved the discarded piece of wood.

"Hey, that was some shot. You get some more control on that, and we've got a real secret weapon here," Beckett skated by as Wilson approached the box.

"Choke on it!" Wilson spat back.

Beckett sighed and skated out to the center of the ice. He caught the puck with his stick and skated back.

He closed his eyes, took a deep breath, let it out, and opened them again.

Unlike in his previous rounds, he didn't wait long to move forward. Instead, he darted forward quickly and grabbed the puck with his stick's quick movement. He moved side to side in the same quick, fluid motions that Wilson had pulled off in the first round.

'*He's showing off,*' Rowan thought with a grin. He looked over at Briggs, and the grin faded. '*But won't he be ready for this? He's already seen it; it's the same thing.*'

Beckett moved forward quickly and gracefully, drastically reducing the gap between himself and the net with each passing moment. Briggs gently slid side-to-side with each of Beckett's movements, ready to pounce.

Beckett approached the net and got his stick behind the puck. Biggs tensed up and went into an even deeper squat than before.

But Beckett quickly adjusted, moving his stick to the other side of the puck while he kept moving forward. His stick moved quickly from one side of the puck to the other, back and forth in rapid succession. Briggs moved with it, obviously not looking to fall for another feigned shot.

Finally, as Beckett was just over a foot from the net, his stick settled on one side of the puck. Briggs reacted, dropping to his knees and covering all the possible openings.

Beckett slid the puck to the other side of the net and smacked it with the back of his stick.

The light behind the net lit up.

The bench roared. So did Wilson, who immediately burst from the box.

“That’s bull! You got lucky!” he shouted. Beckett turned and stood tall in front of the angry player, who abruptly stopped on the ice.

“You did well, Wilson,” Beckett said with authority. “But you lost this fight. You’ll get another chance, but I don’t want to hear it until then.”

Wilson stood on the ice for a moment before grunting and skating to the side. Beckett skated over to Briggs and helped him up off the ice.

“Good effort there. You’re getting better at challenging; keep it up,” The captain said. Briggs came up with his usual grin on his face, though he looked surprised that Beckett was talking to him. “Thanks, cap. You did great, too!”

The rest of the team waited near the door from the ice, mouths still dropped from the action-packed match. Rowan skated up to Beckett excitedly. “That was awesome! I knew you would win, though.”

Beckett smiled and said, “Thanks. He could have gotten that last one, though. If he could just control his temper.” He shook his head.

A loud, “Alright, ladies,” came from the other side of the ice. Everyone turned and saw Coach Archer skating across the ice toward them. “If you all are done questioning your captain’s abilities,” he said before glaring at Wilson. “And my judgment in choosing your leader...”

"Whoo! Beckett!" Rowan exclaimed as he threw his arms into the air. He looked at the rest of the team, who continued to stand in silence. He dropped his arms. "I mean, uh, yeah. You heard him."

Archer pinched the bridge of his nose and groaned. “As I was saying, if you’re all done playing 'who shot it best', it's time for your actual practice to start. Everyone on the ice! Line up!"

The team skated out, single file, and lined up on the blue line. Rowan followed the rest of the team and fell in with them.

"Briggs, I saw your work today in that shootout," Archer said. Briggs stood up a little taller. "Good glove work, so we're going to focus on your stick work today." Briggs nodded and went into the net. Archer turned to the rest of the group.

"The rest of you, we're starting with accuracy training today. Beckett," The captain looked up. "Set up the targets."

Beckett nodded and skated away. He brought back five little targets and put them in different parts of the net.

"It's like a carnival game!" Rowan said excitedly. Archer glared over at him.

"Yes, West. And maybe if you can hit them all, you'll even get a stuffed animal," he said sarcastically before looking back at the group.

Rowan grinned, filled with confidence after seeing Beckett's performance in the shootout. He made it all look so easy, and the blond felt like he had a contact high. "I'm gonna win a bear."

Rowan didn't win a stuffed animal that day. But by the end of practice, he was able to hit the bottom two targets...some of the time. He was still proud of the improvement.

Archer had lined them all up on the blue line again. "Okay, not bad today, everyone."

"Thanks, I'm exhausted," Rowan said. Beckett looked over at him.

"You didn't even take half the shots the rest of us did."

"Yeah, but I did ten times the improving!" Beckett rolled his eyes and smiled a little.

"West, if I could please wrap this up, we can all get out of here," Archer said. Rowan apologized and folded his hands in front of him.

"Anyway, we have a long series of games coming up starting tomorrow, so I want everyone to rest up tonight. No parties, no pizza, no play time," Archer said as he looked back and forth across the line of players. He was met with understanding nods.

"Good, get off my ice."

It took some wrangling, but Rowan convinced Beckett they had to celebrate every win they got. After changing, the two skaters found themselves at a food truck near the end of campus as Rowan mimicked Beckett's earlier moves with a crushed soda can, kicking it up and into the trash can across from them.

Rowan did this all the way back to the dorm, even bumping shoulders with the alpha as he complimented him constantly.

Reaching their room, Rowan noticed Beckett's face in a perpetual state of red as he pulled his shirt over his head to change into his pajamas. "What is it, Beck?"

The captain glanced up. "I just..." He paused as if rethinking his words before continuing, "Never had someone so excited for me, outside of my family."

Rowan felt his stomach twist as he squinted his eyes up at the college student, nervously looking down at their food as if avoiding eye contact. The more Rowan saw past this quiet persona, the more he wondered what caused it.

Instead of asking and possibly ruining their night, he let a giant grin pull at his face as he ran across the small room and took Beckett's hand into his own. "Beck?"

The alpha looked down, and Rowan pushed out his most calming scent, an omega trait he usually avoided, but for Beckett, he would do it. When he was sure the alpha was enraptured by the scent and his smile, he tilted his head and closed his eyes tightly. "I'm so proud of you!"

When he opened his eyes again, the glassy look in the alpha's eyes was heartbreaking. Rowan wanted nothing more than to hug him.

So, he did. He jumped up to wrap his arms around his shoulders and pulled him down. "So proud!"

After several moments, Beckett reached his hands up and rested them on Rowan's waist. The blond could hear the slight inhale of Beckett taking in his scent as Rowan did the same to the alpha's coffee, home-like feel.

After what felt like an insanely long bro hug, Rowan pulled away and motioned with his head to the food. "Come on. It'll get cold." Then, he picked up his pajama bottoms and rushed to the bathroom to change, throwing Beckett's own pajama bottoms back to him.

Once he was shut in the bathroom, Rowan leaned against the wood and pressed a hand over his racing heart, smelling their mingled scent clinging to his skin.

# CHAPTER SIXTEEN

## ~~~~~~ BECK ~~~~~~

Good things didn't usually happen to Beckett.

That wasn't an assumption or exaggeration. Beckett knew it was true; it was his whole life story. Experience told him that good things just didn't happen to him, and he had accepted that.

But over the past few days, Rowan just refused to accept that. Instead, he broke down the walls of expectation and warmed Beckett up with the bright rays of sunshine contained in his beautiful smile.

Beckett now woke up every morning to Rowan stumbling around for his stuff. He tried to be quiet, but it was hard when nine out of ten times the omega would trip or start mumbling to himself about where he left something. The blond's morning routine then prompted Beckett to get up and accompany him to his practice.

At first, he was nervous that he was intruding. That was until he saw how the blond lit up when Beckett asked if he could tag along. That was enough for him to go to every single one without question.

Emily was alright with it, even allowing Beckett to skate along the edges of the ice while Rowan practiced. Apparently, the blond got tired of asking the alpha how he did on a particular jump or move and only receiving a nod or a smile. He insisted that it was imperative to his progress to have accurate feedback, so he dragged the captain onto the ice to get actual words out of him.

Now, when Rowan would ask for his opinion, Beckett could be the sarcastic yet bold bitch he was on the ice.

"How was THAT?" Rowan had once asked after completing two sequential jumps, one after the other.

Beckett nodded, skating backwards with his hands in his front hoodie pockets. "It's like watching Disney on ice."

"Oh yeah? Who am I?" Rowan struck a pose, with his signature finger guns and a wink.

"Rapunzel."

Rowan blinked at him for a few seconds before flicking his small ponytail with another exaggerated wink. "Punzi with the good hair? Yes! I love it!"

It was one thing to watch Rowan from the sidelines, but to actually be on the same ice with him while he performed was breathtaking. Beckett's heart leaped to his throat whenever Rowan pulled off some complex move or jump. Beckett sometimes felt like he was the one flying through the air instead of the small omega.

Rowan had been getting better at hockey; not playable, but he could at least skate around the action while the team was working. It was nice to have the calming scent of an omega in the rink when it was usually filled with alpha testosterone stinking up the place. Rowan's sunflower and sugar cookie scent was something Beckett looked forward to every time he dashed past the captain, leaving an air of him in his wake.

Their routine didn't stop at Rowan's practice. It also stretched to random coffee trips and convenience store runs for snacks. And, of course, dinner time.

They would take their food back to the dorm every night to get sucked into another episode of the X-Files on the alpha's bed. Beckett wasn't really a conspiracy kind of guy, but Rowan was so energetic about it. The way he loudly commented on Mulder and Scully's observations was comical enough to keep Beckett invested.

His time with Rowan so far may have been short, but Beckett couldn't imagine giving him up. Ever.

Rowan now felt like a constant presence in his life, and Beckett wouldn't give that up for anything. It was exactly what he'd always wanted.

A friend.

While Rowan promised to help him make friends, he was perfectly fine with never making another friend as long as he had Rowan.

At that moment, Rowan was running around the dorm, looking for his phone. Beckett looked at his watch and grunted at the time. "I know, I know, it's time for the game. I just need to find my phone!"

"Why?" Beckett moved their gym bags to his other shoulder, watching half of Rowan disappear under his bed, tossing random socks out from under it. He stifled a laugh because, while Rowan went to bed every night with socks on, he was somehow always barefoot by morning.

"I don't wanna be bored during the game!" He gave a triumphant shout when he slid out with his phone. "Plus, I wanna get some cool pics of you to send to my friends!"

Beckett blushed at the mention of pictures and tried to address Rowan's first point. "Archer," he warned, and Rowan caught on with a loud scoff as he attempted to take his bag from Beckett, but the stubborn alpha turned and walked with it, closing the door behind them with a lock.

"He doesn't like phones out?" He groaned at Beckett's nod. "Guess I'll have to find another time to secretly take your picture."

Beckett held his hand out for the phone, which Rowan relinquished. Beckett tapped at an icon in the corner, opening the picture app. It might have been bold, but he gave his famous killer-looking smile, holding up two fingers while the other hand snapped a pic before handing it back to Rowan. "That one's free."

Rowan had the most adorable blush on his cheeks as he thanked the alpha and quickly played with his phone, possibly texting the picture to his friends.

They walked to the arena, seeing a small crowd walking in. Rowan stayed close by his side as they made their way through the side door to the locker room. Some members are already there changing, so Rowan grabbed his stuff, giving small greetings intermittently before disappearing to change.

The captain wondered if Rowan changed in there because he felt uncomfortable around the team or if he actually thought someone would watch him. The blond had no problems throwing his shirt off the second they got back to their dorm or walking around in his towel when he got out of the shower. He hoped Rowan did that because he felt safe around Beckett. Maybe he could ask him later.

Beckett started changing, hearing Wilson huff as he got into his pre-game mood. He always hyped himself up before a game, ready for a fight. It was actually kind of funny how excited Wilson was to spill first blood. It was a cacophony of grunts, cracking knuckles, and neck pops.

Briggs blasted some rap song from his phone while he and McAllister tried to rap along to the hard parts, wrapping their sticks with tape. Jeon was bent down, slapping his stick on the ground quickly, practicing until the last second.

Beckett smiled to himself, looking back in his locker as he slid on the padding. His team was good, but they had to pick up the slack for being down one player tonight if they wanted to be better. Hopefully, they wouldn't take it out on Rowan too much.

He had noticed the blond wasn't entirely as successful at winning over the team. McAllister and Briggs seemed friendly enough with him, but he could see the disappointment on Rowan's face every time the team ignored him. And if Beckett had them run a few extra ball-busting exercises for making his friend sad, well, that was his cross to bear.

He would bear it in secrecy, of course.

Rowan came walking out in his gear, taking a seat next to Beckett. Archer entered a moment later, and the locker room chatter and music instantly fell silent.

Archer stopped near the front, looking impossibly tired. "Alright, you all know the drill. For first lineup, I want Kage, Wilson, Briggs, Jeon, Jones, and Cooper.

After that, I'll pull you in succession with how you're doing."

He went over some plays with the team as Beckett nodded. They were good plays, and as the team's captain, he needed to show his support.

Archer sighed at the end. "Alright..." He looked at Rowan. "Let's have a good game. Anyone who screws up will fear my wrath. Hands in." He motioned as everyone leaned forward. Beckett was in first, followed by Rowan's smaller hand on top of his.

“On three,” Archer said tiredly, not at all pumped like the others.

"One, two, three!" Briggs shouted, and everyone threw their hands up in a shout of the school's mascot.

Making their way out to the ice for a game was something Beckett didn't ever think he'd get tired of. The prospect of putting everything behind him to focus on the ice, on the game. He couldn't help but look down at Rowan, who was looking up in wonder at the arena as they came through the opening to see it all lit up. It wasn't a big game, so the seats were sparsely filled, but Rowan still had his mouth open in wonder.

It was adorable.

The team went out onto the ice and did their warm-ups; some skated around to stretch while others passed a puck back and forth. Rowan backed out of the warm-up, instead going with Archer to the bench and taking a seat. Every time Beckett looked up from his skates to the blond, he found that megawatt smile waiting for him.

At one point, Rowan held up his hands and made a weird gesture. It was enough to have Beckett skate over as the blond leaned across the wall.

"What was that?" Beckett asked, smiling at the cute look Rowan made as he did the gesture again.

"Just taking some mental pictures." He made a click sound with his tongue. "You know, since I can't bring my phone out here with me."

Beckett shook his head, chuckling as he turned back to the group at Archer's pointed look.

The music from the DJ booth blared some current pop songs as the other team skated along their side of the rink. Beckett couldn't help but notice all eyes on Rowan. The voices weren't hard to hear over the music.

"Is that an omega?"

"What're they doing with one of them on their team?"

"Is he a mascot or something?"

One whistled loudly, catching Rowan's attention as he waved, and Rowan looked away back to Archer. Beckett bristled at the laugh as someone from the other team called out for the figure skater to look over again.

The horn blew, signaling the game would start soon. The players not on the starting line went to the box with Rowan and their coach. Beckett lined up with the alpha that called out to Rowan. They both leaned down, squaring their sticks up as the referee skated to them with the puck.

"So, you guys got an omega on the team?" The alpha asked in a low voice while the ref skated.

Beckett just glared, looking down, waiting for the start.

"Is he, like, a player, or just here for fun?" The intentions behind the words were enough to make him bristle, but he kept his head down.

Finally, the ref arrived and stood beside them. When he dropped the puck, Beckett wasted no time swiping it away to Wilson, who was already dashing for the line. It had to have been a record with how fast the puck flew into the opponent's net. The horn blew, signaling the first point.

Beckett stood upright, feeling the burning glare of the alpha that spoke to him while also hearing the audience's cheers.

"Ya! Kick their ass, Beck!" Rowan called, and the alpha looked over his shoulder at the small blond standing up and waving at him.

"Alright, fucking no more Mr. Nice Guy," the opposing alpha spat.

"Aw, you went easy on us that time?" Wilson chided as he skated by and overheard the words. "What, you got a knot for us or something?" He chuckled darkly.

"The only one getting a knot is your fucking omega!" He said as the ref came back and lined up the puck. Beckett smirked when it dropped, and he slapped the guy's stick away, shooting it back to Cooper.

The game was going great until, all of a sudden, it wasn't. Their team was up by three points in the last period. Archer had already swapped out the players and brought Beckett back on the ice for the final plays.

Normally, Beckett was one of the most level-headed players next to Jeon. That was until the other players started teasing him about Rowan some more.

“Hey! Can you get me his number after the game?” One shouted over to Beckett, who gritted his teeth and focused.

"I think I saw it on the bathroom door." Another player skated by. "Something about calling for a good time." He laughed, "That must be him."

“Or your mom’s!” McAllister snapped back, gliding past the players to get into position.

Waiting for the whistle, Beckett focused on the ice, remembering to breathe.

"Bet he can take the whole damn team on," The guy in front of him said, his tone dripping with confidence. "Might have to see him after the game."

When the whistle blew, Beckett went right for the player instead of going for the puck. The captain slammed him with his stick, knocking him over.

The ref blew the whistle, stopping the game.

"Cross-checking! Five-minute penalty!" He pointed to Beckett while motioning to the box.

“Come on, Kage!” Archer shouted in annoyance. “Ten minutes left, and you do this?” He snapped.

Beckett sullenly made his way over to the box that faintly smelt of Wilson from how often he found himself there. Thankfully, they were up by three, and his team could hold that lead even with a five-minute penalty. Beckett took a seat in the box and looked across the ice at Rowan. The omega was wagging his finger at him playfully. He couldn’t help but crack a smile, but it didn’t last long when his coach caught his eye with a disappointed shake of his head. Beckett lowered his head in an attempt to look penitent.

The whistle blew as the team took a moment before the next start. Archer was talking to his team when Beckett noticed a new, unfamiliar face join their huddle.

# CHAPTER SEVENTEEN

Rowan had tried to focus on Archer's talk to the team, but his eyes kept drifting back to their captain in the penalty box. That check looked personal, and he was dying to know where it came from.

"Coach Archer," A voice said, and the benched team all turned to see a small man in a white suit. "Do you have a moment?"

“Dean Prescott,” Archer grumbled, looking back at the ice as he held his clipboard. “To what do I owe the honor?”

Prescott looked around the ice before settling his gaze on Rowan with a tight smile. "Why haven't you played our secret weapon yet? We talked about this when I let him have the scholarship."

Archer didn't even need to look to know what he was talking about. "Kid's not gonna win us any brownie points when we're short on the ice already."

Prescott hummed, "I've heard quite the ruckus in the stands over-" He cleared his throat. "The type of player you have."

"Kid's an omega. So what?" Archer finally looked at him in annoyance. "He's also a damn figure skater. What do you want from me?"

Prescott looked to Rowan. "I'm aware of your situation, Mr. West. I hear you're quite the force to be reckoned with on the ice."

Rowan scratched the back of his head nervously. "Um, yes, sir. But with all due respect, this isn't figure skating."

"No," He agreed. "No, it's not. But it is still a hockey scholarship you're on." Prescott looked back at Archer. "And isn't there a clause in the scholarship that the recipient actually plays?"

Archer looked down at the small man with a twitching eye. "Yes," he bit out.

"Then play him," He said, still smiling. "It'll be so exciting. Imagine the talk we'll get with this." He looked to Rowan, holding up a fist. "Good luck, son."

Dean Prescott walked away, leaving a dumbfounded group of players as Rowan stuttered, "W-wait, i-is he serious? Sir, I can't play!"

"He seriously can't play," Cooper said from the seat next to the omega.

Archer groaned, looking out at the rink, holding his hand up as the ref blew the whistle for another quick moment before they started. He inhaled deeply before looking at Rowan. "Get out there." Then, he pointed to the side. "Jones! Come back!" He shouted as the large blocky beta skated over, confused.

Cooper panicked as he looked back and forth between Rowan and Archer. "Coach," he said tersely.

"I know," Archer bit out. "But he's right." He looked at Rowan. "You're playing wing. Stay off to the side and out of the way."

Rowan nodded, dumbly looking back at Beckett as Archer pushed the helmet from the bench on Rowan's head, clipping it for him.

"Wait-" Rowan stopped as Archer pushed open the door for Jones to walk in as he stepped out, looking over his shoulder. "Seriously? I'm playing?"

"Unfortunately," He grunted, motioning with his head. "Go."

Across the rink, Beckett stood, staring out at the ice as confusion shrouded Wilson, Jeon, Briggs, and Walker's faces.

"Yo, what the fuck?" Wilson shouted, looking from Rowan to Archer, holding up his hands. "Coach, what the fuck?" Archer waved him to look back at the game as the ref held the puck up, and Wilson reluctantly turned his attention back to the action.

# CHAPTER EIGHTEEN

Beckett watched as Rowan stood closer to the wall than a wing usually does, nervously holding his stick. Beckett bit his lip, wanting to shout at him to center himself. The hungry eyes of the players watched, some looking at Rowan while others looked at the easy win just handed to them. With the team down a player and subbing Rowan in for another, they were down to four. Beckett cursed his box time.

When the whistle blew, it was like open hunting season. While three players went toward the game, one circled toward Rowan, eyes blazing like a predator who found a meal. He circled the omega like a shark in deep water. Beckett saw him talking but couldn't hear what he said as he got closer.

Just when he was reaching out to touch Rowan's face, the alpha was thrown to the side in a harsh check by none other than Briggs. The redhead left the goal unattended long enough for the other team to score.

"God damn it!" Wilson shouted, throwing his stick down and pointing at Briggs. "Get the fuck back in position!" He screamed and looked at Rowan. "You! Stop being a goddamn rabbit!"

Beckett bristled. “Wilson!” He snapped, and the sandy-haired alpha looked at him, apparently shocked the captain spoke off the ice. However, Beckett found the words die on his throat as he pleaded with his eyes to help Rowan. Wilson seemed to understand because he flipped him off before skating into position. Beckett growled under his breath while he looked at Rowan, who nervously slid backward and hugged his stick. He looked absolutely terrified.

"Coach!" He found his voice, looking at Archer, who was glaring out at the rink. There was no way he could be heard, but the alpha managed to catch his eye as Beckett mouthed, ‘Pull him,’ motioning to the omega out there.

Archer sighed, shaking his head in a ‘No can do’ kind of way.

He looked up at the clock. Just four minutes left. Beckett cursed loudly, looking out at the ice as the ref blew the whistle again.

Apparently, the other team saw that last goal as a strategy. This time, two alphas came around Rowan, jarring and shouldering past him as the blond tried skating away, but they wouldn't stop.

They did this until an opportunity opened up. Being down two players, Wilson lost sight of the puck, and the opposing players took it to the net. The other team scored again, bringing the game to a one-point difference.

Wilson skated over to Rowan, grabbing the omega by the jersey and shaking him.

"Get your fucking shit together, Twirl Hurl! If I lose my first game of the season because of you, I'm gonna kick your ass!"

Beckett looked at his timer and saw he had thirty seconds left when the next play started. The players got back into position, and when the puck dropped, it was another play to get Rowan. Beckett waited, and the second his penalty was up, he just flew onto the ice, blocking the alpha targeting Rowan.

But it was too little too late as two alphas broke away toward the net. One charged forward like a battering ram, ready to take Rowan out, while the other went for Briggs, the puck at the end of his stick.

It all happened so fast. Beckett had just rounded around when Rowan projected himself up and to the side out of harm's way with a high double lutz, narrowly missing the guy's stick. When he landed, he managed to swing his stick and slap the puck out of the other player's path to the center of the ice.

Everyone stopped.

The players, coaches, and crowd fell into silence. It was so quiet in the arena that you could hear a pin drop. It only lasted a few seconds before everyone made a dive for the puck. Wilson got there first and, after some quick motions, scored a goal on the other team just as the buzzer sounded.

The crowd was instantly on their feet, screaming. But not for Wilson. They were cheering for Rowan and his fancy skate work that helped them score the goal. Beckett glided to a stop before the blond, who was looking up around him, taking in the cheers and applause.

"Is… is that for me?" He asked.

Beckett felt his stomach tighten with pride and smiled down at him. “Yeah, all for you.”

Rowan looked between Beckett and the crowd before throwing his hands up, cheering himself. “I didn’t die!”

Just as he said that, an alpha from the other team barreled into him, checking Rowan to the ground. His face smacked the ice.

"Rowan!" Beckett shouted. He glared over at the alpha as he tossed down his gloves. For once, it was Beckett’s turn to start the fight on the ice.

# CHAPTER NINETEEN

## ~~~~~~ ROWAN ~~~~~~

"Owwww," Rowan whined, squeezing one eye shut while the other looked up at Beckett as he held an ice pack to the bump on his head. "Is it noticeable?" He could feel the bruise forming on his face when he peeled himself off the ice.

Beckett smiled weakly, shaking his head while simultaneously moving Rowan's bloody napkin in his limp hand back to his nose. "Hold it," He said firmly, not wanting any more blood to spill onto Rowan's jersey.

The words were so simple and in no way an actual alpha command, but Rowan found himself obeying as if the captain was controlling his brain like a puppet on strings. He could tell Rowan to jump, and the omega would ask how high or just him?

The blond felt his face heat up as Beckett tapped Rowan's chin to keep his head up, looking at him. The black dots in Beckett's eyes took in every aspect of Rowan's face. After that alpha from the other team checked him, Rowan hardly remembered anything except Briggs and McAllister helping him up while Wilson,

Jeon, and Walker pulled Beckett off the guy who started it. Rowan bit his lip, trying not to think about how hot and angry Beckett was, and the way his eyes heated up as he set his jaw. Even in a fight on the ice, he was graceful.

The omega remembered the feral growl Beckett emitted as they pulled him off the ice. It sent his little omega heart in a tizzy that had him almost fanning himself like he was a flustered Scarlet O'Hara in the summer vapers.

“How ya feeling, West?” McAllister walked from the showers with a towel around his waist, smiling at the pair.

Rowan looked up at Beckett as the alpha looked over the bump more. Honestly, Rowan didn't want to look at anyone else. He was allowing his inner omega to preen under the attention of such a caring and protective alpha.

“Honestly?” Rowan’s voice cracked as a giant smile pulled on his face. “Pretty good.”

"That's that skating high," McAllister snapped his fingers and pointed as he started changing with the others, who poured out from the large showers. Rowan tried not to focus on how many dicks were around him as he kept his eyes up.

"Nahhh, I've felt that high before." Rowan closed his eyes, remembering how his chest constricted when he watched everyone fly to their feet. "This was… different," he said softly at the end. It was euphoric the way his stomach hadn't let up since it nearly climbed out of his throat.

In figure skating, the cheers were never that loud; Rowan would receive polite clapping at best. No one leaned over the rails, shouting at the top of their lungs.

Rowan felt the goofy grin come back.

“What was that move you did?” Briggs, just in some jeans, asked as he did a mock jump over the low bench, trying to imitate Rowan. “Like some ninja shit!”

"It was just a double lutz." Rowan laughed along with him.

“But the way you caught that player off guard! It was sweeeeet!” McAllister sang the last part.

“I will say,” Cooper spoke up from his corner, already slipping on a black hoodie. “It was an effective move.”

“Agreed,” Jeon spoke for the first time since Rowan had met him. He almost commented on it, but held back.

Rowan turned to talk, but Beckett took his chin and forced it back up, which was also hot in a dominant kind of way. He stared up at the ceiling and some of Beckett's profile as he spoke, "Thanks! I'm just glad I could help."

"Pfft, it wasn't even the winning goal, and you didn't even make it!" Wilson snapped, pulling on some pants. Rowan pouted, wishing Wilson could give a single word of praise without swinging that big dick energy all around.

“Damn it, and stop stinking up the place!” Wilson slammed his locker, bringing the back of his hand to his face. “You’re making the whole damn place smell like a fucking bakery!”

"I don't know," McAllister and some of the other players sniffed the air. "I kinda like it. It's a nice change from sweaty balls."

"Yeah, the little guy's just happy!" Briggs walked by Rowan, slapping his shoulder and jostling him as he looked over at the redhead with a grin. His face was quickly pulled back to Beckett.

The force behind this pull was enough for Rowan to wag his brows up at the captain suggestively, as a joke, of course, who blushed and let his face go. However, his hold on the ice bag never went limp.

"How do I smell?" Rowan asked Beckett. "Imani once said I smelled sweet, but Julie said it was more floral."

Beckett hummed and shrugged. "Sugar Cookies," He mumbled. "Sunflowers." His voice strained, obviously reaching his limit as he clamped his mouth shut.

Rowan scrunched up his nose. "Huh, cool. I mean, it's fine."

The captain gave him a look like he was crazy, as Rowan shrugged. The door to the locker room opened, and all eyes fell on Archer and Dean Prescott. Archer looked pissed as he stood with crossed arms and a frown on his face. Prescott, meanwhile, couldn't have been any more excited as he waved his hands for their attention.

"Great job out there, team! You really made our school proud!" His small, beady eyes looked at Rowan, who was looking at the dean from the corner of his eyes. "Especially you, young man."

Rowan gave a thumbs up, not really knowing what to say.

Archer spoke up next, eyes glaring down at the omega, "Well? Are you proud of your little stunt out there?"

Rowan's smile returned as he nodded, dislodging Beckett's bag of ice from his head. "Yes, sir!" From the way Archer's vein nearly popped, Rowan flinched and lowered his voice. "I mean- no?"

"I thought it was amazing. No, better than amazing! It was a spectacular spectacle! All those eyes on our school for paving the way for all omegas. This is just what the school needs to put us on the map!"

"Listen, Prescott," Archer grunted, head leaning to the side with a tired roll. "Rowan wasn't meant to play tonight, or ever, really. He's a figure skater."

"And as I said before, I'm well aware of the predicament." Prescott had a glint to his eye that matched his smile. "I'm the one who signed off on the paperwork, wasn't I?"

Rowan wasn't sure where this was going, but he was confident his nosebleed had stopped as he lowered the napkin to feel it. He could feel Beckett hovering, looking over his shoulder to check that it was dried up, leaving just a dried red smeared under his nose.

"I want more of Mr. West playing in future games." Prescott turned around, hands behind his back. "With him out there, I guarantee we'll be selling tickets hand over fist! There will be 'sold out' signs already up in the window before game day!" There were practically dollar signs in the old man's eyes.

"But, sir," All eyes went to Rowan as he nervously twisted the bloody tissue in his hand. "I don't know the first thing about hockey."

"You'll learn, my boy." He started to walk out. "This is a school, after all. I have no doubt in my mind that you'll bring a lot to the table." He waved a hand over his shoulder. "Congratulations on the win, boys!" he called over as the locker room door shut.

Archer grumbled about an early retirement as he dismissed the team, telling them to be ready for tomorrow night's game.

“Another game? Tomorrow?” Rowan’s eyes widened. “So soon.”

"We play a lot of games each week. Sometimes it's practice games, other times it's part of the roster lineup. You get used to it," Briggs said as he walked by Rowan and Beckett with Jeon, Wilson, and McAllister. "Good game, guys! Night!"

The omega thought of something and looked up at his roommate, "Back on the ice, the hit that got you that penalty. What did he say to make you go ape shit on him like that?”

Archer, who was wiping down the whiteboard, looked behind him to add, "Doesn't matter if he pissed in your Cheerios and called it soy milk. You're better than that, Kage."

Beckett nodded. “Yeah, sorry.” He smiled, watching as Rowan shook his head, mouthing to ignore Archer. He gave the omega a look that said he wasn’t going to spill the beans. It made Rowan pout, but he accepted it easily enough.

Slowly, the team poured from the locker room, leaving the alpha and omega alone. Beckett pulled the ice bag away and brushed Rowan's hair from the bump before nodding and setting the bag of mostly melted ice to the side.

Standing up, Rowan made his way to the showers, offering to let Beckett go first, but the alpha let him go as he settled down, looking at a cat video on his phone. Rowan wondered if he was still calming down after that fight.

After a quick shower, he rushed from the steamy tiled room to his locker to grab his bag. Beckett walked toward the showers, now in nothing but his towel. Rowan would be a liar if he didn't admit to two or three glances at the passing captain to see what he had going for him, which happened to be everything.

Rowan nodded to himself in appreciation.

# CHAPTER TWENTY

The two left the nearly empty arena and strolled out into the cool night air.

“How’s your head?” Beckett asked when the door slammed behind them.

Rowan smiled up at Beckett, noting the worried look the alpha wore as Beckett brought a hand up to touch his own cheek. Rowan knew he was motioning to his own bruised cheek from his fall and shook his head. “It’s fine. Hey! Wanna celebrate?” He looked across the campus at a pizza food truck parked by the lot for after-game snacks.

Rowan put their order in and, much to Rowan's protests that he could cover it, Beckett tapped his card to the machine. They found a stone flower bed that people used as a bench to wait for their food. Rowan sat down and groaned. "My feet hurt. Jumping in that heavy gear really did a number on my ankles," he pouted.

A couple sitting near them looked nervously at Beckett before the other alpha placed a hand on the girl's back, and she leaned in to whisper, "Oh my goodness, look at that poor omega's face!"

"Do you think he did that?" A beta girl nearby with her phone asked another girl.

"Should we do something?"

Rowan could hear it and knew Beckett could, too. Huffing, Rowan scooted closer, resting his head on his shoulder. "I hope the pizza is swimming in grease."

Beckett, who was also privy to the whispers around them, looked down at him with a scrunched-up nose. "Why?"

"I like to dip my breadsticks and crust into the pool at the bottom of the box." He shivered. "It's delicious."

"Hey, um, excuse me." They turned to see a small group of college students, most likely out on the town. The girl in front must have been their chosen speaker because she looked nervously from Beckett to Rowan. "Are you alright?"

"I'm fine?" Rowan cocked his head innocently. "How are you?"

She glanced at Beckett and flinched when his eyes narrowed as she forced herself to stand in front of Rowan, cupping a hand around her mouth to whisper, "Do you need help? You can come with me and my friends if-" Another glance to the alpha. "If you want. We can walk with you."

Rowan tried to make himself as positive as possible, because people who did things like that did so with the best intentions. "I'm fine. I'm waiting on our food with my friend."

She nervously looked at Beckett, who looked just as uncomfortable and ready to bolt the second he had an opening. Rowan wanted to avoid that and squeezed his arm around Beckett's. "We just won our first hockey game," he pointed to his bruised face. "Not without consequences, of course! Courtesy of the other team."

The girl and her friends' eyes went wide as a beta boy stepped out of the group. "Wait, are you the omega that played tonight?"

“Yeah, that’s me!” Rowan gave a dazzling smile.

“You’re trending!” The guy held up his phone. “I thought it was a joke!”

Rowan pouted, straightening himself up. “No joke, all real.”

The girl who originally spoke gave him a soft smile, though she still seemed concerned for new reasons, and she took a step back. "Oh, well, congratulations, I guess. Um… bye?" She waved, walking over to her friends as they whispered loudly among themselves, looking at their phones.

Rowan looked up at Beckett and saw the face he made as he hugged his arm tighter. "Ignore them," He whispered. "They just don't know what a total softie you are under all that roguish smolder."

"Roguish smolder?" Beckett asked, cracking a tiny smirk as he looked down at Rowan, who blushed at how handsome he was.

"Yeah! I'm coining the phrase for you. If you ever get a hockey card, that's totally going on there as a stat, and it'll be sky-high. Way bigger than anyone else's."

The food truck employee called their names, and Rowan jumped up to accept the food with a thanks. He returned to Beckett with the three large boxes. "Let's go! I have the urge to get into my pajamas and stuff my face."

Beckett looked relieved as he nodded and picked up their bags to walk them back to the dorm.

"Don't let the whispers get to you," Rowan said once they were away from the onlooking eyes of the food truck circle. "They're all wrong about you."

Beckett just hummed, and Rowan wished he could hug the doubt out of him.

"We'll show them," Rowan said as they passed by a jogging couple who looked back at Rowan with the same concern but kept going. "This whole campus will know just how amazing you are. Or my name isn't Rowan West!" He proclaimed to the sky.

Beckett just chuckled, and Rowan was glad he could pull that from the alpha at least.

"Come on! I'll race ya!" Rowan began jogging but wore out within seconds. He huffed and puffed on the campus walkway. "Nevermind! Too tired! Feet hurt!" He said, pulling another laugh from Beckett.

Nearly half an hour later, the two skaters found themselves in their pajamas, sitting on Beckett's twin bed with their backs to the wall, watching their usual show. The large pizza boxes sat to the side as they munched and relaxed.

It was getting late, and Rowan knew he had practice in the morning, so they wrapped it up after an episode. Rowan dropped onto his bed, bouncing on the cheap mattress as he kicked his socks off the edge. It had been a difficult evening, and the omega felt quite cuddly. Most omegas nested only during or near their heats. Rowan, though, loved nesting all the time. His bed was his everything, coupled with his soft comforter and a hand-sewn quilt his grandma made him a long time ago.

At the head of the bed were some stuffed animals made from shirts of his friends back home. Juliette was a master of the needle, and when she came over to see his childhood room and saw a mess of random borrowed shirts from their friends, she went to work. She asked everyone for old shirts, which she fashioned into soft plushies for him to cuddle. Rowan even managed to throw in one of Beckett's shirts to the pile, though it was under his quilted comforter, hidden from the prying eyes of the alpha.

It was one of the main reasons they always watched their shows on Beckett's bed. An omega's nest was sacred, and you were only allowed in with the owner's permission. Rowan thought of offering access to Beckett, but the thought honestly made him flustered, and he could never get the words out. Besides, Beckett had never asked, and every time they got ready for their nightly binge-fest, Beckett always crawled into his own bed.

Rowan's bright pajama bottoms and black t-shirt were a comfortable contrast to Beckett's plain black pajama bottoms. The alpha folded up the now-empty pizza box and set it aside to take out later. Rowan snuggled into his nest, pulling a pink bunny made from Imani's old shirt to his chest and hugging it, sniffing at the faint scent of his bestie.

"Hey, Beck?" Rowan asked, looking at the ceiling as he rolled onto his back.

The hockey player hummed, signaling he heard the question as he made his way back to his bed and sat down.

Rowan had a faint blush on his face as he sat up on his elbows and smiled at his friend. "Thanks for defending my honor and all that out there."

Beckett's nose tinted a light pink as he nodded.

Of course, it should have ended there, but Rowan had no filter, so he kept talking, throwing himself flat on his bed again. "It was kind of hot seeing you go all alpha back there. Like, I bet you even made Wilson piss himself a bit." He pinched his fingers together to indicate an amount, laughing.

At the continued silence, he popped his head back up to see Beckett full-on blushing as he pulled back his covers and slid into them, lying on his back. Rowan noted the light in the bathroom was left on, but Beckett had shut the door, casting the room in a soft glow. He'd never say anything, just roll to face his new best friend, and smile at the silhouette of his form.

"Hey, Beck?" He asked again.

No hum came, but Rowan knew he was listening, "I'm glad we're friends. A long silence followed before his deep, scratchy voice replied, "Me too."

At that moment, Rowan got a small rush of what it felt like back on that ice with the standing ovation. Happy that Beckett could reciprocate that feeling to him.

"G'night!" He snuggled into his bed, hugging his stuffed bunny to his face while he pulled the covers up and snuggled into his nest.

"Night."

# CHAPTER TWENTY-ONE

## ~~~~~~ ROWAN ~~~~~~

Rowan couldn't believe the buzz around campus just one day after his first debut on the team.

Things had seemed normal when they woke up the following day. Well, not completely normal. He was sore and mildly shocked when he looked in the bathroom mirror to see the pronounced bruise on his face. Of course, he had fallen and had accidents when he was still learning the finer details of figure skating, so he was no stranger to the pain. However, he hadn't seen an injury on his face like this one in a long time, certainly not since he started performing for any significant crowd.

"Ugh, Coach Emi's not gonna like this," Rowan said as he examined the injury under the bathroom lights.

"Hm?" Beckett hummed from the other room, peeking around the corner to see blond in the bathroom.

“Nothin’,” Rowan said, bringing some of his usual pep back into his voice. “I can’t do anything about it right now, anyway. You ready?”

Beckett nodded and grabbed his sweater from the back of a chair. As they walked out of their dorm into the hall, something smacked the back of Rowan's shoulder. Beckett immediately turned and focused his gaze on the source of the sound, his icy stare landing on another student patting Rowan on the back.

"Oh, wow, it's you! The omega hockey player!" the student exclaimed. Rowan smiled back at him and tilted his head while he waved.

“I go by Rowan these days. I guess you were at the game last night?”

The student shook his head, "Nah, I had class. But I didn't need to go to the game to see what you pulled off, my man. Congrats!" The student looked at Beckett, and the excitement rushed out of him like air from an untied balloon. He backed up and waved to Rowan before turning and walking briskly down the hall. “S-sorry, I d-didn’t see you had company.”

“Weird,” Rowan said. “I guess that video from last night really made the rounds, huh?”

Beckett looked back at the small blond and his gaze softened. He let out a small snort of air and shrugged.

Rowan returned the shrug before adjusting the bag on his shoulder. "Well, I guess we'll see later today. The tough life of a trending celebrity," the blond said jokingly with an exaggerated toss of his hair. He nudged Beckett with his elbow, earning a slight smirk for his efforts. “If my friend Imani were here, she’d steal the spotlight. Did I tell you she's verified on all her socials?" Rowan said proudly.

The alpha blinked at him, and when Rowan saw he wasn't going to get much of a reaction, he rolled his eyes, nudging him. "Come on, let's get to the arena before Coach Emi does. I can at least try to earn some brownie points by getting a bit of practice in before she shows up."

It wasn't until the two of them stepped out of their dorm building that they realized just how many people had heard about the game. The fact that anyone was even awake at such an early hour was impressive, and Rowan took in the strange sight of student clusters in the break-of-dawn light.

They started running into small groups as they walked across campus, all of whom seemed to gravitate toward the two players, as if magnets were involved. Some of the on-campus businesses had changed the lettering on their marquees to show support for their new player.

The ice cream shop that said,

'NOW WE'RE NOT THE ONLY ONES
WHO LOVES A SWIRL ON THE ICE.'

Or the Bookstore that displayed,

'WE HAVE A-Z, AND THE TEAM
NOW HAS ALPHA-OMEGA.'

It was a lot to take in. People Rowan had never seen before came up to him, holding a school newspaper, to congratulate him.

On the cover was a black-and-white picture of Rowan slapping the puck away from the other team after he finished his jump.

‘Omega Hockey Player?’ the article said in big, bold letters. The article praised the team for allowing an omega to play for them. While there were no comments from anyone on the team, there were several quotes from Dean Prescott, boasting about the school’s progressiveness.

According to the game's reporter, the dean had put together an impromptu conference after the game to address any questions from the press. But Rowan knew better than to assume it was spur-of-the-moment. The omega wasn't even going to play until the dean intervened, and there was no guarantee that it would go well.

"We don't like to think about things like gender when we're selecting our competitors and athletes," the small dean had said in the interview. "Instead, we focus on nothing but talent and dedication. That's how you get star athletes like young West. Not only is he an exhilarating player behind the puck, but he even finds time to compete as one of our premier figure skaters, too!"

The story went on for much longer than Rowan would have expected, with snippets of the interview sprinkled throughout.

*'How many skating competitions have I won with nothing more than a single sentence in the local paper?'* Rowan thought to himself as he looked up from the article. It was even worse to have the dean, who made it abundantly clear the night of the game that he was aware

of Rowan's situation, say that Rowan "even finds time" for figure skating.

He wanted to be upset that his real passion was taking a public back seat to his free ride to school, but his fellow students' beaming smiles and congratulations helped suppress that frustration. He knew it wasn't right, that he was getting the attention for the wrong reasons but seeing people happy and excited always pulled Rowan out of his slump.

Beck, on the other hand, looked about as uncomfortable and out-of-place as someone could manage. For as strong and dominating as the alpha was on the ice, the attention and conversation in the open seemed to shove the team's captain right into his shell.

Countless whispers plagued the two as they passed the surrounding onlookers.

"Who's that guy following the omega hockey player?"

"Is that his alpha?"

"No, he's another hockey player! I saw him at the game last night," one girl announced to her gaggle of friends. "He started a huge fight with the other team."

"Ya, the guy looks like he can fight."

"He looks like he WANTS to fight. So scary."

It hurt Rowan to hear it, too. Here was his team's captain, who led those players all night, and had taken a stand for Rowan, no less, and he couldn't enjoy or appreciate the adulation they received for their performance. He was just known as the scary-looking alpha who got into a fight.

"Come on, CAPTAIN!" Rowan emphasized the title for others to hear as he took Beckett's hand and squeezed it. "We gotta get to practice."

Why should Rowan be openly accepting the admiration from the fans if long-time players like Beckett couldn't bask in it, too?

Rowan didn't really know how to feel, so he decided to take the praise in stride as he pulled the captain through the light crowd of people to get to practice. He would try to appreciate the acclaim, even if the captain found it difficult to do the same.

Unfortunately, Emily didn't seem too thrilled about the praise either as she turned Rowan's face left to right. "Aw, kid, that bruise is gonna cost you some points with the press," she whined. "I'm going to kill Archer if it doesn't clear up before your first debut."

"I'm fine, really." Rowan sat on the metal bench, allowing his coach to look over his face. Beckett was already on the ice, skating in lazy circles.

Emily released his face and shook her head. "No, I can't believe they played you! Archer said he wouldn't do that! Ugh, I'm going to go have a talk with him."

"Good luck," Beckett called from the rink, looking up and giving a smirk that made Rowan's stomach flutter. "He usually sleeps pretty late after a late game."

"While I appreciate the pro-advice, I've got a bone to pick with that puck-head!" She stormed from the arena. Rowan would have chased her if he weren't already standing in his skates.

As the omega leaned against the wall of the rink, Beckett glided over and placed his hands on the top next to Rowan's, their fingers brushing slightly. Rowan gave him a half-lidded look. "Do I even wanna know how you know Archer's sleeping schedule?" He wagged his brow at him, "Something you wanna tell me?"

Beckett's face scrunched up in this cute display of grossed-out. "No, he's, um… my dad. Adopted dad, really."

Surprise filled Rowan's face as he opened his mouth. "Oh, so that's why you two seem so close!" Rowan leaned forward, feeling Beckett's pinkie brush up against his own. "For a second there, I thought you were stalking him or something."

The captain snorted, pushing back from the wall and gliding backward. "I've heard that theory in the locker room. Jeon has more of an active imagination than you'd think."

Rowan reached down to the phone connected to the sound system and hit shuffle on his ice playlist. He went out onto the ice and did a few stretches before performing a big axel and landing near Beckett, who responded with soft golfer claps.

"Aw, thank you, thank you. You're too kind." The omega projected his happy scent of sugar cookies and sunflowers.

Beckett turned sharply on the ice, and Rowan had a thought as he kept practicing. "Hey, Beck?"

"Yeah?"

"You ever thought of being a figure skater?"

Beckett snorted again while he shook his head. "Nah, I always wanted to be a hockey player." He paused for a bit and smiled at his skates. "My mom, my birth mom, used to skate. Nothing professional, though, just for fun."

Rowan was excited to hear about Beckett's life and didn't want to waste an opportunity. He skated closer to the alpha. "Yeah? I see she got you into it."

"Yeah." His smile widened, and Rowan wondered how anyone could find such a handsome smile creepy. "She took me a few times when she could." He seemed hesitant to add more, and after a moment, he decided it must have been alright, "I don't have a lot of memories of her smiling, but the few I do have are always out on the ice."

"What about your dad?" Rowan bent at the waist slightly to get a look at his face.

Beckett shrugged. "Never knew him; he left when I was a baby. My adopted dads are the only fathers I've ever known."

"That's so sweet," the omega preened at the idea of their gruff coach having a soft side for his adopted boy.

"Don't tell him I told you," Beckett groaned. "He likes to keep it on the down-low. His life is super private."

Rowan made a zipper motion across his mouth. "Mum's the word."

"But anyway, no, never considered the ice skater thing. I'm not as graceful as you," He motioned to his height. "Plus, I think I'm too tall."

"Nonsense! You're perfect!" Rowan felt his whole face flush. "I mean, you would be perfect as a skating partner." He scratched behind his head, his hand then slipping into his yellow hoodie.

"You think so?" Beckett asked playfully.

"I know so!" He leaned forward, lifting one skate behind him as he looked at Beckett. "Try this."

Beckett managed to lift his leg off the ice in a similar pose, but wobbled a bit as he leaned forward. Slowly, Rowan brought his leg higher and higher till it was way over his head, and he was grabbing onto his other leg. "This is a spiral."

"Show off," Beckett said, but his voice was laced with an impressed tone. Rowan smirked at the tone, looking over to see Beckett's eyes glued on the small skater. "You're so bendy."

"The better to please you with, my dear," He stuck his tongue out to the side. He was rewarded with a blush and a deep laugh that made all these years of intense yoga and gymnastics worth it.

"But for real, it's not hard. I can show you. If you did yoga with me in the mornings, I swear, I could get you in all kinds of positions by the end of the year." His face burned a cherry red as he snapped his pointer finger at a laughing Beckett before swinging his small fists against his arm. "Not what I meant!"

"Okay, okay!" Beckett relinquished as Rowan continued to hit his arm. "Stop trying to beat me up."

“I don’t have to try!” Rowan swapped his taps to punches against the tall alpha’s side. “These babies are lethal weapons. I got them registered last summer.”

"Lethal, are they?" He reached out and took his hand, the momentum pulling them both into a lazy spin. Rowan reached out, taking his other hand as they spun and laughed.

They goofed around, transitioning into an intense game of tag on the ice that involved a lot of dodging and zigzagging, which left them huffing for air. Rowan couldn't help the happy pheromones he was producing, probably filling the whole arena with his happy omega scent. He could smell Beckett's equally happy alpha scent, too. It was coffee and rain, and it encased him into warm cocoon.

“You cold?” Beckett asked as they stood along the railing to catch their breath.

"That's my secret, cap… I'm always cold." Rowan winked, hiding his hands back in his sleeves. "What gave me away?"

"The constant sweater paws," He motioned to the long sleeves. "You also breathe into your hands to warm your nose."

"My face gets so cold!" Rowan pouted, knowing his nose was probably red from their time on the ice. Imani always used to poke it, making ’boop’ sounds in varying tones from a tiny mouse to a deep baritone giant.

Beckett laughed, bringing his bare hands up and cupping the omega's cheeks. "Here, I always run hot."

Rowan's eyes drooped as he was encased in the warmest hands ever, leaning into the touch. "Wow, you have the magic touch."

Fluttering his eyes open, he smiled up at Beckett. "If you could do this more often, I would greatly appreciate it."

"I'll keep that in mind," Beckett said, his voice low as he looked over Rowan like he was trying to memorize every detail of his face. If Rowan died right then, he could honestly say 'no regerts,' because that Snickers commercial would always be the funniest thing on TV. He just felt so warm and wanted. It had been a long time since someone looked at him and actually saw him.

It broke his heart to think of living in that house with his grandma. She would always look at him like she didn't know who he was. Sometimes she had good days, but she had some bad ones, too. It was even worse when she looked through him like he didn't even exist.

Those had always been the worst days.

It made this kind of attention damn near addicting, and he didn't want it to end.

It could have been the warmth coursing through his veins or the murky fog casting over his brain function, but he opened his big mouth again.

"I like hearing and learning things about you." He blushed. "Opening up to friends is… pretty cool, ya know?"

Beckett hummed, looking across Rowan's face as if searching for something. "Yeah?"

"Yeah." Rowan smiled.

"Well," Beckett let his mouth curl up into that murderous smile that made so many people quake in their shoes. It gave Rowan a whole different set of quakes. "Did you know I have a little sister?"

Rowan did a stage gasp, mouth and eyes blown wide. "No way; you're a big brother?"

Beckett nodded, hardly even moving his head as his fingers twitched on Rowan's face, his thumb almost moving back and forth in a soothing motion. "You?"

"I don't have any siblings. Sad, I know." Rowan sighed. "But I like to think I'd be a good big brother."

"Hmmm," Beckett narrowed his eyes down at him. "You have little sibling energy, sorry to break it to you."

Rowan let out the cutest snort, scrunching his nose up as he grinned at the captain. "You jerk!"

Beckett matched his laugh, though it was deeper, and it did things to Rowan's insides.

Of course, Emily had to come back right at that moment, her loud voice breaking them apart before she even entered through the ice arena doors. Their faces turned red as they faced opposite directions, their hands shooting to their pockets as if they had been caught doing something.

"I swear, that grumpy cat is gonna get more than a fisting if he ignores me one more time." Her angry look melted away into an insane laugh as she covered her mouth. "OH MY GOD, DID I SAY FISTING?" She snorted more, holding the railing and bending over it in uncontrollable laughter. "I crack myself up!"

Rowan smirked at Emi's childlike laugh, skating over to her as she composed herself. "Alright, kid. Ready for some real work?"

Rowan nodded as she took the device and turned on his choreography song. It was a song Rowan could already recite by heart, even in his sleep, but he still loved it. “Let’s take it from the top!”

The omega skated to the center ice, taking his starting pose as he slowly began his movements. He could feel the heat of Beckett's eyes on him. His face still felt warm from where the hockey player had held him just moments before. It was intimidating and also kind of hot to have him so close. Rowan didn't plan on putting any distance between them anytime soon.

Glancing over his shoulder to Beckett, he swore he could almost read the alpha's face as he leaned against the railing, watching with so much want in his eyes. It nearly made Rowan trip over his own skates.

"Focus, Rowan!" Emily called.

"Right!" He looked forward again, hearing Beckett's deep voice chuckle, and trying to keep his whole body from catching on fire.

# CHAPTER TWENTY-TWO

Everything until the evening of their next game was a whirlwind for Rowan.

Everywhere he went on campus, people stopped him for pictures or to ask if he was really on the hockey team. It felt weird to be like a sideshow attraction, with people poking and asking invasive questions.

"How do your parents feel about that?"

"Isn't that an alpha sport?"

"Are you dating any of the players?"

"How did you make the team?"

These questions constantly surrounded him until he eventually found himself in the locker room, already dressed and sitting on the bench. He laced up his skates while passively listening to everyone around him. Briggs was once again blasting some rap music while McAllister drummed on the lockers in his gear, hyping everyone up.

Rowan looked up at Beckett as the captain shrugged his jersey on, his stick leaning against the wall beside him. They hadn't talked since leaving their dorm to get there, and Rowan was starting to feel the familiar pull at his gut, wondering if they really were going to play him tonight.

The door opened as if to answer his question, revealing Archer as he walked in with his familiar clipboard and serious yet tired face.

Briggs stopped the music, and everyone looked to their coach. A sense of Deja-vu washed over Rowan as he looked up at the coach to find his eyes on the omega. He looked as if it pained him to speak, but he finally started.

"Given the… attention-" The word was like burning lava in the man's mouth as he blanched it out. "From our last game, the stadium is more packed than usual. Not that it should matter, but we don't normally play full houses this early in the season." He looked around at everyone before lifting his clipboard. "I went over the plays with your captain, and we're going to use this as our starting lineup: Kage, Wilson, Briggs, Walker, Cooper... West."

"What? Fucking seriously?" Wilson groaned loudly, but Rowan was only looking at the coach.

"Are they serious about playing me?" Rowan stood up on his skates. "Coach, last night was a fluke."

"It's what Prescott wants," The coach groaned at the challenge his players provided.

Wilson was up on his feet, eyes blazing. “This is fucking hockey! Not a goddamn ballerina recital!”

“Hey!” Rowan pouted up at the sandy blond. “It’s called figure skating. The name won’t poison you.”

Wilson flipped him off before looking back to Archer. "I came to this school to play with the best. I have offers from other schools." The threat was clear, but Archer didn't back down to it.

"You're free to do what's best for you, Wilson. But I can guarantee your attitude won't go unchecked elsewhere like it does with me. I let you have your tantrums because, at the end of the day, I can reign you in and teach you." He quirked a brow up, "Any other team will just dump you."

Wilson flinched as his heated glare turned to Rowan. "Don't fuck it up for us out there, Twirl Hurl."

Rowan scrunched up his nose in a forced smile. "Wouldn't dream of it, Parole." Archer turned to the rest of them, “You know the plays we’re starting with.”

Rowan slowly raised his hand, and Archer sighed, rubbing his eyes. "Kage, talk to him."

“Pfft, because he’s so talkative,” Wilson mumbled loudly from his locker as he slammed it shut.

Giving Wilson a glare and sticking out his tongue, Rowan turned to Beckett and smiled. "You can fill me in on the warm-up."

"Let's get out there, team. Hands in." Archer put his hand in, and Rowan and Beckett followed, but no one else did. Archer looked around at them. "I said, hands in."

Instantly, everyone else came over and did their usual countdown before breaking apart.

The cheers from the arena were much louder than before as they made their way to the ice. When Rowan appeared from the walkway, everyone went crazy. Rowan pushed out onto the ice and looked around at the arena, which was mostly full. Some had signs with their team name, while others had signs showing Rowan's name. It was crazy to think he gained overnight fame from just one move.

While he was taking it all in, he felt someone come up next to him and looked to his side to see Beckett looking around at the signs and support. "It's crazy, huh?"

Rowan blushed, nodding. “I’ve never had this much attention.”

“What about at your figure skating contests?” Beckett looked down at him curiously.

The omega shook his head. “Never this much.” He brought a gloved hand to his chest. “My friends had a sign for everyone we would hold up at competitions, but that was just us being supportive. Never… this.” He motioned out to the crowd.

“Well, get used to it. You’re a lovable guy.” Beckett smiled.

Rowan felt his face flush as he bit his lip and looked down, bringing his shoulders up to try and hide it.

"Come on, let's go over the plays real quick."

Beckett led Rowan over to a small whiteboard that Archer always kept on hand for quick changes. It already had an outline of the ice lines permanently drawn onto it. Beckett grabbed a marker and popped the cap off with his thumb. Still on the ice, they stood near the wall where the team usually sat while everyone skated.

“Okay, when it’s time for the face-off, I’m going to be here,” he said as he drew an X next to the dot at the center of the ice.

“Our two defensive players, Wilson and Cooper, are going to hang back here,” he drew two more X’s closer to the blue line.

"And there's the wings, you and Walker," he said as he drew two final X's, one on either side of the X that represented Beckett. They were just a little further from the center of the ice than his X.

Rowan nodded his head. “Cool. What happens after the face-off?” Beckett looked back at him from the whiteboard. “The game, Rowan.”

He looked back at the board and said, "You'll know once play starts; everyone'll be moving around. I need you to go here." Beckett drew an arrow from the X that represented Rowan over to the boards on the right side of the rink.

"And just...stay here…" he said while he circled the spot a few times.

Rowan smiled and nodded. "Can do, cap!" His face fell slightly, and he asked, "What if they come after me?"

Beckett turned back to face Rowan. “As long as you don’t have the puck, that shouldn’t be a problem.”

Rowan’s face scrunched up slightly. “Shouldn’t?”

Beckett shrugged and replied, “Shouldn’t.”

Rowan thought about it for a moment and nodded again. “Alright, yeah, I can do that,” he said before skating forward a bit. He grabbed the marker from Beckett and approached the board.

"But, if I end up in trouble, I could always skate over here, maybe throw in a backward crossover for some pizazz, and then back here," Rowan said as he drew on the board. Beckett raised an eyebrow and tried to see

Rowan's apparent master plan, but it was hard to make out past his hand and marker.

"And when all's said and done," Rowan said before spinning to look at Beckett and stepping to the side. "I think everyone will love my performance!"

Rowan stood there, arms outstretched to show the big heart he had drawn on the whiteboard. Beckett sighed and erased it from the board. "You keep that up, and the main thing you and a heart will have in common is all the beating."

Rowan's grin grew wider until Beckett looked at him and said. "No, the bad kind." The grin fled Rowan's face. Beckett hit him on the shoulder playfully, his small, murderous smirk creeping in to obviously try and comfort the omega.

"Ready?" Beckett asked.

"No."

"Too bad, it was rhetorical. Let's go, Rookie."

"Wait, Beck." Rowan reached out and grabbed the captain by his sleeve before he could skate away.

Beckett looked back at him with a raised brow, and Rowan fiddled with the stick in his hand, "What if… What if last night really was a fluke, and I mess you guys up?" He looked away from the captain to the crowd all around them. "What if I'm the reason you lose the game?" Finally, he brought his eyes to look up at Beckett like a sad puppy. "Are you gonna be mad?"

Rowan wasn't sure what he was expecting, but it wasn't the strong hand on his shoulder and that adorable smile he was crushing on so hard. "You'll do great. I've seen you on the ice. These guys don't know what's coming for them."

It felt like electricity shooting through him, like landing a perfect quadruple lutz or scoring that final point to push you in the lead. Having Beckett around was like having a live wire stuck into his insides and electrocuting his whole body. Rowan was instantly addicted to the feeling. Beaming up at him, he showed his perfect smile, nodding. "I'll do my best, Captain!"

"Good, come on, let's get into place," Beckett said just as some cat calling started from across the ice. The captain handed the board over to Archer, and they pushed away from the wall.

Looking over to the other entrance, the other team stepped forward, their players crowding the ice. Some howled while others whistled, and Rowan blushed as he glared at them, already familiar with toxic alpha masculinity.

"Come on." Beckett tapped his arm, and Rowan skated with him. "Just ignore them."

“Wish they’d ignore me,” Rowan huffed. “Jerks.”

"Hey, baby!" One guy waved at Rowan as the blond lifted his nose to him. "Awww, that's cold."

"Don't let them get to you," McAllister skated to the box with the other players. "Good luck, though." He held his fist up, and Rowan excitedly bumped it with his own.

He turned and nervously looked at center ice.

It was game time again.

# CHAPTER TWENTY-THREE

## ~~~~~~ ROWAN ~~~~~~

Rowan lined up in his position, lowering his stick to the ground and staring at the player across from him. The guy made a kissy face at the omega as Rowan scrunched up his face in disgust.

The referee skated to the center, holding the puck over the ice between Beckett and the other captain. Beckett had his face leveled with the other alpha across from him. He was in his element, and it showed with the intense focus. It was almost hypnotizing to watch a level of concentration that rivaled Rowan's own when he was in the zone.

Seconds ticked by until the ref blew the whistle and dropped the puck, starting the game. Rowan was so focused on watching Beckett and the puck that he didn't see the player in front of him rush forward, knocking him back. Rowan's back connected with the ice as he looked up at the arena ceiling.

The crowd booed the guy as he skated around Rowan. "Awww, did da widdle omega fall?" He teased while the others skated around them for the puck.

Rowan rolled onto his side and got on his knees just as the other player stopped before him, looking down at Rowan. "Just where you need to be." He touched Rowan's helmet, the omega's head at crotch level with the other player.

Just then, a form busted by, knocking the guy away. Rowan glanced over to see that it was Beckett as he kept chasing Wilson and the puck. Rowan smiled, standing back up with the help of his hockey stick.

The guy was on his ass, hissing from the pain, and Rowan smirked down at him, "Awww, did da widdle alpha fall?" He winked. "Maybe stay in your lane." He shrugged, pushing off to get away from the action like he was told. The crowd cheered as he turned, skating in a backward crossover.

At the other end of the rink, the players were battling for the puck. Rowan waited patiently, even leaning against the wall.

"Hey! Kid!" Archer shouted, and Rowan looked over at his frowning coach. “Yes, sir?” Rowan straightened up, caught leaning.

Archer motioned for him to stand up. "At least look like you're trying!" He shouted, and Rowan waved to let him know he heard. Just as he did that, he noticed the small black puck sliding toward him, and he just watched it with surprise.

"Get it! Get it, fucking get it!" Archer shouted along with his teammates, who pounded on the half wall, calling Rowan's name.

"Oh!" Rowan swatted at it with his stick to Wilson, who was closest, and he went on to the other end with it. The crowd went crazy, and Rowan held his hands up as if he had scored a goal.

Just as he was celebrating, he caught sight of the guy from earlier approaching him, and he squeaked before turning tail and skating away. He did a loop of their half of the rink before seeing Wilson and attaching himself at his side when he didn't shake off the other alpha chasing him.

"Are you fucking running from that guy?" Wilson skated next to him as he diligently watched Beckett and Walker pass the puck back and forth.

Rowan looked over his shoulder to see the guy coming closer. "Yes!" He shouted, retreating back toward Briggs, who was cocking his head at the scene. All the other players were by the opponent's net since Rowan's team had the puck, and their formation almost exactly matched the setup they practiced the other day

Rowan skated around Briggs's net as the guy followed, and Rowan shouted over at him. "Leave me alone!"

"Not 'til you realize this is no place for an omega bitch!" The guy was closer, and Rowan spun around him quickly; the crowd screamed louder as he went back to the net behind Briggs.

"Oh my god! Are you seriously hiding BEHIND the goalie?" Briggs asked, looking back at him before facing forward again.

"I'm hiding anywhere that keeps me from that guy!" Rowan pointed his stick at the guy rounding back on him. The crowd was eating up the game of cat and mouse, cheering for Rowan to do some elaborate trick to get away once again.

"That's it! Rowan!" Archer shouted, motioning for him to come over, which he did gladly. He didn't even get a chance to open the door before he was forcefully pulled over by the coach by the back of his jersey and put on the bench. Jeon jumped over the wall and skated toward the action without hesitation.

Rowan gasped for air as he crawled onto the bench. "Thank you!" He shouted. "My whole career flashed before my eyes!" He sat down on the bench, accepting the water bottle from McAllister.

The crowd started booing when Rowan was pulled, chanting his name. “Please, sir! That was all I got in me,” Rowan pleaded.

“Just sit there and shut up,” Archer growled out, watching the game.

The game continued with no goals as they all battled over the puck. Rowan cheered for Beckett and his other teammates, but mostly Beckett.

They were still zero to zero in the second period, and Rowan continued to stay off the ice. He was sure he was good to bench warm for the rest of the game as Archer swapped other players here and there. He had just pulled Beckett to give him a breather, and the alpha sat down beside Rowan with a huff. Rowan handed him his own water bottle, which Beckett squirted on his head after taking a few sips and spitting some of it out onto the matted floor. The omega bit his lip at how hot Beckett looked, out of breath and sweaty.

His green eyes were on the game as more players came through, still trying to score a point.

"Coach Archer!" A voice called out, and Rowan could hear the coach groan, but he kept his eyes on the ice.

“Yes, Dean Prescott?”

The small, stubby dean leaned into the box with a disgruntled look. "Why haven't you played Mr. West?"

“He played the first period,” Archer said as if it were obvious.

“The crowd wants more! People are talking about leaving.” He hissed the last part. “I want him in now.”

"Sir," Rowan turned around to face him. "It's dangerous out there. I can't risk getting hurt. At the end of the day, I'm a figure skater."

Prescott smiled supportively while he nodded. "Of course, and at the end of the day, I still get to say who gets this hockey scholarship. Soooo… get in there." He looked back to Archer and turned away.

Archer groaned as the buzzer rang for the end of the period, and the team went back to the locker room. Once there, Archer began writing on the large whiteboard on the wall and started planning out the third period. The team sat around on the benches and watched as their coach laid out the plays. "Wilson, you're here for the puck drop. West, same spot as before-"

The team groaned, and Rowan blushed. "Yeah, yeah, I hate it, too."

"McAllister, you'll be the other wing. Rhodes, you take over for Briggs. Jeon, you and Jones take the back." He capped the pen and glared at them all. "And for God's sake, someone watch the kid, please. I'm embarrassed my player was playing tag on the ice."

"It wasn't tag!" Rowan pouted, poking his index fingers together. "The guy was scary."

"Put me in, coach," Beckett said, and a room of shocked eyes looked at their usually silent captain.

Archer grimaced. "You're exhausted. Sit this round out."

Beckett looked like he wanted to say more, but Archer held up a hand. "We need you for the end if they get any points on us, or if we can't get any on them."

Rowan patted Beckett 's arm. "Yeah. Rest up, cap!"

Archer looked at the screen in the locker room and saw the Zamboni clearing the ice on the live feed. "Alright, everyone, take ten. West, get your shit together," Archer threatened before he walked towards the exit of the locker room.

Rowan took a few deep breaths before sliding up to the coach before he left. "Uh, sir?"

Archer glanced over his shoulder at the young blond. "What?"

"I-I don't wanna let you down." Rowan felt his eyes burn, but he held back the tears. The scent of sad omega crept up on the coach, whose left eye twitched. "But those guys out there are ruthless with me. I-I feel like I'm just-" He couldn't even finish the words, taking a shaky breath.

As if at all possible, the ordinarily hard man softened, his shoulders lowering as he cursed, leaning down to get to eye level with the omega. "You like skating?"

Rowan nodded quickly. "More than anything."

"Then skate," he said solemnly. "Don't let anyone take away the feeling you get when you're skating. And don't let someone chase you in your own element. You belong out there just as much as he does." The alpha looked back at the team, all taking their break to center themselves, and back at the omega, "At the end of the day, on the ice, it's about what you bring to the game." He raised a brow down at him, "So what are you gonna bring, West?"

He wasn't sure why, but his eyes widened, and it just clicked. It was a moment that made so much sense, and it all came together. As much as he didn't want to be there, he also did. Ice was ice, and Rowan knew ice. It was his safe haven, his home.

Rowan nodded dumbly as the coach put a hand on his helmet. It was a very fatherly gesture, and Rowan wondered whether he had done the same for Beckett while he was growing up.

A few minutes later, the team walked out to the arena and slid onto the ice. They did a few quick laps before settling on the bench.

"Alright, let's go, team!" Archer shouted when the music died down, and the whistle blew to get back on the ice.

Rowan got out of the box and watched his team skate into place. He looked around at all the people, and his heart warmed. They were here to see him skate; maybe it was to see an omega play hockey, but they came to see him prove himself, regardless.

Taking a deep breath, Rowan skated forward as everyone watched, and just as quickly, he leaned forward into a spiral, sticking his leg straight up. The crowd jumped to their feet, screaming and cheering. It was a simple move, but he did a quick spin around his team's net before stopping with a flurry of ice.

Looking over to his teammates, he saw a mix of impressed looks and confused head tilts. Then he saw those green eyes and found a warm smile as his captain nodded.

Staring ahead, he found the player from earlier. The player lowered himself down with his stick, and Rowan did the same. When the whistle blew, he didn't make the mistake of watching Wilson, instead locking onto the guy in front of him as he dodged the impending check. Rather than skating away from the guy or the puck, Rowan followed the action closely.

“What are you doing?” Archer called when he got close to the players.

Another player checked McAllister as they chased the puck, but Wilson barreled into him like a freight train, sending the guy sprawling out away from the puck. The alpha enforcer grinned, "That's how you do it!"

Jeon then managed to score a goal as their team cheered. Rowan evaded and dodged the pushes and checks for as long as he could, skating backward and sticking his tongue out at the guy chasing him, riling them all up. He even heard Wilson laugh when Rowan jumped over a stick that was obviously meant to trip him.

The game was going well, given the situation. Rowan was confident he could stay out of the way without outright running away, and they could cruise by on this one point to win. That was until Rowan noticed another player skating toward Wilson, who was facing the action, waiting for the puck to come to him.

"Wilson!" Rowan shouted, and before he could think, he raced forward.

Maybe it was all the violence he'd been exposed to finally coming out, but Rowan plowed into the alpha just before he reached the sandy blond, sending him back on his ass.

Just like before, with Rowan's 'fluke,' the crowd went silent as the game went on. Wilson turned just in time to see it, and Rowan looked down at the alpha, who glared back up at him. The stands went berserk. Feet stomped, people screamed, and the foundation of the whole building seemed to shake. Rowan, though, was more concerned with the heated glare and fangs elongating from the alpha on the ice. Wilson broke out into the loudest laugh Rowan had ever heard from the alpha. He grabbed his side, pointing with his stick to the alpha. "You got checked by him!" His laughter was bringing tears to his eyes. "You fucking suck!"

"You're so fucking dead," the opposing alpha sneered, scuffling to get up. When he managed to stand, he flung his hands down, gloves flying off as he left his stick on the ground and pushed toward Rowan.

Rowan knew he had mentioned never running away again, but that didn't mean anything at that moment. With a loud squeak, he turned tail and skated away as the alpha gave chase.

“Come back here, you fucking bitch!” He shouted.

"Hey! There's no running from fights in hockey!" The angry second in command, Wilson, pushed off next, chasing the alpha chasing Rowan.

The crowd was beside themselves, cameras flashing and voices screaming. Rowan could only look over his shoulder at the seething face and fangs threatening to rip him apart. The ref blew the whistle to signal everyone to stop since a fight was bound to happen, but he made no attempt to stop the alpha from chasing Rowan.

"Can we talk about this?" Rowan called over his shoulder.

Just before reaching him, the guy was tackled from the side by an equally angry Beckett. Fists started flying as everyone started shouting.

"Beck!" Rowan called, not even noticing another player skating up behind the omega.

"Oh, no you don't!" Wilson saw this one coming, though, and met the guy right behind Rowan, throwing the other player's jersey over his head and landing several punches into his stomach as they toppled over to fight.

The players from opposite sides of the rink crawled over the barrier and flooded the rink. A full-on brawl broke out as everyone went down, punching and cursing. Rhodes and McAllister dog piled onto a small lump of players scuffling on the ice. Cooper and Walker were trading fists with two other opposing teammates on the far side of the ice. It was the biggest fight Rowan had ever witnessed, and the crowd was eating it all up. Archer stood to the side, rubbing the space between his eyes in exasperation.

Rowan ducked away from the fight before finding that he was the only player standing. He looked at the carnage as the ref kept blowing his whistle to get control again.

"Hey, Rowan!"

Rowan looked to the call's source to see Briggs holding some guy in a headlock on his knees. "You're officially a member of the team! Welcome aboard!" He punched the guy again, wearing a giant shark-like grin.

Rowan smiled as brightly as the sun among the brawl of alphas and betas wrestling for dominance.

He was finally accepted, and it felt wonderful!

# CHAPTER TWENTY-FOUR

## ~~~~~~ BECK ~~~~~~

"Hold still," Rowan pulled Beckett's chin back, holding an ice pack to his head. Then, after a second, his concentrated eyes showed amusement. "Wow. Deja vu, am I right?" With his head tilted, he winked down at Beckett, who blushed and looked away.

“M’fine,” The alpha mumbled.

"First of all, you're hot; get it right. Secondly, I'll be the judge of whether you're alright or not." He smiled brightly down at him. "Doctor Rowan's got you."

Beckett felt like his face went tomato red with the images of playing doctor with the omega, and he held up the back of his hand to his lower face to try to hide it. Based on the excited giggle he heard, though, he had a feeling Rowan's whole point was to fluster the alpha as much as possible.

'*Cheeky.*'

The locker room was alive with shouting and cheering, mostly from Wilson and Briggs, who were pumped after the game.

"Did you see us! We were gods!" Briggs punched the locker, his sharp alpha teeth gleaming. "I'M GOING TO LIVE FOREVER!" He shouted to the roof. It reminded Beckett of when his little sister ate too much candy before bed.

"Yeah, I love this energy!" McAllister laughed along with them, lifting his hockey stick up. "And it's all thanks to the guy who started that fight!"

All eyes landed on Rowan as he flushed and shook his head. "I didn't do a damn thing." He kept the ice pack on Beckett's head. From where Beckett sat on the bench, the standing omega was now able to look down at him for a change. Not too far down, but a little at least.

Frankly, Beckett liked this position as the small blond stood between his open legs that spread to allow him in closer.

"Pfft! You saved Wilson's ass!" Briggs said, already shirtless, his spiky red hair damp with sweat. "After all that running you were doing at the start, I never thought you'd have our back like that."

Rowan smiled up at him, ever the ray of sunshine, as Beckett resisted holding his heart. "Of course. We're a team!"

This, however, didn't stop some others from clutching their chests as Rowan spoke. In that moment, Rowan not only gained some friends but also official teammates who viewed the small player as their new little brother.

"Alright, I love him," McAllister admitted. "Can we keep him?"

"Yeah! I'd take a bullet for him!" Briggs pounded his chest like a gorilla. "He's so wicked!"

Rhodes agreed loudly as he and Briggs butted heads energetically. The sound of their thick skulls smacking made the omega flinch. Beckett noticed his shoulders rise and fall before smiling at the two alphas.

"I agree," Cooper said darkly. "While Jeon was the one to get us the winning point, Rowan's distraction on the ice played well into our favor."

“Yeah, it’s like he’s a magnet for all those alphas,” McAllister said, putting a finger to his chin. “We should use that!”

“Like a secret weapon!” Someone shouted, and the chatter rose in the locker room.

Rowan glanced down at Beckett, who gave McAllister a death glare that must have looked comical, because Rowan pulled Beckett's chin back and held the ice there. "I might have to put a pin in that thought for later." The omega muttered nervously.

The team broke out into laughter before Wilson's locker door slammed and he looked over at them. Everyone paused, wondering what he would say; he had been quiet since they got back in the locker room.

"You!” He pointed at Rowan, and Beckett readied himself to defend his best friend if Wilson said anything mean.

Wilson's grimace turned amused as he smirked, showing his fangs. "I ever catch you running from a fight like that again, I'll take you out myself. But…" He narrowed his eyes. "Good job out there. Thanks for backing my ass up."

"Of course," Rowan smirked, and Beckett could tell there was something else coming. "Your ass is the only thing nice about you."

A chorus of 'oohs' filled the room as they waited for Wilson to shout and pick a fight. Instead, he barked out a laugh and picked up his bag, already showered and changed. "You're alright, Twirl Hurl. Just don't get on my bad side."

With that, others made their way from the locker room, while some were walking to the showers for a quick rinse to get the sweat off. Beckett was still reeling from Wilson's compliment. He had known the other alpha for several months and had heard nothing but backhanded comments from the guy, even to his closest friends. Looking up at Rowan, Beckett felt his eyes nearly sparkle as he took in how perfect Rowan truly was to subdue a dragon like Wilson.

Rowan was perfect.

The omega lifted the ice and looked at the captain's hair as he brushed it aside, smiling tenderly. "Awww, we match." He poked the spot with the slightly raised bump, and Beckett winced as Rowan apologized, leaning down to give it a soft kiss. "There, all better."

"Yeah?" Beckett asked. "Just like that?" He cocked his head.

Rowan nodded, hands on his hips. "Of course. Never underestimate the power of a kissed boo-boo." He winked, turning around to take off his jersey. He already had his skates off and leaned them next to Beckett's.

"Wow, that was such a rush! Just like yesterday! Does it always feel this way?" He asked, sitting on the bench while Beckett stood to strip off his own gear.

Beckett nodded. “Sometimes.”

Rowan hummed, kicking his feet back and forth animatedly. "I think I could get used to this."

Beckett wasn't sure why, but watching Rowan happily playing hockey did something to his insides. It was something they had in common, and the more he had in common with Rowan, the more he felt like he had earned his friendship. The omega turned away when Beckett wrapped a towel around his lower half and went into the showers, while he went to the storage closet to change. He was quick, not wanting to hog it, and when he came out, Rowan was going in, wearing his own towel. Beckett tried to keep his eyes forward, though it was an arduous task.

At one point, when they passed, he let his eyes catch Rowan’s to see the omega looking up at him before passing a wink and a sly smile. Beckett froze by his locker, staring down at his open bag. ‘*What the hell was THAT look for?*’

Changing into his black zip-up hoodie and jeans, he was lacing his combat boots when Rowan came out, a towel around his waist, while another ran through his wet hair. Beckett knew Rowan didn’t like taking long locker showers. Just enough to get the sticky sweat off to get him home to his own shower.

Just then, McAllister, who was one of the slowest to finish getting changed, lifted his own bag, texting on his phone. "Hey Rowan!" He called, and the blond stopped to look up at the skinny beta. "The team's going to get burgers at this local diner. You wanna go?"

Beckett felt his heart clench as Rowan's face lit up, and he nodded. "Yeah! I'll meet you outside."

McAllister left, and Rowan dipped back into the equipment room to change. He was barely in there three minutes before coming out in just his jeans and sneakers, shaking out his folded shirt and slipping it on. Beckett blushed at the sight of how truly cute the omega was. He knew it was just a matter of time before the team accepted Rowan and swept him away. Of course, the alpha would miss their late dinner runs and X-Files binge-watching.

"Ready to go? You hungry?" Rowan asked Beckett before laughing. "Wait, dumb question. You're built like a house, of course you're hungry. Let's go, I want a milkshake!"

Beckett stared down at him with blinking eyes. "Me?" He even pointed to himself as if there were another person in the now-empty locker room.

Realization crossed Rowan's face, and he playfully glared up at him, punching his arm gently. "Of course! Did you think I would go without you? Wow, what do you really think of me?"

'*You don't wanna know,*' he thought.

Rowan took the alpha's hand and squeezed it. "Come on, it'll be fun!"

"I don't think..." Beckett bit the inside of his cheek before continuing nervously. "They meant to include me."

"Of course they did!" Rowan gasped as if the other option was too crazy to consider. "You're our captain! You're coming." He pulled at his strong hand, and Beckett followed.

Once out of the arena's back doors, he saw the whole team gathered, talking. Beckett felt his skin tingle and his throat tighten. No one wanted him there; he should just leave Rowan to his fun and-

"Alright, we're here!" Rowan held up their entwined hands. "Let's eat!"

"Yeah!" Briggs shouted loudly. "I need at least ten burgers!"

"You get one." Wilson snapped, not even looking up from his phone.

"Aw, but I need to carb load!"

"You need a doctor with all that shit you guys eat."

Rowan laughed at their team's playful nature and looked up at Beckett. The captain could only force a smile back, knowing he would do anything for Rowan. Even endure an evening's dinner that he was totally not invited to.

# CHAPTER TWENTY-FIVE

The team walked along the street, cars honking and passengers screaming about their victory as the team cheered and chanted the school fight song. Rowan didn't know it, but he was excited to learn as McAllister and Briggs went over the verses. Rowan never released Beckett's hand and actually squeezed it several times whenever Beckett seemed to be drifting off in his mind.

It was endearing to see how much the omega wanted him there. Beckett almost forgot all the nagging doubts in his head whenever the blond aimed his perfect smile his way.

They got to the diner quickly. The place was modeled after a fifty's vibe, with vintage cars out front and the staff dressed like some old sitcom. The team saddled in, and the staff scrambled to connect tables for the large number of customers who had just entered.

Rowan released Beckett's hand to hold the menu, and the captain mourned the loss as he picked up the plastic menu to look over the food. It was all standard with shiny pictures depicting each classic item.

"Ooo, I love burgers!" Rowan swooned, "A double deluxe… a bacon burger? Look, a triple-decker!" He pointed, his mouth falling open in shock.

"More like a heart attack on a bun," Wilson said across from him as Rhodes and McAllister laughed.

"Well, if having a burger every now and then is going to kill me, I'll die a happy man!" Rowan said proudly.

"I thought you twirl hurls were super strict about your diet," Wilson commented, not even looking at the menu. He raised a brow at Rowan as if trying to figure him out.

'*Good luck,*' Beckett thought. Rowan was literally a surprise wrapped in a mystery, confined within a riddle. Beckett was still trying to solve him, but the omega kept surprising him.

"We are, but we also burn a lot of calories on the ice. I have an insane metabolism for such a small guy. It's like my body has all this energy, but if I don't eat enough, I'm sooo drained." He whined as the waitress came over, smiling at all the rowdy players.

"Everyone ready?" She asked, and Beckett panicked, looking at his menu. He knew what he wanted, but he didn't have the capacity to say it. If it had just been him and Rowan or even his family, he could have mustered out his order.

The thought of the words coming out as everyone from the team watched him made his throat tighten up. Maybe he could just shake his head and hand back the menu. They didn't need to know he was starving. But would that be rude? Weird?

She went down the line, and Rowan looked at him, reading the panic on his face as he leaned over. "Whatcha want? I can order for you."

The alpha blinked down at him, affection swelling inside his chest. Relief poured through him as Beckett shyly pointed at a picture, and Rowan nodded as the waitress came to him next. "And you, sweetie?"

"I'll have a double bacon cheeseburger with fries, please, and a strawberry milkshake! Also, to save you some time, my friend here will have a cheeseburger with no pickles and onion rings instead of fries. Oh, and a Coke, please." Rowan gave her a charming smile as she wrote it down.

"You got it!" She winked and moved on to McAllister, who was trying to shoot his shot at flirting his way into free ice cream, but it wasn't really working.

Beckett felt his heart flutter as he looked down at the table. Rowan ordered for him and did it knowing how he liked his burger.

No pickles.

It was such a simple thing to remember, but it meant so much to him. He looked at the smiling blond as he kept talking to Wilson and Briggs.

Was this love?

Remembering that he didn't like pickles?

Beckett cracked a smile but stopped when he noticed a weirded-out Cooper next to him.

"Sorry," Beckett muttered, and the other player shook his head.

"Don't be. Your smile… I find it positively dark. It's metal." He threw up a rock-on sign with his hand as Beckett blinked at him. Both their faces were stone-cold neutral as they regarded each other.

"You don't talk much," Cooper said, and Beckett nodded. "I'm fine with that. I usually prefer solitude. But-" He looked down the table at his friends. "Every now and then, we introverts sometimes need to come into the light."

Beckett seemed to understand his cryptic words as his head bobbed in agreement. He looked back at Rowan as the omega snorted and giggled at something McAllister said to Walker; he couldn't help but feel close to the light at that exact moment. Looking back at Cooper, he smiled again, and the wing returned it. "I'm glad you came out with us tonight, Captain. Some of us were wondering if you even liked us."

The alpha's eyes widened as he shook his head. He actually thought they didn't like him. Cooper seemed to understand, strangely really good at picking up Beckett's silent looks. "I see. Well, it's good you're here. We need to understand our leader to work under him. Hopefully, West will bring you out more often." He turned away when Jeon asked him a question.

Beckett looked around the table at his smiling teammates and felt warmth fill him as he looked down at the Coke set before him.

It was the happiest he had been in a long time.

The food came, and the team of ravenous hockey players dove in, getting chided by Wilson for their piss-poor manners. At one point, Rowan turned to Beckett to ask if they could share their sides.

"I just love fries and onion rings," he said as Beckett nodded, pushing his plate closer.

"Hey, Beck," Rowan said, slipping an onion ring onto his finger. "Did you like it, so you put a ring on it?" He wagged his brow.

Beckett blushed but laughed through his nose, rolling his eyes.

Rowan joined the laugh as he drank from his milkshake before offering Beckett a sip from the same straw.

McAllister gasped something about an indirect kiss when Beckett drank from it, but he was silenced when Briggs threw a fry at him.

"What? They're oddly sickeningly cute together!" McAllister whined, and Rowan snorted.

"Of course we're cute together. He's, like, my best friend." He leaned into Beckett as the captain blushed, but he smiled at being called Rowan's best friend.

"Awww, so the best friend title is already taken?" McAllister pouted, leaning his head on Rowan's shoulder. "I was gunning for it."

Beckett leaned over and raised a brow at the beta as the table filled with joking 'ooh's' and 'you better watch it, McAllister.'

Rowan dug his spoon into the milkshake, pulling out the cherry. He held it up to Beckett by the stem. "Want my cherry?"

The captain looked down at it before opening his mouth and allowing Rowan to place it on his tongue. Beckett closed his teeth before Rowan plucked the stem back. The blond then placed the stem in his mouth as Beckett paused mid-chew and raised an eyebrow at him.

Rowan's face distorted as his mouth pressed closed and he moved his jaw left to right.

"What the FUCK are you doing?" Wilson noticed, slammed down his water, drawing most of the team's attention to him.

Rowan looked up and grinned as he spoke around the stem. "My friends back home and I always tie our cherry stems up into knots with our tongues."

Wilson looked like he was trying to process how anyone could procreate when children like this were the risk. "Why?"

"Oh, I know!" McAllister shoved his hand up, leaning over the table. "I heard if you can tie a cherry stem with just your mouth, it means you give great head."

"No, it means you're a good kisser," Dominguez said from down the table.

"How does tying a cherry with your mouth prove anything?" Briggs asked.

"Duh!" McAllister scoffed, waving his hand. "It's all about tongue action, bro!" He looked at Rowan. "Can you do it?"

Rowan opened his mouth and plucked out the now knotted stem. "KNOT only can I do it, but I can double-knot it." He presented them with the stem as someone giggled.

A wave of 'ooo' filled the table as several players golf clapped while Wilson snorted.

"It's not like it's hard!" He reached over to Jeon's milkshake and plucked his cherry from the top before shoving it in his mouth.

"Heyyyy," Jeon hummed as he mourned the loss of his treat, though he didn't seem particularly offended.

Wilson's mouth moved rapidly as they watched. Finally, he spat it out into his hand, standing up and presenting it as if it were the Stanley Cup.

"Ta-fucking-DA, bitches!"

McAllister leaned forward, squinting at it. "It's no double knot."

"Fuck off!" Wilson threw the tied stem at his face. Beckett, meanwhile, was secretly burning up over the very idea of what kissing Rowan would be like.

'*He can double-knot cherry stems with his tongue.*' Beckett took in a deep breath through his nose, trying to look as casual as possible. '*Don't think about it, don't think about it, don't think about-*'

"Beck?"

"Hm?" Beckett looked down at the blond next to him to see him leaning forward.

"Can you do it?"

Realizing he was talking about the stem that everyone was trying to tie, he quickly shook his head. Rowan's eyes lowered as he leaned closer, giving the alpha an almost sultry look as he cupped a hand by his mouth, making sure no one could hear what he was about to say.

"It's alright, I can teach you."

Rowan leaned back with a final look before looking at Briggs, who was trying to tie the paper straw sleeve.

Beckett, meanwhile, felt like his brain just went offline.

Everything was going great until the diner door opened, and another large group of guys walked in.

"Oh, you gotta be kidding me," Wilson groaned, and all eyes turned back to look at eight of the twenty hockey players they faced off against standing at the front of the dinner in their letterman jackets.

The group of visiting alphas made their way over, and Wilson shot up with the rest of the team. Chairs scraped, silverware clanked, and shoes squeaked on the linoleum. They all squared up, the twenty-five of them against the eight players. Naturally, Wilson and Beckett stood up front with their arms crossed.

"Well, well, well, I didn't know this is where losers ate." The opposing captain sneered at Wilson.

"Nah, it's where winners eat," Wilson smirked dangerously back, eyes glinting for another fight. "The losers wait for the scraps out back. I'll be sure to leave some food for you to gum down. Not sure how many teeth we knocked out."

The other alpha sneered, and Beckett instantly recognized him as the guy Rowan checked to protect Wilson. His sharp eyes turned to Rowan and darkened angrily with recognition, pointing a finger at him. "You."

Beckett shifted, ready to stand in front of him if needed. The alpha scowled in disgust. "What kind of omega plays hockey? You think you're too good to be lying on your back taking knots?"

Rowan, with more confidence than he probably should have had, stepped forward ahead of the alphas on his team. It was a total power move as he crossed his arms just like Wilson's and cocked his head.

"You would know a lot about being on your back. Considering that's where this omega put you." He gestured to himself.

"Damn, son!" McAllister laughed loudly as Briggs hissed, asking if that burned as badly as he thought it did.

The alpha blushed, hands going into fists as he leaned forward, bumping his chest to Rowan's. "You wanna go outside now and finish what you started? Your fucking alphas have to fight all your battles?"

“Figure skaters don't start fights.” Rowan didn't back down to the challenge. “But we can finish them.”

"I'll beat your fucking head in-" The guy stopped when the rest of Rowan's team stepped up, their large mass of bodies against the eight players. Beckett gave his meanest glare, making the other alpha gulp.

"You got two options here, buddy," Wilson said, motioning to his crew. "Either we fuck you up again, or you leave to go lick your wounds in the shitty hotel you're no doubt staying in." He leaned forward. "I'd ask that you choose the first, but it's not an option if I pick for you."

The captain snarled at them all before taking a step back, knowing when he was defeated. "Screw you guys. You're fucking weird for having an omega on your team anyways."

The team turned and walked from the diner, leaving the winning team to laugh and high-five. Beckett looked down at Rowan, who was receiving pats from all around, congratulating him on his first official post-game showdown. If Rowan had a tail, it would undoubtedly be wagging like an energetic golden retriever as he looked up at Beckett with a big grin. "We showed them!"

Beckett smiled, nodding. "Yeah, you did."

Rowan blushed at the compliment, and the team went back to finishing their food. After paying, they parted ways on campus, splitting to their dorms.

Rowan hummed the school fight song all the way to their dorm, practically glowing with excitement. When they got inside, he kicked off his sneakers and jumped onto his bed, gently bouncing on the squeaky mattress. Beckett took off his own shoes and set his bag by the door, smiling at Rowan's childlike wonder.

"I'm too excited to sleep! Today was awesome!" Rowan threw his hands up as he kept bouncing.

Beckett sat on his own bed, watching Rowan bounce and recap that close call at dinner with exciting details.

"I seriously thought that guy was gonna hit me! But bam! I had my own scary Pitbull crew behind me!" Rowan giggled loudly.

Beckett sighed dreamily at Rowan as he kept going, feeling his heart race as he fell more in love with the blond every second.

Yeah, he admitted it; he was falling for the rookie.

# CHAPTER TWENTY-SIX

## ~~~~~~ ROWAN ~~~~~~

Ever since their incredible second win, Rowan felt his world tilt on its axis in the best kind of way. It had been two days since that amazing night, and Rowan had started receiving more hockey training; Beckett was tasked with double practices to get him into shape before the next game. Dean Prescott insisted that the last game drew so much press they might have to host more games to accommodate ticket demand.

Rowan wasn't complaining; it meant that he got more time with Beckett and on the ice. It was a win-win, really. He didn't have time to go home to see his friends or grandma like he wanted, but he got something equally exciting there. His teammates quickly became like a second family to him. He was never alone on campus, not anymore.

On an even more positive note, they also accepted Beckett. It was almost like a stipulation for having Rowan: they had to have Beckett, or it was a no-go.

Rowan got along with all of them, and they all treated him like one of their own. Rowan needed the camaraderie with the attention he got from campus and outside reporters.

Wilson nearly beat away a crowd of people asking Rowan one afternoon.

"I'll smash every camera if you don't get outta our way!" Wilson was ready to windmill his arms through the small crowd as he and Rowan went to get coffee after a class. Beckett stood in the back, nudged there by reporters who got between them. He just gave his famous death glare to the people as they slowly backed away.

Of course, Rowan would always pull him back to join him when they were separated.

Meanwhile, McAllister and Briggs had this game where they wore matching sunglasses and acted like the president's security guards, leading him around.

"Ksh," McAllister made a fake walkie-talkie static, holding his watch to his face. "Blond Lighting is secure." He said as they each framed his side on their way to their shared class. Beckett had another course at that time, but Rowan wished he could be here to see their teammates in action.

"Ksh," Briggs mimicked the sound, nodding. "Roger that, Putty. Security confirmed."

"Ksh, copy that, Red Wall," McAllister nodded.

"Putty? Red Wall?" Rowan had asked. "Where do you guys come up with this stuff?"

Briggs gave him a big goofy grin. "Oh! Those are actually our hockey names!"

"Hockey names?" Rowan cocked his head.

"Yeah, all the great hockey players have nicknames." McAllister began listing off on his fingers, "There's Mr. Hockey."

"Also known as Gordie Howe," Briggs jumped in. McAllister ticked off another finger.

"The Kid."

"The one and only Sidney Crosby," Briggs fired back like a kid in class who's excited to have all the right answers.

"The Great One, of course."

"All respect for Wayne Gretzky."

"Ohhh, Penncakes!"

"Now I know you're making that one up," Rowan laughed.

"Nahhh!" Briggs jumped in to come to McAllister's rescue. "Dustin Penner, one of the best players with the best name background story! He made up a story to cover up how he really got a major injury during the season. Basically, he said he got hurt diving into a stack of pancakes."

"What really happened?" Rowan cocked his head.

"He threw his back out at home, no pancakes involved," McAllister chortled. "But he's a great sport about it."

"So, Putty?" Rowan pointed to him. "And Red Wall?" He moved his finger to Briggs, who nodded. "Alright, you've piqued my interest. Why did you two pick those?"

"We didn't." Briggs threw open the door to their class as they walked in, finding three seats together in the middle. "In hockey, you don't get to pick your name. Your team does."

"Ohhh, so how'd you get those names?" Rowan pulled out his pen and notebook, but gave his full attention to the two players.

"Well," McAllister blushed, scratching the end of his nose. "At first, they called me Tape Dispenser. You know, 'cause I stuck to people on the ice, like tape." He shrugged. "But it didn't really have a ring to it until

Wilson one day shouted, 'Yo, Putty, stick with it!' and like that it just stuck… like tape." He snorted, slapping his knee as Rowan joined.

"What about you, big guy?" Rowan looked up at Briggs. "Red Wall," He tasted the name again. "Is it for the hair, orrrr-" He held out his hand, circling it at the wrist for him to pick up.

It was the giant red head's turn to blush as the alpha lowered his head and brought his shoulders up. "It's kind of embarrassing. McAllister, you tell him."

McAllister gave a snap and a wink, "I gotcha covered, big guy." He turned in his seat to face the omega between them. "Picture it, Sicily 1922-" Rowan slapped the beta on the arm, before rolling his eyes as he shook his head. "Okay, but for real?" He looked over to a still-blushing Briggs. "He showed up to the first day in the locker rooms wearing every… bit… of Detroit Red Wings merch." He broke out in snickering, tears in his eyes as Briggs blushed harder. "He seriously had Red Wings crocs! Red Wings sweats! A Red Wings jersey, not to mention a Red Wings backpack and key chains! He was even filling his locker with like a dozen Red Wings posters." He snorted once at the memory, "We teased him for it, but that day on the ice, he was a damn wall in the goal. Hence the name, Red Wall."

"I love that team!" Briggs literally had stars in his eyes. "I grew up in that area, and those games were my life. You know they've won the cup eleven times? They're one of the original six teams!" Briggs held up six fingers.

"Yeah, we all have teams we worship, but-" McAllister raised a brow, "Detroit boxers?"

Briggs blushed again. “My mom got them for me!”

While McAllister poked fun, Rowan rested a hand on Briggs’s arm. “I think it’s sweet.”

“Really?” Briggs peeked up at him. It was rare to see a shy alpha outside of Beckett, so Rowan found it positively adorable. He resisted smooshing the alpha’s cheeks together and cooing.

“Really! I’m a huge fan of Emily Star, especially when I was growing up! She went to the Olympics two times, too! Gold, of course!” He turned to the alpha with just as many stars in his eyes. “I have, like, a hundred posters of her in my room back home and in my dorm.” He bobbed his head from left to right as if in thought. “She doesn’t have boxers or sweats, but I do have a shirt with her on it, and a cute keychain!”

Briggs’s eyes widened as they flashed with happiness. “That’s so cool!”

“It is! And the fact that you’re named after your team is such an honor!” Rowan went on as Briggs gasped.

“I never thought of it like that!”

Rowan saw the gears turn as the alpha closed his eyes and began humming to himself in excitement. While the redhead thought about it, Rowan turned to look at McAllister. “Soooo, I’m Blond Lighting?”

“Eh, we’re still working on the name.” McAllister lifted his pen as the professor walked in. “Don’t worry, though. We’ll pick something good.”

“Just as long as it’s not Twirl Hurl.” Rowan giggled.

The beta laughed with him. “If Wilson had his way with everyone’s name, Kage would be Bitch Face,

Walker would be Big Mother Fucker, and Cooper would be Bird Brain."

"Well, good thing we only listen to him sometimes," Rowan pointed out as the professor began the lecture.

Frankly, it was nice having Pitbull privileges with his friends, but nothing compared to the way Beckett stuck by his side.

They were rarely apart, and Rowan was slowly becoming very used to him as a permanent fixture in his life.

Rowan always considered himself like glue, sticking to his friends. If anything, the alpha was the clingy one, always walking Rowan to his figure skating practice and workout sessions. Rowan even convinced the alpha to join his morning yoga at the park, which McAllister and Briggs had also joined. His hockey family really seemed to be coming together.

# CHAPTER TWENTY-SEVEN

## ~~~~~~ ROWAN ~~~~~~

All in all, things were going great for Rowan. He thought of how fortunate he had been since he arrived at college during his next practice. He smiled as he landed his jump and finished it off with a fast-paced two-foot spin in full hockey gear. Clapping echoed when he struck a pose and smiled over at Dean Prescott, who was so excited that the short man was practically sparkling.

"Yes, yes! I want to see more of that!" The old man cheered.

Behind Rowan, he could feel the eyes of his teammates as McAllister and Briggs joined in the clapping while Wilson rolled his eyes. Archer stood next to Prescott, growling.

"Can we please get back to practice?" Archer grunted.

"In a moment! I just wanted to see our star player in action." He smiled at Rowan once more. "You're making this school very proud!"

Rowan gave a nod as he fell back in line next to Beckett, who gave Rowan a smirk. "Nice twirl," he bemused.

Rowan blushed before he elbowed him with a puffed-out face like a pufferfish. "Shut it."

"No, really. It was so pretty," Beckett said again, his cat-like smirk never leaving his face. "I couldn't take my eyes off you."

"I'll kick you in the knee with these skates." He motioned down to his figure skates that Archer hadn't replaced yet.

"Duly noted. At least you don't bite." He nodded, though he did offer a wink to the omega. Rowan's flush deepened as he fought down a giddy smile, turning away from him.

It was so crazy; Beckett on the ice could sometimes be just as flirty as Rowan, and it drove the omega up the wall. To have him do things like that and say those words to him, it was enough to almost make Rowan purr. But off the ice, the alpha refused to back up those words and got all shy. It was like being on the tilt-a-whirl, going between weightless excitement to mind numbing dizziness.

But Rowan wouldn't trade either version of his alpha for anything. He liked Beckett for who he was, and if ice Beckett truly was a flirt, then Rowan would profit off that.

In retaliation for the wink, the omega made a biting motion towards him, his teeth giving a loud clack as he looked up at the Alpha. Beckett raised a challenging brow but shook his head with a laugh.

"Anyway, I'll let you all get back to it! I have a meeting with a reporter.

Good luck on your away game! Do us all proud!" Prescott made his departure as Archer sighed in relief.

"Finally. Let's get back to it. Kage, you know the drill." He jutted a thumb at him and Rowan, and the blond felt an exhilarated zap to his system as he followed his crush/roommate to the far side of the ice.

"So, what's on the agenda today, cap?" Rowan asked suggestively. "Something handsy, preferably."

Beckett laughed, and it was a semi-loud one that went right to Rowan's heart.

"The only time you get handsy is when you fight. We'll be practicing your passing." He tossed the black rubber piece on the ice. "Ready?"

"As I'll ever be!" Rowan took the position.

Beckett pushed the puck across the ice. There was a solid crack sound as the rubber snapped against the wood of Rowan's stick. He recoiled a little but recovered quickly.

"That was pretty hard for a pass. Are you trying to score a goal on me, too?" Rowan asked, moving his shoulders up and down in a teasing manner.

Beckett shook his head. "A pass should be confident and certain. You don't pass to another player when you don't have any other options; passing is the first option." He skated a little closer to Rowan.

"Go ahead, pass it to me."

Rowan looked down at the puck, up to Beckett, and back down again. After a moment, he leaned into the stick and slid the puck across the ice toward Beckett.

Unfortunately, 'toward Beckett' seemed to be as accurate as Rowan could describe. The puck looked like it was going to miss the captain by about six feet. Beckett pushed forward, intercepted the puck, and spun back to where he had been originally.

"Were you afraid the puck was going to grow wings and fly away from your stick?" Beckett asked. The omega was certain it was a joke, but Beckett said it with a serious dryness.

"No," Rowan replied sarcastically. He then added in an equally sassy voice, "Should I have been? Does that happen?"

Beckett shook his head. "No, you don't need to worry about that. And, because that isn't a concern, you don't need to stare at where the puck is. Focus on where you want it to be."

He pushed the puck back to Rowan, whose stick greeted the puck with the same loud crack as before.

"You don't need to pull back the stick or anything; the strength can come almost entirely from your wrists," Beckett said loudly as Rowan positioned himself to make the pass. "Just focus on where you want the puck to go and will it there."

Rowan nodded, took a breath, lined up the shot, and passed the puck over. It went right to Beckett, stopping by his skates.

Rowan raised both fists into the air. "I passed it!"

Beckett nodded. "Much better. However," he said. Rowan dropped his arms.

"However?"

"Yes, however. This isn't soccer, I don't kick the puck. Your target shouldn't be me; it should be my stick." Beckett said as he smacked his stick against the ice. Rowan looked at the wood on the ice.

"But...that's so much smaller."

Beckett shrugged. "If it was easy, everyone would do it. And we would call it baseball." He passed the puck back to Rowan and said, "Again."

The rubber cracked against the wood. "How long are we just going to pass the puck back and forth?"

"How long do you practice a move for your figure skating?" Beckett asked in return.

"Oh, until I could do it with my eyes closed," Rowan said without hesitation.

Beckett nodded, a thoughtful look on his face. “Well, how about we get this right with your eyes open first? Small goals, you know?”

Rowan blushed, smiling as he bobbed his head up and down quickly. Beckett was always so patient and calm with him, always lending a gentle hand to the proper ways of hockey. And if he was a little sassy, it only added to his appeal.

They continued their practice until a whistle blew, and they joined the team in some workout drills. By the end, Rowan was sure his jersey was as wet as a fish tank with sweat. He collapsed into a sitting position on the cold ice.

"Alright, team, that's it for today," Archer skated lazily by them. "Be packed and ready for tomorrow. We leave at noon with or without you."

After cleaning up, the team left the ice, the whole locker room abuzz with talk of the first away game of the season.

"I hear the town has a cool food truck exhibit near the hotel! We should go!" McAllister said, shrugging his pants on.

"I hear they have a DJ and a bubble pit at their rink!" Briggs cheered, already pumped. Rowan could see him taking out a cardstock picture of a Red Wing’s player that he apparently tapped several times before each game for good luck. The alpha shoved it safely into his bag to make sure he took it with him for his trip.

Rowan laughed, nervously wiping the sweat from the back of his neck as he waited for his turn in the shower.

“You excited, dude?” McAllister asked the blond.

"Yeah, I'm totes ready!" Rowan gave two thumbs up, but he was actually kind of nervous.

By his calendar, he should be starting his heat soon. Lucky for him, he was on the pill for that. Not because he was out sleeping around, but to help reduce the effects of the heat. While the media portrayed omegas as sex-crazed, withering flowers craving a knot, it was far from the truth. Rowan just got feverish, light-headed, and kind of horny. Nothing like the ones you find on cheesy, dirty websites on their knees begging to be knotted by the first alpha who came their way. People read too much into the stereotypes about omegas being desperate instead of focusing on the reality that heats are a normal, manageable part of life. But of course, many people didn't see it like that, so Rowan was hesitant to say anything at all.

Looking down at his phone, he checked the calendar and saw it should start tomorrow. So, if he stopped by the pharmacy today, he could pick up some scent patches and ride this thing out, maybe even finish it before he came back. No issues there, right?

"Shower's yours," Beckett said as he and Walker wandered out in their towels.

The omega peeked up at the two large alphas who walked by. He bit his lip as he realized the number of sweaty, half-naked men around him. His face heated up as he glanced at a shirtless Briggs and McAllister wrestling while Wilson stood in his boxers, brushing his hair at his locker. Somewhere down the line, Sanchez and Walker dropped their towels as Rowan shot up, turning away.

Normally, he was totally fine, but he didn't want to risk any bits of his pre-heat scent slipping out and everyone getting weird around him. They all just got comfortable around him, so if any of them got a whiff of heat or slick, he'd probably get the hockey name of nightmares.

'*Figure Heat, or maybe Dick Slick.*' Rowan shuddered at the names in disgust.

Rowan picked up his stuff and ran past them, shouting his thanks. And if he turned the shower pretty damn cold to flush out the heat from his face, that was between him and the shower head.

The next morning was hard for the omega… Literally. Rowan groaned, already feeling the early effects of his heat. Looking to the side of his nest at the large lump across the room, he sighed, feeling a pull at his lower stomach. The scent of alpha was heavy in the air as he felt his arousal push into the mattress where he lay on his stomach. After allowing himself a couple of seconds to grind into the bed, he sat up, not wanting to get carried away.

Crawling from the bed was achy and annoying as he fished around his backpack for the scent patches. Taking them out, he ripped them open with his teeth and slapped one on his neck near his scent glands. His long blond hair hid it for the most part as he shoved the box into his backpack, which he planned to take with him on the trip.

Loud sniffing pulled his eyes to Beckett as the large alpha sat up, sleepily blinking, while sniffing the air. His hair stuck up in each direction, and the way his eyes squinted up at the ceiling made Rowan's heart lurch.

Nervously, Rowan picked up the trash by the door while sliding his sneakers on. "Morning, Beck!"

“Rowan?” He sleepily rubbed his eyes as he blinked them at the small omega. “What are you doing?”

Rowan held up the trash, hoping that if he left, he could air himself out a bit. "Taking the trash out before we leave. Can't have this in the room while we're gone, ya know?" He quickly turned, walking out the door. When it shut, he leaned against the heavy, cold metal and exhaled.

Walking out to the dumpster was enough to clear his head. It was getting colder, and the figure skater couldn't help but sigh when his heated skin met the cold breeze. Tossing the trash into the dumpster, he leaned against the brick wall for a bit, basking in the weather before heading in.

Opening the door, he found Beckett already up and in the bathroom. Walking to his bed, he half-made it, which consisted of straightening his nest walls. He already noticed Beckett's neatly made one and resisted snatching up his pillow to take a long whiff. Throwing his duffel bag on the bed, Rowan began to pack, shoving clothes from the clean laundry basket he had yet to fold.

Pushing the window open, he got to air out the room a bit and allow that sweet, crisp cold to sneak in. Stepping away from the window, his gaze lingered on the bed across from his own.

“Damn it,” Rowan whispered, looking to the bathroom door and back to Beckett’s bed. In three quick steps, he jumped up onto it and shoved his face into the alpha’s pillow. Taking in several big gulps of air, he sighed, nuzzling into it. “Oh yeah, that’s the good stuff,” He breathed out heavily.

After satisfying his inner omega needs, he jumped off the bed and went back to his bag just as the water shut off.

Stepping back to admire his packing, the door to the bathroom opened, and a shirtless Beck walked out, rubbing a towel on his head. He gave a pointed look at the messy bag and back at Rowan, raising a single brow in a silent question.

"I know, I know. You told me to pack yesterday. Give me a break; I was tired!" He whined. "It's done anyway!" He pointed to the shower. "You done?"

Beckett nodded, and Rowan was thankful to get away from the damn perfect sight of his shirtless roommate. He slammed the bathroom door shut to get ready while Beckett finished changing.

Two hours later, the captain and rookie found themselves outside the school, bundled up from the cold. Rowan was getting a talking to from Emily while the team stood back and watched.

Emily was adjusting Rowan's knit hat, trying to cover his ears, but his wild blond hair wouldn't allow it. "Make sure to take it easy."

"Totally," Rowan said quickly as she moved to pull the hood of his hoodie over the top of his head.

“And don’t forget to do your stretches every morning and night.”

"Mhm," he nodded.

"And don't stay up too late." She smoothed out his hoodie before moving to ensure he had everything in his skate bag. "Don't get into anything dangerous."

"Coach Emi." Rowan felt his already hot cheeks heat up as his team snickered behind him, and he looked over his shoulder to see most of them covering their mouths to hide their smiles. Others, like Wilson, were grinning like the cat that caught the canary.

“Vegetables, yeah, those sound good. Something an adult should suggest.” Emily lifted up a bag of candy. “But I got you some peach rings for the ride.” She paused before putting them in his bag, pointing to him like a stern mother. “Share.”

“Emmiii,” Rowan whined.

McAllister was practically on his knees, wheezing while Briggs and Rhodes held his arms to keep him from going all the way down. Beckett even smiled his 'scary' face at Emily's motherly obsession.

"Do you want me to come?" Emily finally asked, her big brown eyes wide with worry. "I brought an overnight bag just in case." Her eyes then flashed with excitement just as fast. "We can stay up rewatching my old skate videos!"

"As much as I would love that," Rowan said as he took her hand and gently patted it. "And trust me, I’m going to try and talk you into watching them with me when I get back, I gotta go." He motioned with his thumb to the team. "I'm a big boy."

"Awww, my little Ro-Ro." She sighed, ignoring the loud crack of laughter at the nickname. Rowan felt his whole face go cherry red as Emily gave him a quick hug before leaving with a final threat to Archer to take care of her star student.

Turning around to the team, the omega was met with a sea of grinning faces.

"Not a word," He threatened. Deep down, he hoped this wouldn’t come back as a suggested hockey name.

"Anything you say..." McAllister squeaked. "Ro-Ro."

And like that, the team collapsed in on themselves with a laugh that roared louder than the bus. Rowan sighed, walking by Beckett, who was trying to cover his small laugh with the back of his hand as he followed Rowan onto the bus. Archer took note of each of them as they passed.

“Wilson, Briggs, McAllister… Ro-Ro," His monotone voice called, counting them off.

A whole new wave of laughter haunted the blond omega as he gave a long, hard look to his coach, who gave a barely-there smile, pointing with his pen to get on the bus.

"Figure skaters have so much more class," he snorted, flipping his ponytail before carrying his bags onto the bus.

Beckett and Rowan sat near the back. With Beckett's extra height, he needed more legroom, and the back seat was the place for it.

As the last player got on, Archer stood next to the driver and glared at them. "Alright, we’ve got a two-hour drive on our hands. Let's make it as painless as possible, and no one bother me," he said before sitting down and leaning against the window to try and get some sleep.

Rowan wanted to say it was a cute bus ride like in all the books he read; the protagonist would lean their head on the other person's shoulder, and they grew predominantly closer. But instead, it was Rowan fighting off crumpled-up pieces of paper McAllister was throwing at him while fending off more jokes about Emi's cute pet name for him.

The two hours flew by, and the blond flinched when the bus slammed on its brakes at an ordinary-looking hotel. Then, one by one, they filed their way off and waited in the lobby as Archer got them all set.

He called for their attention, which took some threatening before he held up a handful of keycards. "As I call your names, come get your keys. We have a strict curfew to be in your rooms by nine o'clock and in bed by eleven. If I catch any of you out of your rooms, you'll be doing burpees 'til you bleed," he threatened before starting the names.

Rowan, as much as he loved bunking with Beckett, was looking forward to having a room to himself. Finally, he could ride out this annoying heat with just him and his hand. And he could finally take off that godforsaken itchy scent patch. It had been bothering him since he put it on.

He scratched it again.

"West… and Kage," Archer said, and Rowan's eyes flew open in terror as Beckett picked up the key from his dad.

Rowan coughed into his hand as he followed Beckett. Rowan, Beckett, McAllister, Briggs, and Wilson all flooded into the elevator and pushed their floor numbers. McAllister, being a dick, pressed three extra floors, making Wilson shout at him. Rowan would have joined in on the fun had he not been nervously looking in the mirror wall of the elevator at the alpha behind him. Beckett looked amused at McAllister as the beta tempted fate and hit another button, earning a slap on the back of the head.

"Can't believe I'm stuck with you two," Wilson groaned, having been given both Briggs and McAllister as bunkmates.

"Chill, my man." McAllister looked over his shoulder at him. "As long as you let me be the big spoon, I'm actually easy to stay with."

“I AIN’T NO ONE’S LITTLE SPOON!” Wilson shouted, making the thin beta snort in laughter.

"Fine, you talked me into it, I’ll be the little spoon," McAllister said through his hands, and Wilson lunged forward, but he was held back by Briggs. “I didn’t realize you were so passionate about spooning. What a scandal.”

The doors opened, and Rowan jumped out as if his feet were on fire; looking back, Beckett followed, and the blond waved to his friends. "Don't kill each other," he said just as the doors shut.

Rowan looked up at Beckett and smiled. "Roomies for life, huh?" He asked, trying to play off his nervousness.

The alpha smiled as they walked down the long hall to the last door. Swiping the key card, the door opened to a relatively large room. Two queen beds sat side by side.

Rowan sighed in relief, dropping his two bags by the door. "For a second there, I was worried it was going to be the one-bed trope." He laughed, taking off his jacket to fall back on the plush bed with a loud groan. "Aw, man, this is nice. Better than our beds at home."

His roommate set his bag on the luggage rack and started taking off his jacket, dropping his wallet on the TV stand. “You good?” He asked, looking back at Rowan.

Rowan blinked up at him before leaning up on his elbows. “Yeah, why?” He laughed nervously.

Beckett came over and leaned one knee on Rowan’s bed before positioning himself over him slightly. Rowan felt his face heat up as one of those impossibly warm hands touched his forehead, gently brushing his hair away.

“You’re warm,” He said quietly. “Been warm all day.”

Rowan swallowed the dry lump in his throat and looked up at Beckett leaning over him on this soft bed. His arousal jumped ten times the legal limit as he pulled away from the hand and sat up, pulling one knee up onto the bed and hugging it to his chest to hide the evidence. "Yeah, I'm great! Kind of hungry, though. What about you?"

Beckett lifted one shoulder in a shrug. “Yeah.” He stood and looked at his phone. “I can get us food.”

Rowan bobbed his head excitedly. "I saw a pizza place a few blocks away. We can go."

The alpha shook his head. “You should rest.” He seemed to hesitate but opened his mouth again. “I don’t want you getting sick.”

Rowan was surprised by the sheer amount of vocality his friend was giving him as he nodded. "Yeah, sure. Thanks, bro."

Beckett slid his shoes back on and walked to the door. “Be right back.”

Once the captain left, Rowan flopped back on the bed as he ripped the old patch off his neck and sighed in relief. "Oh, sweet, sweet relief." He leaned into the bed.

Rowan wondered if he could jerk off a few times before Beckett got back to get it out of his system.

Usually, a few orgasms helped clear him right up during his heats. He was pretty familiar with his limitations and knew how to work his body to keep it going. And those vivid images of Beckett in all their locker room moments were enough for his spank bank to last him three lifetimes.

"Just one or two should be fine." He assured himself, figuring he could open the balcony door and air the room out before his roommate got back.

Reaching down his stomach, he felt the tingles of a familiar heat pull up into his chest to his throat. Popping the button on his jeans, he felt the warm drip of slick come out, and he shivered at the feeling. Sliding the jeans down an inch, he bit back saying the name on his mind at that very moment. Sighing in excitement at what he was about to do, he stopped when the door opened.

"Forgot my wallet-" Beckett opened the door, taking several steps in and froze as the unmistakable scent of aroused omega mixed with slick slapped him in the face.

Rowan sat there, thumbs hooked at the side of his jeans, legs bent with his feet down on the mattress, his obvious arousal standing at attention in the denim material. He forced a smile, but his heated cheeks flushed more when the scent of an equally aroused alpha met him. His slick became heavier as he grunted. "MM– I can explain."

At Beckett's wild eyes, looking back and forth between Rowan's hands and his face, the omega gave a forced smile. "I'm in heat. Surprise." He sang the last word as if it indeed was, in all its glory, a surprise.

Beckett audibly gulped, eyes going even wider as the door shut behind him with a soft click.

# CHAPTER TWENTY-EIGHT

~~~~~~ BECK ~~~~~~
~~~~~~

Beckett didn't know what to say. For once, his shy nature wasn't the main reason for his loss of words.

Rowan looked down at his own thumbs hooked on the edge of his pants before going back to the nervous-looking alpha. Beckett looked away moments after Rowan announced his predicament. Quickly, Rowan readjusted his pants, buttoning them and sitting up, obviously trying to will his arousal to go away.

But like a bad party guest, it stayed well past its welcome. Folding his hands in his lap, the blond cleared his throat.

"I'm not gonna, like, jump you if that's what you're worried about," Rowan said, looking down. Embarrassment clawed at his face and neck as the pink flush crept across him. "I'm perfectly in control of my heats."

"I know." Beckett's response came out flat. His voice seemed deeper, strained almost as he kept his eyes averted. He just couldn't look at Rowan, smelling like he did, sitting in that... position. In the back of his mind, he began reciting hockey stats to try to calm himself down.

'*Draisaitl: 55 goals. Gaudreau: 111 points. Um...*' He flinched, trying to remember more and not linger on the image of the omega spread out on the bed. '*I think Kaprizov did 45 goals last season. Um–'* His eyes strained on the wall, swallowing the lump in his throat.

"The media hypes up heats," Rowan said, trying to defend himself to someone who wasn't even arguing back. "We don't- we don't act like that anymore! We have control of our bodies now." He held his hands out as if begging Beckett to understand. "I'm in perfect control of my body. Just a little horny."

Beckett flinched, finally looking back at him, and, for once, it seemed Rowan could not read his face or the silence surrounding him. Panic surged into the alpha's chest as Rowan stood quickly. "I can go! I can- um, get my own room if it bothers you." His eyes glassed over, looking around nervously for his stuff as if trying to piece together a thousand thoughts jumping at him.

'*No, no, no, no, no, no.*'

Beckett's eyes widened, and he shook his head, a frustrated look crossing his face as the captain looked around as if trying to find the words that escaped him. Then, after a few moments, he sighed and looked back, "No, it's… fine."

A laugh forced its way from Rowan's mouth. "Really? Because you seem kind of uncomfortable." He crossed his arms self-consciously, and Beckett hated that he was making this beautiful, kind, intelligent being feel anything but happiness. He was fucking this up just like he did everything else in his life.

"It's," He took a shaky breath when another whiff of that damned arousal slapped his face. "Fine," he finished, determined to get it through. He just needed to collect himself. Looking at his wallet on the table, he pointed to it. "Forgot my wallet," he managed, grabbing it.

After momentarily pausing without speaking, he pointed to the door. "I'll. Be right. Back," his voice grew softer as he turned around, paused, and whipped back, pointing at him. "Don't go–" His eyes flickered to the side as if second-guessing himself. "Anywhere." Finally, after a few pointed seconds of a stare-off, he opened the door and walked out.

Leaving the room felt like running away, and as much as he hated that, Beckett knew he had to or who knew what he might have done. Not that he couldn't control himself from pouncing on an omega in heat, but he might give his feelings away with his own scent, or even a look. Rowan was so perceptive about Beckett's feelings just by looking at him. One time, he knew Beckett was about to sneeze before even he knew or felt it. Rowan even managed to say 'gesundheit' right before the alpha scrunched his face up and sneezed.

Oh god… Did Rowan smell his arousal?

Beckett paused inside the elevator, looking at his reflection, and blushed bright red. He recalled Rowan sprawled on the bed, fingers hooked on his pants, showing a sliver of skin. His face flushed from the heat radiating from his body.

Except, in his vivid imagination, he pictured the omega mewing his name, 'Beck,' as he pushed the fabric down further.

Familiar arousal pulled at his stomach, and he tried to shake the image from his mind. That image didn't belong to him. He happened upon a private moment that Rowan hadn't meant for Beckett to see. It would be wrong to draw pleasure from it, despite his desires. Twisting it to fit his own sick fantasies was just a below-the-belt shot that he didn't want to drag out.

Heading out into the city, he walked the short distance to the pizza place. He forgot to order ahead and nervously stuttered out a cheese pizza order to the small beta behind the register. When asked for toppings, Beckett shook his head, and the beta shrugged, ignoring it as he put the order in.

"Fifteen minutes," He was told, and Beckett stepped out, walking to the pharmacy across the street.

Walking around the store, he felt his mind go on autopilot. He grabbed a basket and began filling it with things Rowan might like. He called it an apology in his mind. Or, maybe it was an alpha desperately trying to prove he could provide, but he wanted to do it for the blond omega. So he dropped in some electrolyte drinks, protein bars he had seen Rowan stock up on in their dorm, and some chocolate. Why not?

He stopped at the cash register. As the young woman rang him up, he looked behind her at the display of condoms. His face flushed even more red as he looked down, stretching his mouth into a thin line. Then, when she gave him the total, he shoved his card into the machine and waited for it to beep before accepting the receipt and nodding his head at the woman.

The pizza was ready to pick up by the time he left the store, so he grabbed it and made his way back to the hotel.

On the walk back, he practiced what he would say in his mind.

'*It's alright. What you're going through is a natural part of life. I'm sorry if I made you uncomfortable. Just tell me what you need, and I'm here for you,*' He thought with a firm nod. That wasn't so bad;

it was short but to the point, and he felt he should have the power to get at least that out of his mouth, right?

It's Rowan! Beckett could talk to Rowan about anything– even this!

Arriving at their hotel door a lot quicker than he expected, he held up a hand and knocked.

After a few seconds, he heard the voice of the omega call out to him. "Dude, seriously, you don't need to knock. But come in."

He swiped the lock using the key card until it turned green and pushed the door open. Peeking his head in, he sniffed the air against his better judgment and sighed in relief when it was mostly gone. His inner alpha mourned the loss of the amazing scent, but he sucked it up and walked in. He toed off his shoes by the door as it shut behind him.

Rowan sat curled up on the bed, a blanket wrapped around him like a cape. He was obviously freshly showered with two scent patches on either side of his neck. Rowan looked up from where he was adjusting his nest-like bed and pouted. "So you came back, huh?"

The comment slapped him, but he deserved it as he tried to offer a soft smile and held up the pizza box in one hand and the bag in the other.

Rowan's look turned into a slight tilt of his head. "You brought gifts?"

Beckett nodded, stepping forward and setting the bag before him while placing the pizza on the nightstand between their beds. He heard Rowan shuffle through the bag before the blond snorted out a giggle. He turned to face Rowan as he sat on his own bed, sliding his jacket down, wondering if he had done well. Rowan's nose was scrunched up in that impossibly cute way as his tongue stuck out between his teeth. He held up the electrolyte drink and protein bars. “How much do you expect me to jerk it? Enough to deplete my body of all my energy?”

The alpha choked on air as he coughed, and Rowan laughed. “I’m kidding,” he lowered the stuff to the bed and looked sweetly at the captain. “This is sweet. Thanks, Beck.”

Beckett looked at him, trying to will out the words he practiced.

‘*It’s alright. What you’re going through is a natural part of life. I’m sorry if I made you uncomfortable. Just tell me what you need, and I’m here for you.*’

But nothing came out, and the captain scrunched his own face up in concentration. The space between his eyes pinched, and he felt his mouth tick to the side as the words never came.

After several seconds of nothing coming out, Rowan's eyes widened with that same glazed-over look. Beckett panicked, thinking he had offended him again, and Rowan placed a hand over his heart. "You're so sweet. Apology accepted."

Beckett felt his chest ache and resisted grabbing at it himself. Rowan knew without words what Beckett was trying to express.

Nobody… absolutely nobody in this world besides his adopted family ever could read him, and even then, Rowan had his pops beat by a mile. Sometimes Beckett wondered if the figure skater could read his mind.

After watching the omega reach for a slice of pizza, Beckett stood up. "Shower." He motioned to the cracked bathroom door as Rowan waved him away and turned on the TV, slice in hand.

Going into the bathroom, Beckett nearly choked at the scent of aroused omega captured around the tiled room. Shutting the door behind him, he took a moment to take it in. His own arousal strained as he leaned against the counter. He turned on the water and quickly stripped, dropping his travel clothes into the small hamper by the sink. Before he dropped them in, he caught sight of Rowan's shirt on top and blushed as his lizard brain suggested they get a whiff of the 'good stuff,' and no one would need to know. His hand twitched towards the fabric, but he froze and quickly dropped his clothes on top to stop the temptation.

He kept the shower short, mostly using the cold water. As much as he wanted it warm, it was the appropriate thing to do. Afterward, he changed into his pajama bottoms and walked out, drying his hair with the towel.

Rowan was huddled on the bed, leaning against the headboard with the blankets and pillows around him like a cozy nest. Beckett looked to see that he was watching some old action movie. The captain walked across the room and sat on his own bed.

Rowan offered him a sweet smile, though the tension was still hanging between them. He'd never seen Rowan so quiet as he ate, fixated on the TV as if it provided him a lifeline to distract himself.

Pulling out his phone, Beckett looked up how to make omegas comfortable. He wasn't surprised that a lot of porn and sexual suggestions on pleasing your omega popped up. But he eventually found an actual article on comfort tips for alphas to help omega friends.

After half an hour of debating and second-guessing, he sent a text to Rowan, not at all trusting himself to actually say these next words.

Rowan's phone chimed, and he looked down at it. When he swiped to unlock the screen, his face lit up as he smiled at Beckett.

**Beck:** Feel free to say no, but I read that an alpha scent is sometimes comforting. Did you want to borrow one of my shirts to sleep in?

Rowan pointed to his phone before putting his hand to his cheek in a mock swoon. “Awww, you’re researching how to make me comfortable?”

Beckett blushed as he gave a jerky nod, and Rowan giggled. His blue eyes trailed to the side.

"Actually…" Rowan made a thoughtful look before nodding, "Can I? Is that alright? It's not weird to you?" He asked hopefully. Beckett quickly shook his head, and Rowan jumped up, rushing across the room, pouncing on the alpha's bag and ripping it open. "I already know what shirt I want!"

Beckett watched him pull out a big cotton jersey with cat paw prints on the chest with a hockey team, ‘Panthers’, on the back. Rowan ripped off his own shirt before shrugging into Beckett's. It swam on him, coming down past his waist. He had to push the sleeves up, but he brought the front of it up and over his nose as he inhaled deeply. "Oh yeah, that's the good stuff," he said, flopping back on the bed. It reminded Beckett of back in the bathroom when he wanted to sniff at Rowan’s own clothes for that ‘good stuff’ hit.

Never in his whole life had Beckett been more flustered and aroused. Was it possible for human flesh to cook under the heat rushing to his face?

"It's sweet, you know," Rowan turned on his side, looking up at Beckett, propping his head into his hand. "You doing all this." He motioned to the food, snacks, and shirt. "Thanks."

Beckett nodded, wishing he could do more. As if reading his face, Rowan blushed and played with the hem of his new shirt. "Um… if it's alright… Can I ask a favor? Something that helps me?" His eyes once again darted to the side. "You know— since you're so interested in making me comfortable."

The quick up-and-down motion of Beckett's head probably made him look like a bobblehead. Rowan laughed and stood up. "Um, well, when I was in my heat back home, my friends would come over, and we'd cuddle and watch movies." He peeked up at the alpha, the most adorable pink tint to his tan features. "I guess I just crave touch, ya know?" His head cocked. "Wellll, that and praise. I've kind of got a praise kink that I've been harboring for a while."

Beckett was sure he had died and gone to heaven. Swallowing the lump in his throat, he didn't trust himself to even give a simple 'yes' as he sat back and pulled the blanket aside as a silent invitation. Rowan took on a predator-like smirk as he jumped over, shouting in victory at winning the alpha over. He pushed against the alpha so hard he nearly slid him a few inches across the mattress. He snuggled up to Beckett, cheek nuzzling his chest as he wrapped around him like a boa constrictor. Beckett wasn't sure where to put his hands, but Rowan helped with that. He moved one hand to his shoulder, and then he handed him the remote if he wanted to change the channel. He didn't, so he let it rest in his lap.

It was amazing how the omega fit up against him. It was like a missing puzzle piece that finally brought the picture together. Beckett closed his eyes and rested his head on the blond tuft of hair, inhaling the sweet scent of sugar cookies. With Rowan's heat in full swing, there was a wisp of something else that he couldn't quite place, but it was so welcoming. Beckett couldn't get enough of it and knew this was a new addiction he would secretly harbor. He wished the omega would take his scent patches off so he could become engulfed by it, drown in it.

Rowan, never one for awkward silence, provided commentary for the old movie. Going on about what his friends used to do on movie nights and how they could maybe talk the hockey team into a slumber party before the end of the season.

"What are the odds that Wilson can braid hair?" Rowan ran a hand through his hair. "I could get a super sick Viking look before a game. Really make the other team piss themselves."

Beckett nodded along, looking between the omega and the TV. He wondered if he smelled like content alpha, because he was more relaxed than he could ever remember.

Rowan was squirming here and there, and near the end of the movie, Beckett cleared his throat. "The game… tomorrow." He managed, and Rowan looked up at him. "You… gonna be alright?" Rowan looked proud that Beckett got all that out and gave him a dazzling smile as a reward.

"Yeah, totally! I've done competitions in heats before. It's not a big deal." He snuggled back to Beckett's side, looking at the TV. "I'll just jerk off a few times before the game to get in the zone."

He must have felt Beckett stiffen next to him, because he laughed and slapped the alpha's shoulder. Beckett was flustered and way out of his element as the captain opened his mouth and, for once, said the first thing that came to mind without overthinking it.

"Let me know if I can help." And, of course, it had to be that.

As soon as the words left his mouth, he felt dread fill him. He tried to form the words to take it back and say, 'I didn't mean it like that!' or 'You know, I mean, like, if you need food or another shirt or like a fucking soda!'

He didn't mean it like how it sounded: 'Let me know if I can help jerk you off!'

But instead, he said nothing. What is wrong with him? How was social communication so hard that he had to open his mouth and say that! He worried that Rowan would see him as another disgusting alpha.

"Oh, thank goodness!" Rowan sighed as if a huge weight had been lifted from his shoulders, and he turned in Beckett's hold to look at him fully. "I was worried that asking you to fuck my heat out of me was off the table for bros." His eyes shone with excitement, a wide smile on his face. "But since you offered, I'm happy to accept!"

'*What*'

The pupils of Beckett's eyes shrank as he replayed the omega's words in his head. Did he hear him right? That perfect smile shone at him as Beckett could only blink back before Rowan's eyes lowered in a seductive look. "Bros helping bros through their heat is so attractive. Didn't know you had it in you to offer."

He reached back and pulled off Beckett's borrowed shirt, tossing it over to his bed before looking back at him. "You good to go right now?"

Blinking several times, Beckett looked down at the omega's toned chest and back to his face before feeling his head nod quickly. "Y-yeah, I'm good."

Rowan reached out, placing a hand on the back of Beckett’s neck and pulling him forward. “Bet.”

# CHAPTER TWENTY-NINE

## ~~~~~~ ROWAN ~~~~~~

Rowan didn't realize how starved he was for that connection. His already heated body was excited by the simplest touch. His cock had never gotten harder than it did when he straddled Beckett's waist. Rowan brought his arms up to rest on the sitting alpha's broad shoulders; his eyes were heavy as he thought about Beckett.

'*Such a great guy! How did I get so lucky?*'

Beckett would only have offered to assist if he wanted to help his friend out. It showed the omega how much the alpha cared. "Could you get any more perfect?" He asked with a huff of a laugh. "Whatever site you looked all this research up on, I'll need to leave them a five-star review." He rolled his hips against the alpha's lap, feeling the swell of his own hardness under him.

"I want to help you," Beckett said, his voice several octaves deeper than Rowan had ever heard. He was so glad he wasn't standing because he would have dropped to his knees.

Rowan hummed. "You are." He moved his hips, hearing the hitch in the alpha's breathing. "But don't get it twisted. This doesn't make me a panting mess of an omega." He moved again, loving Beckett's noises. Rowan drank them up. "I can stop at any moment and be just fine. It just so happens that this helps me get by." Leaning down, he bit Beckett's earlobe. "Keep your alpha side in check, and we'll both have a good time."

Beckett nodded stiffly, and Rowan felt an immense sense of power he had never felt before. The fact that there were no questions about him being in charge made Rowan heady with desire.

'*It's like he's willing to do anything.*'

Rowan waited for him to do something or say something, and slowly the power ebbed away, and he felt a bit self-conscious. The desire to please the alpha bubbled up in his mind, wanting to make him feel just as good. Looking down at their bodies smushed together, he looked back up and placed a hand on Beckett's chest. "W-what do you like?"

'*Because I know what I like, and what if it freaks you out?*' He thought, a blush creeping up his heated cheeks.

The alpha glanced to the side as if thinking about something before tentatively bringing his eyes back to Rowan. Then, ever so slowly, he brought his head down, and Rowan's eyes widened as their lips pressed together. It was soft and cautiously slow, like Beckett didn't want anything to be overwhelming.

'*Oh, my god.*' Rowan squeezed his eyes closed. '*This is so fucking sweet.*' He felt his heart clench. '*No one's ever been so- so-*' He broke away from the kiss for a second, breathing heavily.

"Good to me," he whispered, finishing his own thoughts before he surged forward, kissing Beckett again.

Rowan leaned hard into it, deepening the kiss into something more sensual. His heart was pounding, moving his hands from Beckett's shoulders to his black hair, digging between the soft tresses to keep him close. Their mouths moved leisurely, and Rowan felt those large, strong hands move to his hips and gradually pull him forward. The friction caused Rowan's mouth to fall open enough for the kiss to delve into territories unknown with tongues.

True love's kiss would probably be a cliché in describing Rowan's current predicament. It was probably his elevated hormones romanticizing the moment. But he couldn't deny that he felt something awaken inside him as he closed his eyes, feeling that hot tongue lick against his own slowly. Every brush of his lips and touch of his hands brought parts of his body to life like a fire. Heat blazed across Rowan's skin where their bodies pressed together.

"Mm–" he whimpered, the sounds slowly moving from the creak of the bed to their own vocal additions. Beckett groaned, and it vibrated in his massive chest as Rowan slid a hand down from his shoulder to rest over his pectorals.

He had never had an all-consuming experience like that before. He'd never been kissed like that, either. He'd never been kissed in a way that caused every single nerve ending in his body to electrify itself like a live wire.

Rowan soon realized that they had been making out a lot longer than he expected. Honestly, he thought the alpha would throw him down and give him a good time, no doubt. But it was as if he couldn't get enough of just kissing Rowan senseless. The omega swooned, feeling so wanted and treasured; he didn't want it to stop, either. However, his growing arousal was driving him up the wall with insanity. And, of course, this was meant to be a no-strings-attached kind of situation.

'*Besides–*' Rowan peeked his eyes open enough to see Beckett doing the same, and their eyes connected in a heated stare. '*He doesn't need to know I could get off from this alone.*'

Pulling away, Rowan laughed softly, loving the way Beckett leaned forward to chase another kiss, but Rowan leaned back to stop him. Those damned perfect green eyes really grounded him. They looked into his very soul, making him shiver.

"You… alright, Ro?" Beckett asked, eyes looking over him to ensure he was fine and not overwhelmed.

'*Ro!*' Rowan's inner omega screamed. '*He said Ro!*'

Rowan squeaked, but it was so small he doubted Beckett heard it.

'*Say it again! Say it again!*' He wanted to beg.

It was entirely unfair that Beckett could cause such a reaction with just a little nickname, but it did the trick. The omega inhaled through his nose, trying to maintain a relaxed air as if that name didn't shoot right to his dick and make a quick stop to his heart on the way.

"All good. Great, even." Rowan leaned forward, giving in to his urges to kiss him again. He felt wet desire pulling him as slick escaped and let his body know it was getting ready to take in an alpha. The thought of Beckett inside of him was enough for the omega to moan again.

The first thrust of Beckett's hips was sedated, just to measure Rowan's reaction. The omega pushed down onto him, letting him know it was indeed fine by him, and the alpha gripped his hips harder, making Rowan gasp. The look on Beckett's face quickly made him nod. "MM– No, no, that's good… You can– get a little rough with me." He smirked. "I don't mind."

'*PLEASE get rough! Get rough and call me Ro!*' He begged with his eyes. '*Send my face to pillow town and-*' He inhaled, giving the alpha a sweet smile. "I promise," he whispered.

Beckett seemed hesitant but pulled him closer, sliding down the bed to lie on his back while Rowan sat atop his hard dick. Rowan's smile turned devious. "Orrr, I can get rough with you?"

From the red dusting across Beckett's face, Rowan wondered what he was thinking and trailed a hand down the alpha's long chest to the hem of his pants.

"My, my, Captain," He admired Beckett's toned body, while his hands twitched at the prospect of touching. Rowan felt his mouth salivate as he leaned down, pressing his lower half into Beckett's. The first swipe of his tongue up Beckett's chest had the alpha letting out a shaky breath. Rowan wanted to hear more, so he bit his skin, making Beckett grab at his shoulders as he looked up at Rowan.

Rowan smirked, "Slow down? Speed up? I could use a little help here." He shuffled down, latching a hand on the top of his pants. "The silence can only get me so far." He dipped his fingers into the hem of the pants, tugging them down. "Tell me what you want," Rowan could feel those heated eyes on him as he eyed the outline of his alpha's bulge. "I'll accommodate you."

Beckett glanced away again, and for a moment, Rowan thought he wasn't going to get anything until those eyes found him again with newfound confidence. "I… I want you-" He paused, and Rowan felt his heart skip a beat. "To feel good."

The fact that he was so intent on Rowan having a good time proved that Beckett was absolutely perfect. Any other alpha would already have Rowan on all fours with his ass in the air to receive. Beckett, meanwhile, was dead set on pleasing him in his heat. As if he wasn't already head over heels for this guy. Rowan sighed dreamily, "You know what? I know something we'll both like."

Sitting up, he pulled Beckett by his hand to follow and sit him at the edge of the bed. The alpha seemed curious and was about to open his mouth to try to say something when he stopped. Rowan dropped to his knees before the sitting alpha and reached behind to tie his blond hair back to keep it from his face.

'*Ah, yes, the universal sign for I'm about to give you some good head,*' Rowan thought with a slight smirk.

"I kind of have a kink for this," Rowan admitted, looking up at the alpha as he pulled Beckett's pants down, freeing his cock from his pajama bottoms.

"Holy shit!" Rowan's eyes widened at the dick before him, standing at attention, ready for anything. He looked up at the alpha and back down, mouth opening and closing before breaking into a wide grin. "For once, you knocked me speechless. All you had to do was show me that monster cock." He gripped it with one hand, and Beckett let out a shudder of breath. "I knew you were packing, but damn. If I knew you were this large and in charge, I'd have suggested we do this on my first night in the dorms."

At Beckett's continued silence, Rowan leaned forward, swiping his tongue up the underside, getting acquainted with his length. Beckett hissed, hands holding tightly onto the bed sheets. Then, ever so slowly, after feeling acquainted with the length and calculating what he could fit, he popped the tip into his mouth and gave a gentle suck. Beckett threw his head back, looking at the ceiling. Finally, Rowan popped off the tip, giving it two slow pumps. "Show's not up there, big guy. And I want you to watch."

Rowan flicked his tongue out to collect a bead of cum right at the top. The salty liquid spread as he smoothed it out on the roof of his mouth, and he moaned. His hair nearly stood up like a cat as the omega looked back down at the thing he would choke on momentarily.

Beckett flinched but looked back down as Rowan latched on again, this time moving further down, bobbing to accommodate his throat. His own arousal was straining in his pants. Spreading his knees, Rowan lifted himself ever so slightly up and down as if he were still on the alpha's lap. The figure skater's hand went to his own dick and pulled it from his sleep pants to get in on the action. Looking up at his alpha, Rowan was pleased that those brilliant green eyes were watching everything. A glazed look shifted over Beckett's eyes, taking in Rowan's every movement. Going deeper, Rowan released his own dick to reach for Beckett's left hand and move it from the sheets to the back of his blond head. He came up for air and looked at Beckett.

"I like having my hair pulled." He swallowed. "Just… just fucking use me, okay?" He begged, loving the idea of Beckett fucking his face to take what he wanted.

Without waiting for an answer, he went back down, swallowing the dick a little faster, bobbing harder. The hand in his hair tightened around the ponytail, and Rowan moaned loudly, hand going back to his dick to pump.

"So good," Beckett panted out.

'*Oh, FUCK me!*' Rowan moaned, eyes nearly going crossed as the words played on repeat in his head. He would remember them to his fucking dying day.

There was a physical reaction in Rowan's body to Beckett's praise. Between that and all that heavy kissing and grinding, plus the fact that Beckett was praising his mouth, was enough for the omega to salivate like it was a four-course meal. Beckett gave Rowan's head a heavy push, shoving it down until the tip of his cock pushed to the back of the omega's throat and beyond.

Rowan never stood a chance against this fucking fine-ass alpha of a man. Rowan moaned as Beckett gasped his name, hardly getting past the first syllable. The blond stuttered in his rhythm but tried to remain calm, so he literally didn't choke to death on the cock in his throat.

Not that it would be a bad way to die.

Beckett must have known what Rowan was doing because he threw his head back and gave a stuttered gasp as he tapped the back of Rowan's head. Rowan shot his hands up and made him tighten his hand back into his blond hair. It was as if he was saying, '*Don't you dare be polite!*'

With that, Beckett gasped Rowan's name, cumming down his throat, and Rowan swallowed as much as he could before some dribbled down his chin. The choking sensation momentarily had his throat spasm as tears built up in his eyes. His cheeks felt so full he popped off, letting the rest coat his face as he closed one eye to avoid getting any in it. It pushed Rowan into his own over-the-edge feeling. He felt the sticky mess coat his hand and shivered as he slightly bounced on his knees as if chasing that now-gone feeling of completion.

Panting as the last of Beckett's mess leaked down Rowan's face, he looked up at Beckett, heaving his shoulders as he came down from his own climax. The captain looked down at him with such want that it made Rowan glad he was already on his knees.

'*Is it weird I want to take a picture of myself right now?*' Rowan thought. But there was no need, because Rowan would remember that night for the rest of his life, no doubt.

# CHAPTER THIRTY

After several minutes, the fires of his heat finally died down from the release, and he smiled. "Thanks." He swiped his tongue to the side to get some cum leaking down his cheek before looking back up at him. "I really needed that."

Beckett pulled Rowan up and back into his lap, attacking his mouth with fierce kisses. Pulling away, Rowan purred. "Man, I'm covered in cum. Not a good look." He blushed, reaching a hand up to wipe at some of the sticky, cold stuff from below his eyes. Beckett shook his head, pushing Rowan's fallen hair from his ponytail out of his face and behind his ear.

Rowan leaned into that hand, ready to try and kiss him again, when something hard poked his thigh, and he turned cherry red. "You recover fast." He giggled before looking sideways at the open bathroom door. "I know we just took showers buuutttt-" He made a motion with his head to the side, and Beckett smirked, picking up on it.

He'd deny it if anyone asked Rowan if he squeaked when being picked up. But he totally squeaked like a toy when the alpha picked him up and pulled him to the bathroom.

They didn't even make it to the shower before Beckett propped Rowan onto the counter of the illuminated room, pulling the pants off the omega and dropping them by the sink, kicking them aside. Rowan was about to open his legs for him when Beckett leaned over, took a washcloth by the sink, and turned on the warm faucet, dampening the cloth.

'*What's he doing?*' Rowan blinked down at the action. '*I thought he wanted more.*'

He watched as the alpha turned back and tilted Rowan's head up as he wiped his face with the warm cloth. The act itself made Rowan quiver at being so taken care of. Everything Beckett did for him made the omega part of Rowan want to submit. Maybe the captain wasn't aware of everything he had done, but so far, Beckett had fed him, given him one of his shirts, and bought stuff for his heat. It was enough to make Rowan swoon and wish this wasn't just to get him through an annoying heat.

'*It's how someone with a mate would act.*' He thought, turning his head to the side to allow that warm cloth a swipe up his neck. Some might've seen it as an act of submission, but Beckett just focused on getting all the release off his heated skin.

When he was finished, Beckett tossed the cloth to the hamper and was about to turn back when Rowan reacted first, wrapping his legs around the alpha, and brought his crotch flush against his own. The omega felt positively drenched downstairs, and being covered in Beckett's scent was making him feel drunk. Rowan smirked deviously as he looked up at the alpha, leaning back on the counter. "So, I started the last activity. Your turn," He said with a wink. His small hand came up and peeled away the scent patches on his neck. He hated them anyway, and he hoped Beckett wouldn't mind.

The alpha inhaled deeply, watching Rowan discard the patches to the side by the sink. Beckett leaned forward and kissed him again. Rowan mewed under the tongue that licked into him, memorizing his mouth.

Rowan was slowly growing accustomed to the kissing. '*He must really like it, too.*'

It didn't stop there, because those large hands rested on his hips, pulling him back, so Rowan was grinding against the alpha. The blond slid back with half his back against the full mirror while nearly hanging off the counter, but Beckett's hips pushed back. He still had on his low-hanging pants, pushing that bulge against Rowan's entrance. The blond hissed, turned on by having a single piece of fabric separating him from what he craved. He closed his eyes and gasped, pulling away from the kiss to look at Beckett.

"I can't wait," he begged. "P-put it in."

Beckett grabbed his chin and pulled him back into a kiss, pushing his hips harder against Rowan's lower half. The slick there made the front of Beckett's pants wet. Rowan nearly sobbed into the kiss as Beckett's strong hands gripped his waist so hard, he knew there might be a mark.

"B-Beck-" He paused when he was again picked up and flipped around before being pushed forward on the counter. He was bent at a ninety-degree angle on the cold counter, hands pillowed under his chin. A hand went to the back of his half-tied-up hair, forcing him to look forward at their reflection in the mirror. Beckett was breathing heavily, looking at the omega bent over for him.

Rowan pressed his ass back into Beckett's hard cock. "Come on… give me that knot, alpha." He looked at the captain's reflection. "I can take it all, I swear."

'*Fucking breed me,*' he bit back, nearly choking on another moan as the cold counter felt good against his heated skin.

Beckett looked down at the omega's reflected eyes, and the most devious smirk came to his face. A smile that screamed, '*I know what you're thinking.*'

'*Does he know?*' Rowan felt his heart lurch up into his throat, his erection twitching between where it was pressed against the counter.

Rowan shivered in anticipation as he jerked his hips forward, annoyed that the alpha was still in his fucking pants. Finally, Rowan slammed a hand onto the counter, panting. "Fuck! Come on! I-I want it!"

Beckett ground his hard cock into Rowan's backside, and the omega mewed out, babbling unintelligible words. Fuck, it was all so hot, and nothing was even penetrating him.

"I like it when you talk," Beckett uttered in a deep voice, and Rowan preened under him. Beckett's voice did things to him that should be impossible as he pressed harder into the counter.

"Good, because I cannot imagine shutting the fuck up right now."

Beckett chuckled, and the blond slapped a hand to the mirror, "Please tell me you at least plan on fucking me tonight. I can't take much more of this."

The captain pulled him up by the back of his hair, which wasn't so hard given that Rowan went willingly, and wrapped his arms around him while Rowan braced against the counter. Their eyes locked on each other's reflection as heated fingers trailed down the omega's chest, touching more skin. The omega blushed in embarrassment but couldn't look away from the full-on display of their carnal lust.

Those large hands roamed his body, one going lower to wrap around Rowan's dick while the other scratched up his chest, thumb flicking his nipple, making the blond flinch. Rowan hissed, leaning back into that toned chest, letting the captain pleasure him. Once again, it didn't take long, and Rowan soon had his stomach and Beckett's hand covered in cum. The hand on his dick eased it slowly; he already knew how sensitive it was from another release.

Rowan looked into his roommate's reflection and smirked, panting heavily. "You're going to make me cross-eyed tonight, I can already tell."

Beckett kissed the side of Rowan's head before pulling him into the shower, flipping it to hot but standing with his back to the cold spray to protect Rowan until it warmed up. As the shower took its time, they indulged in more kissing. Rowan thought Beckett must really like that, as the alpha memorized Rowan's mouth. Every time the omega went to pull away, Beckett's hand was at the back of his blond head, pulling him back.

The shower was short and tender, mainly because Beckett wanted to ensure Rowan was cleaned up from their earlier deeds. The alpha was obviously hard, and every time Rowan reached for it, he was detoured into another kiss or soft touch. Once finished, Beckett dried him off and wrapped the towel around the figure skater's waist before grabbing one for himself. Finally, they walked into the main room, and Rowan was slapped with the scent of sex. His desire built all over again. Two times within the night should have been enough to satiate him, but when it came to Beckett, Rowan could tell he was already addicted.

Sitting down on the bed, Rowan looked up at Beckett with heated eyes. "Down for more?" He winked up at him.

Beckett smirked and pushed the blond onto his back before ripping the towel off. Rowan shivered in the cold air. He closed his eyes, ready to feel Beckett crawl on top of him, but he instead felt his pajama bottoms slide onto him. Looking down, Rowan saw that Beckett had adjusted the fabric and sat back to look up at him. Rowan found it insanely cute how much the alpha took care of him. The small blond blushed. "I can– you know… go all the way."

Beckett nodded and pulled on his own pants, still looking hard as ever. But he crawled into bed next to Rowan and pulled him close to spoon. Rowan didn't realize he needed this just as much as he needed the sexual release, and he sank into the hold, closing his eyes.

"Thank you," Rowan whispered.

The captain hummed his acknowledgment, nuzzling his nose into Rowan's hair, huffing every time the hair tickled his nose. Rowan could admit he might have been scent-drunk off the alpha, but obviously not as much as Beckett.

Rowan fell asleep feeling wanted and protected in the arms of his best friend. It was the first time he felt wanted in a long time.

The lull in his heat was enough for him to get a full night of restful sleep.

However, he wasn't expecting his eyes to crack open to his member at full attention or for his backside pressing against the sleeping alpha.

Or, Rowan quickly realized, Beckett might not have been asleep at all. As soon as Beckett realized Rowan was awake, the alpha pulled him around, setting the figure skater on top to straddle the captain.

Rowan blinked his sleepy eyes, half asleep and horny as hell, making for a sloppy combo as he rutted his hips against the alpha's.

"Please," Rowan whispered at an equally tired and horny college student.

Rowan pulled his pants down, throwing them to the side before moving Beckett's down enough for him to kick off. Fumbling around, they touched and teased, kissing and panting. Rowan reached behind and felt how ready he was; his answer was soaking wet.

He felt his body adjust itself to take a knot, and he inserted a finger into himself, moaning at the jolt of pleasure it brought. He looked down at Beckett as the alpha watched him pleasure himself, slowly opening himself for what they had coming. Rowan arched his back, leaning forward to give his hands better access. The look of sleep deprivation and lust on the alpha's face made Rowan coo because he knew his hands had the alpha's full attention.

Rowan barely got a third in before he shook his head, removing his hand and nearly collapsing on his shaky thighs. "I-I can't take it anymore." He moved down and grabbed Beckett's cock in hand, forcing it to his entrance. "I need you in me." Searching his face, he asked, "Are you–" He gasped at the feeling of the cock twitching in his hand. "Still DTF?"

'*Please, please, please, please,*' He begged with his eyes.

Beckett only nodded, his sharp eyes letting Rowan make the first moves. Though the hard hold on his waist was enough to slow Rowan, even though he wanted to move faster. He sank ever so slowly down, down, down onto his thick cock. The method he used was for every two inches he took, he pulled off one before sinking down again. This left Beckett a panting mess, looking up at Rowan as he allowed him to take whatever he could handle.

His mouth opened in a silent scream until he managed to finally bottom out, hands pressed against the alpha's toned stomach. He got used to the girth quickly enough before nodding his head.

"I might need you to move me, b-because I can't feel my legs," Rowan whispered as if being filled to the brim was enough to make him forget how to function.

And like an answer to his prayers, Beckett lifted the omega as if he weighed nothing before slamming him back down. Rowan choked out a gasp, his sleep haze lifting, being totally filled with desire. "Fuck, do that again."

In the back of his mind, he remembered the drops of precum from the night before. Every time Rowan pumped, a bit more came out.

'*His cum is inside me, right now. I can feel it leaking,*' Rowan whined, screwing his eyes shut to hold back from finishing in seconds like a goddamn virgin.

Beckett did as he was told, picking him up and slamming him back down, though this time, he didn't stop and repeated it again and again. Rowan threw his head back, gasping out a mixture of words and Beckett's name. Rowan begged him not to stop, and every bit of that was answered. He pictured that hard cock leaking more into him with every drop.

'*He's going to fill me.*' Rowan felt his face heat up with a blush, shame coursing through at the idea of Beckett blowing his load inside him and how he would savor every drop.

At some point, Rowan found himself on his back, legs wrapped around Beckett as the alpha slammed into him. The headboard slapped the walls, and the feet of the bed scratched on the floor. Rowan felt like his soul was getting fucked from his body.

"M-my guts are all mixed up," Rowan gasped, hands flying up over his head to grip the pillow. "Fuck, you're so deep!"

Beckett slapped his hips harder, and Rowan mewed again. "Fuck, fuck." He looked up at Beckett. "Fucking fill me!"

The alpha didn't need to say anything; his eyes conveyed precisely what he was going to do. He pushed into Rowan with three giant thrusts, grinding him onto his cock as he clenched his teeth together. Rowan felt the knot swell, filling him even more as his mouth dropped open. "Beck," he stretched out his name, feeling a gush of hot liquid fill every crevice of his insides, painting him. Beckett let out stuttering breaths as Rowan felt himself cum, white-hot ropes down Beckett's chest. It was possible that Rowan blacked out for a couple of seconds from the intense feeling. It was all so sloppy and quick; they both looked at each other, and Rowan let a wide grin spread across his face as he came down from his high, even while he was still stuck on Beckett's knot.

"It's official..." He gasped, feeling that hard cock pump another round of cum inside him. "I'm your fuck buddy for life."

Beckett released a deep chuckle, gripping Rowan's waist to grind upwards, lifting him up before dropping his hips down, making the omega push down into the mattress. Rowan whined, feeling intensely aroused but completely spent as he looked up at Beckett, "How long you gonna go for?"

Beckett looked up in thought before shrugging, and Rowan chuckled.

"Take what you want, Captain. I'm spent." He flopped back onto the plush bed under him. At the unsure look Beckett gave, Rowan nodded tiredly, "Honestly, it's cool. We're kind of locked together, so go to town. Besides-"Glancing to the side shyly, Rowan swiped his tongue on his lower lip. "This is the best part for me. Besides the finale, of course." He winked.

Beckett seemed to think about it for a moment before pulling Rowan's tired legs back around him and gently rocking. They were locked together, but the motion itself was enough friction to rub against Rowan's sweet spot continuously, making the omega turn his head into the pillow to sigh and moan.

The few times Beckett's name left his lips, the alpha would thrust sharply, and Rowan sang his praise. Rowan felt like he gained a pound in cum alone as another pump pushed into him, and he drooled at the warmth. The look Beckett gave him as he babbled about being filled didn't go unnoticed.

Eventually, the knot died down, and he was able to pull out with one final spurt. When he did, Rowan groaned at the loss of Beckett's warmth as he felt so much cum spill onto the bed. Rowan looked up at him as Beckett stared down at his handiwork, a smile on his face. It must be an alpha thing to take pride in cumming in an omega, knowing your seed is in every crevice of their being, and you were successful in your chase.

'*Oh well, I have my kinks, and he has his,*' Rowan thought.

Of course, while Beckett was a full-blooded alpha, he always managed to surprise Rowan. He reached over to the discarded towel from the other night and wiped Rowan down.

"Damn, Beck," Rowan breathed out, lifting his hips to better assist the alpha. "You trying to make me swoon?"

"Something like that," Beckett said, and it was a shock to the senses to hear him say anything after that.

Once cleaned up, the captain leaned over him and gave Rowan the softest kiss he had ever received. It was damn-near heartbreaking when he remembered they weren't actually a couple.

A chime broke the moment as they pulled away from the kiss. Beckett, though, changed direction and began planting kisses across his chest while Rowan reached for his phone by the bed. Pulling it over, he read the message and sighed.

"Team wants to go out for breakfast."

Beckett bit down on Rowan's hip, and the omega jumped. "Whoa, whoa, I'm not on the menu, big guy." He laughed as Beckett nipped at him again.

Sitting up on his elbows, he looked down at the alpha, who was resting his head on Rowan's stomach, his ear pressed down. It was a subconscious thing alphas did to omegas, but it still made Rowan's face heat up.

"Come on. I want waffles." He scratched Beckett's dark hair, and the alpha nodded, standing up, ready to get the omega anything he needed.

Rowan stood on shaky legs and walked to the bathroom, but he paused as he glanced at Beckett. The alpha had just moved their towels to the pile by the door. He smirked and clicked his tongue to get his attention.

"Wanna maybe conserve water and shower tog-Woah!" He didn't even get to finish before Beckett swept by him, picking him up in a fireman's carry.

Rowan giggled, feeling the giddy bubble of arousal pull at his stomach again.

He hoped this would go on, even when his heat would eventually end.

## CHAPTER THIRTY-ONE

Beckett had a tough time keeping his hands off Rowan while the blond got ready. Once out of the shower, Rowan put a ban on sex, because they would be late if they got caught up again. Beckett was alright with tardiness, but from the pout on Rowan's face, he knew it meant a lot to the omega to get out with the team.

The team was blowing up the group chat with memes about which players got lucky last night. Shortly after Rowan was added, he added Beckett to the chat, and while the alpha didn't really talk, he did enjoy watching Rowan fire off gifs and memes faster than anyone else.

Beckett leaned against the door frame, already dressed, watching as Rowan brushed his hair in the mirror over the dresser. He held a hair tie in his mouth as he shuffled his hair from his face and detangled it. The omega looked into the mirror at the alpha over his shoulder and winked. It was so simple, yet it sent Beckett's heart into overdrive.

He kept replaying what they did in his mind, and his fingers itched to touch the omega again.

Rowan took the hair tie from his mouth and smiled as he tied his hair up. "You know you can still touch me." He turned around, leaning back on the dresser. "I don't want whatever this is to come between our friendship." His eyes lowered as he smiled nervously while he played with the front of his jacket. "Um...I know we haven't known each other long, but I consider you one of my best friends." He swallowed, and Beckett felt his skin prickle at the blush on the omega's face.

Ever so softly, in a way that was so un-Rowan-like, the omega tilted his head to the side. It might be seen as submissive to some, but to Beckett, it was a sign of trust. Those blue eyes slid over to look at him and gauge his reaction. "I appreciate you helping me and all. So, promise me this won't make us weird around each other?" He pushed off the dresser and walked forward, taking Beckett's hands into his own and squeezing. "I mean, I'm totally fine if you never want to do any of that again."

A sharp pain etched in Beckett's chest at the idea of never holding his omega like that again. The look must have been clear as Rowan giggled, eyes looking relieved. "Dude, I WANT to do that again, and again... And again." He wagged his eyebrows at him, making Beckett snort in amusement. Rowan continued, "Last night was kind of crazy, and we didn't get to fully talk it out." Rowan's phone pinged with another text tone, and he sighed, releasing one of Beckett's hands to grab his phone and glance at it. "The team's waiting downstairs."

He pocketed the device and retook Beckett's hand. "I know talking isn't really your thing, but maybe we can find some ice time to work out anything you might wanna say?"

Beckett wished he could say it all right then, but the lump in his throat made it too difficult. He nodded instead, leaning down to place a gentle kiss on Rowan's soft lips. Rowan returned it just as eagerly before pulling away with a whine. "Come on, it took me forever to get that scent off me! Don't make all my hard work go to waste!" He motioned to the three scent patches spread across his neck and body. It would undoubtedly be pure torture; Beckett remembered Rowan mentioning how itchy they made him.

Nodding toward the door, the duo left, heading to the elevator. The whole ride down, Beckett kept glancing at Rowan's hand, having a massive urge to hold it. It got so bad that he had to shove his hands into his jacket pockets.

In the lobby, a whole team of rowdy college students bounced around, talking and taking jabs at each other. McAllister spotted them and called out, "Whoaaa, here comes the newlyweds!" Rhodes, Briggs, and McAllister wolf whistled as the two skaters blushed. Some of the other players barked while someone moaned, really making the scene that much more embarrassing.

Rowan pouted, “If anyone is the newlywed, it’s little spoon over here.” Rowan jerked a thumb to an obviously sleep-deprived Wilson.

“Shut up! I hardly got any sleep last night!” The sandy-haired alpha snapped.

"Oooo, that good?" Rowan wagged his eyebrows, shooting finger guns at him.

"No! These two idiots kept me up all night!" He pointed an accusing finger at McAllister and Briggs, who looked like angels with their perfect eight hours of sleep.

Rowan giggled behind his hand. "You made your point. You had the best night out of all of us. No need to make us all jealous."

If Wilson were a bomb, he would have exploded as he shook his fist at the omega, shouting obscenities.

"Let's go! I'm hungry!" Rhodes shouted, accompanied by several groans of agreement.

“I saw a diner down the road,” Cooper said, holding up his phone. “It looks adequate.”

"Tally that hoe!" McAllister pointed forward like an adventurer, and the whole team took off, much to the relief of the hotel staff, who had endured the rowdy group.

On the walk, Beckett kept looking at Rowan, who animatedly talked with McAllister and Rhodes about some game coming out soon. The morning sun made Rowan's hair shine like gold, and his skin soaked up every bit. They were nearing winter, so the air was chilly, but the skaters were no strangers to the cold. Beckett wondered how Rowan felt; was he still feeling the effects of his heat, or did their morning activities satiate him for now?

As if reading his mind, Rowan looked to his right at Beckett and gave the most sexual wink. His tongue peeked out from the edge of his mouth as he bumped shoulders with the alpha, wagging his brows at him. Beckett's face heated up, and he looked forward after Rowan caught him staring again.

They got to the diner, and like their previous outing, the tables were smooshed together longways so they could eat as a team. Rowan took his rightful place by Beckett, never leaving the alpha to fend for himself. Though Cooper seemed to take it upon himself to sit on Beckett's other side most of the time.

Beckett liked Cooper. He was quiet like him, and he seemed not to get annoyed when Beckett gave short or nonverbal answers. He wondered why they never spoke before Rowan came along, and it was probably because Cooper hadn't had a chance, or maybe the solemn player was just a tad shy.

Beckett knew he wasn't in any place to judge someone for keeping quiet.

The waiter came around to take orders, and Rowan leaned over, pressing his shoulder to Beckett's as he looked up at him with that pure, innocent smile. Beckett recalled the open-mouth gasps Rowan gave while bouncing on his cock; those blue eyes that reminded him of winter nearly brought to tears as he choked on Beckett's dick. Those images were night and day compared to how the omega was swinging his feet in the high-top chairs they all sat at, looking at the alpha's laminated menu.

"Whatcha thinking? Gonna join me on my pancake adventure? Or will you go for the old-timer's meal like Wilson over there?" He jutted a thumb at Wilson, who glared back.

“Hey! Don’t come to me when all you toddlers get heart disease before your thirties!” He held up the menu.

The waiter came over, and Beckett quickly pointed to a selection. Rowan nodded. "Okay, cool, cool, um," He looked up at the waiter, "Hey, I'll have the chocolate chip pancakes with chocolate milk, and my bestie here will have your finest western omelet." The beta wrote it all down. "Hash browns are fine, and wheat toast?" He raised a brow at Beckett, who nodded, and Rowan hissed in celebration, handing the menu back to the waiter. "Oh, and a coffee."

The waiter nodded before heading off to the next person as Rowan went back to folding his paper straw holder into a tight triangle to flick at McAllister’s goal he made with his fingers.

"So, it's true, huh?" Rhodes asked, and Beckett looked over, feeling he was the one being addressed. He was correct as the auburn-haired alpha leaned his chin onto his hand, "You really don't talk?"

Beckett felt his hair bristle like a cat and looked over to see Rowan concentrating on shooting his paper puck into McAllister's L-shaped fingers. Looking back at the other alpha, he noticed Wilson watching him, too.

Beckett pressed his mouth together in a thin line before nodding. Damn, he was gonna look dumb again. Why couldn't they have this conversation out on the ice?

"Rowan says you can only really talk on the ice," Cooper spoke up next, and Beckett was relieved someone knew. Beckett nodded, and the goth skater hummed.

"Why?" Rhodes cocked his head. "You have, like, a talking issue?"

Wilson squinted his eyes, scrutinizing Beckett, and the captain felt sweat on the back of his neck as he swallowed. With all those eyes on him, he felt like he was ten years old again, standing before his peers as they waited for him to say anything. Opening his mouth, he was struck with an anxious shiver that rolled down his spine, and he swallowed. "I..." He looked down to the wooden tabletop. "I just-" He wondered what they would all think of him. Would they challenge his standing as a captain again? Would they make fun of him in front of Rowan? Would Rowan get embarrassed that he spent the night with an alpha who could hardly speak?

Just as he was about to panic and excuse himself to the bathroom, a hand reached over and took his. Looking at Rowan, the blond was already inserting himself into the conversation, having lost their paper puck under the table. McAllister was currently fishing around for it. "Beck's just shy." As if that was the end of it.

"But why do you always look pissed?" Briggs asked, and before they knew it, most of the attention was on him, and Beckett itched for the feel of ice under him.

"That's just his lovable face!" Rowan reached up and cupped his cheeks, shaking them gently to show each end of the table. "Homeboy here's got a smolder that could make any hockey player run for cover. Frankly, you all should admire it!"

McAllister put a hand to his chin in thought, abandoning the discarded paper puck. "Hm, you're right. I've seen it intimidate quite a few players."

Briggs lit up like a Christmas tree. "If we can all channel Beckett's look, we'll make all the other teams piss themselves!" He took on Beckett's blank look but came off looking like a constipated statue.

"No, no, it's more like this!" McAllister took on a stern glare, but his cheeks were puffed out.

"Nahhh, that looks like Wilson," Walker offered with an attempt to imitate Beckett's look, and McAllister nearly shot his water from his nose laughing.

"Would it be like this?" Jeon said in a monotone voice, and Rowan gasped.

"Whoa, you're the closest by far!" He said, giving a golf clap that was echoed by several other players who agreed.

The table erupted in talking, and Beckett felt relief, grateful for Rowan's intervention. Feeling eyes on him, he looked up and met Wilson's glare. He sat upright, not wanting to appear weak before his rival and teammate.

Wilson crossed his arms and squinted his eyes at him as if reading beyond Beckett's silence. Thankfully, they were interrupted by the food, and chaos ensued as the food and sticky syrup passed back and forth.

Rowan's pancakes had a whipped cream smile on the top, and the blond swooned as he took a picture, saying he needed to text it to Imani.

He smiled down at the omega, wishing he could smell that wonderful scent of sugar cookies and sunflowers. Deep down, maybe he wanted to smell his own scent on the heat-stricken omega, but that was his deep secret to hold onto.

They ate as a team, and Beckett found it calming when the attention wasn't on him any longer. Once finished, Jeon was generous enough to put the bill on his dad's card, stating it would be funny in the most monotone voice ever. The whole team already knew about his strenuous relationship with his father, but nobody was going to say 'no' to a free meal.

Leaving the diner, they were all chatting about plans before the upcoming game.

"Coach wants us all to take it easy," Cooper reminded them, since they did have a game that night.

"How about a warm-up at the rink? We can get a feel of the place." McAllister offered, and the others echoed agreement.

Heading back to their hotel, Rowan offered to run up and grab their skating bags as Beckett waited in the lobby with Wilson, who shouted at Briggs to grab his bag. The captain tried to insist with his eyes that he could go with him, but Rowan said the two elevators were already going to be packed.

“Just chill with Rye-Rye!” Rowan had said, taking off with the others, squeezing into the large elevator between McAllister and Walker.

“Don’t call me that!” Wilson yelled at the omega, who ignored the outburst with a wave of his hand.

Once the team was thoroughly packed into the closed elevator, Wilson snapped his gaze back on Beckett with a hard look.

"You," he said, and Beckett pulled his shoulders back, ready for another Wilson berating. "I just want to say..."

‘*Here it comes.*’ Beckett prepared himself for the threats, the insults, and the constant challenge of his title as captain. He was honestly in too good a mood for this shit, but it’s not like he could tell the alpha to back off.

"Sorry," Wilson bit out, and Beckett felt like he was in the opening of the X-Files with the theme song playing as he fell through a void of chaos.

Beckett cocked his head, and the alpha snapped, baring his teeth. "Fuck, don't make me spell it out!" He shook his head before sighing loudly. "I thought-" He groaned, running a hand through his hair. "That you assumed you were better than me– or at least better than the team." He looked down. "You'd talk to us on the ice, but off of it," He looked away as if remembering something. "Do you remember the first time I approached you after our first practice?"

How could Beckett forget? On the first day of practice, they had all shown their skills and did several hours of drills before it was announced that Beckett would be captain. Wilson had been obviously disheartened, and when they were in the locker room, the alpha tried to talk to him. Beckett remembered freezing up and looking at the sandy blond and just staring. After a few seconds, Wilson screamed several curses and punched his locker before storming out.

Ever since, Wilson had hated his guts. For a guy with as bad a temper as he had, it was a wonder the whole team gravitated to him. Deep down, Beckett wondered if he should give up his captain title to the blond. But Archer told him on several occasions that Wilson wasn't ready for that position.

Beckett nodded, and Wilson scoffed, running a hand through his hair. "My old man… he's, like, super fucking shy." He groaned. "It's almost embarrassing how much my mom has to talk for him. But I get it. Talking isn't for everyone. And with your mean-ass mug, it can't be easy." He looked off to the side. "I shouldn't just assume because you're an alpha that you should be like everyone else."

The captain felt his stomach knot up as Wilson sighed, finally meeting his eyes. "Point I'm making is… Twirl Hurl is alright, and if he vouches for you, then I guess that's what I'll accept." His hand quickly shot up to point at him. "But damn it, you're our captain! You need to get it together. We rely on you to lead us, and you can't exactly do that if you can only talk on the ice."

That was true. Beckett nodded. "You're right."

Wilson nodded at the verbal confirmation. "We're on a winning streak, and I wanna keep it like that. So, if you promise to try and talk more, I'll back off." He held up a hand. "Just more than three fucking words, alright?" He raised a brow. "Can we do that?"

Beckett swallowed the lump in his throat as he nodded. "I'll do whatever it takes, Wilson."

That seemed to calm the alpha, who gave a single nod, eyes set in a heated glare. "Alright, that's the fucking captain we need." He turned away, shoving his hands into his jacket as the elevator doors opened and the rowdy team appeared in the distance.

"Oh, and by the way." Wilson looked sideways at him, and Beckett took his eyes off Rowan to look back at him.

“Hm?”

“I don’t give a shit if you and Twirl Hurl are fucking. Just don’t let it interfere with the game.”

Beckett's face turned bright red as he opened his mouth and closed it several times, trying to find words to say.

"Whoa, what are you two talking about?" McAllister said as the team stopped before them. "Did Wilson drop an emotional bomb on our dear captain?"

“A confession?” Briggs gasped, eyes sparkling. “How cool!”

"I ain't confessing shit! Let's get going!" Wilson snatched his skate bag from the redhead and led the way out of the hotel. "Come on! I need to burn off that fucking food!"

Rowan bounced up next to Beckett and handed him his duffel bag. “What were you two talking about?”

Beckett gave a strained look, blushing as he faced forward. Rowan giggled, “Alright, keep your secrets– for now. But on the ice, you’re mine.” He bumped shoulders with him.

The walk to the ice rink turned into a long line of muscular hockey players jostling each other in a rowdy game of shoulder knocks. Rowan got tired of being nearly knocked off his feet by the larger players. He tugged on Beckett's sleeve and looked up at him with the most pitiful pout. "Can I ride on your back?"

Beckett felt his heart jump into his throat as he nodded stiffly. He was about to crouch down, but the omega was spry and full of energy as he jumped and climbed Beckett's back like a tree. Those legs wrapped around his stomach while his arms took their rightful place on his shoulders. Rowan leaned upwards to tower over the others. "Ha, ha! Now I am the tallest! How's it feel now to get looked down upon!" He boasted in a booming voice.

"I don't know, shorty, you tell us," Wilson smirked up at him, and Rowan pouted, leaning down to rest his head on Beckett's shoulder.

"Beat them all up for me?" He asked in a sweet voice. And damn it, Beckett knew he would take them all out if it meant Rowan would keep smiling.

"Awww, they're so cute!" McAllister sighed, looking at Briggs. "Carry me, alpha?"

Briggs, already in on the joke, laughed and let the skinny beta jump on, carrying him in a similar fashion as the two moaned, obviously mocking the duo.

"You're all just jealous because I got the best alpha!" Rowan stuck his tongue out and tightened his hold on Beckett as he leaned down and whispered in his ear, "Right, Beck?"

Beckett held onto the thighs squeezing his sides and nodding stiffly, trying not to get too aroused and have everyone smell it on him. The fact that Rowan called him the best alpha made him preen. Rowan never made him feel bad about his lack of communication and, instead, made it seem like it wasn't a big deal. Why is it so easy for Rowan to break down his walls when he spent so many years building them?

They arrived at the rink, and Beckett was remorseful when Rowan slid off his back, but not before he gave Beckett's butt a slap and winked as he thanked him for the lift. Then, Rowan took the lead of the group of alphas as he rushed inside. He stopped and gasped at the large rink.

"Wow! I'll never get over seeing other cities' rinks!" Rowan said and called everyone over to a bench he commandeered for them all. They slid on their skates, and Beckett felt the familiar prickle of ice nearby. He smiled.

Rowan was the first on the ice, and thankfully, it was completely deserted, except for the rink master, who sat by ice skate rentals with his eyes glued to a book. The blond called out for them to hurry up as he circled around the rink and followed it up with a jump and twirl. He landed on one foot, and some of their teammates gasped in awe.

"Dude! I've seen figure skating before, but you know, I've never actually watched it," McAllister admitted, and some agreed with him.

"It looks quite challenging," Cooper stated, and Jeon hummed.

"Oh, please! How hard can it be?" Wilson snorted, but was covered in ice as Rowan did a quick stop, spraying his teammate with his ice dust.

Rowan raised a brow and piqued Beckett's interest in more ways than one. "Oh yeah, Rye-Rye? Think being a twirl hurl is all skips and daisies? I'm flattered you think I make it look so easy. So, come on..." He motioned with his arms. "Care to show us how it's done?

A chorus of ‘ooo’ filled their group as a blushing Wilson scoffed and stepped forward, gliding like he was born on ice skates, too. “Gladly! But don’t call me Rye-Rye and try not to cry when I make your craft an utter joke.”

"Yeah, uh-huh." Rowan nodded. "Let's start off easy, then. Humor me." He skated around Wilson before gaining momentum, spinning three times on one foot before launching himself up into the air in a spin before landing, pulling one leg out and slowly up over his head while turning in place quickly.

When he finally stopped, he smirked at all the mouths practically on the floor, including Wilson’s, who looked like he had just eaten glass.

"That was a butterfly with a quick spin." Rowan exuded confidence, and Beckett couldn't stop the smirk as he pushed off onto the ice with his team. Beckett crossed his arms and watched with humor as Wilson closed his mouth with a snap.

"I added the leg lift for style, but I don't think you're as flexible. Don't let that stop you from showing us what you got, though." Rowan stuck his tongue out in a cheeky grin, poking it from between his teeth. He skated over, stopping by Beckett and holding his hand out for a fist bump, which Beckett gladly returned.

"Whatever! I can do it!" Wilson backed up, skating to the very end. The team howled and hooted, cheering as he broke into a sprint-like skate.

When Wilson reached the center ice, he pushed himself up, and that's about how far he got before he slid forward onto his face. A collection of empathetic hisses echoed out from the team as they watched the impact. Briggs and Walker skated forward to try to help him up, but the sandy blond shoved them off as he got up and glared at Rowan.

Beckett was worried this would cause an argument until Wilson sneered, "Fucking show me how you did that!"

Rowan perked up in excitement, skating forward. "Gladly!"

Several players skated out, wanting to learn as well. Rowan obviously channeled his inner Emily and began showing them the process of a butterfly step by step. Beckett passed on learning to jump and instead skated around with Cooper and Walker.

"You need to get your balance on one skate," Rowan said as Wilson wobbled again.

"I am balanced!" He snapped back.

Beckett chuckled, and Cooper looked at him. "He's a great addition to the team."

"Yeah, he's perfect," Beckett said it in a tone that was a lot dreamier than he wanted it to sound.

"Now that you're on the ice..." Cooper cleared his throat, and the captain looked down at him. "I've been meaning to ask you." He scratched the back of his head nervously. "Would you mind giving me a breakdown on my progress? I feel Archer's strict teachings might come better with a second opinion. Wilson just tells me to be better. Might you elaborate on what I can do to improve?"

Beckett felt proud that his teammate was coming to him for help, and he nodded. "Yeah, I have a few suggestions."

"Same here." Walker sighed, "I feel like I'm repeating myself when it comes to relying on my singular moves. Any suggestions?"

“Of course. Let’s go over it.”

And like that, everyone split into two groups. Half the team learned to butterfly jump, while Beckett took the others to the side to give advice. They borrowed some sticks from the rental station and shot around the puck as Beckett gave loud and clear instructions, watching them improve.

Beckett looked over at Rowan and found the blond already staring at him with a pride that made Beckett's heart ache. With a smirk, he winked at the blond. The omega flushed a deep pink and turned around to adjust Briggs's position.

After an hour, Wilson managed to get the lift and landing. He wasn’t even half as graceful as Rowan, but it was enough for him to shout in victory to his teammates, who still couldn't do it.

"Yeah! Fuck you guys! Eat my shit!" He laughed evilly as he jumped again.

Rowan clapped, not at all put off by Wilson's earlier teasing about how easy his sport was. That was another thing about Rowan; he was so kind and supportive, ready to give the shirt off his back to anyone who needed it.

Wilson looked very pleased with himself, turning to Rowan with a newfound smirk. "Alright, Twirl Hurl! I'll admit you got some moves. Now it's only fair I teach you something."

Rowan took on that flirty smirk he did with Beckett, and it made the alpha's hair raise as he wanted to suddenly check Wilson into the wall.

"Oh yeah? Whatcha gonna teach me? How to use big boy words? How to pick nicknames to taunt my enemies?" Rowan snickered cheekily.

"Nahhhh, let's start with something easy." Wilson's eyes gleamed as if ready to go to war. "I'm gonna teach you how to fight."

"Fight?" Rowan looked positively shocked, looking over to Beckett and back. "Like, fight-fight?"

Beckett came to a quick stop next to Wilson and crossed his arms, wearing a smirk that matched Wilson's. "I agree. It's time we taught you the fundamentals of ice fights."

Rowan gulped and forced a smile. "Oh joy."

# CHAPTER THIRTY-TWO

## ~~~~~~ ROWAN ~~~~~~

Most of the team had taken their seats on the bench off to the side of the rink. Rowan glanced at them enviously, wishing that he could join them and avoid the upcoming lesson.

Wilson and Beckett stood in front of him with wide stances, typical of alpha's in charge. Despite all of Rowan's protests, they seemed adamant about showing him how to hold his own on the ice.

"Can't I just avoid fighting?" Rowan had pleaded as the two seasoned players figured out the best lesson plan. Maybe if he hadn't been wearing so many scent patches, he could have gotten out of this with a bit of a distressed omega scent, but he was pretty screwed.

"Not if you want to keep playing on my team," Wilson replied, and Rowan knew that was the end of that. He was going to need to learn to fight.

It all seemed cruel and unnecessary to Rowan. Everyone was playing the same sport, they knew the rules, and they were all just trying to win. Why did they need to trade blows? Rowan had been disappointed and frustrated when he lost competitions before, but the thought of clobbering the other skaters never crossed his mind.

"Pay attention, loser," The blond alpha said, and Rowan snapped to attention.

"We're gonna teach you what you need to know out there. We'll demonstrate first, so pretend I'm you."

"Blond boys forever," Rowan said with a smirk and two thumbs up. Wilson growled in return, looking like an angry Pomeranian.

"And Kage here is your opponent who wants to kick your ass."

Wilson jerked his head in Beckett's direction. Beckett, in turn, gave a small glove-on salute to Rowan.

"How do I know Beck wants to fight?" Rowan asked.

"Well, if you keep tackling people on the ice, you can be damn sure they're gonna want to fight you," Wilson said. "But there is one tell-tale sign you can look for."

Wilson raised both hands up and swung them down. Both of his gloves slipped off his hands and landed on the ice with a dull thud.

"Oh, Wilson," Rowan said, pointing at discarded equipment. "You dropped your gloves, silly boy."

"Yeah, that's the sign, lightfoot," Wilson said. "Tossing the gloves off tells the other player that shit's about to go down."

Rowan squinted a little as his head moved back an inch. "Really? And everyone does that?" He was trying to recall the other fights he'd seen to remember that ever happening. Usually, it was all a blur as he tried to escape the fight.

To answer, Beckett lifted his hands up and swung them down as well. The gloves slid off his hands as the momentum carried them away from his body.

Rowan looked back and forth between the two players. "Is there a reason that they do that?"

"We want to hit with our fists, not some soft gloves," Wilson replied in a macho tone, punching his fists together for emphasis.

Rowan raised his hand. "Can I request that they leave their soft gloves ON for the fight? That seems like the less painful option."

"That's kind of the point, Rowan," Beckett said. "We're going for pain."

The blond omega's face scrunched up. Surely the other player would still get the point if the gloves were on, but Rowan felt like he had protested enough already. He decided to hold that question for later and let the two of them continue.

"Okay, so what next?" He asked.

"Best idea is to take a fighting stance," Wilson said. He turned toward Beckett, shifted his body sideways, and balled his hands into fists. He lifted his hands, with his left hand out in front of him and his right hand locked back near his head. Beckett turned and mirrored this stance.

"Your weaker hand will be doing a lot of the light hits. It can also do a bit of blocking and shoving," Wilson said, shaking his left fist around while maintaining eye contact with Beckett. "Or, you may end up grabbing the other player's jersey with it."

"So now I'm attacking their clothes, too?" Rowan asked. Wilson slowly turned his head toward Rowan with a look that said, 'There ARE stupid questions, you know.'

"It will help you stay balanced as you trade blows," Beckett said calmly, cutting off whatever Wilson was going to say. "It also ensures that your opponent stays within arm's reach."

"Ah," Rowan replied. "Got it." He gave Wilson a small smile. It wasn't returned, but Wilson gave the small skater a roll of his eyes and left it at that.

"Anyway, those are the basics. From here, you just wail on the other guy until, hopefully, he falls to the ice. He might take you with him since you'll both be holding onto each other's jerseys, but going down doesn't mean you didn't win," Wilson said.

"That's it?" Rowan asked in genuine surprise. "There's no, I don't know... finesse? No tricks to it?"

Rowan expected another non-verbal thrashing from Wilson, confident that it was a stupid series of questions as soon as the words left his mouth. '*It's a fight,*' he thought. '*It's barbaric; obviously, there's no style to it.*'

He was surprised, however, when the blond alpha glanced at him from the corner of his eye and smirked.

"Now I didn't say that, did I?" he asked. He looked back at Beckett and asked, "You mind?"

Beckett sighed and shook his head. Rowan wasn't sure what was going to happen, but he didn't like Wilson asking permission for anything.

Beckett held his stance and skated toward Wilson. He reached for the blond's jersey, though Rowan could tell he was moving more slowly in order to demonstrate, and Wilson reached behind the captain. In one swift movement, Wilson pulled the back of Beckett's favorite NHL jersey over his head, forcing the captain to lean forward.

"This," Wilson said as he pulled the jersey up. "Is a dirty fighting move.

Probably the most disrespectful thing you can do in a fight. But if you really pissed someone off and need an advantage, this move will disorient them and make it more difficult for them to fight back."

Wilson feigned uppercutting Beckett's head and face with his free hand while the other hand held the jersey in place. Rowan saw how trapped a player could be in that position and how degrading it must feel to be there.

Beckett pulled back and twisted out of Wilson's grip like it was a well-practiced move, allowing his jersey to fall back into place.

"It's not a sure thing or inescapable, mind you," Beckett said, picking up for Wilson. Rowan stood in astonishment at how gracefully his captain had pulled himself out of that hold. Beckett continued, "and you will piss off whoever you do it to even more. So, if you're going to do it, you have to be ready to strike them. A lot."

Rowan was taken aback by this. Beckett, the guy who could barely speak to people when he wasn't on the ice, talked about the proper way to trap someone and beat the crap out of them. He said it with the casual authority that can only come from experience.

The omega nodded, "Got it. So, what do I get if I win a fight, anyway?"

"Pride," Wilson said boastfully.

"And a five-minute penalty," Beckett followed with a very Archer look that he'd probably seen a thousand times.

"But it's a PROUD five-minute penalty," Wilson emphasized.

Rowan's face scrunched up again. "Uh-huh." He shook his head and shrugged. "Well, thanks for the lesson. I'll keep it in mind."

Rowan turned to skate away, but Wilson's hand was instantly on his shoulder.

"Not so fast, there."

Rowan turned his head to look at the other blond. "What? Another lesson?" He asked.

Wilson smirked. "Kind of. Tell me, how do you get to Carnegie Hall?"

Rowan shook his head, bewildered. "A plane to New York, I assume."

Wilson's smirk quickly faded. He sighed as he shut his eyes, angling his head down to the ice. "Practice, Rookie. Practice."

The veteran player skated back, leaving Rowan and Beckett facing each other. There were just a few feet between them, and Rowan didn't like where this seemed to be going.

"Fight," Wilson said with just a bit more enthusiasm than normal.

Rowan's open hands immediately went up in front of him. "What? No! I'm not fighting Beck."

There was no masking the frustration in Wilson's voice. "We JUST taught you how to fight. Now you need to fight. Better to try it here than against someone who's looking for blood."

"Yeah, but I can't fight Beck," Rowan said, gesturing at the captain with both hands. Wilson squinted at him.

"Why not?" He asked. Rowan's eyes darted over to Beckett, whose gaze was starting to wander to the side to leave Rowan to explain this himself. Rowan realized that mentioning that they had...been intimate...might not go over too well in their current setting. He wondered if there might even be rules against a captain and a player hooking up.

'*Well, if there are, it's too late.*' Rowan thought and bit back a smirk. '*And I'm doing it again, so fuck it.*'

"Well, er, he's my captain!" Rowan said, glad to have come up with an excuse on the fly. "I can't hit my captain; it would make things weird."

Wilson stared at him for a moment, and the omega felt like the blond player was staring directly into his soul. It may have only been for a few seconds, but Rowan would have sworn that entire civilizations had risen and fallen by the time Wilson said, "Fine, wimp. Jeon!"

Rowan breathed a quiet sigh of relief and turned his gaze to the bench of onlookers who were shouting words of encouragement to the figure skater.

"You're fighting blond and bashful here," Wilson said as Jeon approached.

Jeon lifted his arms up, swung off his gloves, and said, "Come at me." The team hooted and hollered like it was a damn rodeo.

As thrilled as Rowan was about not having to fight Beckett, he was uncomfortable with how nonchalantly Jeon took to the idea of fighting him. Jeon didn't seem phased about putting Rowan on the ice and keeping him there.

"I mean, we COULD, but where would we really get with a fight?" Rowan said nervously.

Wilson was thoroughly annoyed. "Come ON! You're past using your words here, Rookie."

Rowan lifted a finger and shook his head. "No, I was raised to believe that any problems can be solved with words."

“Hurt him!” Wilson shouted.

Rowan turned to Jeon, took in a deep breath, and said, “Your hair looks stupid.” He looked back to the crowd and motioned to his partner.

There was an audible "Oooo" from the bench. It was cut off like a scratched record with one stern look from Wilson.

“I didn’t choose it, you know,” Jeon said, unimpressed by the insult. Rowan didn’t think he'd ever seen Jeon give anything but his bored look.

“Oh my God, really? I’m so sorry,” Rowan said apologetically. “It’s nice, I swear.” The guilt swam over Rowan as he shook his arms. “I even think you’re a trendsetter with the way you style it!”

“Holy shit, please,” Wilson pleaded, looking back at Rowan. “Attack him! Hit him where it hurts!”

“Okay, okay!” Rowan said as he held his hands up to Wilson. He turned to Jeon, took the fighting stance he had just learned, and said, “Jeon, I think you have some real unresolved daddy issues.”

Color crept into Jeon’s face as the alpha didn’t seem to know how to take that. Rowan looked to his assistant captain and could practically see the cartoonish smoke spilling from his ears. His fists shook with rage as he took in a breath to shout at Rowan again. He was stopped, however, when Jeon replied, “Ouch.”

Wide-eyed, Wilson slowly turned to look at Jeon. “I don’t need you feeding this, okay?”

Beckett snickered behind Wilson. Rowan looked over at the captain, who was covering his face with his hand. Seeing Beckett smile, even hidden away, brought Rowan out of the situation. He realized he was happy to know that he could get Beckett to laugh. He wanted to do it more.

"Nevermind!" Wilson shouted. Jeon shrugged and skated back to the bench. "New lesson!"

Rowan looked back at Wilson, still feeling the warmth of getting that laughter out of Beckett. However, the feeling cooled down quickly as he saw Wilson approach him.

"I call it, 'how to take a hit," Wilson said as he swung a fist, knocking Rowan to the ice.

# CHAPTER THIRTY-THREE

Rowan and Beckett walked away from the rink, an ice pack on Rowan's cheek.

"How's it feeling?" Jeon asked from the back of the group.

"Like I was just attacked by some weird mix between a dick and an asshole," Rowan replied, wincing slightly as he moved his jaw.

McAllister let out a short laugh. "That is the most accurate description of Wilson I've ever heard," he said with a smile. "To be fair, though, you knew you were pushing his buttons."

Rowan put a hand to his chest indignantly. "I'm sorry, are you blaming the victim here? Or did you forget that I was just assaulted by a rabid Pomeranian?"

"Yeah, well, Wilson's like an animal," Beckett said, and it surprised Rowan as he looked up at the handsome alpha's smile. "If you poke a lion, you've gotta be ready for the claws."

Rowan pouted as he watched the rest of their teammates congregating around the entrance, though he was so proud of Beckett putting together so many words off the ice. "What are you guys gonna do 'til the game?"

Briggs offered a supportive smile. "Some of us are gonna go check out this giant sports shop nearby. I wanna get my dad something for his birthday, and this place has, like, every team for every sport. Wanna come?"

Rowan waved him off, feeling the warmth of his heat lick at his insides, and he would rather take a break from the scent of multiple alphas until the game. "Nah, I've had my fill of bro time. You guys go on ahead."

Briggs laughed before waving, and the rest of the team turned around, leaving in the opposite direction. Rowan glanced up at Beckett, who stayed put and smiled, "You can go with them if you want."

Beckett shrugged, looking back down at Rowan, and the blond gently punched his arm. "Aw, you wanna make sure I get back alright? Don't you know I'm a lean, mean fighting machine now? Got the bruises to prove it and everything," he joked, lowering the ice pack to show the shiner he had.

Beckett smiled, which Rowan returned. The small blond was about to walk when Beckett blushed and scratched the back of his head. "Wanna ride?" He asked softly.

Rowan blinked his wide eyes up at him before a giant grin spread across his face. "Fuck yeah, I do!"

He shouldered his duffel bag around his back and jumped on Beckett's back. The alpha wrapped his arms around Rowan's legs as the omega lowered the ice pack to hold Beckett's neck as they walked.

Rowan rambled on about the fight and how next time he'll see Wilson coming.

"Betcha my main bitch Imani would flatten his ass! She's got two settings, lean with it and rock with it, and both pack a punch," he said proudly.

The body under him was so warm, though not in an uncomfortable way. Rowan snuggled his face into the head of hair, inhaling. "Anyone ever tell you that you smell amazing?"

"No," Beckett said, and Rowan hummed.

"Well, you do."

The hands on his thighs tightened, and Rowan squeezed his legs on the alpha's waist, biting his lower lip as he cleared his throat. "Sooo, how long 'til we gotta be at the game tonight?"

"About three hours," Beckett responded, as monotone as ever. Rowan felt a bit of pride again that the alpha spoke more around him than he used to.

Maybe he could reward him for it…

Smiling slyly, he rested his head next to Beckett's ear and whispered, "What do you think we can do to pass the time?" He let out a long purr, feeling a shiver go up Beckett's spine. "Maybe we can even get another lesson in before- WOAH!" Rowan tightened his hold on Beckett as the alpha broke into a jog, rushing to get them back to the hotel. The omega laughed, blushing bright red at the fact that Beckett was just as excited as he was. He cried out Beckett's name, holding onto his alpha and his duffel bag strap.

# CHAPTER THIRTY-FOUR

## ~~~~~~ ROWAN ~~~~~~

And what an amazing three hours it was!

Rowan was sure his brain had short-circuited after round four, and he was now forever in a sex haze that he would never recover from. Beckett was an animal, tossing Rowan onto the bed the second they got into the room. He barely had his shoes off before Beckett was on him, mouth and all.

Currently, Rowan was lying sideways on the bed, breathing heavily, eyes nearly crossed as he felt the cum inside him move around. Beckett was still balls deep, fucking at a slow pace, drawing all kinds of sounds out of the spent skater.

"My god, Beck!" Rowan groaned, "If you keep this up, I don't know if I'll be skating tonight as much as I'll be sliding across the ice on my back." He groaned when the alpha licked up his neck, biting down on the soft skin.

Beckett didn't seem phased, adjusting the omega's position, his eyes concentrating as he slid his arms behind Rowan's shoulders to jerk his hips up and Rowan down simultaneously, slamming into him harder but at the same slow pace. Rowan felt tears prick his eyes as he gasped around another soft orgasm, his dick nearly sore from the attention it had been getting the past three hours.

"Fuck, fuck, fuck," He hissed, looking up at the alpha who was staring down at him and panting. He had sweat dotting his face, but otherwise looked so composed. It wasn't until Rowan felt him tense up and close his eyes that he realized what was coming.

"Oh god!" Rowan closed his eyes, feeling another round of cum fill him, arching his back off the bed to press against Beckett. After several long seconds of Beckett riding out his release, he finally pulled out and looked down at his handiwork with a mixture of pride and arousal. Those damned horny eyes trailed up Rowan's spent body to his face as the omega blushed.

"You trying to turn me into a Bavarian cream donut?" Rowan gave a weak joke, even though his heart and mind were short-circuiting, "Extra filling?"

Beckett huffed out a laugh, rolling beside the omega to collect him in his arms, bringing Rowan into his space for after-sex cuddles. Rowan discovered shortly after this all began that Beckett was actually a cuddler after sex. He would bury his nose into Rowan's hair to sniff and huff until he was content with the happy omega scent. Rowan wasn't going to complain because he was just as much of a cuddle slut and ate up all the attention.

Looking up at the clock on the nightstand, Rowan sighed. “Beck, we gotta get ready for the game.”

Beckett nodded with a grunt, though he didn’t release his grip. “You… you good to play?” He asked, bringing a hand up to card through Rowan’s wild hair, making the omega yawn.

"You literally fucked my heat right out of me. I think I'm good for the next three heats." He laughed and managed to squirm away before Beckett could latch onto him again. Jumping off the bed, he walked fully nude to the bathroom door and paused, looking over his shoulder at Beck. "But I wouldn't say no to a little shower make-out."

The grin that spread across Beckett's face would look murderous or deranged to some people. But to Rowan, it was the most handsome smile he had ever seen.

Beckett got up and walked over to the bathroom as Rowan smiled brightly at the amazing body his best friend/captain had and proudly showed off. "Fuuuck, maybe you missed a spot. I suddenly feel a tad bit of heat." Rowan wagged his brow as Beckett swooped down and kissed him, pushing the omega back into the walk-in shower.

A short time later, much too short in Rowan's opinion, the omega finished lacing up his second skate and sat up on the locker room bench. He looked around the room to see the rest of his team suiting up for the game.

There was some chatter among some of the players while others performed their pre-game rituals. Cooper and Jeon sat on another bench, and Rowan thought both of them looked like they were competing in a brood-off, possibly trying to channel their inner Beckett glare. Wilson, on the other hand, was competing with Briggs to see who could do more push-ups.

As different as the practices were, Rowan didn't need to be a lifelong hockey player to understand that they were all doing the same thing. They were prepping, excited about the game, and doing what they needed to do to control their energy and emotions.

"Alright, team," They heard from the door, and the locker room instantly grew silent. Coach Archer walked through the door, clipboard in hand. "Big game tonight, and just the first of two against this team. So, I hope you all took the afternoon easy."

"Oh, I took it, alright," Rowan whispered to Beckett as he nudged him. Beckett mostly suppressed a small grin, and Rowan felt pride again in getting even the slightest smile out of him. His eyes moved past Beckett to Wilson, who stared at them with wide eyes and his jaw on the floor, obviously hearing it. He shuddered after a moment before focusing back on the coach. However, a scowl remained planted on his face.

“Starting lineup time. In goal, Briggs.”

“Naturally,” the red-haired player said with a toothy grin.

“Defense: Cooper and Dominguez.”

The two defensemen looked at each other and high-fived.

“On center ice, your captain, Kage.”

Beckett looked around the room and forced a small smile. Rowan was a little surprised to even see him give everyone that. He was glad to see the captain open up, even if he was taking baby steps. The omega smiled slightly as he took a sip from his water bottle.

“And on the wings, we’ve got Jeon and West.”

Rowan's eyes shot over to the coach as he choked on the water. Beckett turned and patted him on the back.

“Excuse me, Coach Archer. Which lineup is that? The back-up for the back-ups?” Rowan asked hopefully. He knew he had to play at some point, but he didn’t think he would be in the starting lineup again. Not after the last game.

"Yeah," Wilson said angrily. "That can't be the starting lineup. I'm not on it."

"It is the starting lineup," Archer said, his eyes darting toward Wilson. "And I don't recall asking for feedback on it."

Wilson's expression held the anger, but he sat down.

Archer continued, "West's become a draw for the crowd. Which is what Prescott wants in order for him to stay. He's also been showing some improvement in practice; I want to see if he can use some of those new skills in a real game."

"Aww, thanks, coach," Rowan said, touching a hand over his heart.

"Also," Archer interrupted. "It makes strategic sense. We start with West on the ice to lure them into a false sense of security. They may get sloppy, thinking they don't need to push too hard because he's an omega. Once that happens, we can strike."

"Jeez, thanks, coach," Rowan said sarcastically under his breath.

Beckett patted him on the back again, though it was lighter than before.

"Hey, you get on the ice early, and we can take it from there. You'll get off the ice early, too, right?" McAllister asked, nervously smiling at their coach for assurance, who nodded once, and the team collectively sighed.

Rowan nodded. That made sense, but he was worried about starting the game off as a target or, worse, messing up enough to throw off the rest of their game.

“Alright, team. Watch each other’s backs, get the puck in the net’s back, or don’t bother coming back. Got it?”

“Got it!”

“Hands in.” Archer moved a hand forward as everyone put their hands in.

Rowan felt practically squished between all the bodies, but he loved every second of it.

“Asher U on three!” Briggs said from the far side. “One, two, three-” All inserted hands were thrown into the air with loud battle cries, “Asher U!”

# CHAPTER THIRTY-FIVE

Just like before, Rowan was greeted by bleachers packed with fans. He stood center ice, looking around him while his team warmed up. The arena played classic rock this time instead of the pop that their stadium stuck with most of the time.

The only difference he could see was the signs with his gender on them and phrases that he wasn't sure if he should find offensive or humorous.

'Feel the Heat!'

'My type = Ice Omegas'

'Call me!'

A hand on his shoulder pulled his attention to his captain, who glanced at the signs before looking down at him. "You good?"

The worry was there behind those eyes, and Rowan swallowed the lump in his throat. Because of his damned heat, all he could picture was two hours earlier, being bent over in the shower, taking-

"Yeah, never better!" Rowan gave his award-winning smile. In his paranoid state of mind, he might have emptied half a pack of scent patches down his chest and neck. There was no way he would let anyone here besides Beckett get a hint that he was even close to his heat.

"You're gonna do great," Beckett gave a comforting smile, which Rowan felt all the way down to his toes.

The ref blew a whistle, signaling it was game time, and the benched players cleared the ice. The crowd went wild when Rowan stayed and took his spot. A player skated across from him, and Rowan tensed at their massive size. His padding made him look even more like a giant as he looked down at Rowan with indifference.

In an attempt to lighten the situation, Rowan huffed out a laugh. "Someone took their Flintstone vitamins," he joked.

The alpha in the green jersey raised a brow before the whistle sounded, and he shot forward. Rowan flinched, readying himself for the hit, but soon cracked his left eye open when a gust of air blew by him without even touching him. Looking over his shoulder, he saw the player completely ditching him, making a skate for Beckett.

Standing there blinking, he heard Archer shout his name. Looking back over, he saw the coach motioning with his arms. "What?" Rowan cupped his large, gloved hands over his ear, unable to hear anything over the crowd. "What?"

"Get in the game!" Archer shouted, face red in annoyance.

Rowan, unfortunately, still couldn't hear the coach, but he felt like whatever he was saying was vitally important. The blood vessel in his head seemed to confirm his suspicions as it threatened to burst.

The small player decided to skate over and see what was so important. Leaving the action of the game behind, he moved over to the bench and stopped with a small flourish. Nothing that took effort, but it was never a bad time to practice in his mind.

"What's up, coach? You got a special play for me?" Rowan asked earnestly. The unwavering glare that the coach leveled at him informed him that an earnest attitude may not be the best approach. He turned and saw Wilson on the bench beside the coach, displaying a very similar rage.

"I'm gonna punch you again if you don't get in the damn game!" His red matched the coach's as Rowan did a quick 180 and skated back out to the game, pouting.

"Jeez, sorry!" He noticed the puck sliding out, and his face lit up as he dove for it. "Dibs!" He circled it, taking it with his stick as the crowd went wild. Skating out, he noticed two players from the opposing team coming in on either side of him. Rowan knew within seconds he would be a splatter on the ground as he yet again closed his eyes for impact.

Once again, it never came, and he opened his eyes in time to see one of the alphas snatch the puck and skate right by him. The other did check Jeon, who tried to come to his aid. Rowan skated and helped him up. "Yo, what's that about?" He asked the alpha, handing him back his stick.

Jeon was too into the game as he shrugged and was off to the other end to try to get the puck back for their team. Rowan hummed in thought, skating forward to follow. Beckett and the other captain were hashing it out. It was pure electricity between them, eyes glaring and ice shavings flying from the quick stops and the changes they performed. Rowan looked around the rink to see another player in the wings getting ready, should his team send the puck to him.

After several quick looks at the game, Rowan skated over, taking position next to him as if he were copying the player's stance. "Hey!" He offered.

The player looked at him before going back to the game. “Hey.”

Rowan clicked his tongue in mock boredom, pretending like they were anywhere but in a wild game. "How's it going?"

“Good.”

"I'm Rowan." Rowan smiled brightly up at him, and the player blushed, turning his face forward.

“Cool.”

After not receiving much, he sighed, "Sooo, is there a reason your team is treating me like I have cooties? Because I can assure you, I've had all my shots." He laughed, but it died in his throat when the player's face blushed more. "Oh god! Do you guys seriously think I have cooties?"

“No!” The player said quickly, finally looking at Rowan.

“Then what’s the deal?” Rowan stood upright, tired of hunching over, “Usually other teams seem to like running me down or chasing me around like some goddamn yakety sax. You know, like it’s some sick game to them.”

The player sighed, looking back at the game. "It's just… our coach told us it's not cool to hit omegas," he muttered with pink scratching his face.

Rowan felt a twinge of anger as he narrowed his eyes. "Seriously? We're playing hockey!"

"Yeah, and coach said we need to go easy on you." He pushed off, noticing the puck's position. "Not like you're an actual threat or anything."

Watching the player go, Rowan felt his face heat up as he heard cheering and looked up at the fans around him. A slow chant of 'Omega' filled the arena, and Rowan felt more embarrassment cloud his features. The heat under his skin wasn't helping the situation as his cheeks tinted pink in shame.

"Omega!"

"Omega!"

"Omega!"

Did they all think he was some joke?

Rowan felt his heart race and the heat climb up his throat as his eyes burned. Were they all laughing at him?

*'Not like you're an actual threat or anything.'*

"Omega!"

"Omega!"

Squeezing his eyes shut, Rowan tried to remember how to breathe, but it was hard when he was begging himself not to cry in front of everyone. What was he doing here? He wasn't an ice hockey player! He's a figure skater!

Somewhere, he heard a whistle blow.

"Omega!"

Hands grabbed Rowan's face, and the blond looked up, blinking his blue eyes at a soft green gaze staring down at him.

"Rowan," Beckett's calm voice washed over him, making his shoulders sag and the heat clear across his skin. He took a shaky breath as he felt his chin quiver, not trusting himself to talk. Is this how Beckett felt off the ice? That if he opened his mouth, he would say something completely wrong and mess it all up? It felt like every set of eyes was on him. Watching, listening, waiting for him to do something so they could laugh.

Beckett's eyes narrowed, and he said again, "Rowan."

He assumed that the game must have been paused because his whole team was crowded around him, shielding the omega from the onlookers.

Embarrassment threw him as he gasped. "The game! Oh god! Did I- did I space out?" He felt tears prickle in the corner of his eyes. "I'm so sorry, guys!"

"No, don't worry," Beckett released Rowan's face and let the omega compose himself. "The other team got a penalty, so the ref called time." He looked at the team around them. "We all just… saw you weren't doing good."

"We wanted to see if you were alright," Briggs announced, his eyes filled with worry. "You looked like you were panicking."

"Did that player say something to you?" McAllister said from next to him as the team closed in on the huddle.

"Want me to kick his ass? Perfect demonstration of our lessons." Wilson kindly offered. The threat of enjoying violence was somewhat disturbing but sweet.

Rowan sniffled, shaking his head. "Sorry! I just… I think I freaked out from all-" He motioned around him to the arena. "This. The whole omega thing."

“What do you mean?” Rhodes asked, cocking his head. Of course an alpha wouldn’t understand, so Rowan searched for the right words to express it to them.

Taking a deep breath, Rowan released it and shook his head. "I guess I just got overwhelmed. Won't happen again."

He saw their concerned looks, and he forced a smile to try to assure them, but Wilson stopped him. "Don't smile if you don't mean it, Twirl Hurl."

Rowan's smile dropped, and he looked at the angry alpha with wide eyes. The ref blew his whistle, and Archer shouted over at Rowan, motioning for him to come back. With a nervous look to the team, he nodded and went back to the bench with the off-ice players, except for McAllister, who replaced Rowan on the ice.

The omega took a seat on the bench between Wilson and Rhodes while the crowd booed at losing their entertainment. However, it was short-lived when the game started back up. Rowan watched from the bench as Beckett dominated the ice, leading their team through their plays.

"So… we gonna talk about that meltdown you had?" Wilson asked. When Rowan looked at him, he could see the co-captain watching the game intensely as if he didn't say anything.

Rowan faced the game, leaning forward in a slump, mostly to hide his face from the cameras he knew were taking pictures and people pointing down at him. “Can we just pretend it didn’t happen?”

“Sure… but it won’t help.”

Flinching at the real talk, he sighed. "It just kind of hit me. The fucked-up way the world works, I guess?"

"Seriously? Just now was your 'the world sucks' moment?" Wilson huffed in a laugh, still watching the game. "So what? The world is fucked up."

"I know, but it's always been fucked up in my lane." He screwed his face up. "Does that make sense?" And he sighed when Wilson looked just as confused and shook his head. "Yeah, of course it doesn't," He hummed, slipping his hands out of his large gloves to take off his helmet and run through his hair. "I know the world has this precognitive view of what an omega is supposed to be like. Small, quiet, dainty, submissive-" He counted off on his fingers. "But I've always tried to break that mold. It doesn't help that my passion is something not out of the ordinary for an omega, but still."

Wilson chuckled, "Thought you said figure skating was ten times harder than ice hockey." His voice took on a mock dopy tone as if to imitate Rowan before his gaze sharpened and he shot up and shouted at the ice, "Jeon, get your head out of your ass! Cooper, watch Kage's six!" He sat back down and sighed.

“It is! But to the untrained eye, it’s-” Rowan tried to find his words. “When they see it-” He motioned to the crowd, “It’s all ballet and twirls, flowers, and pop songs.” He lowered his hands. “But it’s hard work. Hours of practice and weight training, not to mention the fucked-up things it does to your feet.”

“Yeah?”

“Yeah! And no one ever questioned why I did it! I didn’t fill stadiums at my shows or have people chanting ‘Omega’.” Rowan’s eyes turned down again to the floor as the ice melted off his blades onto the rubber. “But now that I pick up a stick and skate with some alphas, I’m suddenly a freak show? How is it so hard to believe someone like me could want this?"

"Do you want to play?"

The question was so natural, but for Rowan, he snapped his head to look at Wilson. "What?"

"Do you want to play?" he repeated, looking at him with a raised brow.

"I have to play… I-If I want to skate," Rowan reasoned.

"I didn't ask that, Twirl Hurl." Wilson leaned in. "I asked if you want to play."

Rowan looked out onto the ice at his teammates. Beckett was shouldering past two players on either side while Jeon came in for a save. Beckett shouted Jeon's name, and the player didn't even need to look up to see the puck coming toward him and just accepted it, taking off towards the opponent's net. Rowan felt his heart rate increase as he and his fellow teammates stood up, holding their breaths.

Jeon made the shot, scoring the first goal of the night. The crowd cheered as the alarm went off. Their teammates on the ice raised their sticks in victory, as did the team on the bench. Rowan was practically jumping in excitement as he leaned over and slapped the metal wall like the others did. Heart racing and sporting a smile that hurt, he shouted as loudly as he could over Wilson's own howl of praise. It definitely wasn't something one would see or hear at one of Rowan's competitions.

Settling down, the ref blew the whistle to get back into place as Rowan and the others took a seat, and Rowan remembered he hadn't answered Wilson.

"Yeah," he said, and Wilson looked at him with a raised brow. "It's barbaric and scary, and maybe I'm not the best at it… But-" Rowan offered his co-captain a real smile. "I will admit, I do have fun. Especially with my team supporting me. Makes me want to do better for them."

Wilson nodded. "There might be hope for you yet, Twirl Hurl." He smirked. "Now, if only we can get you some actual balls to match."

Rowan knocked Wilson's shoulder and laughed as the alpha ruffled his hair roughly.

"Who cares if you're an omega who plays hockey or spins his guts out to Lady Gaga on the ice?" Wilson shrugged, lowering his hand to his hockey stick. "On this team, we only care about winning. Which is why I guess I gave you such a hard time when you got here." He rolled his eyes to the game. "So, fuck what they all think and just play."

Rowan felt a real kinship as he looked at his new friend. A newfound admiration filled him as he realized this must be why the team gravitated around Wilson, even though he was kind of an asshole. He was a great guy under all that anger and rage.

"Wilson," Rowan said breathlessly, feeling his chin quiver. "Are we having a bro moment?"

"Shut up." Wilson looked at him with comically angry eyes. "Tell anyone what I said, and I'll fucking chop you into sushi."

Rowan laughed, sniffling as he pulled himself together. "Yeah! Okay, Rye-Rye, you big softie!" Rowan wagged his brows. "Who knew you had such a motivational-speaker way of talking people off a ledge."

"I'll kill you!" Wilson's threat was interrupted.

A loud alarm sounded, and both teammates looked up to see that the other team had scored on Briggs, who looked devastated.

"What the fuck, Briggs?!" Wilson was up and growling as he pointed to the redhead. "Don't make me come over there to show you how to do it!"

“Sorry!” Briggs sighed but got back into position.

Rowan looked around the ice, taking in all the players and his teammates. When it happened, it was like lightning went off in his lizard brain. Rowan jumped up with a gasp, turning to Archer. "Coach! Put me in!"

Archer looked over at him. “Not after that stunt.” He turned back. “Let us get ahead again before-”

Rowan shuffled around his teammates down the line to his coach. "No, for real! Use me! They can't touch me!"

“What are you talking about?” Archer wore a focused look as if trying to solve a puzzle.

Rowan smirked at the confused look. "Anyone ever tell you sexism is alive and well?"

He asked Archer to lean down and began talking in his ear as the coach's eyes widened the more he spoke. Wilson, who was next to Rowan listening, grinned like a murderer who had just been released on parole.

When Rowan finished, Wilson laughed evilly. "Really? Bunch of pussies were told by their daddy not to clap back on an omega? Wow!"

Rowan shrugged. "Yeah, he said his coach talked to them and told them. I felt like I was invisible out there."

"Coach, you gotta play him now," Wilson said, and Rowan smiled. For the first time, he was excited to go out onto the ice.

Archer hummed, closing his eyes in thought before nodding. "I'm willing to give you one more shot, Rookie," He looked down at Rowan, and the omega felt all the responsibility just placed on his shoulders. "If you're wrong, I'll make sure you're benched for the rest of the away games. Regardless of what Prescott says."

Rowan nodded and turned back to the game, waiting for when he would get tossed in. Through the second period, Archer pulled and added players. Rowan and Wilson were itching to get in; their knees were bouncing in their skates, shaking the bench.

"Can you two, like, not?" Briggs said as he looked at them from where he sat near the end, holding his water bottle.

“Sorry, I’m just so excited!” Rowan said as Wilson flipped him off.

"Ay, coach, you planning on playing us today?" Wilson snapped at the taller alpha.

"Yeah, put your blond boys in!" Rowan gave a peace sign as if it was some signature move the two do, and Wilson pushed his head down to fight the urge to murder.

"In due time," Archer said just as the whistle blew, signaling the end of that period. Waving his hand, he called out. "Kage, Jeon, McAllister, Cooper, haul ass in!" He shouted.

The skaters came over, drenched in sweat, breathing heavily as they piled into the bench area. The team traveled back to the locker room together and sat on the hard benches, away from the crowd. Everyone else left an open space beside Rowan, already knowing to give Beckett the spot. It made the omega blush as he greeted his captain with his water bottle.

"Great hustle out there, Beck!" Rowan held a towel out next as Beckett took his helmet off and accepted it with a nod, wiping at his sweaty face.

"What hustle? We're tied!" Wilson blanched, pointing up at the scoreboard in the locker room with matching ones next to home and away. "Fucking lazy asses, all of you!"

"Well, now it's time for you to put your money where your mouth is," Archer said, pointing over to him. "Wilson, West, Walker, Briggs, and Jones, you're in for the final period."

"Fucking finally!" Wilson stood up, slipping his gloves on. "Time to show you posers how to really fuck shit up!"

Beckett gave Rowan a raised brow. “You good?”

Rowan offered a sincere smile, "Better than good." He stood up, slipping his helmet on. "I'm the secret weapon." He stuck his tongue out between his teeth and winked at the alpha, who sighed in relief that Rowan was back to his usual bubbly self.

After the intermission, the new lineup headed to center ice for the faceoff. Walker stood face-to-face with the other team's center while Rowan went to his left side.

The ref skated between the two opposing centers, the puck in an elevated hand. In the stands, the crowd went wild at the sight of a newly added omega to the ice.

Rowan felt like time slowed to a crawl. He watched as the two players stared each other in the eye for a moment before lowering their gazes down to the ice. In the distant future, Rowan would claim to even recall the smell of alpha testosterone filling the space of the ice like a fog machine. It made his heated body shudder as he focused his gaze to not get lost again.

The ref seemingly waited an eternity before releasing the puck. It dropped to the ice with agonizing slowness.

As soon as the frozen rubber touched the ice, Walker's stick was already on it, cupping it and pulling it away from the opposing player. Rowan took off toward the far end of the ice. Time had picked back up, but the omega still didn't feel rushed. He glanced out of the corner of his eye and saw Walker firing the puck up toward the skater-turned-player.

He would get it. He had all kinds of time.

Rowan reached his stick forward and caught the pass. It wobbled a bit and threatened to bounce off his stick. The nimble omega managed to get it under control before looking up again. He saw a massive opposing defenseman coming right at him, eyes on the puck.

'*He won't hit me,*' Rowan thought, '*but he will try to take the puck from me.*'

He thought of all of the stick work that he had seen Beckett do during their practices and at that shootout, but he knew he wouldn't be able to pull any of that off. He was still impressed that he had been able to receive that pass before.

But what he lacked in stickhandling, he made up for in skating.

Once the omega was close to the other player, he spun around and started skating backward. The defenseman was thrown off by this and knew not to hit the small omega, so he slid sideways into the sideboard. Rowan spun around again after passing the player, then moved forward.

The crowd erupted into a roar. Air horns went off, people smacked inflatable tubes together, and bare hands slapped the glass at the side of the ice. Rowan smiled and continued toward the net. The only thing between him and a goal was the goalie.

The player in the net stared down the small blond as he approached. Rowan realized he hadn't thought that far ahead. He didn't feel confident in his shot accuracy, but he also remembered hearing that he couldn't just run straight into the goalie. That would be a penalty.

Sure, Wilson would be proud, but Rowan wanted more than that.

His mind racing, Rowan searched the net for an opening. He looked at the gap between the goalie's legs and decided to go for it. He pulled the stick back, not too far, and fired the puck. The frozen piece of rubber sailed through the air smoothly, and, to Rowan's surprise, it looked to be heading right around where he wanted it to go.

The goalie's stick moved and blocked the puck, which bounced off toward one of the opposing players. Rowan felt the energy leave him as he slowed down and stopped right near the net.

"Good try," the goalie said to him, grinning through the cage in front of his face.

"Oh, spare me!" Rowan said, turning back to the action. He saw the player with the puck heading toward Briggs.

Only to be checked flat by Walker. The player hit the ice and slid to the wall, and the puck landed right into Wilson's stick. The assistant captain looked up at Rowan, gave him a toothy grin, and made a beeline to the opposing net on the far side of the ice.

Rowan looked back to the goalie, who was following Wilson with his whole body, blocking the player's view of the net as much as he could.

And leaving it all wide open on Rowan's side.

'*There's no way they would expect him to pass to me here.*' Rowan thought excitedly. '*They think Wilson will go for the glory.*'

Rowan backed away from the net a little, out of the goalie's field of view, and bent forward, leaning on the stick. He saw Wilson glance over to him just a moment before he shot the puck, low and close to the ice.

The goalie dropped, expecting the puck to head between his legs just like Rowan had tried to do.

Instead, the puck sailed right past the goal, straight to Rowan's stick. He pulled back his stick before the puck was there and swung just as the rubber piece slid in front of him. It connected with a solid CRACK.

'*I could have played baseball, too,*' Rowan thought smugly as he watched the puck fly into the net. The goalie turned and watched it sail past him, his eyes so wide that Rowan was actually a little worried they might pop out of his head.

The puck struck the vertical bar at the back of the net with a CLANG.

There was silence. It was only a fraction of a second, probably not even noticeable by most. But Rowan felt it. He felt a lifetime of excitement and raw energy surge up through him, starting low in his gut and traveling up through his chest. It radiated through his arms and into his head.

His arms involuntarily shot up over his head, straight toward the sky. The horn behind the net blared as the goal light flashed. Rowan yelled triumphantly, his face forgetting to smile at first out of pure surprise. The entire stadium jumped to its feet and screamed. Rowan looked to his team's bench and saw that they were the most excited of all. Every one of them jumped from their seats, throwing their bodies over the half wall and skating across the ice to him, wrapping him in a team embrace.

Beckett had made a point to be the one closest to the petite blond, wrapping him into his strong arms.

"You did it, you twirly sun-of-a-bitch!" Wilson shouted, an honest-to-god smile on his face. "You scored a goal!"

"Not just any goal," Beckett shouted at Wilson before looking at Rowan. "You scored a one-timer! Who the hell scores a one-timer for their first goal?

It was a question that didn't need to be answered, of course, but that didn't stop the stadium announcer.

"Your Asher away team goal scored by number 24, Rowan Weeeessstt!"

The blond omega beamed, looking at his teammates. They were proud of him for this. He hadn't ever had a whole team to back him up in ice skating; it was much more secluded. And the celebrations were far less energetic. He looked out at the crowd and saw they were pounding their fists in the air. It took a moment for his ears to tune them in, but he was surprised to hear that their chant for him had changed.

"West-is-the-best!" followed by five claps.

"West-is-the-best!" five claps again.

It might not have seemed like much, but Rowan couldn't have been happier at that moment. Tears gathered in the corner of his eyes as he clenched his teeth together in pure joy. In their eyes, he had earned his own name.

Rowan West was now a recognized hockey player.

# CHAPTER THIRTY-SIX

The rest of the period went by in a flash. Rowan was skating on air rather than ice, and the other team seemed to have lost a lot of their morale after Rowan's goal.

Even though Rowan didn't score again, despite a few attempts, he did manage to get an assist for Wilson. As they celebrated another goal, Wilson nudged Rowan's arm and said, "Good, now we're even."

The final buzzer went off, and that was it. Asher U took the victory, 3-1.

The team was abuzz as they took off their sweat-drenched equipment in the locker room. It was the kind of energy that could only come after such a good game, where everyone had put everything on the table.

Beckett sat next to Rowan as they both unlaced their skates. The blond pulled the second skate off and leaned back. "God, I'll never understand why you all don't just use the skates I use for figure skating. Yours are so bulky and heavy."

Beckett rolled his eyes and smiled as Cooper offered a response for the alpha. "They offer more protection. Your other skates wouldn't protect much if a stick or the puck smacked into the side."

Rowan pulled his foot up across his other leg and rubbed it gingerly. "At this point, I might welcome it. At least it would be a different kind of pain, y'know?" Beckett let out a small chuckle as he reached down and grabbed his sports bottle.

He lifted the back end of the bottle and squeezed it, firing a stream of water into his mouth. He tilted his head back, his sweaty hair fell away from his forehead, and he swallowed the mouthful of water in one gulp. He looked over to Rowan and must have noticed the omega licking his lips. It wasn't the water that was making him stare in pure want, though.

He held the bottle out to him. "Thirsty?" he asked.

Rowan stared at him blankly for a moment before registering the bottle in his hand. He quickly grabbed at it. "Yeah, of course. Parched. Maybe dying of dehydration," he said before taking a long sip of water.

He was glad the team was being so loud because he was sure the pounding of his heart would be loud enough for Beckett to hear otherwise. He finished sipping the water and handed it back to his captain. "Thanks."

Beckett nodded. "Happy to help."

Archer walked into the room, and everyone got quiet immediately. The coach cleared his throat.

"Great work out there, team. You took all of our practice and put it to good use. And, of course." He looked at Rowan before continuing, "Congratulations on your first goal, West. You saw a weakness in your opponent and used it. That's not something I can teach you; that was all you."

There was a smattering of applause in the locker room, but Archer put a stop to it with a raised hand. "As a reward for a game well-played, I'm pushing your curfew out an hour. Enjoy your R&R time, but don't get too crazy," the coach said before turning and leaving, obviously ready to go back to the hotel to sleep.

Once they heard the outer door shut, Wilson turned to the team with a devious smile. "Who's ready to get crazy?"

# CHAPTER THIRTY-SEVEN

The locker room was just as loud as the stadium had been. Briggs and McAllister were howling, 'We are the champions,' while Fitz, Rhodes, and Sanchez sang along way off-key.

Rowan was in the center of it all yet again. Congratulations were shouted, arms were punched, and hair tussles were given as the omega soaked up all the attention like a sponge. Beckett was first to shower while his team celebrated.

Rowan had hardly moved when the captain got out, nodding his head to something Cooper was saying, though he looked dazed.

"Aw yeah, extended curfew! What should we do?" McAllister looked pumped. "Archer never lets us stay out late! We gotta do something fun!"

"I saw an arcade nearby! We can all go!" Fitz suggested, and the team eagerly agreed.

"I could devour my weight in pizza right now!"

"Let's hurry!"

The team sprang into action as Beckett stopped by his duffel bag. The blond omega looked up at him and gave Beckett the softest smile. The alpha nearly choked on his breath at the pure, innocent look, holding his chest in shock.

He cursed scent patches because he was sure the omega would be producing the most wonderful, happy scent with the warm hues of his heat if he wasn't wearing so many. Beckett could imagine himself getting scent drunk off it as he instinctively sniffed the air, sad to find nothing but alpha and sweat.

"You good, Beck?" Rowan asked, his voice breathy and soft. The tint of pink on his cheeks hadn't left since they got off the ice, and it was so damn cute.

"Y-yeah," he scratched the back of his head and went to change as Rowan stood up, leaving his skates there. Rowan walked over to the bathroom stall along the side to take his clothes off.

The team all showered and changed in record time as McAllister shouted for Rowan to hurry.

"I'll meet you guys there! Go on, I need to actually shower off this sweat, so I'll be a minute." He called from the bathroom stall.

"Fine! Just hurry!" McAllister ran out, announcing loudly to everyone to go on ahead.

Beckett sat on the bench waiting, and after a few seconds of silence in the once-noisy room, the door clicked. Rowan walked out, wrapped in a towel, looking around. He noticed Beckett and blushed as he tightened his hold on the towel. "H-hey, they all gone?"

Beckett nodded, eyes sliding down to the scent patches on Rowan's chest and neck. He could almost smell him like a phantom scent. It made him slightly more irritable on the ice when he couldn't catch a whiff of the sugar cookies and sunflowers.

Rowan looked down at them and sighed. "Yeah, I'm not a fan either, but they do their job." He turned and strolled past the half-wall that housed the communal showers. Beckett looked back down at his feet as he listened to Rowan shower. Slowly, the scent of sugar cookies and sunflowers filled his nose, and he sighed, closing his eyes. After a few minutes, the water turned off, and Rowan came strolling out with the same towel on his waist as he ran another through his fluffy, wet hair.

Walking over to the bench where his bag was, Beckett froze and tried to keep his eyes down on his phone as he looked up the arcade. He could see from his peripheral vision as Rowan dropped his towel and got changed. The sounds of the blond changing paused, just long enough for him to notice. He could feel his cheeks warm up as the omega stood in front of him in just his jeans, staring down at him. Beckett looked up, blinking as Rowan glanced at the locker door and back, biting his lower lip. His blond hair was down from its usual updo and framed his face ever so perfectly. It reminded Beckett of the way it fanned out around the omega like a halo on the bed.

"You know, Beck," He said in a low voice, eyelids lowering as he stepped forward between Beckett's spread legs. Those small hands rested on his shoulders, going up the back of his neck to run through his wild hair. "I have another idea on how we can celebrate that win."

Rowan hardly finished before Beckett pulled the blond forward to straddle his waist. Those blue eyes went from flirtatious to surprised as his hands latched onto Beckett for balance. The alpha dove forward and pressed their mouths together. It only took Rowan seconds to reciprocate, pulling their bodies flush together, hands tugging at the root of his hair. Beckett bit back a feral sound at the harsh tug, liking it more than he should. Honestly, any time Rowan touched his hair it made the alpha turn into a purring kitten.

He'd been wanting this all evening; to hold him, kiss him, worship him like he deserved. Rowan was pure sunlight in Beckett's usual dark presence, and he had come to crave the warmth and brightness. In all honesty, it scared him to feel so attached to a single human being. It was different from the way he was attached to his sister or dads. It was a weird example, but he could only describe it as if coming home to a warm house on a cold winter day. Rowan felt like he belonged in Beckett's arms, and now that he'd had his taste, he didn't know if he could ever let go.

But nothing lasted forever. Beckett knew that better than most. His therapist would call it a morbid way of looking at things, but it was just the world he knew.

Rowan pulled away, just barely an inch, as they both panted, sharing the same air. Beckett could feel the omega quivering in his hold and wondered if it was the heat or if Rowan was actually feeling this for Beckett's touch? What would it be like to actually be wanted like this without the disguise of heat?

One of the things he loved about Rowan was his constant smile. Even as Beckett dipped down for quick kisses, he could feel the upturn of the omega's lips. It was nice to know Rowan could smile when kissing someone like Beckett. It made him feel wanted, and he craved more of it. Leaning their foreheads together, Beckett felt his heart swell as Rowan giggled.

"Wanna fool around in the locker room, or am I totally alone on this venture?" Rowan asked with a cute head tilt.

Beckett could only nod quickly, and the omega cheered in victory, swooping back in for another kiss. Rowan broke away to get quick words out before pressing forward for more. "We need-" The alpha bit Rowan's lower lip, making him gasp before pulling in for a quick kiss and away. "To hurry-" Another kiss. "Can you be-" Another kiss. "Fast?"

Pulling away, Beckett gave the omega a look that could only be described as 'challenge accepted.' He hoisted Rowan up, slamming the blond's back against the lockers as Rowan wrapped his legs around Beckett's waist.

Something Beckett had discovered in their short time being intimate was that Rowan loved being manhandled. The rougher, the better; of course, Beckett was hesitant to get too harsh with him.

"Hell fucking yes!" Rowan whispered, closing his eyes as he leaned his head back, letting Beckett grind his lower half into him.

True to his word, or lack thereof, Beckett made it fast, pulling Rowan from his half-undone pants and giving him the pleasure he so desperately chased. It wasn't long before the blond was a panting mess in his hands, looking down at Beckett's work before dropping his head back to thunk against the lockers. Beckett couldn't help but feel a sense of pride in his work.

The omega came soon after. Beckett covered Rowan's tip to spare them the mess, but shuddered at the warm, gooey feel. When done, Beckett lifted his hand to see the clump of white dripping down his palm to his wrist.

Flicking his eyes to Rowan, he saw the blond watching him as if waiting for his next move. Something hot flickered in his chest as Beckett leaned his head down and swiped his tongue up the side of his hand. The taste was salty, but Beckett didn't mind, hardly paying attention to the look of arousal covering Rowan's face. He watched Beckett audibly swallow as he smiled nervously. "You just made me explode ten seconds ago. How are you making me ready to go again?"

Beckett smirked, leaning down and placing a soft kiss on Rowan's mouth as he lowered him to his feet. Rowan wrapped his arms around Beckett's neck, standing on his tip toes to try and keep him close when the alpha attempted to pull away. Chuckling at the needy skater, Beckett granted one last kiss before pulling away, picking up Rowan's fallen damp towel and wiping his hand off while Rowan got dressed.

"Um-" Looking over his shoulder to a flustered Rowan, Beckett felt his heart swoon. "I-I can help you." The blond glanced down at Beckett's clothed crotch, obviously still hard.

Beckett looked down as well before shaking his head. "We'll be late," he said, and shockingly enough, it wasn't hard to say. It was soft-spoken and scratchy, but he managed to say it without overthinking. That shocked him enough to hardly notice Rowan pouting as he shoved his shoes on. "Fine! But next time, I plan on making you see stars!" He joked, giving that charming grin with his tongue poking out from the side. The omega slid on his shirt, followed by a large jacket that probably was a comfort item, judging by how Rowan snuggled in it. He had applied four scent patches to himself, sealing up that persistent scent.

The captain smiled and nodded as he cleaned up their mess, and together they shouldered their bags and left the arena.

If Beckett could channel McAllister, he would call the walk to the arcade flirtatious. Rowan kept bumping Beckett's shoulders as they walked and found reasons to touch him. Either ticklish pokes to the side, brushes of the hand hanging between them, or even just leaning against him to press shoulders together. Beckett absolutely loved every second of it and was disappointed when they got to the arcade.

Rowan's eyes lit up as he took in the massive arcade. "Wow! Check it!" He saw the team had commandeered a table to the side with their large duffel bags piled precariously on top. Rowan tossed his on the very top before running over to McAllister, who was playing air hockey against Jeon.

"You made it!" McAllister said, not taking his eyes off the game. Beckett was close behind after placing his bag under the table next to Walker's. The place was alive with ringing bells, whistles, and the chatter of games. It wasn't as crowded as he thought, but with the team spread out, he could see almost everyone paired off doing things.

Looking down at the air hockey table, he smiled. His sister loved the arcade, and he liked taking her but would constantly get weird stares since he was a large, scary-looking dude standing with the tiny, innocent little girl.

He should ask if she wanted to go when he got back, and maybe they could bring Rowan. The omega hasn't gotten a chance to meet her and Beckett really wanted the blond to get to know her.

"Yassss, suck my DIIIICK!" McAllister jumped, hands pumping up in victory at the goal he scored.

Jeon looked up with a dangerous glint in his eyes. "Two out of three?"

"You're on, padre!" McAllister threw more coins into the table as he looked at Rowan. "Jeon got us all tokens!" He bent down and handed a small pile to Rowan, who squealed in excitement. "Courtesy of daddy dearest."

"Jeon, we seriously need to talk about your daddy issues, but for tonight, I'm alright if he foots my gamer addiction." Rowan winked, grabbing Beckett's hand to pull him to the side while cradling the handful of coins against his chest. "Come on, Beck!"

Beckett let himself get pulled around by the short figure skater. Their first stop was the ski balls. Rowan broke down laughing when he saw Wilson shouting at some little kids for climbing the ramp to cheat.

"Real men don't cheat!" He said, showing them as he slid the ball up and into the bonus slot, making the bells go off.

"Wow, Rye-Rye!" Rowan said, eyes shining in excitement. "You're really good at that!"

"Hell yeah I am!" He said, throwing more. Every shot gained higher and higher points as tickets pumped out. "And I told you to stop calling me that."

Beckett felt a pinch of jealousy as he watched Rowan fawn over Wilson, hyping the other alpha up.

They moved over to the basketball shot, where Beckett and Wilson stood shoulder to shoulder, shooting hoops.

"Whoa, look at you two go!" Rowan hopped up and down, his newly tied-up blond hair bouncing.

Beckett shared a competitive look with Wilson, who smirked, realizing something. "If I knew all it took to get you to take my challenges seriously was to get your bunk buddy to swoon over me, I'd have done it day one!" He said, making another net as Rowan, who wasn't listening, shouted loudly.

"Nice, Rye-Rye!"

A glint of anger flickered on Beckett's face as he picked up the pace, making every single basket as Wilson did the same. A small crowd gathered, all watching in amazement as tickets piled around the alphas' ankles.

Rowan jumped back and forth between the two hockey players, hyping them up. He had no idea they were secretly competing.

"Whoa, look at you guys go! Get it, get it!" Rowan was practically made of electricity with how fast he popped up on either side of their games, looking at the scores. "Oh my god, you're gonna beat the high score!"

At the last second, Wilson shot his ball, and it lodged itself between the rim and the wall next to it.

"What the fuck?!" He shouted, taking another ball and shooting it, but the game ended with a loud whistle. Those angry eyes looked at the two scores, and he shouted, "No! It got stuck! God damn it!" He shook his fist at the two-point difference.

"Don't be a sore loser, Wilson!" Rowan picked up Beckett's mountain of tickets that hung over his arms. "You'll get him next time." Rowan winked at Beckett as if to say he wouldn't.

“Rematch! Me and you!” Wilson was practically made of fire as he pointed to the air hockey table. “Let’s go!”

Rowan collected Wilson's forgotten tickets and followed the tired-looking captain to Wilson's claimed table. Rowan dropped the tickets nearby and slid in four tokens before the board lit up. The neon lights around them cast everything in a glow of different colors as loud sounds went off all around them.

"Oh, is Wilson playing the captain?" McAllister asked, stopping on his walk by. "I gotta see this! Hey guys! We got another shoot-off!" He called over, and like moths to a flame, the team gathered around the table, watching as their captain and assistant captain squared off again.

“Whoa, this is gonna be hella interesting.” McAllister brought his thumb and pointer finger to his chin. “Any of you gentlemen wanna place any bets?”

"I got thirty tickets on Wilson!" Briggs said excitedly, waving his only winnings into the air.

"No way! I bet my fifty that Kage wipes the floor with him!" Elton shouted, and Beckett felt a moment of gratitude to the beta he hardly spoke with.

"What'd you say, headband?" Wilson snapped at Elton, who flinched and hid behind Sanchez.

“N-Nothing!”

“My tickets are on the captain!”

“Wilson, you got this!”

“I think you’ll both be winners!”

The team was alive with comments as some took sides of the table while the ones not picking took the middle for a better view.

Rowan gave Beckett's shoulder a pat, "You got this!"

Nodding, Beckett looked bored as Wilson slammed the puck on the table before smirking and glancing those beady eyes at Rowan. "Don't I get a good luck, too?"

Rowan gasped and rushed over, patting Wilson's arm. "Of course! You're both my bros! Good luck!"

Like a fire igniting in a dried forest, Beckett's anger became a blazing inferno as he glared at a smirking Wilson. That blond alpha knew exactly how to push his buttons as he nudged Rowan with his elbow in thanks, which made the omega laugh playfully.

Slapping the plastic handpiece on the table, the buzzer sounded, and the game began. Wilson hit it forward with a heavy shout as his fellow hockey players behind him cheered. Beckett leaned against the table, hunched over as he hit the puck back with as much force as Wilson.

The team watched, eyes going back and forth, following the action. They cheered for their selected champion, and Beckett might've been wrong, but he felt he heard his name get shouted more than Wilson's, and he wasn't sure how to process it.

Beckett scored the first goal before Wilson got back at him with another. This happened back and forth before they were tied with only one more goal to victory. Rowan, meanwhile, was in the middle, hands on the edge, providing loud commentary.

Wilson held up the plastic puck. "This one is going straight up your ass!" He slapped it down, hitting it with the handle. Beckett was just as fast, swiping the plastic handheld paddle across the table, connecting with the puck with a loud smack sound.

It was Wilson's momentary cockiness that wás his downfall as always, blinking when the game buzzed to signify Beckett's victory, and he looked down to see that his hand wasn't placed right. The puck bounced off his own handle into the goal.

Dropping to his knees in a dramatic display, Beckett could practically see Wilson's soul leave his body as Briggs and Sanchez took each side of the blond alpha to get him up.

Meanwhile, Rowan was in a tizzy of excitement. He smiled at the omega before he connected eyes with Wilson. The captain gave a very subtle lift of one eyebrow that caused the second in command to shout out in anger, fighting the hold on his arms as the teammates holding him laughed.

"Wow, that was intense! My appetite is at an all-time high!" McAllister clapped as Beckett felt Rowan skitter around him with praise while picking up more tickets. Beckett basked in the omega's words like the tears of angels, though he looked as neutral as if he hadn't played for the honor of Rowan's attention and praise.

"Let's get pizza!" Briggs pointed over to the pizza parlor attached to the arcade. Beckett watched the stampede of hockey players and was reminded of the one scene in The Lion King where Mufasa died. Wilson would be the dead lion as his team practically trampled over him to get to the food. He stood up and seemed to momentarily forget about his challenge with Beckett as he took off to knock some heads together.

Beckett looked over to Rowan, who was practically covered in tickets. A single strand rested across his head, wrapping around his neck and down to his waist, obscuring his chest. "You're gonna get the best prize here!" The omega laughed, motioning with his head to follow.

The parlor was basic, with most of the pizzas already made and resting under heat lamps. The team cleared out the selection without leaving a trace behind. They hardly stayed long, chugging down pizza and sodas before they were back on the floor to play more games. Wilson demanded a repeat challenge on the ski ball, claw machine, and even the shooting gallery. Beckett dominated him at each stop, and he would admit that the more he played, the less it became about impressing Rowan and more about having fun.

Currently, he and Wilson were hunched over a fighting game, smashing buttons. Both leaned into the small space of the screen as their fighters punched each other's heads in. It wasn't until Beckett's character pulled Wilson's spine from his back and proudly proclaimed victory that Beckett jumped back, hands up in triumph with a wide grin across his face.

“Ha! Take that, Wilson!” He pointed at the other alpha.

Silence met him as he looked to his assistant captain to see his eyes wide and mouth hanging open. Looking around, he saw that the whole team, including Rowan, wore the same face. It was then that Beckett realized how loud his voice was as he blushed and lowered his arms.

The team let out a loud 'OHH,' and he was ambushed from all sides as his teammates jumped onto his shoulders, howling and barking in excitement at their captain's vocal display. Even Wilson was smirking, running a hand through his hair as he shook his head. "Yeah, yeah, eat up the praise for now. I'll get you next time."

Beckett was shaken by the number of hands pulling, pushing, and slapping his back. Looking to the side, he noticed Rowan was the only one not attacking him. Instead, his smile was so proud underneath glassy eyes that threatened tears. Beckett's blush intensified, but he smiled and looked at his team.

"Alright, alright! We got fifteen minutes to wrap it up! Curfew is in forty-five. Just enough time to walk back," Briggs announced as the team groaned, but everyone disbursed to get their last games in.

Rowan bounced up to Beckett with stars in his eyes. "Beck, you had fun! With other people!" He said as if it were the biggest announcement in history. "I'm so proud of you!"

Beckett's blush had yet to leave his face, but he scratched the back of his head. "Thanks. It was... fun." He agreed, and Rowan looked ready to pop from excitement as he picked up the large pile of tickets.

"Let's get you a prize! You deserve one!" He pulled Beckett over to the glass desk, where he proudly dropped the tickets before a young teenager who looked positively terrified of Beckett

"What're our options?" He asked as the girl dumped their tickets into a bin that calculated it and turned back to them.

"Anything on the back wall or top shelf," she said sweetly to Rowan, nervously glancing at Beckett.

Rowan grabbed Beckett's hand and motioned to the wall and shelf. "Whatcha want?"

Beckett looked at his options and raised a brow at all the cheap-looking toys and props. After a moment, he blinked at a particular shelf and pointed. Both Rowan and the girl looked up at it, and while Rowan's eyes lit up like stars, the girl looked confused. She stepped up the ladder and pulled it down, handing it over to him with a bow. "C-congratulations on your prize."

Beckett blinked down at the two plushies sitting side by side. “A bunny and a cat!” Rowan nodded. “Good choices!”

Beckett looked between the black and yellow creatures before turning to Rowan and holding it out. At that moment, which Beckett would never forget as long as he should live, Rowan's face took on a pink tint as he looked down at the offered plush before pointing to himself.

“For me?”

Beckett nodded, and Rowan gently reached out and accepted it. He blinked down at it, and Beckett momentarily panicked that what he had just done was considered weird. Do bros sleeping with their bros to get them through their heat give them gifts? Would he know Beckett was feeling more than he should? Was Rowan trying to piece together how to turn the captain down?

All his internal anxiety and panic died the second that sweet smile came back, and he hugged them. "I love them."

Letting out a sigh of relief, he smiled at the adorable image before him, wishing he could take a picture of Rowan without appearing weird.

His tender moment was short-lived when Rowan pulled the two plushies apart and made them kiss. Their mouths stuck together, and he gasped. "MAGNETIC

KISSING ACTION!" He said as if it were a 90's toy commercial.

Pulling them apart to kiss repeatedly, the magnets in the stuffed animals' mouths clicked every time they connected. Beckett's face went ten shades darker as he turned around, bringing his shoulders up to his ears.

'*Fuck he's so cute!*' He thought, closing his eyes to replay that adorable look over and over.

"Alright, last call! Line em' up!" Briggs called from the front with his own swag bucket of candy he got for his tickets.

The team filed to the front, some carrying dumb souvenirs or pizza boxes to eat back at the room. They collected their bags, piled them up, and went on their way. They took up the whole sidewalk as they paraded down like the proud team they were. Beckett took the lead with Rowan and Wilson, listening as Rowan showed Wilson his stuffed animals. Wilson looked as interested as a coma patient, but he listened to Rowan go on and on about his collection of stuffed animals from various competitions. Beckett, however, hung on to his every word. This lasted all the way back to the hotel, where the rowdy players broke off into several groups to take separate elevators up.

On their floor, the doors opened, and the team began barking and wolf-whistling as Rowan and Beckett stepped off. The captain looked to the six players in the elevator, and he wondered if they knew. Was it possible that Wilson wasn't the only perceptive one? Were his feelings for the figure skater so obvious?

"Yeah, yeah, get going, you horny dogs!" Rowan stuck his tongue out at them as the doors closed, and he finally looked up at Beckett. The alpha noticed a dust of pink on Rowan's cheeks as he took off toward their room near the end of the hall.

They took turns showering because locker room showers weren't meant to fully clean you, just to clear the sweat and chill from the ice. Rowan came out in the oversized shirt Beckett lent him, which he practically swam in as he jumped onto the bed and turned on the TV. Beckett wasn't far behind, coming out to see Rowan snuggled into the covers of his bed, looking content.

Housekeeping obviously came and disassembled Rowan's makeshift nest, putting all the extra blankets away and leaving the room perfectly fresh. The two stuffed animals on the nightstand next to him continued their kissing.

Rowan didn't seem uncomfortable or in need, so Beckett walked around the bed to his own. Just as he pulled the covers back, a soft whine emerged from behind him. Looking over his shoulder, he saw Rowan sitting up, pouting.

"You're sleeping in your own bed? Brooo, you hate me that much?" His tone was teasing, but the pout looked real.

Beckett panicked, turning around and dropping onto Rowan's bed. The blond bounced as he shuffled over, lifting the covers to let Beckett crawl under.

Beckett did just that, letting Rowan take the lead in everything. The small figure skater cuddled up to him, entangling their legs and using him as a pillow.

"I had such a great day!" Rowan sighed happily, and Beckett inhaled the scent of content omega, intermingled with the light scent of heat. It was intoxicating, and Beckett was practically scent drunk from it as he reached a hand up and carded through the blond's hair. He hummed an agreement.

They lay like that for a while, just watching an old rerun on TV, basking in the warmth. Beckett felt like his jaw hurt from smiling so much and couldn't remember when he had done so much in a single day with people who weren't his family.

It was all thanks to the small blond in his arms.

If Rowan weren't here, Beckett would have likely bunked alone or with his dad. The alpha had grown to hate away games. The others on his team would always request not to get put with him because he scared them. Archer tried to get him paired with other players in high school, but they would just ditch him and go to their friends' rooms to bunk. Being alone with him always made others uncomfortable or scared for their lives. And yet there was Rowan, nuzzling his face into Beckett as he inhaled the alpha's scent with a grin.

Tightening his hold, Beckett swallowed the lump in his throat. Rowan was very quickly becoming a significant person to him. He found himself becoming protective of him in ways that always made him aware of what the omega was doing. Beckett wanted to always make sure he was safe and smiling. Even if nothing ever came of these feelings, he would still be happy just to have him in his life.

At least, for as long as Rowan will allow.

Beckett grinned as he thought about Rowan's first day on the ice. Beckett had no idea how much the small skater would change his life, or the lives of the rest of the team for that matter. He was a little whirlwind of kindness, empathy, sass, and seductiveness all packaged together.

Even if Asher U lost every other game that season, Beckett would feel like they had won it all by having Rowan West grace their roster.

# Coming Soon!

## Figure It Out: Book 2

Head to cr-ship.com for updates about the next release. Thank you for reading!

www.ingramcontent.com/pod-product-compliance
Lightning Source LLC
LaVergne TN
LVHW100509110826
845146LV00002B/575

* 9 7 9 8 2 3 4 0 6 0 6 2 4 *